PENGUIN
TILL THE FAT...

Sean Hardie was born in Northumberland, educated in Scotland and at Cambridge, and now lives in County Kilkenny, Ireland. He worked as a BBC TV current affairs producer for ten years before moving to comedy as co-creator of *Not the Nine O'Clock News*. He is the author of two other novels, *The Last Supper* (1990) and *Right Connections* (Penguin, 1993).

SEAN HARDIE

TILL THE FAT LADY SINGS

PENGUIN BOOKS

PENGUIN BOOKS

Published by the Penguin Group
Penguin Books Ltd, 27 Wrights Lane, London W8 5TZ, England
Penguin Books USA Inc., 375 Hudson Street, New York, New York 10014, USA
Penguin Books Australia Ltd, Ringwood, Victoria, Australia
Penguin Books Canada Ltd, 10 Alcorn Avenue, Toronto, Ontario, Canada
M4V 3B2
Penguin Books (NZ) Ltd, 182–190 Wairau Road, Auckland 10, New Zealand

Penguin Books Ltd, Registered Offices: Harmondsworth, Middlesex, England

First published in Great Britain by Michael Joseph 1993
Published in Penguin Books 1994
1 3 5 7 9 10 8 6 4 2

Copyright © Sean Hardie, 1993
All rights reserved

The moral right of the author has been asserted

Printed in England by Clays Ltd, St Ives plc

Except in the United States of America, this book is sold subject
to the condition that it shall not, by way of trade or otherwise, be lent,
re-sold, hired out, or otherwise circulated without the publisher's
prior consent in any form of binding or cover other than that in
which it is published and without a similar condition including this
condition being imposed on the subsequent purchaser

For Paddy and Dorothy
and
For Kerry

Main roads
Railways
Borders
Rivers
Mountains
CARIBBEAN SEA
Gulf of Honduras
Bay Islands
Cow Cay
N
GUATEMALA
Trujillo
La Ceiba
Tela
San Pedro Sula
Sico
Jiuba
Paulaya
Caratasca Lagoon
Aguán
La Entrada
Chamelecón
Copán
Ulúa
L. de Yojoa
Patuca
Cedros
Otoro
Tegucigalpa
EL SALVADOR
NICARAGUA
HONDURAS
PACIFIC OCEAN
Gulf of Fonseca
kilometres
0
50
100
150
miles
0
100

I

JUDGE WILLIAM WILDE retired from the Northern Circuit when he was seventy. The day after his farewell dinner he moved out of his Newcastle flat and into a small stone house forty miles up the coast in Alnmouth, a picturesque seaside village with a good GP, no vandals and a mainline railway station. He moved alone: his estranged wife Margaret had been dead almost ten years and his only son Joe was living in London. Good brain, three years of Cambridge, and the boy ends up playing piano in pubs and writing songs for left-wing theatre groups. The waste of it.

Willie loathed retirement. All his life he'd worked, and his job was who he was, from junior to barrister to Queen's Counsel to Recorder. As far as he knew no one liked him, or thought him handsome, or witty, or creative. He drove his wife to drink and divorce, his son avoided him and mocked his values, but no one ever suggested Willie wasn't up to job. When the job went his whole sense of himself went with it.

The house in Alnmouth was neat and practical, with a line of wind-bent ash trees to shelter the well-tended garden from the North Sea gales. A wicket gate led straight from the garden on to the golf course, where his fellow geriatrics spent their afternoons shuffling around the links or walking their dogs on the dunes. Willie didn't own a dog, and he had no time for gardens or golf. Nor were the dog-walkers much interested in commercial fraud, which had been Willie's speciality until he reached the Bench. Tell someone you're a fraud lawyer and their eyes glaze over, they don't want to hear about the Mysterious Case of the Reappearing Basildon VAT Invoice, they want serial sex killers, cannibalism, mobsters, celebrity libel. He should have been a criminal lawyer – could have been, only fraud work was more dependable, the money better, the career breaks came earlier.

The main attraction of Alnmouth turned out to be the railway station. Once a month or so, when the atmosphere of stagnant gerontocracy got too much for him, he would take the morning train to London and spend a night or two at his club, buy some books, see old colleagues. The rest of the time he mouldered, wrote letters, read biographies of Great Lawyers, and watched the news on television. He had few friends, and none younger than himself.

'They shouldn't retire judges at seventy,' he complained to his son Joe at one of their infrequent meetings, which normally took place over lunch on the neutral territory of a Soho restaurant when Willie was down in London. 'They should hang them.'

Not that he meant it. Deep down Willie Wilde wasn't ready for the coffin yet.

He lasted two years in Alnmouth before boredom drove him to travel. He started modestly with an off-season package tour that took him to Florence, Rome and Venice. To his surprise he rather enjoyed the trip. Three months later he was off again, on a Classical Cruise round the Aegean. The next spring he went to China, the following autumn to Jordan and Israel. The company was elderly and parochial, but it provided him with an audience. A good audience is an important thing in old age.

Important, but not enough. With time the destinations seemed to blend into one another. The hotels and coaches were all the same, the sites curiously repetitive. The arthritis in his hips was beginning to bother him, and the foreign food disagreed with his digestion. When he saw a trip to Mexico advertised in the *Telegraph* he hesitated for a month before sending off for the brochure, and only signed up because the alternative was another dreary winter of North Sea gales and half-dead dog-walkers.

They flew to Mexico City first, where a third of the party succumbed to Montezuma's Revenge. Next came Guadalajara and Acapulco, Puerto Escondido, Oaxaca, then the Yukatán peninsula. The company was dull, the climate fierce, the days long, the towns dirty and disorganized. He didn't mind the climate or the dirt, but by the time he reached Merida he'd had enough of global tourism, of air-conditioned buses and fixed-smile tour guides and the company of old people. This kind of travel, he decided, was just another drug for the old, a way of distracting yourself from the painful but necessary task of coming to terms with who you've been and who you are and what you're about to become.

Sitting alone in his hotel room in Merida, contemplating another day of ruins and canned music on the coach, he caught sight of himself in the dressing-table mirror. What he saw was not just a face but a lifetime of evasion. No, not a lifetime: just fifty years – at twenty-five he'd been known as a radical lawyer, a fighter for lost causes. Whatever happened to all that?

'Who the hell are you, Willie Wilde?' he grumbled.

The truth was he hadn't a clue.

I don't want to be here, he told himself. I don't want to be here, but I don't want to go home – the cry of the self-pitying adolescent down the ages. Only Willie was now at an age when self-pity was as dangerous as cancer.

He poured himself a whisky, lit a cigarette, and turned on the television. They were showing the weather forecast.

You didn't need a weather forecast in Merida, the weather never changed. It rained once a day, at nine a.m., you could set your watch by it. Twenty minutes later the sun came out again, and that was that. The following afternoon his group was due to fly to Cancún, where as far as he knew it never rained at all, to spend a week sunning their wrinkled torsos on the loungers by the hotel pool, nothing to do except gaze at the sky or inspect the pottery donkeys and straw hats in the air-conditioned gift shops.

The forecaster was standing in front of a map, jabbering away in Spanish. Willie didn't speak Spanish. His eyes were on the map, idly picking out where he'd been in the previous ten days.

The map was what reminded him of Mike Osborne.

Mike was a school and college friend of his son Joe's. After Cambridge Mike had gone into the BBC and become a television reporter. He'd done well, worked on *Panorama* and *Newsnight*, travelled all over the world. And then, for some reason Willie couldn't remember, Mike had quit the business and gone to live in Honduras, where he ran an aid project on an island off the Caribbean coast called Cow Cay. Joe had been out to visit him there, a couple of years ago, and on his return had spent most of one of their quarterly lunches in London telling Willie about Mike's work. Having someone or something interesting to talk about was a great help at Willie and Joe's lunches, stopped them getting personal. There were times when the two men were fond of each other, but plenty when they weren't, and these fleeting moments of affection embarrassed them both.

Honduras, Willie realized from the map, was almost next door to Merida, no distance at all.

'Why not?' he decided. 'Bugger it, why the hell not?'

Just taking the decision – spontaneously, irresponsibly – was a revelation to him.

The following morning, while the rest of the group were at breakfast, he slipped into the travel agents in the hotel lobby. There was a flight to San Pedro Sula at half past eleven. He left a note at reception for the courier, and took a taxi to the airport. A day to get there, five days with Mike, a day to get back to Mexico in time for the return flight to London.

Only Willie never came home.

The day he was due back he sent a cable to Joe from

Honduras, saying he'd extended his trip. Three weeks later he summoned up the courage to write Joe a brief letter, explaining that Mike Osborne had given him a job. There were two more letters in the weeks that followed, both largely concerned with practical arrangements for the house in Alnmouth.

Then there was nothing.

2

JOE WILDE WAS in his thirties, six foot three and thin as a bamboo, with hunched shoulders, mischievous eyes, a hangdog Dave Crosby moustache and a head of wiry black hair, fast receding. Give it a couple more years and he could get out the Proud To Be Bald sweat-shirt: in the meantime he wore hats. When anyone asked Joe what his old man did for a living, Joe simply said, 'Don't ask'.

He wrote songs that were like little short stories, about ordinary people and ordinary lives, their jobs and relationships and how they saw the world; sometimes wry, sometimes comic, occasionally angry, in styles that ranged from rock-'n'-roll through blues to full-blown ballads.

People liked them, but they were rarely commercial. To pay the bills he sang and played keyboards and guitar round the clubs, did some late-night TV and the odd Arts Festival, and balanced the books by working as a session man on other people's recordings.

He was a musician's musician, easy-going and light on ego, fooled around a bit but never missed a note when it mattered. *The Guardian* once described him as the English Randy Newman, which was fine by Joe. He didn't make Randy Newman's kind of money, but he liked the life, and playing music didn't seem to do any active harm to his fellow citizens, which was more than you could say for judges.

He liked the life because he liked the people, the kids who came to Dingwalls, the old men in Glasgow labour clubs and Manchester pubs who'd fought in Spain and marched to Aldermaston with Canon Collins. He wasn't much of a socialist, but he admired those who were, less for their politics than for their appetite for justice.

His friends were an eclectic and amiable rabble: sitters in pubs, late-night movie addicts, painters of unsaleable paintings, writers of unpublishable novels, mountain climbers, psychiatric nurses and school teachers, defrocked civil servants and superannuated revolutionaries. His recreations were unplanned but mostly urban and nocturnal.

Joe grew up in Hexham, nowadays little more than a mock-rural suburb of Newcastle, but in those days of lost innocence a prosperous little country town set among wooded hills and well-run farms, with a cattle market and a Norman abbey on a low ridge overlooking the river.

The Wildes were among the first commuter families to migrate up the Tyne valley from Newcastle, where Willie was by then a successful barrister. They lived in an Edwardian villa above the town, with stained-glass windows and oak-panelled plush-furnished rooms, and a black Bakelite phone on the waxed table in the hall beside the bentwood hatstand. Hexham 31 – Joe could still remember the number. And there was Boris, a great bear of a golden retriever who spent his days asleep under the laburnum tree by the front gate.

He had a photograph from that time, taken on a warm evening in late summer, the air soft and golden, Joe in shorts and socks and Clarks sandals and an aertex polo shirt, Willie in a loose pinstripe suit, tie undone, a cigarette in his mouth, leaning on his croquet mallet, laughing and cursing Boris as the dog chased his ball across the turf.

To one side Joe's mother Margaret, in a sexless calf-length polka-dot dress, watched from the edge of the laurels, waiting to hand Willie his whisky in a cut-glass tumbler, her own gin and tonic in her other hand. In the background the black bull-nose Volvo was parked under the chestnut tree in the drive.

His parents must have been about the age Joe was now,

the prime of life. Different times, different lives, before the Old God died, which according to Willie was somewhere around 1964.

His mother, he'd realized since, must already have been drinking, quietly and without fuss, just enough to blur away the edges of a life that had somehow slipped away from her. It wasn't that Willie mistreated her: he simply lacked the imagination to understand what was wrong. His long hours at work he saw as a virtue, not a vice. In an age when middle-class women were not expected to pursue careers of their own, he assumed that the blossoming of his career at the Bar would automatically benefit them all, both in terms of material security and of status.

The problem was that Margaret didn't want status or security: she wanted a husband.

She not only wanted Willie, she needed him, because she was a shy woman who'd married too young to have any sense of her own worth. Confronted with Willie's legal friends, she had nothing interesting to say. She wasn't witty and she didn't understand the law or politics, though she read *The Times* assiduously every morning to try and keep up with events; and she lacked the confidence to buy striking clothes or play the graceful hostess.

The concept of shyness was beyond Willie's comprehension: he found it literally unimaginable. Nor could he cope with Margaret's depression. And because these things were alien to his own character, he did what he always did when confronted with problems he couldn't solve: he ignored them.

There were concessions, but they were entirely practical, ways of alleviating the symptoms rather than attacking the disease. They entertained less than he would have liked, and he often went to functions alone. He was careful not to criticize the way she dressed, and routinely praised her dreary Ideal Home cooking. But just as the human ear cannot hear the high pitch of a dog-handler's whistle, so Willie was deaf to the silent lonely scream that filled the house in Leases Lane for almost twenty years.

Joe could hear it, and like all children confronted with adult misery he assumed he was the cause of her unhappiness. He wanted to help, but didn't know how.

Margaret was not a good mother. She went through the motions, made him birthday cakes and read him stories, and knitted him endless misshapen jumpers – if there was one image of Margaret which stood out among his memories, it was of her knitting, sitting on the Chesterfield in the front room, the needles piercing, stabbing, rasping the wool, her body tensed, eyes down, refusing battle, refusing comfort, refusing peace, nurturing her grievances like house plants. But she was always distant, distracted, and he learned not to try to intrude.

He discovered young that it was a waste of time to try to involve her in his enthusiasms. If he came back from school excited by a class project or a new friendship she heard him out, but she never listened, so that if he subsequently mentioned the friend's name or the progress of the project she would look at him with blank incomprehension.

The drink didn't help. When Willie drank to excess, he became merry: when Margaret drank, she disappeared so deep inside herself that sometimes you wondered if she was there at all.

Joe learned to head off her disasters, the untended pots on the stove, the tell-tale sherry bottle left on the kitchen table when the sound of his father's returning car was already crunching up the gravel drive. Tidying up the miserable detritus of Margaret's life became second nature to him, no more remarkable than filling the coal bucket or walking the dog or any of the other mundane tasks children take for granted around the home, or did in those days.

It was all, somehow, his fault: and yet she wept when he went away to prep school. Joe wept too, and wept again fifteen years later when she finally moved out, although he was by then a student at Cambridge and not greatly given to displays of emotion.

His memories of Willie through those years were very different. Willie was also a distant figure, but one to be admired. Where Joe's mother was awkward and withdrawn, his father was utterly self-confident; where she was passive, Willie thrived on action. Because his entire experience of life was of being male – male in a way that it's hard to comprehend in this age of co-education and the Women's Movement – he understood nothing of what it meant to be the drab wife of a successful and gregarious man.

But he knew, when it suited him to remember, what it was to be a boy. From the cradle up Joe was showered with the sort of presents that Willie had wanted as a child – toy trains, cricket bats, fishing rods, adventure story-books. His birthday treats were trips to St James Park to see Newcastle United, or to rain-lashed point-to-points in the boggy fields below the Roman Wall. And though Joe disliked sport and was bored by G. A. Henty, he knew that his father, in his own way, meant well.

Margaret meant nothing at all. It was only later that he began to glimpse the terrible sadness of her life, and to blame his father for failing to see how much a little understanding would have helped her. It was a wretched marriage, and worse than either deserved.

It was also a poor introduction to relationships.

Joe grew up a solitary, self-contained child. He found it hard to make friends, and instead devised his own entertainments, read magazines and wrote stories, built models, painted, imagining himself as a miniature adult. On fine days he took to his bicycle, often covering thirty or forty miles in a day, up the Tyne valley or across the moors into County Durham. Like his father he kept his own counsel, and made sure he was emotionally and materially beholden to no one.

Within its own parameters his strategy worked fine. At thirteen he was sent away to school at Glenalmond, a gloomy gothic mausoleum in the Perthshire hills. He spent his free time walking alone in the mountains, often for days on end, ticking off the peaks and listing his sightings of capercaillie and ptarmigan in a red notebook, competing with himself.

When Joe was fifteen Willie asked him what he thought about religion. Joe said he thought it was a good idea to be nice to your neighbours.

'That's not religion,' said Willie dismissively, 'That's wanting to be liked.'

Joe couldn't see what was wrong in being liked: he just didn't know how to go about it. He wanted to behave well, couldn't stand the idea that people might think him mean, or selfish, or intolerant. He didn't want to sit in judgement on anyone, he didn't want to be famous, he didn't want a CBE or a cellar full of claret or an account with Coutts. He craved friendship, longed for the good opinion of his peers.

Another time Willie asked him what his favourite word was.

'Phlegm,' said Joe.

'And your least favourite?'

'Convulsion.'

'The worst word in the world,' said Willie, sucking on his untipped cigarette, 'is "should". Followed by "ought" and "must". There's nothing wrong with "want to" or "need to". But never "should".'

This from a judge.

Only Willie wasn't a judge then, he was still the young barrister, fighting the underdogs' corners, looking for ways to knock the system. Knocking to knock down, or knocking to get in? Joe often wondered.

By the time he reached Cambridge Joe had begun to relax a little. He joined the student newspaper and worked backstage at amateur dramatics, projects that brought him into day-to-day contact with like-minded students. But he still communicated with the outside world through his deeds not his emotions: through what he did, not who he was. Life was easier to control that way.

Mike Osborne was the exception. He'd known Mike at Glenalmond, but not well. Cambridge brought them closer, two hick Northerners huddling together for comfort in the alien, self-confident world of braying Etonians and supercilious aesthetes. The difference between them was that Mike found it easy to adapt: Joe didn't. But he took Joe along with him, and with time Joe learned to relax, get drunk, misbehave. By the middle of his second year he was beginning to enjoy life.

Music helped. He found he had talent as a song writer, and began performing a little. By the time he left university he was playing professionally. He and Mike took a flat together in Camden Town. Mike was working for the BBC, Joe doing nonsense jobs – bar work, security, bus conducting – and gigging at weekends. Three years later he was a full-time musician, and so it had been ever since.

He still had problems with relationships, not helped by the final break-up of his parents' marriage. It never seriously occurred to him to get married himself. He had few serious lovers, and the only one who really mattered was Marion, a fiery red-headed radio producer with whom he lived off and on for almost ten years until she got tired of waiting and left him to his own indecisions.

Her leaving hurt him, but the alternative scared him too much: he'd seen what his father had done to his mother, and what marriage had done to them both, and despite their differences he recognized enough of his father in his own character to know the dangers. From the age of twenty, the dominant force in Joe's life was a constant desire to avoid his father's mistakes.

Willie's silence in Honduras worried Joe, but not a lot, because Willie had always been inclined to arbitrary action, and once he decided to do something there had never been any point in even discussing the matter with him. And the old took pleasure in worrying their children nowadays, presumably out of revenge for what their children had been doing to them since the youth revolution of the Sixties.

He tried writing to his father, and when that produced nothing he wrote to Mike Osborne.

Mike wrote back to say everything was fine; and then Willie wrote too, three lines on the back of a postcard.

The card, buckled and faded as though it had been left

too long in the sun, arrived on his mat by the second post on Thursday. It showed a statue of a general on a horse in some Central American town square.

'There are things going on here in Honduras,' Willie had written on the back, in fountain-pen italic, 'that are either miraculous, criminal, or insane. Letter follows, W.W.'

Joe took it as a joke. He should have known better.

The following evening, at a little after eight o'clock, Joe was on stage at a barn of a pub called the Saracen's Revenge in Finsbury Park, playing blues piano behind a fat and acne'd Australian lady who thought she could sing like Janis Joplin. Maybe she would one day, but she'd need to get the drink habit first.

They were halfway through 'Underneath the Harlem Moon', Joe taking it slow and moody, when he got the note from Benny behind the bar. Two words: Mike Osborne. He cut the middle eight, took the last verse at ragtime speed and pushed his way through the tables to the phone.

'Joe?'

The line was awful, as though someone was shouting down a long metal tube.

'Mike?' Joe shouted. 'How the hell did you know I was here?'

'*Time Out*.'

'You get *Time Out* in Honduras?'

'Fuck off,' Mike bellowed back. 'You're never home, I phoned them, they checked the listings for me.' And then a pause. 'Have you heard from Willie?'

'I thought he was with you.'

'He was. He went off on a trip last month, never came back. I thought maybe he'd decided to go home.'

'A trip to where?' asked Joe'

'I can't hear you,' Mike shouted. 'You'll have to speak up.'

'*Where was he going?*' Joe bellowed.

He looked around the bar. People were watching him. He signalled Benny to pour him a whisky.

'To the mainland,' Mike shouted back. 'He wanted to visit some ruins up near the Guatemalan border. I wondered if he'd been in touch.'

'He has and he hasn't. I had a postcard, must have been sent ten days ago or so. Nothing since. You think we should be worrying?'

For twenty seconds all Joe could hear was echo.

'Probably not,' Mike said eventually.

That was the moment Joe started to worry. Mike Osborne was an eternal optimist: at Cambridge they called him Wonderful World because his enthusiasms were boundless, the good humour always about to boil over in him. There were times when he reminded Joe of a bird supported on hovering wings of relentless optimism: if the wings ever failed him his whole world would come crashing to the ground. For Mike 'Probably not' was an alarming prognosis.

'Do you think he's in trouble?' Joe asked.

There was another pause.

'I don't imagine so. He probably got the Mayan bug, people do, after one ruin they just keep going, up into Guatemala and Belize, on into Mexico, sometimes they're gone for months. There aren't any phones in the jungle, post offices tear up letters and steal the stamps, buses break down, roads get swept away in the floods. He's probably holed up in Tikal or Copán, looking at carvings and ball courts and waiting for the weather to break. Let me know when he gets in touch.'

'Hold on,' Joe started to say, but the line was dead.

He stood looking at the receiver for a moment, then handed it back across the bar.

'That the Mike Osborne who used to be on the box?' asked Benny.

'Yup. Couldn't stand the heat, ran off to Central America.'

'You're joking.'

Joe swallowed his whisky.

'Yes, I'm joking. About the heat, that is. He's living in Honduras, runs malaria clinics and stuff.'

'I never knew that.'

'You're not meant to know, that's not why he went.'

He flashed Benny a friendly smile, put down his glass, picked up his jacket, walked straight out of the bar and picked up a taxi on the street, leaving the Australian to finish her act alone. Joplin sang 'Mercedes Benz' with no band, Bel McCracken could do the same.

Joe lived in a red-brick terrace in what estate agents call 'Close To Hampstead' and Joe called 'British West Kilburn'. The house in Harvist Road was divided into four flats off a boxed-in central staircase, with junk mail and bicycles in the hall and a pay-phone on the wall.

The ground floor was lived in by a hard-drinking paraplegic art school lecturer called Eddie Scargill. Upstairs from Eddie there were two Spanish students; above them Calum, a long-haired Glaswegian who wore black capes and slept in a coffin. Joe had the top floor, three rooms with skylights and a dormer window looking out over the tops of the sycamores to the dog-infested mud and grass of Queens Park. It was a one-man flat, chaotic and disorganized, with a piano in the kitchen and books and tapes and take-away food cartons scattered around the surfaces.

The cab waited outside while he collected his passport and a bag of clothes and phoned the airlines. British Airways told him they had a midnight flight from Heathrow to Miami but it was full.

Joe told them this was an emergency, he was phoning from the Foreign Office, sounding very Public School about it all. The girl from BA put him on hold, played him two minutes of synthesized 'Greensleeves' then told him he could have a seat but it would have to be Economy.

Joe said that was fine.

The cab was halfway down the M4 on the way to Heathrow before it occurred to Joe to question what he was doing, why he was flying 5,000 miles to look for a man he wasn't even sure he liked. Impulse, mostly, he decided. Impulse, and unfinished business. There would be times in the weeks ahead when Joe would wish he'd left it that way.

He made the flight with ten minutes to spare. His luggage for the trip to Central America comprised three shirts, a spare pair of jeans, a change of underwear, swimming trunks, a ten-year-old sponge bag, £37 in cash and a Visa card. He hoped they took Visa cards in Honduras.

3

ON THE FLIGHT between London and Miami Joe sat next to a bearded dentist with podgy pink fingers called Doug Bisztyga. Doug came from Missoula, Idaho, and fished bass in his spare time. As did all his family: he had Polaroids to prove it.

The in-flight movie starred Bert Reynolds in a romantic comedy. Aeroplanes, as Joe pointed out to Doug, being one of the few places it's safe to show Bert Reynolds' comedies with dignity because there's no danger of the audience walking out halfway through.

'Could you say that again slowly?' asked Doug.

'It wasn't anything important,' said Joe.

Doug opened his mouth to speak, thought better of it, stretched his mouth into a polite dentist's smile, and put on his headset. It was quarter to four in the morning, 26,000 feet over the Atlantic. Outside the clouds were bathed in silver moonlight.

Assume he's dead, Joe decided. Drowned, maybe: anything goes wrong with you in the water at that age and you're a gonner, you can drown in a bowl of prunes. He tried to picture Willie face down among the parrot fish and turtles. Seventy-four years old, with his seized-up hips and wrinkled dugs and his Senior Service cough, 5,000 miles from home. Or murdered: there were places in Honduras they'd slit your throat for a pair of plimsoles. Or maybe his heart packed in.

It's not my bloody fault, Joe reminded himself, he went

there of his own accord. I never forced anyone to do anything in my entire life. Least of all Willie. It's an irreversible law of the universe: fathers decide, sons resent, and obey, and try to please, and then resent some more, until time and age finally castrate the old bastards, and useless resentment inverts itself into equally useless guilt.

He waited five hours in Miami for a connection to Tegucigalpa, the Honduran capital. People who say there's not much to do in the evenings in Ulan Bator have never spent five hours at Miami International.

He filled in the time in the bar drinking beer and admiring the presenters' hairstyles on Cable Network News. Ninety-three People Are Feared Dead In Manila I'm Larry Stay Tuned. He'd already done five double whiskies on the flight from London, as well as two of those doll's-house bottles of wine they give you with the meals, on the principle that if tomorrow's hangover is bad enough you won't notice the jet-lag.

Every once in a while, almost out of curiosity, he'd pinch his emotions to make sure they were still there, search out an affectionate memory of his father to justify to himself what he was doing, and for a while a poignant nostalgia would well up inside him. But it was a mechanical trick, a way of making yourself feel something you think you ought to be feeling when you're not, and he felt ashamed of himself for bothering with it.

All of us have fathers, all of them die. Joe wasn't even sure if he loved his father, but he probably loved him more than anyone else did.

Not that he really believed Willie was dead. If he was there'd be no point in flying halfway round the world to a scruffy island off the coast of a country few Englishmen or women could place on a map. But Willie's disappearance had woken him up to the fact of his father's mortality. And before Willie died there were questions Joe wanted to ask him, not all of them kind.

Honduras was the original banana republic: it lies like a

knee-patch across the bent leg of Central America, bordered by Nicaragua to the south, Belize and Guatemala to the north. It's always been the poorest of the Central American states, too poor to interest the conquistadores, who built only a thin skim of settlements along its mountain ridges as staging posts on the strategic trail between Mexico and Panama.

Less than a fifth of the land is cultivated; the rest is divided between upland forests and humid malarial jungle. Three quarters of the population are barefoot, more than half illiterate, almost two thirds illegitimate.

It was mid-afternoon by the time the shuddering TAL 737 reached Tegucigalpa, the mountainous mud-and-dust, shanty-fringed capital. Two flights up, one to go. Joe felt as if he'd been travelling for a week.

He cleared customs and immigration and checked in for the domestic flight that would take him to Cow Cay. The old Dakota flew low over the clouded hills and forests down to the Caribbean coast, across endless plains of banana and tobacco, and then a long white beach fringed by palms, at one end of which red mud bled from a river mouth into the clear sparkling waters of the Caribbean.

They landed briefly at La Ceiba, a run-down banana port, one part rotting Fruit Company bungalows to six parts fly-blown *barrio*. A military band met the flight, for what reason Joe failed to discover. Habit, he suspected. Half an hour later he was airborne again. Below him the sea glistened in the sunlight, turquoise slashed with white where the breakers hit the reef. Beyond, a hundred miles to the East, lay Cow Cay.

The Cay, like the neighbouring Bay Islands, belongs to Honduras, but its heart lies elsewhere, across the horizon in the West Indies. It supports a population of 4,000: Afro-Caribbeans whose ancestors escaped from the West Indies, Hispanics and mestizos from the mainland, a dusting of more recent European blow-ins, a few indigenous Indians and Caribs.

From the air the long thin island looked like a leaf whose

rim had been nibbled away by insects, its low ridge of sandstone hills forming a spine from which the land descended to a succession of indented bays and beaches.

Halfway along the south coast Joe could pick out the town of Morgan's Hole. Three miles west along the narrow coastal track, at the end of a thin peninsula, was the old Anglican mission settlement of St Andrews, which Mike had bought and converted into his school and clinic.

The island's runway was a short strip of red clay bulldozed out of the scrub, a wind sock at one end, a long timber hut at the other, beyond it a low ridge of sand and rock, palms and breadfruit trees swaying in the breeze, and then the shimmering blue infinity of the Caribbean. The Dakota bounced softly on its wide doughnut tyres as it hit the ground; the pilot revved the engines, slowed and then taxied back the way he'd come.

This was Joe's second trip to the Cay. His previous visit had been three years ago, on his way home from the Havana Festival of Music and Youth, a week of noise and laughter and misbehaviour in the Hotel Nacional, culminating in a five-hour stadium oration by Castro himself. Even the Grateful Dead didn't risk playing that long.

The following morning Joe had caught a flight out to San Pedro Sula and on down the coast to Cow Cay, and sat up all night with Mike on the veranda of the Rectory watching the electric storms, drinking rum and smoking dope and talking about old times, laughing a lot.

It was some months after, over lunch in Soho, that Joe had told Willie about Cow Cay, never guessing – how could you guess?

Coming down the aircraft steps the humid heat hit Joe like a hair drier. He'd forgotten the Cow Cay heat, the way it forced open every pore of your body, broiled the body in its own sweat.

A small crowd had gathered to meet the flight, embracing relatives, carrying their luggage shoulder high through the dust thrown up by the propellers towards a line of palms. A row of jeeps and minibuses was lined up in the shade. Joe collected his grip and set off to look for a taxi.

Morgan's Hole wasn't really a town, just a thin dirt road separating two rows of shacks and houses, some single storey, some two storeys, with rusted tin roofs and balconies and wooden walls painted faded reds and faking blues and greens.

Bright-flowering tropical shrubs and flame-trees shared the yards and alleys with hogs and chickens and garbage. Behind each house stilted shit-houses projected out over the warm stagnant waters of the lagoon. The seas around most of the island were clear as lead crystal, but the beach at Morgan's Hole was the colour and texture of dog food, six inches deep for as far out as you could walk. Lumps of hanging green and brown fibre floated off into the open water beyond.

The people were every colour and no colour, predominantly black, predominantly anglophone, predominantly children. Animals and drunks slept in the shadows – men who claimed they'd once visited Liverpool or Glasgow, and maybe New York, though it was hard to tell – much of the time they didn't make a lot of sense, and there was confusion about what they'd done, what they liked to imagine they'd done, what they wanted people to think they'd done, and things they meant to do.

Scattered along the street, joined by sagging cats' cradles of power lines and telephone cables, were a general store, an ironmonger's, two bars, a dentist with a terrifying five-foot red-rooted hardboard tooth outside; a pharmacy-cum-fish-tackle shop, Franca's Sala de Belleza, a post office, a bank, and the faded pretensions of The Gable hotel. Occasionally an American jeep rolled slowly by on a visit from one of the diving camps. Behind the town the land rose to low jungled hills.

There was a disturbance outside the hotel, twenty or thirty islanders standing in the road facing the building opposite, a half-built concrete hall with a painted sign hanging from the scaffolding, 'Coming Soon, Praise The Lord,

The Good Book Union of the Americas.' A balding, overweight American stood on the steps, sweating heavily.

Has to be a preacher, Joe decided as he paid off his cab: no one else dresses that badly, the only people who dress worse than evangelists are golfers. He wore department-store leisurewear – a short-sleeved yellow shirt, sky-blue slacks and Nike trainers and carried a briefcase. At his side was a big-arsed woman in a turquoise tracksuit and trainers. She looked like his wife. The preacher was red-faced and angry.

'Therpent!' he lisped at the top of his voice. 'Blath-themer!'

'Amen!' shouted an ill-looking, spidery black man in a trucking cap, loose-jointed as a puppet, with high cheekbones and bad teeth, dressed in a check shirt and old black trousers held up with a snake-buckle belt. He was swaying slightly on his heels, whether from ecstasy or drink it was hard to tell.

Joe watched mesmerized.

There were three sides to the dispute: the preacher and his supporters, a similar number of antagonists across the street, and a larger crowd who stood in the middle, following the action like a tennis rally. In the background a uniformed sergeant leaned against the door jamb of the two-room police post, a cigarette between his teeth, mending a pair of sunglasses, looking up once in a while to make sure no one needed him. Dogs yawned in the shadows, sounds of salsa radio came from inside the hotel.

Mike Osborne wasn't arguing at all. He was leaning against the rail of the Gable, tanned and lean with curly salt-and-pepper hair and aquiline features that were midway between youthful good looks and distinguished middle age. He wore sandals and shorts, a bush shirt and a wide panama hat, one hand holding a bottle of beer, the other tapping against his thigh in time to the music from inside the hotel, a cigarette gripped between his teeth, a wide smile on his freckled face. He looked like something out of a Camel commercial, the noblest of savages.

The clergyman called him Beelthebub, Mike just grinned. The crowd laughed too.

'You gonna leave this town,' the preacher waving his arms now so that dark sweat stains showed under the armpits of his polo shirt, 'You gonna leave this island, you gonna leave this country, you gonna leave these people in the hands of the Lord 'cause if you don't the Lord gonna bring his Wrath and take you away Himself.'

'Amen!' shouted Spiderman.

'You got nothing to say?' the preacher shouted.

Mike said nothing. He took the cigarette out of his mouth and ground it under his heal, still smiling.

The crowd loved it.

The audience were a motley bunch, schoolgirls in navy skirts and white blouses, a dozen or so West Indian men in trucker caps or trilbies, beer bottles dangling from their hands, a fat Spaniard in shades with a moustache and an embroidered Mexican shirt, open and untucked, an old woman with withered walnut skin carrying a scarlet parasol. A girl with braces on her teeth giggled, took a swig of beer from a bottle, and passed it to a neighbour.

'You beware!' the preacher screamed. 'Remember Babylon, remember Lot . . .'

'Thave me!' mimicked the girl with the tooth-brace, waving her arms like a windmill. Good-looking girl, Joe decided, once you got over the teeth.

The Reverend had more to say, but his wife had had enough. She had a face like a sheep and tinted glasses in red plastic frames. She took her husband by the arm and led him back into the building.

Joe picked up his bag and set off towards the hotel, where Mike was now talking to the old woman with the parasol, leaning against the balcony, scratching the back of his neck.

Joe couldn't hear what he was saying but it made the woman laugh so loud she had to put her hand up to her mouth to keep her dentures in place. The girl with the braced teeth still giggling, doing grotesque imitations of the preacher, Spiderman swaying uncertainly, steadying himself against the half-built veranda of the mission hall.

Then, as Joe watched, Spiderman bent down, picked up a beer bottle and threw it violently across the street towards Mike. Someone shouted a warning, Mike ducked, but had no need to: the bottle smashed harmlessly on the tin roof of Sala de Belleza. The policeman put his sunglasses in his shirt pocket, walked slowly across the road, and spoke quietly to Spiderman: a tired-looking woman in a housecoat joined them. Mike was standing in the doorway of the hotel, lighting another cigarette. He gave them a friendly wave.

There was something terribly English about Mike Osborne. A particular kind of English, as though Rupert Brooke had grown up in the Britain of the 1960s, equal parts public schoolboy and reckless hippy. As a student he took drugs, listened to Hendrix, spent his summers backpacking in Thailand or Morocco, revelled in trash – cheap music, clothes, films, pulp TV, fast food – anything he could get his hands on so long as it had no meaning, no seriousness, no sense of purpose.

He loathed pomposity, dismissed authority, yet possessed immaculate manners. He had that rare combination of innocence and high intellect. Everyone liked him, many loved him, because his presence would lighten a room.

Joe had now known him for more than twenty years. It was the kind of relationship that failed to notice interruptions, and they stayed close even when their lives diverged, Joe to music, Mike to television.

Mike had done well in the BBC, travelling the world as a current affairs reporter. But corporation life didn't suit him, and at twenty-eight he moved to the States and took a job with WGBH, a public service TV station in Boston. Only Mike called it WGAS: when people asked him what it stood for he said, 'Who Gives A Shit?' He never got tired of the joke.

One day four years ago he was sent down to Honduras to make a documentary on what the Evangelical Christians were doing to the Mosquito Indians. What the evangelists were doing to them, Mike soon discovered, was turning a stone age civilization into a race of twentieth-century zombies. Whole tribes were dying of imported Western diseases.

While they were filming Mike met Amos Lipstein, an elderly Jewish doctor from the coast who told him about Cow Cay, and after the shoot Mike decided to take a week off and see the Cay for himself.

The first time Mike saw the island, he thought it was paradise. The climate was hot, but tempered by sea breezes, the soil fertile, the beaches deserted, the population benign. Cascades of vines and tropical flowers tumbled down the canyon walls, parrots and humming birds peopled the woods.

Close up, the mirage began to fade. The people were poor, and apart from a little shrimping there were no industries to employ them. A few tourists came in the Sixties and Seventies, but the wars in neighbouring Nicaragua and El Salvador drove them away, and only the divers came now. The young emigrated, and the old drank.

Dysentery and malaria were endemic, and when Mike arrived there was no hospital. Schooling was minimal, illiteracy almost universal. Most of the women got pregnant in their early teens and stayed that way for twenty years. The average family size was fourteen; infant mortality and deaths in childbirth were a weekly plague.

For Mike Osborne, Cow Cay was the Road to Damascus. He'd made films in Bangladesh and the Sahel, helpless countries where the scale of the problems was so great all you could hope to do was apply a little first-aid in hell. But Cow Cay was helpable, the scale possible, real progress achievable. Not Paradise Found, but Paradise Possible.

A month later he sold up his apartment in the States and used the money to buy the redundant Anglican mission at St Andrews.

That was four years ago. By the time of Joe's first visit, eighteen months later, the project was well underway. There was a clinic and dispensary at St Andrews, and a free school. Mike had gone to work on the island's water supplies, and had brought in nurses from the mainland to run prenatal courses and a birth control programme. Amos Lipstein, the Jewish doctor, flew over from the coast twice a week to work in the clinic.

The men still had no work and drank too much, babies still died, and there were ongoing problems with malaria. There was also a certain amount of local suspicion, particularly in the early months. But looking at St Andrews you could see the future, and it was beginning to work. Mike was excited, and so was Joe.

The crowd was dispersing, the old lady shuffling off down the road with her parasol, chuckling out loud. Joe waited until he was maybe ten feet away from Mike before calling his name.

Mike turned and blinked, the blink of a short-sighted man without his glasses on. For a moment a look of surprise that could have been dismay passed across his face like a wind-squall on water. Dismay became delight as his eyes found their focus.

'Joe! You fucker!'

He dropped his cigarette and ground it under his sandal.

The two men embraced in silence for what must have been a full minute. Then Mike put his hands on Joe's shoulders, held him at arm's length and looked him up and down like a farmer examining a cow at market.

Joe just smiled. Maybe it was the journey, but his eyes were wet with emotion. Big emotions, twenty years of them.

'What the hell . . . why didn't you phone?'

'I'm sorry, I should have. Impulse.'

'You come looking for Willie?'

'Yup.'

They looked at each other. Mike shook his head.

'You've heard nothing?'

'Nothing.' He picked up Joe's bag. 'Come on, let's get out of here.'

He led him across the street towards an old Land-Rover parked outside the bank. Two faded cotton towels hung over the seats to keep the vinyl cool. There were empty cigarette cartons and Coke cans on the floor, and a jumble of music cassettes in a box under the dash.

'You need to change money?' Mike asked.

'I would if I had any,' said Joe, settling into the passenger seat. 'I left in rather a rush.'

Mike's generosity was legendary, always had been: he gave away his possessions at the least pretext, often to people he hardly knew. He fished a wad of notes out of his back pocket and passed them across.

'Let me know when you run out. What did you think of the cabaret, by the way?'

'The preacher? I thought the government had put a stop to all that evangelist stuff.'

'They have and they haven't, the usual story. He's quite something, Bobby Burgess. Thinks I poison the natives, corrupt their daughters, obstruct the Word of the Lord. Actually I quite like the man, it's his wife I can't stand – imagine being married to that.'

Mike drove with his elbow out the window, his hand raised to catch the breeze.

'Tell me about Willie,' said Joe.

'Not a word. He took off two weeks ago, didn't take much luggage. The rest of his stuff's still here. He was living at at B. J. MacIntyre's place, out at Reef's End. You met B.J., didn't you?'

Joe nodded. He remembered B.J., a massive West Indian with pebble glasses who ran a fried chicken shack and rented chalets a couple of miles along the beach.

'Willie flew to San Pedro Sula,' Mike continued. 'Up the coast. That was the last we heard.'

'Did he tell anyone where he was going?'

'Copán, the ruins. Up country, in the hills, on the border with Guatemala. He was there okay, I checked with the police. Stayed a night, took a bus back to San Pedro. That's all we know. The immigration people say he's still in the country, but I wouldn't put much faith in that.'

'Do you think he's dead?'

Mike reached forward and took a pack of cigarettes off the dash, his eyes still on the road. He offered one to Joe.

'I don't know. I suppose it's possible.'

'Two days ago you said, "Don't worry".'

'I know. Half of me still thinks the same.'

'And the other half?'

'The other half simply doesn't know.'

He took a lighter out of his shirt pocket.

'I know this might sound queer in the circumstances, Joe, but it's good to see you.'

'You too, Mike.'

They drove slowly through the town. Where the main street ended the countryside began again, groves of palms and mango trees dotted with tin-roofed wooden bungalows, painted in richly faded shades of green and blue and red. The road was unpaved and heavily rutted, and there was little other traffic, just the occasional cyclist or one of the old jeeps which doubled as buses between Morgan's Hole and the smaller settlements, Reef's End, Dixon Ridge, West Beach.

St Andrews lay three miles from town and as much again from Reef's End, at a point where the land ran out like a finger into the sea, bordered on both sides by white beaches, and culminating in a flat rocky headland fringed with palms. Elsewhere in the Caribbean a site like that would by now have been bulldozed into a resort hotel or a golf course, but the leisured classes weren't ready for Honduras yet, nor Honduras for them.

Mike slowed down to cross an empty riverbed, steering the Land-Rover with one hand in and out of the boulders, eyes on the road, cigarette between his teeth.

'Tell me about the postcard.'

'He said there was something going on here which was either miraculous, criminal or insane.'

Mike smiled, straight off, not a hint of hesitation.

'Maybe miraculous, certainly insane.'

They turned a corner.

'Fuck me,' said Joe. 'What happened?'

4

St Andrews, when Mike first arrived, was a jungle of weeds and creepers, fallen palms and old oil drums, alive with snakes and lizards and the ghosts of the Scots missionaries who had built the settlement. The two-storey wooden Rectory was abandoned, its veranda overgrown, its balconies broken. The corrugated iron chapel had rusted through. Rafts of snails clung to the peeling paint on its sun-bleached notice board; dogs scrounged among the rusting pilchard tins on the midden; bone-thin cows grazed the thorns. The stilted timber boardwalk that had served as a jetty had rotted and collapsed. The skeletal ribs of the mission's cutter lay upturned and half-buried in the grass.

Mike and his hired helpers had hacked away a clearing in the undergrowth with machetes, rescued the harmonium and generator from the weeds, erected a fence to keep out the cattle, repaired the guttering, and tied down the roofs with fisherman's ropes and boulders against the hurricanes.

The Rectory became Mike's home and offices. The roughly restored chapel doubled as schoolroom and clinic. They used whatever materials came to hand: wooden crates and pallets, oil drums, hardboard, flotsam from the shore.

And that was how Joe remembered the place from his previous visit: makeshift, improvised, a triumph of energy and ingenuity.

Not any more: St Andrews was transformed.

The Rectory was still there, but the chapel had been torn down and replaced with a row of low cinder-block buildings arranged at right angles on either side of a wide asphalt path, bordered by shaved lawns and flowering shrubs. There were more new buildings among the trees on the headland, single-storey bungalows with steel-framed windows and wide eaves against the sun, timber storerooms and a handsome brick schoolhouse. Two nurses were helping an old man down the clinic steps, a youth in a straw hat was hosing the flowerbeds, the sound of chanting voices came from the school.

Mike parked the Land-Rover under the palms.

'We got most of the building materials from the US military on the coast,' he explained. 'They had a training base, counter-insurgency, only as you know there aren't any communists left in Central America. The Americans finally pulled out a couple of years ago. I went to see a colonel there, asked him what they were doing with their construction materials. He said "Help yourself". We brought it all over in trawlers, took us the best part of a month.'

'Isn't that what's called sleeping with the enemy?'

'Statutory rape. It's the name of the game in this business. You beg, you steal, you borrow. Not just from the army, from anyone.'

'Anyone?'

'Anyone.'

Mike would be brilliant at that stuff, charming and utterly unscrupulous. It was the way he'd worked as a TV journalist, cutting out the crap, ignoring PRs and press officers, presenting himself unannounced at the homes and offices of industrialists or generals or government ministers and asking for what he wanted face to face. His cheek had disarmed men and women regarded by his colleagues as untouchable. Admirals lent him helicopters, politicians admitted their shortcomings, lawyers showed him confidential documents, revolutionaries took him to midnight rendez-vous to meet their leaders, all because of the way he asked them: politely, reasonably, and with an intrinsic assumption of mutual trust.

Joe followed him down the path between the buildings.

Humming birds hovered among the hibiscus, guinea fowl pecked in the dust, a warm breeze blew in from the sea.

The Rectory was timber gothic, built in the 1920s, with a tin roof and pitch-pine floors. The doors and windows were all open, and the brass storm lantern in the hall swung gently in the breeze. It was eccentrically furnished, spare, a mixture of late-colonial missionary remnants and eclectic souvenirs from Mike's travels — heavy mahogany dressers, the restored harmonium, a ten-foot dining-table with carved legs, a pre-war dentist's chair, a glass case of stuffed fish, an elephant's-foot umbrella stand, carvings from North Africa and Nepal.

Boxes of medical supplies and equipment were stacked in the hall and halfway up the stairs, and through the open door of the study Joe glimpsed a laptop Apple computer — top of the range — open on the desk beside a small fax machine. A line of wetsuits hung in the hall above a heap of flippers and snorkels and diving cylinders, and a stripped-down outboard motor was laid out on the dining-table. The general impression was of lightly planned chaos.

'What happened to your housekeeper?' asked Joe.

'Virginia? She died. A couple of years ago, she was over on the mainland, up country from the Mosquito Coast, visiting friends. She caught malaria. A village called Jiuba, a couple of hundred miles east of here — a wild place, very remote, mostly Indians and a few settlers. Plenty of Indians, including refugees from Nicaragua who decided to stay put when the war ended. If she'd been here we could have done something to save her. Jiuba's the next project, but that's another story.' He ran his hand back through his hair. 'I was going to get someone else but in the end I opted for privacy.'

He got beers from the fridge, and they wandered down to the sea and sat on the end of the new pier, legs dangling, looking down through the clear green water, watching the crabs and needle fish feeding. Fifty yards offshore the swell was breaking over the reef.

Joe remembered the last time he'd been here, the two of

them sitting out in the moonlight, laughing as they argued over the lyrics of an old Everly Brothers' song that Joe had forgotten in mid-verse. Good times.

Mike took the last cigarette out of his pack, tapped both ends on his knee several times, put it in his mouth and then crushed the pack in his hand.

'Tell me about Willie,' said Joe.

'He just arrived one afternoon. A taxi dropped him off, he walked up the path, knocked on the door. He had his back to me when I opened it, I hadn't a clue who he was. Honestly, Joe, it must be fifteen years since I'd seen him. He was wearing an old cotton suit and a trilby. Cigarette hanging from his lip, wanted to know what the guinea fowl were for, whether they were wild or pets or if we ate them. Even when he turned round I didn't recognize him, he had to introduce himself. "Willie Wilde. You know my son." And that was that.'

'He didn't want a bed, he'd already booked in at The Gable in Morgan's Hole. It's a whorehouse, God knows what he made of it. It took me a week to persuade him to move into the Rectory.'

Joe smiled. Willie always hated staying with people, hated being beholden to hosts, even family and close friends.

'He wouldn't budge until I offered him a job,' Mike continued. 'I told him to relax and have a holiday, he wanted to work. Crazy, a man that age signing on in a place like this. I spent days trying to dissuade him, but in the end I ran out of excuses.'

'What was the job?' Joe asked.

'I made him bursar. Looking after the petty cash accounts, dealing with local suppliers and government officials and so on. I'd been handling all that business myself, it was getting out of hand. This place has grown, Joe. It used to be just me and a couple of local people, I've now got a full-time staff of twenty. And there's the Jiuba project, which takes up a lot of my time now.'

'What's happening at Jiuba?'

Mike picked up a hank of rope off the jetty and ran it through his fingers.

'You know much about malaria?'

'Only that I should probably be taking something for it now. I left in rather a hurry.'

'Used to be something you could take, but most of that shit doesn't work any more. The parasites got smart. First they figured chloroquinine, which was the old cure, so the chemists came up with something stronger, but the parasites got that figured too. And on and on. They reckon a new drug's good for roughly a year before the immunity sets in. Not an attractive proposition to most drug companies. Malaria's the biggest killer on earth, 500 million cases a year world wide, 2 million deaths, and getting worse all the time. The World Health Organization ran a global eradication programme on it, same way they did with smallpox, only with malaria they had to give up.'

'So what do you do?'

'Keep trying new drugs, it's the only way. But we seem to be making progress, it's not a big problem on the Cay any more, but on the mainland it's a hell of a thing. And I've got hold of funding to run a pilot project at Jiuba.'

'This is because of Virginia?'

'That gave me the incentive, but once we started working up there it took on a life of its own. The Indians are in a pretty rough state, fucked around by the Contras, fucked around by missionaries, they've lost their old way of life and no one's raised a finger to help them find a new one. A lot of disease, a lot of poverty, not much else. We've bought land and built clinics, I've managed to get funding out of an American agency, Third Aid. But there's a long way to go. One way and another it takes up a lot of time. So Willie took over the day to day administration back here. It's not the easiest of jobs, you spend days sitting around offices in San Pedro Sula and Tegoose, arguing with officials, bribing suppliers.'

'Willie managed your bribes for you?'

Mike laughed.

'No, I spared him that. Or most of it. You have to bribe everyone here, from the postman to the minister of health.

He handled the postman, I took care of the fat cats in the ministries.'

'Bribe them for what?' asked Joe.

'To get things into the country and to get them out again. Some medicines we bring in the official way, through Tegoose or San Pedro. But it takes for ever. If we need something in a hurry we bring it in the same way the drink and tobacco comes in, by night, on back roads from Guatemala. Slip the border guards a few quid to go out to the flicks for the evening. You also need to pay to make sure no one gets arrested for whatever trumped-up offence the police care to dream up when they're short of beer money. To get a pilot to take medicine to where it's needed, to get work papers for a paramedic from the States, to get a phone put in. Anything. It's not too bad on the island but on the mainland backhanders are a major industry. No one gets too upset about it.'

'How did Willie get on?'

'It took him a while to settle in and for people to get used to him. You know what he's like when things aren't done the way he wants. But once he got into the swing he was brilliant at it, honestly. Most Europeans haven't a clue how to handle the Hondurans, they act so bloody nice to those guys, fall over backwards not to appear racist or colonial, either that or they blow their lids all the time. Willie wasn't unpleasant, but he was firm. He didn't pretend to speak Spanish, he didn't wave his arms or lose his temper, he just gave orders, quite loudly, in English, over and over again, until he got what he wanted. Coming from you or me that kind of behaviour would be disastrous, but the Hondurans liked him. Maybe he reminded them of old times, maybe it was his age. I think it quite shocked him that people got fond of him. He took over all our paperwork, bulldozed it through the system.'

'Heaven help the system,' said Joe. 'Tell me something, Mike. Are you worried about him?'

'I was to start off with. But I'm coming to think no news is good news. He certainly knows how to handle himself in this country. And he never seems to consult anyone before doing anything, at least he never did while he was on the Cay. If he felt like pushing off for a week or two I honestly don't think it would occur to him that anyone would worry about him. But you'd be a better judge of that than me, Joe.'

Mike was right: Willie never told anyone what he was going to do, he just did it, always had.

'Unless he's dead,' Mike added, almost as an afterthought.

'If he's dead he's dead,' said Joe. 'The problem is if he's alive and in trouble.'

'That's why you came?'

'That's why I came.'

'Then we'd better find him.'

Mike smiled and put his hand on Joe's shoulder.

The sun was setting, and the sea had turned a white gold and the palms to black silhouettes. Two children, agile and thin-limbed like spiders, were playing with a thin sickly dog among the trees. A generator started up somewhere.

They walked back up to the Rectory, and Mike improvised dinner, frozen fish with tinned beans and tinned potatoes and a six-pack of Mexican beer.

They ate on the veranda, listening to the waves sighing up the beach and the frizz of insects frying themselves on the blue tubes of the fluorescent fly-trap, watching the bats flicker through the shadows. The lights from the house threw long bright shafts across the grass, silhouetting the rustling branches. There were fireflies too, flickering in the darkness. Land crabs scuttled in the undergrowth.

Mike took a mouthful of beer and wiped his mouth on his sleeve.

'So how are you, Joe?'

'I'm fine, all things considered. I seem to have got my hands on most of the trappings – regular work, a place to live, friends, reasonable health.'

'You happy?'

'Yea, I suppose I am. I get the feeling I should be doing

more than I am but I suspect that's just Work Ethic crap. I like my friends, I like talking to people in bars, I like playing music. Same old story.'

'Are you still with Marion?'

'Nope.'

'You're nuts.'

'I know. The trouble is she isn't.'

'Bullshit,' said Mike. 'The trouble with you two is that you can never synchronize your emotions; you take it in turns to decide to get married, but never at the same time.'

It was true: for almost ten years they'd stalked each other, but every time one of them decided to get serious the other ran away; except that now Marion had gone for good. She was thirty-six, and wanted to try someone else while she still had time.

'No, she decided to get married for real, got hitched to a guy who gave her a Golf GTi as a wedding present. Last March. That chapter's over.

'Do you mind?'

'Of course. I mean I don't blame her, but I mind, yes. It's hard to summon up the energy to go looking for someone else.'

'You're just scared of commitment,' said Mike.

Joe winced.

'*Et tu, Brute?* No, you're probably right – fear of the unknown. How about you?'

Mike shook his head.

'I'm too busy for any of that nonsense these days.'

'Which nonsense – sex or relationships?'

Mike grinned.

'Never too busy for sex. You get a very good class of bedmate out here when you need it, but no one's too fussed about the long term. Let me know if you get lonely, I'll arrange some introductions. All tastes and ages catered for.'

Joe was pouring himself another whisky.

'All ages? You don't mean . . .'

'Willie? Absolutely.'

'You're joking.'

'Not at all. Hold on a second, I'll show you.'

Mike got up from the table and went inside. He returned with a Fujicolour envelope of pictures.

They showed Willie in a pair of sensible knee-length shorts and a bush shirt standing bolt upright and staring expressionless at the camera in front of a clinic; similarly upright and unsmiling with two West Indians on a beach in his ancient bathing trunks, wearing his horn-rimmed glasses under a wide panama hat; posing formally with B. J. MacIntyre, his landlord at Reef's End, outside a tin-roofed hut; studying an old Seagull outboard motor in a dug-out canoe.

There was nothing significant in the lack of smiles: Willie came from a generation which treated a photo-call much like a visit to the dentist, and you needed a long lens to catch him off his guard.

Joe stopped when he got to the picture of Willie and the two West Indians on the beach. One was B.J.; the other was a black girl in her early twenties, slim but big-breasted, with laughing eyes and high cheekbones and braided hair tied back across her scalp. She wore tight red trousers and a patterned green and blue blouse. Circular silver earrings hung from her lobes, and she had a string of antique coins on a red cord round her neck and a man's watch on her wrist. Her only flaw, if it was a flaw, was her teeth. She had a mouthful of enormous dental work, metal braces and silver caps, which bared the gums clean up to the nostrils when she smiled. She looked like a girl who laughed a lot, when she wasn't mimicking the Reverend Bobby Burgess in the main street of Morgan's Hole.

'Who is she?' asked Joe.

Mike looked at his glass.

'That's Sarah.'

'And she and Willie . . .'

'I'm afraid so.'

'Jesus,' said Joe.

Who the hell did Willie think he was – Paul Gauguin? His father had had many vices, but as far as Joe knew womanizing wasn't one of them. He'd tried one woman – Joe's mother, Margaret – and when that didn't work he sort of gave up, ticked it off the list. Had a wife, fathered a child, done it.

'How old is she?'

Mike shrugged his shoulders.

'She must be about twenty-two. Early middle age in these parts.'

Joe was still looking at the picture.

'Was he living with her?'

'Not exactly. She lives with her mother, an old witch called Omangatu, what they call a *brujo* here. Mexican Indian, from Veracruz, with a dash of something darker. Her father was West Indian, from the Cayman Islands, but he fucked off years ago. They have a cabin about a mile up the hill from B.J.'s.'

'What's a *brujo*?'

'They're what people round here had before they had doctors. Wise women, witch-doctors, whatever. Dry herbs, fix potions, mumble a lot, you know the shit. There's nothing secret about them. There's one works in the kitchens at The Gable, another keeps hogs up on Dixon's Ridge, three or four more up and down the island. You get them everywhere in Central America. Harmless old women, up to now I've got on with them fine. So did Joe.'

'Sarah's why he moved out to B.J.'s?'

'Partly, I suspect.'

'Did Willie say anything to her about where he was going?'

'Only what he told the rest of us.'

Mike was rolling a joint. It was such a familiar image to Joe, Mike spreading out the papers, licking the seam of the cigarette, splitting it open and mixing the tobacco with a fat pinch of grass. Mike always did a lot of dope.

'I'm sorry about all this,' said Joe.

Mike lit up, inhaled, and passed the joint across to Joe.

'About what?'

'About Willie.'

'Don't be. Willie's the least of our problems.'

Joe looked at him, waiting for the smile, but it didn't come. Instead Mike ran his hand back through his hair, and Joe noticed for the first time how weary he was looking. The skin beneath his eyes was grey, the muscles tense.

'We lost a boat about a month back,' Mike said. 'The flotation tanks started taking in water a mile off shore. I'd lent it to a couple of guys from the clinic to go fishing, luckily they were strong swimmers. Could have been an accident. Then there was a fire in the stores. Nothing serious, could have been an accident too. And there have been rumours in town, the odd graffiti, people whispering about White Man's Medicine.'

'Has this got anything to do with the Reverend Burgess?' Joe asked.

'That was one of Willie's theories. But I don't think so. Burgess is harmless, really. Preaches a lot, but I can't see him taking the law into his own hands.'

'What do you mean, one of Willie's theories?'

'He's an old man, Joe, you know how the old are. They like to think the worst of everyone. He had it in for all sorts of people – the God Squad, people who wouldn't use lights on their bicycles, teenage drinkers, supposed drug traffickers. When you get to Willie's age the lid comes off and you start speaking your mind. Not just about here, about everything.'

'He thought you never forgave him for what happened to your mother. She never enjoyed sex, incidentally – did you know that? He also disapproves of the way your uncle brought up your cousins. England's finished, Christian values have disappeared from public life, no one believes in Duty and Obligation any more – all that shit.'

'Did people resent it?'

'Not at all, they loved it. And God knows they complain enough themselves. Willie was very well liked. They expect old people to have their eccentricities.'

Joe drained his glass.

'What were his other eccentricities?'

'Oh, the usual. His memory's a bit wobbly these days, he

forgets names, loses things, wanders off and forgets where he's going. But you know all that.'

'Do you think that's what's happened to him this time – he's wandered off and forgotten where he is?'

'I haven't a clue, Joe. I really haven't a clue. He left here on a morning flight to San Pedro Sula, on his way to the ruins at Copán. He said he wanted some time off.'

'How long does it take to get to Copán?'

'A day, I suppose. Mostly by bus. A couple more days to look at the remains.'

'And then?'

'You could keep heading up across the border to Guatemala but it's a shitty road. Or back the way he came.'

'Is Copán one of your smuggling routes?'

Mike looked him straight in the eye.

'It is and he wasn't. I promise, Joe.'

The weariness was getting to Joe now, adrenaline fighting a losing battle with jet-lag. They began to tidy away the dishes.

'Do you known what Willie wanted as a retirement present?' Joe asked as he rinsed out the glasses. 'A bloody washing machine.'

'What did they give him?'

'A Waterford decanter and a framed caricature of himself. Hideous, both of them. What's happened to Amos Lipstein, by the way?'

'Retired. Still living in Teila, he comes over once in a while. But his eyesight's going. We've got a full-time doctor now, young guy called Frank Carreras from New Orleans, a US foundation gave him to us on lend-lease for a year. Frank's over at Jiuba on the new project at the moment, he'll be back tomorrow. You'll like him.'

Joe's room was deep in dust but cool and breezy, with a wood floor and white walls and a white-sheeted bed under a grey mosquito net, a chest of drawers and a bookcase stocked with airport fiction. Before and after photos of St Andrews hung in clipframes beside the door. Directly opposite the bed a set of double doors opened on to a balcony, and the sea beyond.

He got undressed, showered and lay down on the bed, naked under the mosquito net, listening to the hum of the generator. He tried to sleep, but the heat and the jet-lag conspired to stop him. For a while he could hear Mike moving around downstairs, then footsteps on the stairs, a door closing, and silence.

After half an hour he got up, wrapped a towel round his waist and went out on to the balcony. To his left, inland, lights showed in two of the bungalows, but the rest of landscape was in darkness. To the south the black outline of the hills was silhouetted against the starlit sky. He turned and looked across the bay towards Morgan's Hole.

'Bloody Willie,' he said out loud. 'Where the hell –'

The force of the explosion shook the house. For a frozen moment the whole settlement was bathed in a flare of brilliant white light. The remains of the Land-Rover burned fiercely beneath the trees.

As the flare faded, Joe could see a figure in a baseball cap, halfway between the Land-Rover and the house, hesitate for a moment then sprint into the undergrowth.

5

MIKE WAS ALREADY halfway across the clearing as Joe cleared the Rectory steps. Lights were going on in the buildings.

'That way!' Joe shouted.

Mike stopped and turned. Joe was pointing towards the headland. If he was on the headland he was trapped, the only way out back through the settlement.

There were maybe a dozen of them on the hunt now, settlement workers, men and women, some in pyjamas, the rest in jeans and T-shirts. They spread across the narrow isthmus, watching the headland. The moon was out, casting blue shadows among the palms.

'He got a gun?' asked one of the paramedics.

Joe wasn't sure.

'I have,' Mike said quietly.

He had a pistol in his hand, holding it uncomfortably, cautiously. Joe wondered what else had been happening at St Andrews to make a man like Mike Osborne go out and get himself a gun.

He looked up at Mike's face. Gone was Camel Man: in his place was a lost child, fearful, confused, innocent. What you love most in your friends is not their strengths but their weaknesses, the moments when they admit or cannot hide their vulnerabilities. Despite the gun, Mike looked as helpless as a puppy.

Joe took control. He shouted at everyone to stay where they were while they waited for the police. He sent for torches. One of the paramedics suggested they send two men down to the pier to launch a boat in case the intruder tried to swim for it. If he made it to the reef he could work his way along the coral parallel to the beaches and chose a place further down the coast to come ashore.

Someone had switched on the line of lights along the asphalt path, and a plume of black smoke drifted across the settlement. The air was thick with the smell of burning rubber. What remained of the Land-Rover was still smouldering. The force of the blast had thrown the vehicle thirty feet across the flowerbeds, depositing it upside down on the lawn.

'Last time I saw one of those,' Mike said to no one in particular, 'was in Southern Lebanon. Time before that in South Armagh. Culvert bombs, land mines, mercury tilt switches.' He handed Joe the gun, an American Walther P.38. 'You know how to work this thing?'

Joe weighed it in his hand. His only experience of firearms was the same as Mike's, the school cadet corps at Glenalmond twenty years before, where they'd drilled in the Perthshire drizzle with old Lee Enfield rifles that pre-dated the First World War. Didn't like guns then, didn't like them now.

'Where did you get it?'

'It was Willie's idea. He bought two off a fellow on La Ceiba last month.'

'And kept the other?'

'I presume so.'

'Why?'

Mike looked at him blankly.

'Has something like this happened before?' Joe asked.

'Not exactly.'

'What the fuck does that mean?'

Mike didn't answer.

A siren was approaching from the direction of Morgan's Hole. Headlights were moving on the coast road, flashing between the palm trunks.

'Talk to me!' Joe demanded.

Mike was lighting a cigarette. He said nothing.

'What the hell is going on?' Joe asked again.

'I don't know, Joe. I really don't know.'

'This is to do with Willie, isn't it?'

'It's to do with me.' He sucked on his cigarette. 'Later, Joe, we'll talk about it later.'

Captain Luther Mendes drove a Chevvy 4WD pick-up, white with a blue stripe down the side, two fluffy cotton footballs hanging from the mirror and a spotlight welded to the roof. He was a short man, almost top-heavy, on thin legs, like a barrel on stilts. A mestizo, Joe guessed, black hair and pockmarked skin, more Spaniard than Afro-Caribbean. The watch on his wrist had a metal strap two inches wide. His now mended sunglasses were clipped to his shirt pocket.

The policeman got out of the jeep and stood for a while looking at the crater, then walked over to join them. Joe explained what had happened.

'He armed?' Mendes spoke in a high-pitched, squeaky voice, like a tyre going down or a balloon stretched at the mouth.

'We don't know,' said Joe.

The captain collected a megaphone from the jeep and tested it by tapping his finger against the mouthpiece.

'You out there,' he squeaked. 'You got two minutes to come out.'

No one moved. Offshore they could hear the sound of an outboard, the two paramedics patrolling the waters between the shore and the reef.

Joe watched Mike stub out his half-finished cigarette and light another. Mendes looked at his watch.

'Okay, let's go. He got a gun, don't do nothing or say nothing, leave him to me.'

They moved off in line, five yards between each man, Mendes in the centre, Joe and Mike on his left, playing their torches over the shrub. The ground was treacherous, thorn shrub interspersed with boulders. Some of the party had brought machetes, slashing a way clear through the undergrowth.

'You get snakes here?' Joe asked cautiously.

'A few,' said Mendes. 'Nothing too dangerous, 'cept the yellow fellow, thin like a stick, hides in the branches. No use worrying about him, no chance you'll see him this time of night.'

They were twenty yards from the open sea when something moved in the shadows to Joe's left.

'Stop!' Mendes shouted.

The figure was in the open now, dodging the boulders, making for the beach. Joe made a run for him, but the orderly on his left was faster. There was a splash, shouting, and then silence.

They waded out to where the orderly was standing waist-high in the warm water, his elbows under the armpits of the unconscious intruder. Fluorescent ripples ran over the black surface of the lagoon as he moved. The water seemed somehow heavier in the darkness.

'He alive?' asked Mendes.

'I guess,' said the orderly. 'Hit him in the mouth, he ain't said nothin' since but he breathin' okay.'

Joe took the legs, and they carried the body back along the shoreline to St Andrews and laid it out on the grass in front of the Rectory. Only when they reached the light of the porch did he recognize the face.

Their catch was Spiderman. His lips were swollen where the orderly had punched him and there was blood coming from his mouth. But the most obvious thing about him was that he was drunk.

'Vaz,' said Mendes.

Everyone knew David Vaz.

His story was the story of half the island: illegitimate, raised by his grandmother, went away to sea, came home, married, fathered nine children, went to sea again, came home again, fathered three more, argued with his wife, shouted at his children, moped around town, drank, kept a few hogs, fished, caught crabs, sold a bit of dope to tourists.

Then he got ill. None of the doctors knew what of, he

just said he felt bad all the time, agues and sweats and tiredness. The worse he felt, the more he drank, until no one could tell if he was ill any more or just drunk. He hung around town sponging off tourists, doing a bit of labouring. Always a beer bottle in his hand, dangling behind his back.

Half a bottle of whisky would buy anything from David Vaz. For ten dollars he'd blow up the whole town if he didn't get distracted in the liquor store on the way.

He was awake now, sitting on the grass with his knees to his chest, nursing his busted mouth. His eyes flicked across the crowd, clocking faces.

'Who told you to do this, David?' Mendes said quietly.

'No one told me do nothin'.'

Mendes shook his head.

'Empty you pockets, man.'

Vaz didn't move.

'I said *open you pockets*!' the policeman shouted, so high it sounded like a falsetto.

It was a pathetic hoard: a clasp knife with a broken handle tied with tape, a bottle opener, a few coins, a box of matches. Mendes picked them over one by one by his flashlight. Mike had collected cotton wool and iodine from the Rectory, and was trying to dress the wound.

Vaz pushed him aside with his arm. He still wasn't saying anything.

'You been seen running off the time it blew, David,' Mendes persisted 'We got a witness. You ain't the kind to go blowing up vehicles, not 'less someone suggests it to you.'

Vaz dropped his hand from his mouth.

'What witness?'

'Friend of Mr Osborne.' Mendes pointed to Joe. 'He seen you.'

Vaz's eyes turned to Joe, trying to get him into focus.

'You Willie Wilde's boy?'

Joe nodded.

'Told me in town you was out here.' He shaded his eyes from the jeep's searchlight. 'Yea, I reckon you's Willie's boy. Same way he stands, same stoop, some people see these things, some don't.'

And then he looked away.

'That all you saying?' asked Mendes.

'That's all,' said David, his hand back over his bleeding mouth.

They put him in the police jeep and Mendes took him into Morgan's Hole.

Back in the Rectory Joe made coffee and they sat in the kitchen, Mike stretched out in the old dentist's chair, Joe perched on the edge of the table.

'You'd better tell me what all this is about, Mike.'

Mike's hands hung over the arms of the chair, fiddling with the chrome handles. He looked a little better than he had outside, but not a lot.

'I wish I knew, Joe, I really wish I knew. All I do know is that someone wants us out of here.'

'Apart from Vaz?'

'Apart from Vaz.'

'Then who set him up?'

Mike shook his head.

'I don't fucking know, Joe. Things keep happening. Aside from Bobby Burgess no one says anything to my face, no notes, no phone calls. Unless you're careful you start believing everyone's in on it. But you can't afford to believe that. And anyway it's not true, people value this place. They wouldn't use it if they didn't.'

'Was all that business in town yesterday unusual?'

Mike shrugged.

'Happens once in a while. Burgess is very anti the aid agencies, Third Aid in particular, and Third Aid is our major source of funding now. They've got a long history of rubbing missions up the wrong way, I'm glad to say. You know what Burgess and co are like, they use radio telephones and video recorders and computers, but deep down they're medieval, flat-earthers. I've never said a word against Burgess in public, I swear. But the very nature of what we do here's a threat to him. He doesn't give a shit about health, not his department, all he wants is souls. Once they're saved the sooner they get to heaven the better. Guaranteed heaven's bloody tempting if your experience of this world is anything like David Vaz's.'

'Tell me what else has happened.'

'I told you about the boat and the fire, they're the most obvious. Most of the rest is Chinese whispers. Some of the trawler owners are keen to bring in tourist development, hotels and casinos and so on. Extend the runway to take jets, bring sun-lovers in from the States. I'm not against it in principle, but I think you have to plan these things carefully if you're not going to end up looking like Puerto Rico. That's not a popular view in certain circles. They say I'm blocking jobs, keeping the dollars out.'

He got up from the chair, collected the whisky from the side and poured two glasses.

'The rest's quite vague. The race thing surfaces sometimes, White Men coming in here and organizing everyone's lives for them. There's a bit of that, but not much. Then there are people who think our being here gives the Cay too high a profile — always been a lot of smuggling along this coast, they don't like outsiders around, period. And the government has an innate suspicion of intruders too. Because of the way we operate we're not popular in government circles. We bribe, you have to. But only on a very modest scale. What those guys like are nice fat grants from US Aid and the EC, plenty of cash and hardware coming in so they can cream off enough to keep them in Mercs and swimming pools. Low-key, low-cost projects are a threat to their way of life. We exist on a knife edge here, they could close us down tomorrow on the slimmest pretext. They can't be seen to obstruct us, but I don't think they'd be upset if we moved out.

'People look to us for miracles, too — expect us to cure any illness then get bitter when we can't. David Vaz is a case in point, when I come to think about it, always complaining he was in pain, why the hell couldn't we fix him.'

'What's wrong with him?' Joe interrupted.

Mike tapped the side of his head.

'Whatever suits him. Amos did tests, Frank too, nothing showed up.'

'You got any friends at all?' asked Joe.

Mike laughed, finished his whisky and put the glass on the floor at his feet.

'Oh yes. Hundreds. I wouldn't be doing this if I hadn't.'

'You could do it somewhere else,' Joe suggested. 'There must be plenty of other places you could set up.'

'There are, and I won't. The Cay's become my life, Joe. You don't know how it feels to be doing something constructive after all those years farting around making TV programmes. I suppose I've become obsessive about it, but you have to be if you want to achieve anything. I honestly believe that. Even small things, and God knows this is small enough. But it works, it really does. Not perfectly, we've made mistakes, but everywhere you look you can see the evidence. Nothing I did in TV changed anything, not at the level of individuals. This is different. I suppose you could call it doing something with my life.'

This was a whole new Mike. Previously, the avoidance of commitment had been almost a religious tenet, the idea of a Cause total anathema. Such politics as he'd possessed had been generalities: on the side of the poor, against greed, violence, snobbery. But you could never nail him down to specifics. He'd listen, empathize, try to understand other people's ideas and beliefs, but whenever he was in danger of owning an idea he'd undercut himself, turn it into a joke.

'You're no use to anyone dead,' said Joe.

'Maybe not. I'm not sure I'm much use to anyone alive, either – I'm not sure any of us are. But living out here has made me realize you can try. You need to forget all that English middle-class shit, all that reasonable behaviour, if you're going to get anywhere. You need to be a bit unbalanced to achieve anything. I really believe that now.'

'Maybe we're not meant to achieve anything, maybe achieving's a temptation we have to resist.'

'I don't believe that. I don't think you do either.'

Joe smiled. He knew what Mike was saying, knew it from the same source – the careful middle-class values that made England such a safe, stable, dull country to live in.

They moved through from the kitchen to the living room. Joe opened the lid of the old piano, sat down, and started doodling with the keys. It was three days since he'd played music, and he missed it.

'What's all this got to do with Willie?' he asked Mike. 'Was he ever threatened?'

'I don't think so. People like him, Joe. He could be a bit stuffy sometimes, but they gave him a fool's pardon. I've thought about it, but I can't see any motive for anyone wanting to get rid of him. What would be the point?'

'There'd be a point if he'd come across something.'

'Like what?'

Joe didn't know. He'd been here less than twelve hours. His left hand started laying down a twelve-bar blues.

'Did Vaz know Willie well?' he asked.

'I suppose in a way he did. David sort of adopted him. Initially I think he looked on him as a soft touch – you need to watch out for that here, incidentally – there's no shortage of cupboard love around. But even after Willie wised up David still hung around; he interested your father for some reason. He couldn't figure the lethargy here, it fascinated him. David's a perfect case. Willie couldn't work out why the man didn't do something with his life. Not just the drink, the lack of aspiration. David's own father was American, he even had US papers, he could leave any time.'

'Why didn't he?'

'He tried it a couple of times – tried the States, tried the mainland. He didn't like the mainland because he said they chopped each other up there over nothing. He's right, you walk about Teila or La Ceiba or San Pedro Sula they've all got guns. He'd tried America once, spent a year up in Jacksonville working in the docks, said they treated you like shit if you were black, worse still if you were foreign.'

'If he's so scared of guns what's he doing putting bombs in Land-Rovers?'

'Looking for drinking money, I suppose.'

'From who?'

'Fuck knows.'

'Maybe he didn't do it, maybe he was just out there when it happened.'

'At one o'clock in the morning? Doing what?'

They sat talking for another half hour, running over old times, Cambridge, London, shared memories, shared friends. It was after three by the time Joe went to bed. As he lay under the mosquito net, wondering about Willie, he kept rehearing the sound of the explosion on the lawn.

Miraculous, criminal, or insane, the old man had written on his card. Already he'd seen a miracle and a crime, and he'd only been on the island twelve hours. Two up, one to go.

6

JOE SLEPT BADLY, his body unused to the heat, his mind confused by time zones which told him that three in the morning was almost time for lunch. It was ten by the time he eventually woke. Outside he could hear voices, the sound of a tractor, a radio. He got out of bed, pulled on his jeans and walked out on to the balcony.

Morning is the finest time of day on the Cay, the air fresh and pleasant, before the heavy heat of the day has had time to slow all life to the leaden pace of the tropics. Outside the window the sea glistened like a mirror in the sunshine. At a point where the grass met the shore a black woman in a bedraggled housecoat and trainers stood beside a pile of fallen coconuts lighting a fire to make coconut oil.

She shelled the nuts on top of a post with neat, precise blows of her machete, never cutting through to the flesh. Next she grated them on a tin sieve the size of a shoebox, then kneaded the pulp with water. Her large family stood around watching. Her husband, with his arm resting on a young child, walked over occasionally to a pile of rotted lumber and threw a plank on the fire. Two teenage sons, in American T-shirts and trucker caps, posed on the fence and argued politics.

Every once in a while the woman straightened and scolded one of the younger children. She was maybe thirty, maybe older. Not obese, but big, with a fine profile and a startling smile, a confident well-organized woman. None of the men helped her. She took the pot of coconut mulch across to the fire and put it on to boil. In two hours she'd get maybe two bottles of oil from a day's work and a dozen coconuts.

Inland, the settlement was already at work. Medical staff in short-sleeved white shirts came and went up and down the asphalt path; outside the schoolroom a class was sitting on the grass, books on their knees, listening to a young teacher. Under the trees the remains of the Land-Rover were being loaded on to a flat-back trailer behind the tractor. Captain Mendes and another policeman stood in the crater, Mendes poking the soil with a stick, stooping to pick up pieces of metal and throwing them into a pile on the path.

It was only when Joe looked down that he saw the body. It lay face up on the grass directly beneath his window, maybe ten feet away, arms spreadeaged. A white man, big as a bear, with long hair, wearing denim shorts and an Old Kentucky T-shirt.

Joe steadied himself on the rail, opened his mouth to shout out to Mendes. And then the body moved, sat up, yawned, crossed its legs, put its hands palms-open on its knees and began to hum a single low, reverberating note, mani-mani-po, like the men in purple kaftans you used to get in Joseph Losey movies.

When Mike said he had a doctor on loan from the States Joe imagined an earnest young Mormon, or a blue-eyed WASP Peace Corps worker, the kind you met in US Aid compounds from Tierra del Fuego to Angola. Frank Carreras didn't even look like a doctor: if Joe had guessed he'd have put him down as a rock drummer, vintage *circa* 1969.

By the time Joe had showered and dressed Frank was in the kitchen making breakfast. He had the worktop laid out like an operating theatre. His hands moved to and from the stove, juggling food and utensils, oiling the pan, dusting French toast, turning the bacon rashers under the grill, checking the hash browns. Chuck Berry sang 'You

Never Can Tell' on a ghetto-blaster by the open window, Frank beating out the rhythm with his implements as he cooked.

'Hi,' he shouted over the music. 'You must be Joe. How's your appetite?'

Joe was famished.

'There's fresh orange juice in the freezer,' said Frank, cracking an egg single-handed into the skillet. 'Coffee coming up in a minute. I'm sorry I wasn't here when you got in, I caught the early flight this morning, been over in Jiuba for a couple of days. The heat here can be a little oppressive, but at least we have the sea. Jiuba all you have is the fucking jungle. How you like your eggs?'

Sunny side up, Joe decided. He found Frank hard to keep up with. The man wouldn't sit still, kept roaming from cupboard to cupboard, collecting salt and plates and cutlery and sauces, changing his mind, going back for something else.

Close up he didn't look much like a doctor either. He was a vast man, well over six foot, must have weighed close to eighteen stone. His hair reached down over his collar and he had a belly that hung over his thick leather belt like dough.

'Shit, that was some bang you had last night, Mike told me about it on the way in from the airport. He's still in town, be back shortly. I talked to Mendes, doesn't have a fucking clue.'

'Do you?' asked Joe.

Frank put the ketchup bottle on the table and licked his thumb.

'Not really. You get a lot of that sort of thing over on the mainland, some of it political, some commercial.'

'Mike said he thought Vaz might have had a grudge of some kind.'

'Mike said that?' Frank shrugged his shoulders and wiped his hands on a tea towel. 'Possible, I suppose. Sick people get that way sometimes. Go to hospital, the hospital can't help them, they blame the doctors. Happened in Florida a couple of years back, some dumb intern screwed the paperwork on a patient, the surgeon takes off the wrong leg. Two months later the guy shows up at the hospital in his wheelchair, asks to see the surgeon, pulls out a shotgun and blows him away. Him and two nurses happened to be passing. The intern got off scot free. You ready for your eggs yet?'

He put the plate in front of Joe, sat down, put his feet up on the table and got a cheroot out of his top pocket.

'You're here looking for Willie, right?'

'Right.'

'Aren't we all. You got any theories on that one?'

'Not really.'

'Me neither.' The American shook his head. 'Who the fuck would have it in for Willie?' He rolled the cigar between his fingers, stuck it in his mouth, then reached into his pocket for a light. 'Maybe he's just taken a vacation. At least that's what Mike reckons – the old guy went walk-about, same way he did when he wound up here. Give it a couple of weeks and he'll show up some place.'

'You don't believe him.'

'It's possible. I sure as hell hope so. He's some guy, your old man. They certainly don't make them like that any more.'

You can't blame them, Joe refrained from saying. He picked up a heel of bread and dunked it in his egg yolk.

'The old man write you at all?' Frank asked.

'Only when he wanted something doing. Plus the odd card. He's not what you'd call a conscientious correspondent.'

Frank had moved to the sink, rinsing dishes, clawing the inside of the frying pan with his fingernails.

'How long have you been here?' Joe asked.

'Me? Three months or so. I'm with an outfit called Third Aid. Mike tell you about all that? Rentadoc, guilt money from corporate America. You need a special skill in the developing world, you call them up and provided they like the look of you they find someone for you. Free gratis and for nothing.'

Joe asked him what his skill was.

'Number one, tropical medicine. Number two, infectious diseases. Typhoid, cholera, malaria. Spent most of the past five years in Liberia, Cambodia, Chile, New Guinea. Number three, I speak Spanish, which isn't a lot of help on the Cay but sure as shit helps in a place like Jiuba. Number four, I'll do anything to stay out of the States. All you do in the States if you're a doctor these days is fill out insurance forms. Or pump fat out of middle-aged women who eat too much.'

Frank had the American habit of telling you more about himself in ten minutes than an Englishman would reveal cautiously over five years. He was thirty-four years old and came from Louisiana, youngest of a family of five. His father was a surgeon, his mother stayed home and raised the kids.

He went to medical school in New Orleans, married a nurse when he was twenty-six, divorced three years later on the grounds of mutual incompatibility (she decided she was lesbian), did his internship in Houston Texas, and moved on to Mobile when he qualified, specializing in Tropical Medicine. His favourite author was Tolkien, his favourite food clam chowder, his heroes were Bruce Springsteen, Nelson Piquet and Bob Geldof.

'Tell me about you,' he said, settling back in at the table.

'I play the piano.'

'Married?'

'Nope.'

'Gay?'

'Nope.'

'Bowel movements regular?'

'Clockwork.'

'Couple of days here'll sort that out. Keep off the melons.'

A car door slammed, and a moment later Mike came up

the steps, wearing only shorts and flip-flops, carrying a cardboard box of provisions.

'You find yourself a new set of wheels?' Frank asked.

Mike sat down and helped himself to coffee.

'Not exactly new. You know that old Toyota Landcruiser the Belgians were trying to get rid of?'

'That heap of shit? You bought it?'

'Not bought, borrowed. The average life expectancy of a vehicle on the Cay', he explained to Joe, 'is two years. After that the suspension packs in. I reckon we've got about a month.'

After they'd finished eating Mike took Joe on a tour of the settlement.

'What do you make of Frank?' he asked as they crossed the clearing.

'Is he really a doctor?'

'Sure. Don't be put off by all the bullshit, underneath he's solid gold. He may act nuts, but he's a good doctor and he's costing us nothing.'

The philosophy behind St Andrews was very simple. People came because they had an immediate health problem that needed treating — skin diseases, bowel complaints, ulcers, VD, ear infections, gallstones, whatever. Along with a cure, if there was one, they got an education.

If they wanted contraception, they could get a cap or a coil fitted. No compulsion, just the choice.

If their water supply was bad — which it generally was — they were told how to improve it. If they needed antibiotics, they were prescribed, but under strict controls.

'On the mainland,' Mike explained, 'you can buy anything. You don't even need to go to a chemist, you can buy drugs by the sack in street markets. I went down to the market in Comayagua once and bought a suitcase full, just out of curiosity, brought them home and got Amos Lipstein to analyse them. It was astonishing. About a third was harmless rubbish, flour and chalk, Taiwanese and Malaysian placebos.

'Another third was the real McCoy, but years out of date. They might do you some good if you knew how to use them, but they sold them loose, by the handful, you had no way of knowing what you were getting, and no instructions.'

'The rest was actively dangerous, tranqu's and sleepers, anti-coagulants and so on. There are peasants in the mountains hopelessly addicted to pills they didn't need in the first place. The Incas kept the rabble quiet by feeding them coca leaves, we use valium. Same effect.'

They stopped off to talk to Captain Mendes and his crew. The captain was ready to leave, leaning against the cab of his jeep drinking out of a Coca-Cola can.

'You get any joy out of David yet?' Mike asked him.

'Nothing to get yet. The man fell asleep soon as we got him home last night, hasn't woken since. Wife came down first thing with his breakfast, bawled him out, he didn't even stir. I let you know when he does.'

They started at the clinic, where Frank Carreras was back at work, standing behind a steel desk littered with papers and medical paraphernalia, talking to the nursing sister, a diminutive West Indian woman with short black hair. Frank introduced her as Esther Manley.

'"She didn't grow up, she grew out,"' he sang cheerfully. 'And in case you've got any ideas she's married with seven children.'

Esther grinned.

'First that ain't true – I ain't married and I ain't got kids. And second being married and having kids never stopped no one I know from doin' what they inclined to do.' She held out her hand. 'Pleased to meet you, Joe.' Then she stepped back and looked him over. 'You another these Aid guys come to see how the niggers gettin' on?'

'Afraid not,' said Joe.

'Promise?'

'Promise. You got something against Aid people?'

'Not the ones work here, just the ones come visiting. Treat you like shit.'

'She's right,' said Frank. 'Full metal arseholes. But they pay the bills.'

Three electric fans kept up a constant breeze. Against the far wall, under a line of primary health care posters, a pregnant girl was lying on her back, exhausted, one arm covering her face, the other hanging limp over the edge of the bench. Her mother was standing beside her.

'This your first?' asked Frank.

The girl said nothing.

'Third,' said the mother.

'How old is she?' asked Mike.

Frank checked his papers.

'Seventeen. We think.'

Poor man's riches, they called children on the Cay, where breeding was a way of doing something with your life. There weren't a lot of other options.

The girl's name was Charlene, and she came from the North Shore. Joe tried to think what was happening to his own life at seventeen. He was still a virgin, for starters, without the vaguest idea about how you set about seducing a woman, and only a very basic knowledge of the mechanics of sex, which had been explained to him and Mike by their house master one memorable afternoon with the help of a comically coy little textbook. The first time he took a girl to bed had been a fiasco, trying to work out what went where and who was meant to do what. God, the embarrassments of youth.

They moved on to the pharmacy. Mike picked up a clipboard and ran his eyes down a list of drugs.

'If it takes one gallon of iodine seven weeks to travel two hundred miles,' he asked Joe without looking up, 'how long will it take five hundred electric blankets to get from Idaho to Mogadishu?'

Joe smiled.

'What voltage are the blankets?'

Mike put down the clipboard.

'Two hundred and twenty. Africa works on a hundred and ten, not that it matters, you don't need electric blankets in the desert, but they sent them anyway. You wouldn't believe the shit that gets shipped out as aid. Tampons – at the height of the Ethiopian famine the Brits sent tampons. You can see the charity ads, can't you. "Five pounds will keep a menstruating Nubian in Tampax for a year."

'The Finns supplied flush toilets to Somalia. In a drought. The Americans sent frostbite medicine and Lo-Cal Diet Soup, plus a plane-load of medicines which turned out to be discarded sales reps' samples, fifteen years past their use-by date. They went to Somalia too. Nicaragua got laxatives and indigestion pills.'

'You're making this up.'

'Not at all. Food's the same. Chernobyl lamb, BSE beef, anything the West doesn't want for itself. And unvitaminized milk powder, which is actively harmful to babies. Kampuchea got meat that San Francisco Zoo had declared unfit for animal consumption. The EC sent Morocco butter oil that contained four times the EC's own permitted levels of aerobic germs. The Moroccans used it to make soap.

'There are tens of thousands of tons of this stuff wandering round the world looking for vulnerable people to poison. Great business for someone, though I can never quite work out who.'

'Are your lot as bad?'

'No, thank God. Esther's right, they can be patronizing as hell when they come down on a visit, but in business terms they're hard to fault. They give you a hard time until they trust you, but after that it's fine.'

Mike led him across the lawn to the stores and pushed open the door. Inside was an office, a phone, a fan, a steel chair with a torn PVC seat and a stack of industrial shelving lined with box files.

'This was Willie's place?' Joe asked.

'Yup.'

Joe thought of the other offices his father had occupied, the mahogany shelves of leather-bound legal books, the smell of wax polish, the roll-top desks and Persian rugs, velvet curtains and sash windows looking out on to cobbled courtyards, the sherry decanters and the boxed cigars. The buildings he worked in changed, but somehow the offices never did. Not that Joe visited him often. In the early years, when the family lived in Hexham and Willie commuted to Newcastle, and if Joe had to be in the city for some reason – the dentist, a trip to the swimming baths – he'd turn up at the chambers for his lift back home and sit waiting in the outside office, thumbing through the *National Geographic*, listening to voices booming through the walls. Lawyers never talk quietly, even when they're trying to be confidential.

Voices, and laughter. It struck him now, twenty years later, that those were the only times he had ever heard Willie laugh like that, from the gut.

'A place for everything, everything in its place,' said Mike. 'A great one for systems, your father.'

At that moment Captain Mendes appeared at the door.

'Vaz is dead,' he squeaked. 'Hanged himself. You want to come on down?'

The police station in Morgan's Hole was a single-storey concrete building with a flat roof, set back from the main street. A blue and white Honduran flag hung limply from a pole outside the door.

Inside a young policeman sat behind the desk smoking a cigarette. He looked about nineteen. The square window behind him framed the harbour, a tumble of shanties leading down to the water, shrimp boats, the reef beyond. The office was bare, except for a sheaf of documents on a nail – cheap yellowing paper with badly printed government crests at the top, two Roneoed paragraphs followed by a circular stamp. On the desk were a pack of cigarettes, a foil ashtray and an old newspaper. A ring of keys hung on the same nail as the papers.

The policeman got up as they entered and saluted Mendes.

'He still in there?' asked the captain.

The man nodded, his eyes moving from Mendes to Mike and back again.

Joe found it hard to get a fix on Mendes. The policeman spoke in short sentences, neither aggressive nor polite. He used the same neutral tone regardless of whom he was addressing, or what the circumstances might be. His impassive expression never altered, except for his eyes, which missed nothing. He was clearly a thinking man, but he kept the results of his deliberations entirely to himself.

'You cut him down yet?'

The boy shook his head.

'How'd it happen?'

The boy looked at the floor.

'I just gone across the road for cigarettes, I came back, checked to see he needed anything.'

'How long you gone?'

'Time it takes walk from here to the store and back. Two minutes, maybe.'

Mendes made a clucking noise with his tongue.

'Okay. You better go tell the widow, get a preacher. The place still locked?'

'Yes sir.'

Mendes lifted the key off the wall and led them down a hot damp corridor to the cell.

David Vaz had hanged himself with his belt: buckled it round his throat and tied the loose end through a reinforced steel rod that projected from the ceiling. His peaked cap had slipped to one side of his head, making him look like a Confederate soldier in a battlefield daguerreotype. A wooden chair lay on its side beneath him beside a saucepan of cold beans and a mug of water. He'd defecated, and the place smelled of shit.

Mendes limped back to the office to get a knife to cut the belt. Joe pushed past him out into the street and threw up. He was still bent double, retching into the soil, when the young policeman returned with Vaz's widow.

Dora Vaz was a plump woman with pneumatic legs and forearms as thick as her thighs. She could have been anywhere between forty and sixty, it was hard to tell. She wore an old cotton dress and plastic sandals and a frayed panama hat. Everything about her looked tired. She was crying, but not a lot.

They were gathered in the office now, Mendes and the young policemen, Dora Vaz, Mike, Frank, Joe and the Reverend Bobby Burgess.

Mendes lit a cigarette, inhaled and sat back in his chair.

'What time he go out last night?'

Dora scratched her cheek.

'Came in maybe eight, said he ain't been feeling too good all day, maybe go and find himself some Andrews Sel. I told him they're ain't enough of him to be ill any more, he three parts alcohol to one part bone, nothin' else there to feel ill about. Had his supper, went out again maybe nine o'clock, said he had business in town. Next I knew you people call up tell me he's planting bombs. He didn't need no bombs, light a match any time he's breathing he'd go up like gasoline.'

'That ain't no way to speak of the dead, Dora,' said Burgess, a gentle reproach.

'I ain't talking of him dead, I ain't talking about how he was in previous times, I talking about the way he was last night.'

'Did he tell you who he was going to see?' asked Mike.

'Told me all sorts of people. Told me he goin' to see a man about a hog, told me there's some man in town hiring for the States, told me all kinds of shit. Also told me he goin' over to the Rectory about some business, I figure that's what he decided in the end. All that mattered to me he's goin' out, maybe I get some sleep for a change.'

Joe watched her face. She was upset, but she was also used to disaster, the tears running down well-ploughed furrows in her face. Once in a while she wiped her face with her forearm.

The Reverend Burgess knew how to handle situations like this. He stood with his left fist gripping the fingers of his right hand, a slight smile on his lips, his eyes fixed on Dora.

'I think maybe Mrs Vaz would like some time to reflect a little if you gentlemen have finished.'

He unbuckled his hands and put a podgy palm on her shoulder. Dora didn't seem to notice.

'Gonna have to be an autopsy,' said Mendes. 'That something you can handle, Dr Carreras?'

Frank nodded.

'If that's what you want.'

'Save a lot of trouble if you could. Take two days to get a government man over from San Pedro, we ain't geared to storing the dead that long.'

'Defilement,' Burgess objected.

Mendes stubbed out his cigarette.

'Maybe so, but it's the law.'

'Then I'll take Mrs Vaz on home,' said the preacher.

They got up to leave.

'You happy about the autopsy?' Mike asked Frank quietly as they made their way out the door.

'Sure, if that's what they want. At least he's dead. The last year we were in the States, we had an epileptic kid come in, run over by a truck. In a coma but still breathing. We had to keep him alive for three days to let the epilepsy drugs run through his system so we could clean out the organs before we cut them out for transplants. That's modern medicine for you. I'll tell you something about autopsies, though. Three times out of ten when they cut someone up in hospitals they find the patient died from something the doctors hadn't spotted.'

'Is that really true?' Mike asked.

'True in the States. Could be worse than that here.'

Joe went over to where Dora was being shepherded into Burgess's station-wagon. There was an orange sticker in the rear window, 'For lf They Do These Things In A Green Tree, What Shall Be Done ln The Dry? – John 23:31'.

The minister was already in the driving seat, Dora about to get in beside him.

64

'I just wanted to say I'm sorry about what happened,' Joe said gently. 'I gather David was a friend of my father's.'

Dora turned to face him with a weary smile.

'That', she said, 'is what he coming to see you about last night'.

Joe looked at her.

'What do you mean?'

Dora got into the station-wagon.

'Didn't say nothing else, just he wanted to talk to you.'

At that Burgess started the engine and drove off.

7

'NOTICE TO ALL,' said the sign on the roadside. 'Please be informed No Loafers Around The Hotel. The Hotel Is Strictly For Guests no loafers: no visitors. No Dope Smokers Or Peddlers. Anyone is found here doing these things will be called before the Law, Please take advice before these things bring further trouble.

'Orders from the Boss thank you.

'Boswell J. MacIntyre.'

B. J. MacIntyre was short and stout, with white curly hair, and a big smile full of bad teeth. He wore a check shirt and long loose trousers and sturdy shoes.

'You ain't heard nothing 'bout your father yet?'

Joe shook his head.

'Damned if I know where he gone,' B.J. continued. 'Most times he gone it's two days, maybe three, got business in Tegoose or San Pedro. This time – what is it, two weeks? Three? Never even sent a card. Mike Osborne reckon he's up Mexico or some place, maybe so. Time he came back, get in some serious eating.'

He was sitting on his porch drinking patent medicine from a tin mug.

'Gas,' he informed Joe. He patted his wide hands against his paunch. 'You can hear it. I eat, I don't eat, don't seem to make no difference. Doctor here says don't eat no greasy food, don't eat no pork, but I don't get no pork any place. Doctor gave me some German pills, make me feel a lot better, really a lot better. Come on up, I fix you some lunch.'

Gas was far from being B.J.'s only problem. He was saving up for a cataract operation, which prompted a long and complicated anecdote about a Honduran doctor in San Pedro Sula. Meanwhile he was putting Lipton's tea-bags over his eyes when he went to bed at night, and wearing pebble glasses while he waited for the next Methodist Synod in Belize, which he'd attend in his capacity as lay preacher. He planned to have the operation while he was there, because he trusted the Hollander doctor in Belize most. Nothing against Dr Carreras, but cataracts were too much for St Andrews. The gas, however, was more or less under control, thanks to the German medicine.

'Cost fifteen dollars a bottle you buy them in the chemist. Mike Osborne don't charge me nothing.'

B.J. and his family lived around a compound sheltered by a dozen trees, with the 'hotel' behind a fence at the northeast corner, beside a small blue stilted hut with 'B.J.'s Fried Chicken' painted in two-foot letters on the end gable. Seven pairs of white women's knickers, flat and square, hung from a washing line between two trees. Underfoot the sand was intricately decorated with pig shit and fallen mangoes. Twenty yards away through the palms the sea lapped at the white sands of a long, deserted beach.

In the heavy noon heat the island's leisurely pace slowed to a crawl. Three hens and a pigeon scratched in the sand under the trees, a frustrated hog grunted at a fallen papaya too big for its mouth. Four children were swimming in the shallow water by the boardwalk pier, two black, two blond, all brothers and sisters. A big woman in a white frock with a black umbrella against the sun walked slowly through the palms.

B.J. had fourteen children, eight of them by his wife, the others conceived in the days before he found God. All of them were abroad now, except a daughter who looked after the hotel and a son who ran a discothèque back on the road to Morgan's Hole.

'Have you always lived here?' asked Joe.

'Mostly. I's born here in Reef's End, a single-room hut

used to be up yonder.' He pointed inland towards a ridge of low scrub-covered hills. 'Lost my parents when I's fifteen years old, didn't seem no point hanging round so I went to sea, spent twenty years as ship's cook, travelled all over the world, Hamburg, Dar es Salaam, Yokahama, Brisbane, Bombay, Basra. The longest I's away was two years and seven days, and that was too much. Came home to Cow Cay and used my savings to set up here.'

B.J. was a gentle, slow-moving man, good-natured and philosophic, and he didn't need a lot to live on. Business was bad, but the hardships of life now were nothing to the old days, working out of La Ceiba for Standard Fruit for one and a half lempiras a day, cutting coconuts, copra, bananas. Though you could buy things cheap then, sugar or flour, a piece for a penny.

Because of his eyes he couldn't drive a car any more, which meant potential guests and diners from Morgan's Hole had to come over by taxi, if they could find one, same going back. Sandy Inn, next door, had a car, picked people up straight off the aeroplane. Except there was never anyone at the airport for Sandy Inn because of its reputation.

'Belonged to an American gentleman,' he told Joe. 'Sold it to a Nicaraguan, only turns out it didn't belong to him in the first place, plus the Nicaraguan's in some kind of politics, I forget which kind, one day he's flying back here in his own plane, the plane fell out of the sky. Three, four years ago. Since, when there's a lot of talk of money gone, debts, rumours, not good for business. They got a manager up there and a couple of girls but they don't do too much business at all, just hang around, play cards and be rude to people.'

Most of the interior of the Fried Chicken shack was taken up with two long tables, the rest by the kitchen. A copy of the Bible lay open on the counter, and the radio was tuned in to an evangelist station out of Tampa, Florida, a man with a Georgia accent screaming for money. The tables were covered with floral oilcloth, the door and windows meshed against the insects. On the wall, in chalk, B.J. had hand-written a sign:

> Some People Could Eat No Fat
> Some People Could Eat No Lean
> But B J Fried Chicken Such A Treat
> They All Licked Their Plates Clean.

Beneath the sign, also in chalk, was the menu. Chicken Dinner, four dollars, Special Chicken Dinner, five dollars, Cold Drinks a dollar, Extra Fries a dollar, Lobster on Request.

'Ain't no lobster, no one fixing their pots these days,' he apologized, wiping his nose on his sleeve. 'People don't want to work no more, just want to sit down, wait for the cheques the sailors send. Gonna do you Special Chicken Dinner instead.'

Joe sat at one of the tables drinking Fanta, while behind a shoulder-high wooden partition B.J. cooked, neatly and precisely, his materials stored carefully on timber shelves with the tidiness and economy of a man used to ships' galleys. There was a bottle-gas stove in one corner and a fat old kerosene refrigerator against the back wall. Above them in the rafters B.J. had stored an ironing board, two rolled-up carpets, two oil lamps and an old hanging scales. Through the window you could see the balcony of the house next door, where B.J.'s wife, Kitty, was beating rugs with a broom handle. A line of ants processed along the washing line.

'Your father, he like chicken. Least he did when he could eat it. Got a lot of gut trouble one time, couldn't eat nothing at all 'cept plantain water. Soak plantains in a pan, strain off the water, three or four days drinking plantain water and the stomach good as new.'

Joe remembered the last time he'd eaten with Willie – the last time he'd seen him, in fact – at a Hungarian restaurant in Charlotte Street a year before, the old man chain-smoking and studying the wine list while he struggled to think of things to say to his son.

They'd talked about Northumberland, Willie giving him stilted bulletins about old acquaintances neither of them cared a toss about. Long silences in between, then five minutes of generalities about politics and the state of the country, which both of them deplored but for different reasons. In between the judge's visits to London Joe could even feel affection for his father, but when they met the irritations were too much. They rarely argued, but the price was a scrupulous avoidance of any topic which touched on their real lives and emotions. Joe didn't blame the old man, he was who he was, we all are. But he envied friends who could talk to their parents. He wondered what he'd be like as a father himself.

He also wondered if, in similar circumstances, Willie would be doing what he was doing now. Probably not. In Willie's world you took responsibility for your own actions and lived with the consequences. But then Joe had always gone to considerable lengths to make sure he didn't turn out like Willie. It took constant vigilance: these things had a way of sneaking up on you when you weren't looking.

B.J. was frying the onions now, not too much oil, keep them sizzling nicely, add in a few spices. He transferred the onions to the oven and started in on the coleslaw cabbage, hacking it with clean precise blows of the knife. Joe had worked in an Old Kentucky once, in Westbourne Grove, and knew the procedure. In Old Kentucky's they have a huge wall chart beside the fridge, no words, just pictured – cheap labour can have trouble with words. Instead, they show you how to do it with primary school illustrations – a dead chicken, a meat cleaver, the meat cleaver cutting the bird into portions, a bowl of breadcrumbs, a huge spice shaker, a deep-frying basket.

He'd also done bar work, punched tickets at a cinema on Haverstock Hill, driven a mini-cab, delivered gas cylinders to high-rise tenants, worked as a security guard and as an extra on a film about Christine Keeler. He'd do anything provided it didn't offer a Career, paid the rent and left him time to play music.

'You forgive me for the prices,' B.J. continued. 'Potatoes and onions come from the US, also the mayonnaise an' the tinned beans. Jar of mayonnaise cost me eight dollars. Only way you get a Chicken Dinner to taste American is use American mayonnaise. You ever tasted Mexican mayonnaise?'

Joe hadn't.

'Don't know your luck.'

'Willie didn't give you any idea where he was going or how long he'd be gone?'

'Told me he had to go to San Pedro Sula see a man on business, maybe go on up to Copán after. You been to Copán?'

'No.'

'Got some ruins up there, Indian places.'

'He didn't say who the man was in San Pedro Sula?'

B.J. shook his head.

'Just that it's business.'

He carried the plate of fried chicken across and stood wiping his hands on a dish cloth, watching Joe eat.

'You may own General Motors,' screamed the Georgia preacher on the radio. 'But you can't take it with you.'

'He's right,' said B.J. 'Only some days I wish he'd say it a little softer.' He walked over and turned it off. 'You want to come take a look at your father's place?'

'Sure,' said Joe.

Apart from Kitty the compound was deserted. Down on the beach an American woman with a child, abandoning her engineer husband in La Ceiba for the week, paddled in the shallows, and a fisherman tinkered with his outboard motor on the dock. The reef here was close in to the shore, less than twenty yards out, just visible above the surface at low tide.

'Business quiet at the moment – 'part from your father and the American lady. Methodist preacher comes one Sunday a month, rest of the time I do the services.' He waved his paw towards a tin chapel up the hill among the trees. 'Reverend Lennox-Connynghame from Ceiba takes Matins, eats his lunch, takes his siesta in one of the rooms, sleeps maybe an hour, then moves his bowels, never flushes the WC. No manners.'

Willie's chalet was a timber hut on the shore side of the compound, painted green with a veranda and the ubiquitous corrugated iron roof. A hammock hung on the veranda next to a frayed cane chair. B.J. sat down.

'Likes to talk, your father. Comes home at the end of the day, fixes himself a drink, sits out here with a book sometimes, but mostly he likes to talk.'

'What does he talk about?' asked Joe.

'All kinds of stuff. England, things he's done, places he's been, the way the world was when he grew up, work he's doing.'

'Does he enjoy his work?'

B.J. rubbed his stomach.

'I reckon. He grumble some, but mostly I reckon he's happy. He got the manner, you know, he rub people up a little rough sometimes but they don't mind too much, just the way he is. Get into arguments with government people, health people, even Mike Osborne sometimes. But he likes the job, sure. Likes the job, likes the island. Mutual feeling, too.'

'What does he grumble about?'

'Time it takes to get things done, the price of things, business people in town, doctors. And the Reverend Burgess, he got a thing about Reverend Burgess too.'

'Did he seem worried about anything before he left?'

B.J. thought for a moment.

'Not so's I noticed. To be honest I ain't seen so much of him of late. He's been busy, I been busy, way it goes, sometimes you see someone every day, other times you don't see them for a week.'

Especially if they've got a woman.

A coconut fell near by, making a sound like a heavy object striking flesh.

'Someone told me Willie and David Vaz were friends,' said Joe.

B.J. threw him a look.

'Who told you that?'

'Mike Osborne, among others. And Dora Vaz says David

told her he was going over to St Andrews last night because he wanted to see me.'

'Dora said that?'

'Yup.'

'Dora says it, then it's true, she ain't the energy to go telling lies.' B.J. took a handkerchief out of his pocket and dabbed at his brow. 'Yea, David knew your father, came out here and talk sometimes. Looking for money, most times. Your father wouldn't give him money, but he'd talk to him. Said to me one time he missed the criminal classes, David wasn't much of a criminal but he had that kind of talk. Willie said to him one time, you ever need a lawyer, let me know. David looks at him, says you no lawyer, boss, you a judge. Not any more, says your father. Worst thing I ever did was take on the judge job.'

B.J. laughed.

'Why would he put a bomb into St Andrews?' asked Joe.

'Lord knows, Lord knows. Maybe he didn't, maybe he heard you come to town, went looking to see if you lend him a few dollars, same way he did with your father.'

'At that hour of night?'

'Day and night don't seem that different if you got liquor inside you.'

Joe looked at his watch. It was half past three.

'Do you mind if I have a look round inside?'

'Don't see why not.' B.J. hauled himself up out of the chair. 'Be over at the kitchen if you need me.'

Willie's chalet consisted of a single room with a kitchenette and shower. The place was sparsely furnished: a homemade wooden bed, a small table, two chairs. Willie had pilfered an old crate for a bedside table. A battered leather suitcase protruded from under the bed. A row of novels and guides and notebooks were lined up on a shelf inside the door, next to an out of date calendar with a Honduran beach beauty and a packet of cigarettes on it, the colours faded to a single blurred pink. There was a jamjar of dead flowers, an ashtray and a paraffin lamp on the crate. The flowers must have been Sarah: Willie wasn't the kind of man to pick flowers.

Under the kitchen sink Joe found provisions – tins of condensed milk, rice pudding, peaches, corned beef, sardines, processed cheese, three packets of Bath Olivers, a packet of Quaker Oats, half a dozen bottles of Coca-Cola, a jar of Marmite – nursery food, the last refuge of the elderly widower. The Bath Olivers and Marmite must have come from the embassy in Tegucigalpa: only the Brits ate that sort of stuff.

His shaving kit was missing, but there were two old razor blades, caked with soap and grey stubble, beside the sink. This is the man who taught me to shave, Joe remembered: who enjoyed teaching me to shave. Of all the things he could have taught me in adolescence, all the rituals of entering manhood, the only one that Willie seemed comfortable with was bloody shaving. Scrape the hair off your face, you're a man at last. Don't worry if you don't understand about sex, the women will show you what to do. He spent the best part of an hour sorting through the contents of the chalet, breathing in his father's life, sniffing it, fingering it, piecing the bits together. It was an unnerving experience, because of the insight it gave into the petty intimacies of Willie's life: his threadbare underpants, his sleeping pills and laxatives, the half-used pack of Durex Extra-Strong.

The lingering smell of Senior Service was so strong that he kept expecting to see his father walk in through the door. It was a smell from childhood. Willie's clothes had always reeked of tobacco: the double-breasted suits and starch-fronted shirts, the clubman's ties, the weekend cardigans and fisherman's sweaters, the everlasting dinner jacket he wore for functions. But not the shoes, Willie's black office shoes always smelled of male feet, his country brogues of old wool and peat water.

It was the pathos of the clothes which affected Joe most strongly. Apart from a pair of jeans and a cotton sun hat, they were all old and familiar. Willie wasn't a man to change his wardrobe: when a shirt finally wore out, after the collar and cuffs had been turned and gone again, he bought another in exactly the same pattern and fabric. His sweaters were darned and patched with leather at the elbows. Trousers and jackets went on for years. When he did buy, he bought well, from Savile Row or the posher gents outfitters in London and Newcastle.

He'd travelled light, half a dozen shirts, three pairs of trousers, two light sweaters, plus whatever he'd taken with him. Joe checked the pockets, but there were no surprises, coins and fluff and a cowrie shell that must have taken his fancy.

Under the bed, behind the suitcase, Joe discovered a cardboard box of papers. The three letters he'd written his father were neatly tied with a rubber band, along with a school copybook containing Willie's weekly petty cash accounts. Rent, food, buses and taxis, postage, cigarettes – the same painstaking financial records he'd kept throughout Joe's childhood, only the sums now were tiny, a dollar here, a thousand lempiras there, the totals converted into sterling in the final column at the foot of each page.

Willie's medicines were on a ledge beside the window, his bathing trunks and a threadbare towel hanging on a nail outside the shower, stiff with salt. Wherever he'd gone he didn't intend staying away long.

Joe was almost finished when he found the map, dog-eared and much folded, lodged between the bedside table and the wall. He took it out and spread it on the bed. The paper had torn in places, along the lines of the folds, and been repaired with Sellotape. Cow Cay was ringed in red biro, and a series of blue lines ran out from the island to all the places he'd visited during his stay. Each line carried a date. In some cases where he'd made the trip more than once there were several dates.

He'd made six trips to Tegucigalpa, one to Comayagua, three to San Pedro Sula, five to Teila, one to Trujillo, six to La Ceiba. A further line led from Trujillo to an empty space on the map. The date was 22 May, just three weeks ago.

Joe tucked the map into the back pocket of his jeans and went outside. The temperature and humidity had combined to a point where the sweat was starting to run off him like a tap. He walked round the chalet to the back door, paused by the dustbin, and lifted the lid.

Someone had been having a bonfire. The galvanized steel sides of the bin were black with soot, and there was a pile of ash at the bottom. The bin was still warm.

He was also, he realized, being watched.

8

SARAH WAS ON her way home from the gift shop when she decided to drop by B.J.'s.

It wasn't really a gift shop, just a bamboo lean-to up from the shore, with a table and a painted board showing a coral rock with some jewellery draped over it, painted by the Chinaman who ran the grocery-bar on the road back into Morgan's Hole.

The Chinaman was called Chris Long. Chris loved to paint, did it for free for anyone who asked him – murals, shop signs, portraits, anything. His most famous achievement was the blood-splattered five-foot tooth outside the dentist's in Morgan's Hole, but his work could also be seen in the lobby of The Gable Hotel and behind the bar of the Sandy Inn on the North Shore. He couldn't paint shit, but he was a gentle and generous man, and people liked to humour him. The coral rock and its jewels looked like a vertical orange dog turd draped with seaweed. Sarah was waiting for a storm so she could junk it and say it got blown away out to sea.

The gift shop had been Willie's idea: Sarah said she wanted to be an artist and Willie said, 'If that's what you want to be, do something about it.'

He misunderstood her: what she really meant was that she wanted to wake up one morning to find she already was one, not that she should take lessons. But she knew how to make jewellery, string shells and file down black coral into earrings. So they decided on the gift shop, collected up some conches and cowries from the beach, and pieces of broken Indian pottery antiques from up in the hills, arranged the jewellery on pieces of cloth, and got the sign from the Chinaman.

To be on the safe side they also bought a crate of sodas and a couple of cartons of cigarettes to sell on the side, because the jewellery business at Reef's End wasn't likely to take off in a hurry, not until they got some tourists coming through.

So far she'd sold six bottles of soda, three packs of Rothmans and a lump of black coral which she'd planned to make into a necklace but a Canadian diver wanted to smoke. You could smoke black coral like ganja, file it down and mix it with tobacco, had the same effect but left you with a head like an anvil the next morning.

The coral sale was eight days ago, since when she'd sold nothing except the cigarettes and the soda. But what the hell, it was only an idea, not something she planned on doing for the rest of her life. It was Willie's idea, and now Willie was gone she'd think of something else.

She came by B.J.'s most days since Willie disappeared, the same way she had when he'd been living there. It was a hard habit to break. And now, standing in the shade watching the tall skinny balding figure of Joe head down in the dustbin at the back of Willie's chalet, she felt a twinge of jealousy at this stranger come to poke around Willie's possessions.

'Coconut husks,' she said quietly, nodding towards the embers. 'My mother been tidying up.'

Joe turned round. Sarah had on jeans and the same floral blouse she'd worn the first time he'd seen her, outside Bobby Burgess's mission hall the previous morning. She was chewing green bubble gum.

'Hello,' he said. 'You're Sarah.'

She gave him a big grin, two parts tooth, one part green gum.

'Right. Did Willie leave anything to drink in there? Should be something under the sink.'

'Only Coke.'

'Coke'll do fine.'

Joe went inside and returned with two bottles and an opener.

She didn't use the opener, just stuck the neck between her teeth, jerked it down, and spat out the cap.

'How come your mother waits two weeks to come and tidy up?' asked Joe.

Sarah kept drinking until the bottle was half empty, then wiped her lips on the back of her hand.

'No reason, she ain't the kind of woman has reasons to do things. Or not the kind of reasons you'd understand. You the singer, right?'

'Willie told you that?'

'Among other things. What they told you about me?'

Sarah sat down on the edge of the veranda, back straight, legs stretched out in front of her. Joe stayed standing, leaning against the door post.

'Not a lot. Just that you were fond of my father.'

She took another mouthful of coke, grinned mischievously and put the bottle down on the step.

'Uh huh, that's true. He write you about me?'

Joe shook his head.

'Nope. I'm a blank page.'

He was embarrassed, didn't know what to feel or say. The sweat was pouring off him now, staining his shirt.

'You find anything useful in there?' she asked.

'Not really'

'Ain't nothing, I looked.'

Her hand stroked the woodwork, long thin fingers with long scarlet nails, testing the grain of the timber.

'Has anyone else been to look?' asked Joe. The question came out before he'd thought about it. Sarah looked at him.

'Like who?'

'I don't know.'

'Someone helped themselves to the black coral, used to be a block in a tin box by the bed. You tried black coral?'

'For what?'

'File her down and smoke her, like hash, only the hit comes harder. Take away the pain no trouble so long as you don't hit too hard. Had a piece up at the house but she gone now. Tried to take away the pain of Willie but it ain't no good for that kind of pain. Willie liked a smoke in the evenings. Glass of whisky, lie back in the hammock, relax a little. You got any cigarettes? Left mine up the hill.'

He got out a pack of Marlboro and handed it to her. Sarah took one, rolled it in her fingers, then snapped off the filter.

'You going to ask about me?'

'In time.'

She told him anyway. She'd been born on the Cay but moved to New York City when she was eight to live with an uncle and aunt; stayed on there at school and college and got a diploma, she didn't say what in. She came home a couple of years ago to see her mother, but she didn't reckon on hanging around Reef's End for the rest of her life.

'But you're still here?'

'For a while. I got offers of places to go in the States, maybe Canada or Australia. Maybe study art, something like that. Fancy a trip to England, too, only Willie didn't reckon I'd like England.'

I bet he didn't, thought Joe.

Apart from Willie and her mother and her travel plans, the main thing in Sarah's life was The Church of God.

'You too?' Joe interrupted.

'What do you mean, me too?'

'Seems like religion's the main industry round here. Burgess, B.J., the place is crawling with preachers.'

'Maybe we need 'em. And religion don't cost you nothing, unlike most things people do with their time. Anyway, Church of God say there's nothing in the Bible about being Methodist or Catholic or Baptist or Anglican. Just one Church, one God. Same for Mohammedan too, you ask me.' She didn't have a lot of time for Mohammedans. 'Saw them up in New York, pray with their faces on the floor. Men and women not allowed to look at each other before they're married. Shit, it's like you go into a shop blindfold, not allowed to look at the merchandise. You been to New York?'

Joe said he had, five or six times. He was still trying to picture Willie with Sarah, scraping the depths of his imagination for an image of the two of them together making love, smoking dope, but it wouldn't come.

'You like New York?' she asked him. Her hands were on her knees now, moulding them with her palms, fingers splayed out.

'In small doses.'

'You try being black in New York, you don't want no dose at all. Treat you like a hog on the street up there. That's why I come home to the Cay, stay a little time while I figure out a better place to be.'

The afternoon sun was still high in the sky. Up the hill an argument was in progress. A woman's voice drifted on the breeze.

'I thought I was fucking lazy, but boy you're real lazy, boy, you fucking lazy, get out there.'

Sarah took no notice. She was looking at Joe, trying to get a fix on him. He was Willie's boy all right, you could tell that by the way he looked, tall and white and bony – same sharpness in the eyes, told you he was capable of more things than he'd like you to know. Also by the way he hid behind what he was saying, used words like a mask. The only way you got to see Willie for real was in bed, or when he was trying to get you there, and afterwards sometimes, except that afterwards he liked to sleep a lot.

'Where did you meet him?' asked Joe.

'You stand still long enough on this island you meet anyone you want. Plus a lot you don't want.' She didn't know where he'd gone. 'Mike Osborne got plenty of ideas where he gone. Up to the ruins, he reckons.'

'You don't?'

'Don't reckon anything. But Willie never showed much interest in ruins, not so far as I know. Got them here, Indian stuff up the hill, David Vaz always offering to take him up there, find him pots and arrowheads and stuff, never went.'

'You heard about David?' Joe asked.

'Yea, I heard.' She tapped her teeth with the nail of her index finger. 'You knew him?'

'No. But I gather Willie did. Dora Vaz said he was coming to see me at St Andrews last night.'

Sarah looked up.

'She say what for?'

'No. I thought maybe you might have an idea.'

'Ain't none of my business,' she decided. 'How long you staying?'

'I don't know. Until Willie shows up, I guess.'

'Alive or dead?'

'I suppose so.'

'You worried he might be dead?'

Joe shrugged.

'All of us got fathers, all of them die.'

Sarah butted her cigarette and got up.

'Sure. And all of us get screwed up when they do. Come see us sometime, talk about Willie some more.'

'I'd like that,' said Joe.

'You know the house?'

'Not yet, but I'm sure I can find it.'

After Sarah had left Joe went to say goodbye to B.J.

He found the lay preacher suspended in a hammock on the back porch of the hotel, content as a turtle, engrossed in the Book of Job. As Joe approached he took off his glasses and closed the Bible.

'You see Sarah?'

Joe nodded.

'Pity 'bout that girl. She got some education she be all right. Parents too lazy. She never been to La Ceiba or any place to study – all these stories 'bout college – she always been right here. Pity she ain't got education to go with her craft.'

'She never went to New York?' asked Joe.

B.J. smiled.

'Not in the sense you and I been there.'

Frank made supper.

'Conch,' he announced as he put the steaming casserole on the table. The contents looked to Joe like boiled tripe in porridge. 'You know what that means in Spanish? Cunt. Look at the shell and you'll see why. You get tourists sometimes, nice clean-living all-American matrons, walk into the hotel and say, "You have wonderful conches on this island."'

He laughed, grinding more pepper into the pot. Mike brought beers from the fridge. As he collected them Joe noticed the Walther .38 lying on the worktop.

'Talking of conch,' Frank continued as he buttered the potatoes, 'I had a guy in today, complaining his wife's pregnant. Got three kids already, three's enough. But his wife wants more. He tells her fine, doesn't want a row about it. Next day he comes up to the clinic demanding a vasectomy, but don't tell the wife. Esther's on duty, knows the situation, knows the wife, knows she wants more kids. So she gives him a local, makes an incision, only she doesn't do the vasectomy. Man goes on home, thinks he's safe, gets down to business. Now his wife's pregnant, he's hopping mad but he can't do anything about it because he never told the wife he was having the snip in the first place.'

'Why would the wife want to breed from an arsehole like that?' Mike asked.

'Likes having kids, I suppose.' Frank picked up the gun. 'This thing loaded?'

'Yup,' said Mike. 'Mendes advised it.'

'Did he tell you how to use it?'

'Told me how to use it, told me to rig up floodlighting, told me to hire some security.'

'Covering his arse,' said Frank. He aimed the Walther at the light, squinting down the barrel. 'If you see a lion or an elephant charging you, stand your ground and shoot at it. Hippos or buffalo, get behind a termite hill.'

'Which do you think we're dealing with here?' asked Joe.

Frank put the gun back on the side.

'Elephants.'

Joe poked at his food with his fork and took a mouthful. The conch tasted better than he expected.

'What's Mendes doing himself?'

'Fuck all, of course,' said Mike. 'Making enquiries, if you ask him. I think he's been to see Dora Vaz again. There's an army guy coming over from the coast to look at the jeep, see if he can find any clues.'

Mike was jumpy. Not aggressive, but distracted — but then why wouldn't he be? Someone had just tried to kill him. You can get killed as a journalist in the Lebanon, or Iraq, or Belfast, but if you do it's normally bad luck, a stray bullet, a forgotten land-mine, an unexpected riot. Last night was different, last night was specific and personal. When Mike told stories about near-misses in his war-zone days, he'd tell them almost as a joke, shrug them off, knowing he'd survived, that he didn't have to go back the next day and face the same risk again. Now he kept a loaded gun on his kitchen table.

Mike kept looking at the .38, and Joe knew exactly what was he was thinking, because the same thing was going through his own mind: Mike Osborne is not the sort of man who keeps guns. For thirty years he'd been dedicated to the idea of Life as Party. Even though his work might be serious — investigative journalism, Third World Aid — his personal lifestyle was always dedicated to the twin gods of enthusiasm and optimism.

Being around Mike was as near as anyone was ever likely to get to Eternal Youth. His contemporaries grew up, got responsibilities, worried about their work and their relationships and their mortgages. Mike never shirked his responsibilities, but he never let them get him down — or not when anyone was looking. Until now.

Physically he'd aged a little with the years, but not a lot: the laugh-lines round his eyes had became more deeply etched, the hair thinned a little at the temple. What had gone was the confidence. In its place was a look of puzzlement, almost panic. It showed only fleetingly, but the veneer of gaiety which concealed it seemed to Joe to be wearing thin. He looked tired, the enthusiasms more forced.

'How far can you trust the police?' Joe asked.

Mike ran his finger round the rim of his glass.

'About as much as you can trust any authority here. You need to understand how this island works. We're in Honduras, but we're not. Most of the islanders came from the East originally – Jamaica, the Caymans. They're blacks but their ancestors were raised under the British. They're protestants and they speak English, some of them even have icons of Margaret Thatcher stuck up on their walls, God help us.'

'And they've inherited the Brits' low opinion of Hispanics. It's more complicated than that because there's been a lot of intermarriage, but that's the basic social structure. West Indians on top, then the mestizos, then the Hispanics, then Indians, then Caribs. The Hondurans are looked on as a colonial power, they're either despised and ignored or obstructed. The Hondurans loathe them back, fuck them around any way they can. Which is plenty.'

He scratched the side of his neck with the back of his hand.

'That's the sub-text: anything positive that happens here is anathema to the guys in Tegucigalpa. Positive means us. But Tegoose also has to keep things sweet with the Brits and Americans because that's where they get their guns and money from. They can't be seen to be to be fucking us around, but they're very sympathetic to other people doing so.'

Frank had finished eating and was slouched back in his chair, feet together, knees apart, hands behind his neck.

'The only imaginable question in Honduran politics is: who the fuck would want to run a country like this?' He picked at his teeth with a matchstick. 'What ideologue would believe he could do anything to tackle its problems?'

'The kind whose ideology looks after Number One,' said Mike. 'They're not unique to Honduras.' He pushed away his plate and got out his cigarettes. 'So what are your plans, Joe?'

Joe had been wondering the same thing.

'I want to spend another day looking around here. I know it's old ground, but I'd like to talk to people anyway. After that I suppose I'll go to the mainland, see what I can find there.'

'How did you get on at B.J.'s? He do you the Special Chicken Dinner?'

'He did. Served up the Special Chicken, told me about his bowels, told me Willie rows with everyone but no one minds.'

Mike laughed.

'Absolutely true.'

'Did he row with you?'

'Of course. Not serious ones, but we've shouted at each other a couple times. I think he finds it easier if you shout back.'

Maybe that was Joe's mistake, maybe he should have shouted back. Only no one in the Wilde household argued that way, not Willie, not Joe, not Margaret. You plotted, deceived, did things behind each other's backs, but you never shouted. One of the things Joe had found disturbing in his relationship with Marion was that she blew her top whenever she felt like it. Joe always assumed it was personal: only towards the end, when the relationship was beyond repair, did it occur to him that in some families arguments could be insignificant.

'What did you argue about?' he asked.

'Oh, spur of the moment things. I'd tactfully suggest he did a job a particular way, he'd go through the roof.'

'And vice-versa,' Frank chuckled. Mike laughed too.

'Yea, and vice-versa. Then we'd get out the whisky.'

Joe reached into the back pocket of his jeans and got out Willie's map.

'I found this in the chalet. It seems to have his itineraries marked, maybe it's a start.'

They spread the map out on the table.

'Where was it?' Mike asked.

'Tucked in behind the bed, must have slipped down.'

Mike put on his glasses and traced the routes one by one with his index finger. He got up and went through to the study and came back with a desk diary and checked dates.

'Tegoose, San Pedro Sula, those are all business trips.' His finger wandered across the map. 'Comayagua's another old US base, we were looking for beds and latrines. Bum steer, they took them home with them. Tela and La Ceiba, he was in and out of there all the time.' He paused. 'What the hell was he doing in Trujillo, Frank?'

'Fucked if I know. More military?'

Mike shook his head.

'No, those guys are long gone.'

'What else happens at Trujillo?' Joe asked.

'Nothing. Used to be a port in colonial times, but it's mostly abandoned now. There's a ruined cathedral, a few shanties. Even in the old days it was a frontier town. Five miles down the road and you're into virgin swamp and mountains. A few Indians, a few timber people, a couple of Carib villages – Santa Fe, Limon. The nearest proper habitation is at Puerto Castilla, down the coast, that's where we lifted the American army junk from, a couple of years back. There's a meat-packing station there, a bit of shrimping. Rough country, though.' He shook his head again. 'What in God's name was Willie up to?'

'Jiuba?' Frank suggested.

Mike gave him a look.

'He never went anywhere near the place. At least not as far as I know.'

Joe looked at the map again.

'Is that in the same direction?' he asked.

Frank pointed to an area south-east of Trujillo. There was a river, but no roads, no towns.

'Roughly speaking. But it's a hell of a journey, at least a day, provided the road's open and the weather's reasonable and you have a four-wheel drive. Anyone in their right minds flies in. And if he'd been there we'd know, someone would have seen him. He certainly wasn't there yesterday.'

'Maybe he set out and didn't make it,' Joe suggested.

'Maybe,' said Mike. 'But I doubt it. Do you want to go and look?'

Joe shook his head.

'Not yet. It seems to me the logical thing to do is start where he started and see where it leads. That means San Pedro Sula, doesn't it?'

'San Pedro, then Copán,' said Mike. 'Do you mind if I come too?'

Joe blinked.

'Not at all. I didn't like to ask.'

'Give me a couple of days to clear my desk. Frank can hold the fort here. We can leave on Thursday.'

Today was Tuesday.

9

THE REVEREND BOBBY Burgess was raised on a tobacco farm in Jonesville Kentucky. His parents divorced when he was three. The day after his ninth birthday his mother picked him up from school and drove to Huntsville Texas and left him with his grandparents, explaining along the way that she had fallen in love with a lingerie salesman and was moving to live with him in Santa Fe. She'd be back to pick Bobby up in a few weeks when things had settled down.

It was twelve years before he saw her again, by which time she weighed seventeen stone, dressed in pink tracksuits, lived in a trailer home and drank a bottle of Jim Beam a day.

Bobby's grandfather was a warder at Huntsville penitentiary, his grandmother cooked in a nursing home. They were in their early sixties when Bobby arrived: clean-living people who drove an '84 Honda Accord, worshipped every Sunday at the Second Baptist Church in Huntsville, and kept a tidy home, so tidy that Bobby's grandmother sheathed everything in the house – carpets, furniture, beds, pictures, ornaments in industrial-weight polythene sheeting. She dusted and vacuumed the house and scrubbed the kitchen and bathroom with bleach twice a day and changed the sheets nightly.

They beat Bobby when he wet his bed and sewed up the fly of his pyjamas to stop him playing with himself; they drowned his kitten; they told him his mother was a prostitute; they made him eat soap if he took the Lord's name in vain.

All this Joe discovered from Bobby's wife Bunty while they were sheltering together under a wide mango tree at the edge of the cemetery waiting for the rain to lift so they could bury David Vaz.

Bobby was in his teens and working nights stocking shelves at the XtraValu FoodMart across the Trinity River in Pointblank when he first got interested in religion. The man who brought Jesus into his life was XtraValu's owner-manager, Johnny Lee Hardress. When Johnny Lee first took him aside Bobby thought he was going to fire him. Instead Johnny gave him a Bible and a video cassette of Oral Roberts.

After that Bobby didn't mind what his grandparents or anyone else did to him. Johnny Lee paid for him to go to Bible College in Tennessee. That's how it all began.

After college he joined the New Tribes Mission, brand leaders in heathen conversion and quick-fix redemption, but left after a fellow-preacher tried to get into his bed one night in Papua New Guinea. Back in the States he signed up with The Good Book Union of the Americas. They kept him in Florida for two years selling bibles door-to-door round the condos then sent him and Bunty down to Honduras, where he spent another six months shifting paper at the Union's regional headquarters in San Pedro Sula before being let loose on the natives.

'People don't appreciate how hard he's had to struggle,' Bunty complained. 'Or how much he has to give.'

Joe gave her an understanding smile. He'd decided he rather liked Bunty. She was one of those people who was so ridiculous in her dress and her manner and her beliefs that it seemed cruel not to, particularly if you started talking to her as a human being and forgot all the mission crap.

A hundred or more people had trailed up the hill above Morgan's Hole to see Bobby Burgess bury David Vaz. Most of them were West Indians, uncomfortable in their Sunday suits and frocks, heads shaded by hats and bonnets, trilbies and panamas for the men, black straw and sculptured felt for the women. Old-fashioned black umbrellas sheltered them from the sun, and they fanned away the flies with their hands, their voices rising and falling in a soft singsong of whispered conversations. Joe scanned the faces, imagining his father living among these people, wondering what the hell he made of them and they of him.

The cortège had almost reached the cemetery when the rain started. The wind came first, hot and hard, bending the palms and rattling the tin roofs, smelling of rain and dust and decay. Behind it, out to sea, a wall of grey slate moved across the water towards the Cay.

Minutes later a clap of thunder broke overhead and a monsoon of driving rain swept the hillside. Lakes formed in the ruts, rivers of red mud ran down the hillside. The battered pick-up carrying Vaz's plain pine coffin accelerated up the slope towards the graveyard, while the rest of the crowd took shelter under the trees as best they could.

The preacher was in the cab of the pick-up, Bunty Burgess stranded with Joe under the trees. Mike and Frank were further up the slope, sharing a tarpaulin with a group of villagers, Frank telling them stories, people laughing.

Bunty Burgess was a formidable lady in her late forties, short and stout, with broad heifer's shoulders. She had a thick nose, thin, tight, muscular lips and wore no make-up, and her skin had been burned red until it flaked like old paint. She wore a voluminous gingham cotton dress to her ankles and a white cotton hat with 'My Saviour Lives' printed on the band. A vinyl Adidas shoulder bag hung diagonally across her sagging breasts, safe from any muggers that might be lurking among the mourners.

'How long have you been in Honduras?' Joe asked pleasantly.

'Four years.'

'All on the Cay?'

'No. The Lord sent us to the mainland first.'

'You get this kind of weather there?' he asked.

'Sure do. In Cedros it'd rain for a month, wash the roads clean away. La Entrada was worse.'

She was looking past him across the hillside to the

cemetery, where two gravediggers, stripped to the waist in the downpour, were digging the last shovels of red clay from David Vaz's grave. All the time they'd been talking Bunty Burgess had never once looked Joe in the face.

'Do you like it here?'

She shrugged.

'It's kinda nice in ways, the sea, the beaches. I was raised by the sea. But it ain't an easy place. One day you think you gettin' things done, the next it don't seem that way at all. The people here are inclined to get confused about things. You offer them the Lord, they like that. Then someone else offers them porn movies, they like that too, don't seem to see no contradiction.'

Joe wondered how Bunty defined porn. Doris Day, probably.

'What's the argument between your husband and Mike about?'

Bunty looked at him suspiciously.

'Bobby's got a heap of arguments with Mike Osborne. Religious, practical, you name it. White men have a certain prestige round here, people look up to them. Then you get two white men saying contradictory things, people get confused, end up losing respect. You take David, God rest his soul. Mike offers him medicine, the medicine don't work, he changes his attitude to all of us.'

'That's what happened?'

'Sure that's what happened. Happens wherever you get Aid workers coming in, they raise expectations, then they don't deliver. Truth is most of them aren't here to help people, they're here for their own benefit.'

'I didn't realize David was one of your flock,' said Joe.

'He was, praise the Lord. Came to us three months ago. Bobby's been working with him a lot since.'

'Do you reckon he was saved?'

'That's not something any of us know. I hope so. Dear Lord, I hope so. I hope the fight is o'er, the battle won. But you never know.'

As soon as the rain stopped the sun came out again, hot

and hard. Wisps of steam drifted through the tombstones. The cemetery straddled a low ridge half a mile inland from the town. It was a solitary, neglected place, but with its own beauty, rough-cut colonial headstones and simple wooden and wrought-iron crosses overgrown with thistle, and sun-faded plastic wreaths, alive with lizards and ants. Overhead turkey buzzards and frigate birds circled.

The mourners emerged from under the trees. Bunty went off to look for her husband while Joe joined Mike and Frank for the final walk up the muddy track. They didn't talk much, and when they did it was in whispers. Joe watched as the four pall bearers lifted the coffin off the pick-up and carried it down a path through the grass to the grave, which lay at the end of a line of recent interments.

'In the morning it ith green,' Bobby Burgess roared, his slacks and blazer flapping in the breeze. 'But in the evening it ith cut down, dried up and withered.'

Makes him sound like a tobacco plant, Joe decided, cigarette ash to cigarette ash. He tried not to imagine what state Vaz's remains were in after the autopsy. Frank had found nothing remarkable: an enlarged liver, stomach ulcers, par for the course for a man who had routinely drunk himself to oblivion. The undertakers wouldn't have had much time to patch up the cadaver when Frank had finished. In a climate like the Cay's the sooner he was buried the better.

'I heard a voith from heaven,' Burgess continued, his words coming and going in the heavy mid-day heat. 'Saying to me, Write, from now on blethed are the dead who die in the Lord: tho thayth the thpirit: for they're rethting from their labourth.'

Joe doubted it. Despite Bunty's optimism he couldn't picture David Vaz sitting around paradise idly tucking into the ambrosia, summoning a passing angel to order another beer. He got the impression that the people of Cow Cay went to funerals not because they wanted to pay their respects but because it gave them something to do, an excuse not to clean out the hen-shed or fix the roof. No one was likely to be there to pay their respects to Vaz because no one had any respect for him. Maybe they were there for Dora.

Dora Vaz had put on a dress and a black raffia hat, though she still wore her tattered plimsoles. She stood with her children, aside from the crowd among the breadfruit trees, eyes on the ground, her hands across her stomach, fingers struggling with an invisible lock, tears running down her cheeks. Crying not for Vaz, Joe suspected, but for the wasted mess of her life.

There were plenty of tears among the crowd. An ancient black man, white-haired and wrinkled, in a threadbare suit too large for his shrunken frame, let out a wail. Vaz's father, Joe guessed. Others joined in. B. J. MacIntyre moved across and put his arm round the old man.

Sarah was there too, subdued and respectful behind a line of well-scrubbed school children. As Joe studied her she looked up, and for a moment their eyes met. Joe blushed and looked away to her left, where Captain Mendes hid behind his reflective glasses, arms behind his back, his features carved in wood.

There were a few whites among the black and mestizo faces: a husband with a young wife and a child, a solitary American male with the look of a hippy diver, a middle-aged woman in a wide straw hat with a hastily applied black ribbon tied round the brim, a sallow European in his fifties in a panama.

It was hot among the stones. A gecko flicked its tail, paused for a moment on the edge of a tomb slab, then vanished under a faded wreath of plastic flowers. There were Scots and Irish names on the graves, Campbells and Frazers and O'Learys, but in Jamaica and the Caymans, where their ancestors would have come from, slaves took the names of their owners: the inscriptions were no guide to the nationality of the bones beneath them.

Listening to the Reverend Burgess, Joe remembered his mother Margaret's funeral. They'd burned not buried her, at a modern municipal crematorium on the south side of Edinburgh on a grey November morning, with a cold wind blowing down off the Pentland Hills and scattering dead leaves off the neat piles beside the newly tarmacadamed municipal driveway.

A ghastly funeral, formal and silent. Margaret had grown bitter and irrational in her final years, and there were few mourners, almost all of them there for reasons of duty: her bank manager, her doctor, a long-suffering neighbour, the home help, all the human furniture among which she'd bumped and cursed away her later days. The only ones with ties of the heart, however thinly stretched, were Joe and Willie and Margaret's spinster sister Jean.

The ceremony took twenty-three minutes, and Joe could remember every second of them, every pause and cough, the sound of each individual voice mumbling its way through 'Loving Shepherd of Thy Sheep' and 'The Year Is Swiftly Waning'.

Willie had arrived late and stood at the back, expressionless in a homburg and heavy black overcoat trimmed at the collar with brown velvet. For once Joe badly didn't want to know what his father was thinking or feeling, but afterwards, when the ceremony was over and they were waiting together in the crematorium porch to thank the clergyman, Willie had put his hand briefly on Joe's shoulder, and for maybe three seconds they shared a moment of communion. Neither of them had ever mentioned Margaret's death to each other again.

He wondered now if Willie was dead, if this funeral was being watched by another ghost.

Bobby Burgess was coming to the end.

'Who shall change our vile body, that it may be like unto hith glorioth body . . .'

Prompted by Bunty, Dora Vaz bent down, picked up a handful of red clay and tossed it on to the coffin.

'He cometh not that Man shall continue to live in thith world,' Burgess raised his eyes to heaven, 'but will be with him in the hereafter'.

After the ceremony Mike went over and had a few words with Dora. She listened, but she didn't look at him, just gazed over his shoulder at the sea. Joe wanted to talk to her too, but now didn't seem the time.

He felt a hand on his shoulder and turned to find Sarah smiling at him from under her black hat.

'You coming out to see me sometime?'

'Sure,' said Joe. 'When would suit you?'

'How 'bout this afternoon?'

He couldn't see why not.

'Drink some tea, that's what the English like to do on their afternoons, isn't it?'

'They do in movies.'

'I like movies,' she grinned, and was gone.

Joe wandered through the graves to where Captain Mendes stood looking at his feet, lost in his own thoughts.

'Do you have any theories, Captain?' Joe asked him.

Mendes turned and looked Joe straight in the eye, unblinking, the way Scientologists do. It was a disconcerting technique: you could stare back at him or you could look away, but you couldn't relax.

'About Vaz or about your father?'

'Both, I suppose.'

'Plenty of theories. Start with Vaz. One, whoever put the bomb under the jeep used industrial explosives. Fishermen are the only people round here with explosives, use them to stun fish. You see a man round here with one hand missing, he's off a fishing boat.'

He waved towards a Spaniard in a cotton suit talking to Bobby Burgess by the cemetery gate. One arm of the Spaniard's blazer hung limp by his side, the end tucked into his pocket. He was leaning forward with his head down to listen to something Burgess was saying, scratching his nose with his good hand.

'His name is Carlos Duran, he and his brother Fidel have three trawlers, also other businesses here and on the coast. Used to run guns and money for the Contras at one time.' He paused. 'Or the Sandanistas, I forget. He's a man who could find explosives if he needed them.'

'You talked to him?'

'Yes, I talked to him, he's been away for over a week, only arrived back this morning. Plenty of alibis.'

'And plenty of motive,' Joe suggested.

'Motive to do what?'

'Lean on Mike Osborne.'

Mendes looked at him curiously.

'Who told you that?'

Mike Osborne, Joe was about to say, then thought better of it.

'It's probably just a rumour.'

Mendes put his hand on the bridge of his dark glasses. Joe wished he could see his eyes.

'If Carlos and his brother want to build hotels and casinos,' the policeman said quietly, 'Mike Osborne is not in a position to stop them. These things are for the state government, the Ministry of Culture and Tourism, not for him. What's the point in terrorizing a man who is in no position to harm you in the first place?'

They walked down the path towards the cemetery entrance.

'Okay,' said Joe. 'If not Carlos, who else?'

Mendes got out a pack of cigarettes.

'You could say the Reverend Burgess, I suppose. Not likely, but possible, God moves in mysterious ways, as your father is fond of saying. Or you could look around and find someone with a grudge against St Andrews.'

'Like Vaz?'

'Like Vaz. I don't say he'd been mistreated, but he got a thing about doctors. Same way some doctors get mad at people they can't cure, feel the patient deliberately making them look a fool.'

'Dora told me David came to St Andrews because he wanted to talk to me about my father.'

'Is that a fact?' said Mendes. 'She told me David told her he was going over to steal him some drugs from the pharmacy, told Reverend Burgess David lost a hog, must have followed it down the shore.'

'She lie a lot?' asked Joe.

'No, just doesn't listen much any more.'

'But you reckon David did it on his own?'

'So far I don't reckon any more than I know, which is he was there when it happened and didn't choose to give us a reason why.'

'Where would he have got the explosives?'

'If he got them.'

'If he got them.'

'No idea,' said Mendes. 'But I'm working on it.'

'And what about my father?'

'No idea,' Mendes repeated. 'But I'm working on it too. And if you want to know if he's dead, I don't reckon so. Your father always struck me as a man well able to look after himself.'

10

SARAH AND HER mother lived in a stilted house beside the dirt road between Reefs End and Morgan's Hole. Most days, when the gift shop wasn't open, Sarah would sit on the balcony of the house spraying her bare feet with insecticide, polishing and filing coral, leafing through a magazine or pretending to read a book. The house was so close to the road that every car, man or animal that passed would shout out greetings to her, and she'd look up and wave.

'Heh, Sarah, how you doing?'

'Slow, man, slow.'

She didn't mean herself, she meant life. Life on Cow Cay in particular, if there was such a thing, which she often doubted. Other places lived, the magazines were full of them, places with fancy restaurants with waiters who wore ties, all you needed to get into them was a piece of plastic, pay it off sometime when it suited you. Women in magazines were always having a good time. Particularly in the advertisements, you never saw unhappy women in advertisements, they always had rich men crawling all over them, buying them clothes and flowers and jewellery and stuff.

Not on the Cay. All the men on the Cay ever gave you was babies, as many as you wanted, whether you wanted them or not. All over the island the women got melon bellies, plus the pups that came before clinging round their ankles or off at their grandmothers' making trouble.

The house was a single room, curtained off into a living

area and two bed-spaces, one for Sarah, one for Omangatu. A polaroid picture of Willie Wilde was pinned above the doorway beside a lurid portrait of the Sacred Heart. The unwalled area beneath the hut, ten feet wide by twelve feet long, served as an open-air kitchen and storeroom. There was a kerosene fridge and a stove but no running water, just a rain butt and a stock of ice in the Koolaid.

Omangatu spent so much time under the house, bending from the waist to avoid the low ceiling while she prepared food and medicines and dried her *brujo* herbs, that she rarely bothered to straighten up when she stepped outside, so that her posture had locked into a permanent upside down 'L'. She always wore the same black dress, ancient and much pleated, no shoes, and a straw hat pulled low over her brow.

'Like having an old bitch-dog in the house,' Sarah was fond of saying. 'If she ain't sniffing round the kitchens she's curled up in a corner some place so quiet you don't know she's there.'

Omangatu didn't make conversation, she made statements, mostly to the assortment of animals which shared the compound, cats and hogs and dogs and lizards and a creature called a Roatan Rabbit which looked like a king-size rat and ate up any of the garbage the hogs didn't want. The stream of relatives and visitors who passed through the house Omangatu ignored almost entirely, although sometimes, when the living space was crowded with Sarah's friends, her voice would interrupt from behind her curtain. A single sentence, no more, and never asking for a reply. Sometimes Sarah would call back, sometimes not.

She checked her watch. Not long now, presuming he's punctual. Willie was always punctual to the second.

Joe was, he suspected, the only person on the island who didn't know where Sarah lived. He'd walked along the shore from St Andrews, tracing Willie's daily journey, until he reached B.J.'s. He found the preacher washing up in the Chicken Shack, hanging the pots on a line of nails according to size, scrubbing down the cooker with a ball of steel wool.

'Can't miss her,' he grinned. 'Straight on up.'

Joe was taking no chances. A mile up the road he stopped off at Chris Long's grocery-bar to buy cigarettes and check his directions.

The Chinaman was a square, polite, slightly distant man of maybe forty. Between customers he spent his day leaning on his elbows reading an immense large-print *Good News Bible* propped open on top of the kerosene fridge beside the counter. His eyes weren't too good, which a lot of people thought explained the way he painted. Same problem as El Greco, according to Mike, only without the talent. He also had a chronic problem with change: whatever coin or note you produced he nodded sadly, emptied out an old cigar box on the counter, nodded again, then summoned one of his vast tribe of children and sent them out to a neighbour to get change.

Out of curiosity Joe asked him if he stocked Senior Service.

'Ordered a heap of them couple of months back,' said Chris. 'Never came. Now the guy that wanted them cleared off, when they do come I'm gonna be landed with a hundred packs of cigarettes smell like a burning mattress, no one else ever goin' to buy them. Moral is, never try pleasing your customer, they don't even notice.'

'I'm Willie's son,' said Joe.

'You are?' Chris changed his spectacles and peered across the counter. 'So you are. Pleased to meet you.'

'Me too,' said Joe, shaking hands. 'How many packs did he order?'

'Ten times two hundred.'

'This was a couple of months ago?'

'Maybe less, maybe six weeks.'

'Did he tell you he was going away?'

'Didn't tell no one, so far as I know.'

Joe bought two packs of Lucky Strike, and Chris directed him on up the hill to Sarah's. It was two in the afternoon, the sun already overhead, the air hot and still. Maybe you got used to the heat, but he doubted it. The way most people seemed to cope with it was to do nothing, sit around in the shade and watch the lizards doing press-ups on the ceiling. Out to sea a motor cruiser cut a white scar across the water, more divers on their way out to the reef.

Sarah saw Joe a long way off, and slipped back off the balcony into the hut to get herself ready, check the photo of Willie was in place, her magazines safely out of sight under the matting. She stayed inside, watching the road through the curtain of plastic beads which covered the doorway, wondering what he'd do when he got there. No bells to ring, no door knocker: what Willie used to do was wait at the bottom of the ladder and cough. Sometimes she'd leave him there for minutes on end, while he looked at his watch, coughed some more, wiped the sweat off his brow with his handkerchief. She never loved him more than when she watched him without his knowing.

She didn't feel that way about Joe at all, she was just curious. And there was also the question of money. The old man never spent any, but she knew he had it. If he was dead she didn't reckon to inherit the lot, but she was sure Willie would want her to get something.

'Hallo?'

Joe was at the foot of the ladder now, butting out a cigarette under his heel, looking around to see if anyone was home. He was wearing a borrowed pair of Mike's shorts and a pale blue T-shirt with a picture of a turtle on the front, bought that morning. Joe didn't much like the turtle, but in Morgan's Hole it was that or 'Divers Fall Over Backwards To Do It'. In the dust a hen danced a lazy Charleston, her chicks scrabbling at her feet.

Sarah took a last look at herself in the mirror, then stepped through the bead curtain into the doorway.

'Heh, you found us. Come on up.'

Once inside it took Joe's eyes a while to get used to the darkness. There was almost no furniture in the room, just a low plank balanced on four bricks and some homemade stools, and two shelves along the back wall containing a paraffin lamp, a small plastic model of the Empire State building, a souvenir ashtray from San Pedro Sula, an old transistor radio, a tea pot, a conch shell and three paperbacks. The books were English – a Len Deighton, a Graham Greene and a Bernard Cornwell. He knew without asking that they were Willie's. He also knew without asking that Sarah would have read none of them.

The emptiness of the small dark room disturbed Joe, not because he held any sexual ambitions towards Sarah, but because it made for an atmosphere of intimacy, and he wasn't sure how intimate he should be with his father's lover. It wasn't the sort of social situation they taught you about at public school. He needn't have worried: Sarah took responsibility for the etiquette. She offered him a stool, then asked him what he'd like to drink.

'What have you got?'

'Beer, Fresco, herb tea, brandy, maybe some coffee.'

'What are you having?'

'Beer and a brandy.' She suddenly looked him straight in the eye. 'Helps the nerves.'

Beer would do Joe fine. Sarah disappeared downstairs and returned with two bottles, wet from the bucket, and proceeded to uncap them with her teeth.

He wished she wouldn't do that: just watching her hurt him. He wiped the neck of the bottle on his T-shirt before drinking. Ever since catching amoebic dysentery in Nepal ten years before he'd approached all aspects of tropical hygiene with solar-topee caution. Don't eat pork, don't eat melons, boil your water, Say No To Ice – all the boring platitudes of the English in hot climates. Made you look like a wimp, but he didn't want to spend another two weeks like the two he'd spent in the Everest Hotel in Kathmandu, shitting blood and praying he hadn't caught hepatitis.

'You nervous too?' asked Sarah.

'A bit.'

'Willie was nervous to start with, only he didn't like to show it. Sat right where you're sitting now, hands on his knees, asking about all the stuff in the room, where it came from. Each time he asked I told him straight out, and he had to move on to something else. He'd say "Where did you get the ashtray?" I'd say "Stole it off a tourist." Full stop. "And the Empire State?" "New York." Full stop.' She stretched her lips across her gums in a grotesque but affectionate imitation of Willie's English accent. '"And the shell?" "Found him on the beach." Willie been here months, still didn't know a conch from a lobster. You know what "conch" means?'

Joe glanced across at the eight-inch shell with its long thin mouth, pink and glistening.

'Yup,' said Joe, trying not to blush. 'Frank told me.'

Sarah laughed.

'He should know.'

'Should he?'

'Spends his life pawing people's bodies.'

'Professionally or otherwise?'

'Both, I guess. He got a lot of appetites, that man. Get him into trouble some day. At least that's what Willie reckoned.'

'And Mike?'

She wiped her mouth.

'You mean women? Frankly I don't know what's happened to Mike of late. Used to chase woman all the time, lately he don't seem interested. Works too hard, too busy working on his masterpiece.'

'St Andrews?'

'What else? Don't need women no more now he's got something else to fall in love with. Only St Andrews turning out just as troublesome as a woman.'

'In what sense?'

'Willie, Jiuba, Bobby Burgess. Plus he lost a boat a while back, someone messing around with his operation.'

'Do you know who?'

'Nope. Most folks like him fine, he done good work. He got enemies, but no more than anyone else. Anyone tries to get anything done on this island gets enemies. You hear 'em say he just a white man doing white man business, don't give a shit about the rest of us.'

'Is it true?'

'About Mike? Shit no. He done nothing but good here.'

Joe was waiting for her to sit down, but she stayed leaning against the door jamb, arms hanging loose, one hand holding the beer bottle, rubbing her thumb up and down the neck. Her body was in silhouette against the light from the doorway, and he could see the outline of her breasts through the translucent cotton of her blouse.

'So how did you meet Willie?'

'Over at Mike Osborne's place. I done some work for Mike round that time, helped out with the nurses when some girl got sick. Willie was always there, fixing papers, checking what was needed in the stores. He said he wanted to meet my mother, could he drop by some time. Came up the road one morning just like you.'

'Why did he want to meet your mother?'

'Don't suppose he did, just needed a reason to come calling. Someone told him she was a *brujo*. You people suckers for *brujos*, all that Africa magic shit. Willie got some trouble with his hip, heard she good with hips. Only the *brujo* wasn't here that morning, she gone to town, he had to make do with me. Your mother dead, that's right?'

'Yes.'

'He told me that. Men always tell you they got no woman. In New York seems there aren't no married men at all, not till you start looking in their wallets and find the snapshots.'

'My mother died ten years ago. I don't think Willie had anyone since then.'

'How about you? You given him any grandchildren?'

'Not that I know of.'

Sarah didn't believe him. There wasn't a healthy man on the Cay hadn't fathered some child or other. Even B.J. the preacher had sons who must have been born when he was still in his teens.

'You tried?' she asked.

'I've had girlfriends, if that's what you mean.'

He offered her a cigarette. Sarah took another swig of beer, helped herself to a Lucky Strike, and sat down.

'Willie said you couldn't settle with a woman.'

'I've tried. The ones I wanted to settle with didn't like the idea. And vice-versa.'

'Ones or one?'

'One in particular.'

'She got a name?'

'Marion.'

'You still chasing her?'

'Not chasing, no. But I think about her.'

'You write songs about her? Willie said you wrote songs.'

'Not specifically about her.'

'You sing me a song now?'

'Not now.'

For a while neither of them spoke. Downstairs a cock crowed.

'Where did you get your chickens?' Joe asked.

Sarah laughed.

'Got them off B.J., he tried keepin' them but the boas kept taking them. Boa loves to eat fowl, swallow them whole. Except the rooster, rooster's spurs stick in his throat. We don't get so many boas up here, the *brujo* sees to that.'

'You sell the eggs back to B.J.?'

'Sure. Only he tells people they come from the States, reckons he can charge more for his dinners that way.' She was looking at him again, eye to eye. 'What kind of songs do you write? I figure it must be something serious, you don't look like no disco musician to me.'

Joe wondered if she grilled Willie this way. Willie never talked about himself, or not in a way that revealed anything. Feelings and emotions were girl talk, or the last defence of the felon in the dock. They had nothing to do with real living, which was measured not in what you thought or felt but in what you did. If emotions intruded at all, they were treated as an unwanted interruption, an embarrassment. He'd seen Willie in court once, presiding over the trial of a remorseful wife-killer who'd broken down in tears under cross-examination. For five minutes the man had stood there in the dock, whimpering and sobbing. Willie opened a law book and sat there reading, waiting for the accused to get control of himself. He didn't count it against people if they went to pieces, he just ignored it.

'I either write what comes into my head, or what I'm paid for. Sometimes if I'm lucky the two coincide. Given the choice I write about day to day relationships, human folly, ordinary people and ordinary lives.'

Sarah didn't understand what he meant by ordinary.

'Take love songs,' Joe explained. 'Most love songs are about teenagers or single people in their twenties. You sort of assume they're beautiful people, just like the guy or the girl who's doing the singing. If they're not about young people, then they're normally sentimental slush, women's magazine stuff. People write plenty of books and plays and TV movies about real life, but not songs. In songs it's always Valentine's Day.'

Sarah was glad she'd hidden her magazines. Men saw nothing wrong in simple books about war heroes, but they couldn't half shit on books about romance.

'Sounds dull stuff to me.'

'Maybe it is,' said Joe. 'But that's what I do.'

A jeep came along the road, tooting its horn as it passed the hut.

'Willie liked your songs,' said Sarah.

Joe looked up.

'No he didn't.'

Willie liked opera highlights, and Gilbert and Sullivan, Songs From The Shows, the hummable bits of Beethoven and Mozart, perhaps a little Elgar or Chopin. Sometimes, when he was feeling unusually cheerful, he'd sing a line or two from one of the popular songs of his own youth, 'Run Rabbit Run', 'When I'm Cleaning Windows', 'What A Little Moonlight Can Doo-oo-oo'. Not because he liked them but because of the times and situations they reminded him of.

Joe had given Willie a tape of his songs once, but as far as he knew his father had never listened to it. Another time Willie, down in London for some committee meeting, had come to see Joe perform once, on the opening night of a one-man show he'd done at the Donmar Warehouse in Covent Garden, Willie on his own in a three-piece suit among the unwashed fringe audience, sitting at the back with his mackintosh folded on his knee, upright and silent. By the time Joe had come off stage he'd gone. He'd never referred to the evening later, or shown a glimmer of interest in Joe's career.

'You made that up,' he accused Sarah.

'I could have,' she agreed. 'Only I didn't. He said he didn't understand a lot of them, but he liked what he could follow.'

'What else did he say about me?'

The moment Joe asked the question he regretted it. He wasn't here to talk about himself, he was here to find out about Willie, look for more pieces of the jigsaw.

'You want the truth or you want some more stuff to make you feel good?'

'Try me.'

'Said you acted idle but don't be fooled. Said you acted slow and easy but don't be fooled by that either. Said you were lonely. Not on the outside, but when you got home. And not just for a woman. That true?'

'Isn't it true of everyone?'

'Not so's I've noticed.'

Joe was asking himself if he'd ever met a woman like this before. Bits of her, he decided, bits that belonged to hookers, or brain-melt girls in jazz clubs looking for money to buy more drugs, or cock-teasers with serious emotional or mental health problems. Only Sarah wasn't any of those, she was just Sarah. He decided she was one of those rare originals, a person who couldn't help but be herself. Willie, ironically, was just such a man, capable of a certain thin veneer of tactical dissimulation, but beneath it utterly himself in a way he couldn't help, a way neither he nor anyone else could ever hope to change.

How the hell did he manage her? Willie was the type who still stood up to offer his seat to women on the Underground and hurried to cross a fence or a stile ahead of the ladies to spare them the indignity of hitching their skirts in front of him. Who made the first move? Which of them touched the other's arm to emphasize a point, and then let their hand linger a moment after the point was made?

She helped herself to another of his cigarettes.

'You want to smoke something stronger?'

Joe didn't want ganja, but he would have killed for a whisky.

'No thanks.'

'You mind if I do?'

'Not at all. Do you have any more beer?'

'Sure.'

She brought him a bottle from downstairs and sat down cross-legged on the floor pulling cigarette papers from a pack with her long fingernails. Joe wiped the neck of his beer bottle on his sleeve and took a drink.

'Did he tell you much about himself?'

'Sure. He said he screwed up a lot of things. Said he should never have been a judge, or he should have quit when he found out what was involved, only he was too pleased at how important he was all of a sudden.'

'Judges don't resign,' said Joe. 'At least I never heard of one who did. Even politicians resign sometimes, but not judges. Not unless they get sick or go nuts, and not always then. Was he happy here?'

She grinned.

'Yea, I think he was. Got some queer ways of showing it sometimes, he yea, he was. Done him good to be working again, too.'

'He said that?'

'He said that.'

'Did he talk about his work?'

'Not a lot. He'd get pissed off some days, someone messing him around, government people, shop people, sound off about it. Other days he'd come home big grin on his face, have a drink, go inside and work on his papers.'

'Do you know what happened to his papers?'

'Never could figure that. Maybe he took them in to St

Andrews. Had a canvas bag full of papers, carried them all round the place. Maybe he got them with him now.'

Joe lit another cigarette.

'What do you know about the Duran brothers?'

'Carlos and Fidel? Live in a big bungalow out of town, got a satellite TV dish on the lawn and a peon stands there all day with a walkie-talkie, Carlos and Fidel sit inside watching TV, call him up to move the dish when they bored with one satellite, get him to point it at another.' She licked the gum on her papers and sealed the joint between her fingers. 'Why, you reckon they got Willie tied up some place?'

'I don't reckon anything,' said Joe. 'I'm just getting my bearings.'

Sarah was thinking.

'Hard to figure what the Durans got to do with Willie,' she decided. ''cept they pretty thick with Bobby Burgess. Willie's not too keen on Burgess. You know what he calls him? Wobblebottom.'

She laughed. Joe smiled too. It was so like Willie to go back to his prep-school vocabulary for an insult.

'Where did the Durans get the money for TV dishes?'

'Shrimping, freeze them where they catch 'em, run 'em straight into Florida. With maybe a little something in with the catch for the brothers in Miami. People saying in town they looking to expand their business with a little help from their friends in the States, do up the island, build some hotels, bring in tourists.'

'What does Willie think of the idea?'

'He thinks it's shit. Wants to save this place for people like him, keep the natives real. Take some photos, go home and show people this weird place they found ain't got no hotels or casinos.'

'Was he trying to stop them?'

'Not now. But he talked about it. Maybe that's what's in his canvas bag, stuff on Bobby and the Durans.'

'What do you think about the idea?'

'I don't think nothing. Thing about this island is, people

talk a lot, all kind of schemes. All got something in common, none of them ever happen.'

'It's happened in other places,' said Joe.

'Maybe. Maybe we gonna have big condos along the beach. Maybe the Pope got married. Meanwhile I got better things to worry 'bout.'

'What's in it for Burgess?'

'He backs 'em, they leave him alone to get on with his business, maybe even discourage the opposition. At least that's how I figure it. He ain't too keen on casinos, but he thinks that bit's negotiable. At least that's what the Durans tell him. Once they got the hotels up they won't be worrying too much about Bobby.' She reached up and adjusted her bra strap. 'You decided how long you staying yet?'

Joe told her he was off to the mainland in the morning.

'You coming back?'

'I expect so.'

'Next time you coming, rent yourself a place down at B.J.'s like Willie's. See some more of each other.'

'I might just do that,' said Joe.

It was almost four by the time Joe left. By then the dope was beginning to make Sarah confused, so that sometimes when he asked a question she didn't answer at all, just stared at him, watching his mouth move, waiting for it to move some more, like she was watching a fish in a tank.

As he reached the bottom of the steps, a battered minibus rounded the corner. It stopped short of the hut, and through the window he glimpsed a figure whom he assumed to be Omangatu among the passengers, gathering up her bags. Joe slung his bag over his shoulder and hurried down the road towards Reef's End.

11

SAN PEDRO SULA lies 200 miles west of the Cays and forty miles inland from the Caribbean, in a flat valley surrounded by low cloud-covered hills. It's as close as Honduras gets to a thriving industrial city, with an energetic foreign merchant class – North American, Cuban, Israeli, Irish, Russian, Middle-Eastern – dealing in bananas, sugar, coffee, timber, even steel. Together with the nearby port of Puerto Cortes, San Pedro handles much of the country's overseas trade. The climate is hot, humid, often wet, lacking the Cay's sea breezes, and the atmosphere polluted with noise and with dust.

Mike and Joe had been up since before dawn. Frank had driven them to the airport, from where they caught the morning flight, flying low over the coastal plain just as Willie must have done three weeks before on his way to the Mayan ruins at Copán. If Copán was indeed his destination.

They took a cab into town from the airport. Mike was his old self again, and insisted on playing the Tone game, so called because he was tone deaf. He hummed a tune, Joe had to guess what it was. The odds against recognition were horrendous.

'Born in the USA,' he announced proudly after Joe had given up. 'The Boss himself.'

Joe had thought it was Wagner.

'You know the one Springsteen song that really bugs me? Mike asked. '"Wreck on the Highway". Brucie's out driving, he comes across a wreck by the side of the road, some guy being pulled out dead, makes The Boss to realize how much he loves his woman, how he'd feel if she died. Verse one starts "Last night as I was out driving". Last verse starts "Some nights I lie awake and wonder". But he hasn't had any nights to lie and wonder, the song's in real time, he's only just come across the bloody wreck.'

'Poetic licence,' Joe explained.

'Idle fucker's licence, if you ask me.'

They drove through the outer suburbs, past the rich bungalows of the bourgeoisie, metal grilles on the windows, peons tending the shaved lawns and flowering shrubs, Mercedes and Volvos in the garages. As they approached the town centre the bungalows gave way to rows of flat-roofed cinder-block housing, doors open to reveal day beds and kitchens. A block of housing, and then a crumbling concrete factory behind a high mesh fence, overrun with creepers and abandoned machinery; then more housing, then a tobacco shed. Pools of black stagnant water filled the pot-holes and ditches, and the gutters were littered with fruit husks and empty juice cans and cardboard crates.

Mike tried another song.

'"Go Now"?' Joe guessed.

'Whiter Shade of Pale.'

'Written by?'

'J. S. Bach.'

'Only the riff. The rest's by Brooker and Reid.' Joe scratched the back of his neck. 'You know, it depresses me to think how much of the storage space in my brain is taken up with obsolete song lyrics and twenty-year-old band line-ups when it could be stuffed with philosophic thoughts and lyric poetry. Or practical information, frequently used phone numbers, train times, the names of my friends' children. I can tell you who played bass for the Bay City Rollers and recite the lyrics of Sam The Sham and the Pharaohs B-sides, but I don't know what to dial for Directory Enquiries. For twenty years I've been ringing Engineering Faults instead of Directory Enquiries.'

'Maybe it's a sort of brain insulation,' Mike suggested. 'Protects your subconscious from confronting reality. Who did play bass with the Rollers?'

'Alan Longmuir, brother of Derek.'

Mike lit a cigarette and tossed the match out the cab window.

'Directory Enquiries is 192. At least it used to be.'

The taxi stopped at a traffic lights. On the opposite corner two black women were talking, a toddler at their feet, too absorbed in their conversation to notice a mongrel approach the toddler, cock its leg, urinate against the child, then vanish up an alley. The child started to cry, its mother looked down and saw the damp stain on its crutch, and started to berate it. Joe didn't know whether to laugh or cry.

'Odds are that kid'll be dead before he's ten,' Mike said quietly. 'Or sleeping in a box at the bus station. Poverty really upset me when I first got to the Third World. Swanning around with the BBC, staying at the Intercontinental, making a fuss about the air-conditioning in your Hertz car. Then I stopped noticing, everyone does. Since I came to the Cay I've started noticing again. You still can't do much about it, but it gives me nightmares. Why them, not us?'

Joe didn't really have an answer.

'People won't talk about it,' Mike went on. 'It's a great taboo in nice white circles.'

'That's because we feel helpless, we feel guilty but we don't know what to do about it, except bang a few bob to Oxfam once in a while.'

'It's not that, Joe: it's because people find it inconvenient to know what's happening. Or to think about it, because if they did they might reach some morally uncomfortable conclusions. A couple of months ago Willie was over to supper, started talking about his grandmother and the Great War.'

'He talked to you about Grandma Wilde?'

'She had three sons and a daughter, right? Two boys – your great-uncles, I guess – died on the Somme. One was twenty, the other eighteen. He said it hurt her like hell at the time, but in a way it also seemed noble, fighting and dying for your country, all that shit. What really broke her heart was finding out ten years later exactly what had gone on on the Western Front. She found the realization that they'd died for nothing, the senselessness of it, almost impossible to bear. He said he'd read the papers the War Office sent her breaking the news, the letters from commanders and fellow officers, full of insincerity and downright lies. How could people be so crass?'

'Maybe they didn't know any better,' said Joe.

'That's the point. You look at the idiocies of the Great War, the butchery, the jingoism, and you think – couldn't happen now, we know better. But those people were born no less intelligent than us, no less kind, no less thoughtful.'

'I believe that very strongly, Joe – we're no better and no wiser than our forebears. All we have is the benefit of hindsight. Just as we do about the men and women who allowed the potato famine in Ireland, or the bombing of Dresden, or all the crimes committed in the Empire. And what obsesses me is the need to discover what are the idiocies that we're perpetrating now, the things that in seventy years' time the next generation will find incomprehensible. I think the answer's the North/South divide, the refusal of the developed to treat the undeveloped as members of the same species.'

'Il faux cultiver votre jardin.'

'Is that what you believe?' Mike asked.

'Of course not.'

'Nor did Willie.'

Does, did, they were both beginning to trip up over their tenses.

'Sarah says you love St Andrews like a woman,' said Joe. 'Do you?'

'Sarah said that? She's crazy, that girl.'

'But not stupid.'

'She is and she isn't. I'll tell you something about Sarah, she's one of those credulous people who believes that because a fact appears in a book it is *de facto* true – the idea that people put lies or mistakes in books is strange to them. No education at all, or not in the sense we mean it. Half the time she talks pure shit – island talk, all fantasy and wish-fulfilment. Other times she's sharp as a knife. The problem is sorting the shit from the insight. Not just for us, for her.'

'You still haven't answered the question.'

Mike smiled.

'Yea, I suppose she's right. I've got problems, but deep down I've never been happier, nowhere near it.'

The traffic got worse as they approached the city centre. Police in red caps and khaki fatigues struggled to disperse a permanent jam of overloaded construction trucks, buses, taxis and motorcycles. On the pavements market traders and beggars fought for pavement space with the long queues outside the government offices and bus stations, with Indians in town to sell their vegetables and off-duty army conscripts. The warped and rutted streets were lined with cheap hotels and cantinas and hardware stores stacked with tin and zinc baths, sacks and boxes, ropes and baskets, the shop fronts painted in faded primary colours, daubed with crude illustrations of irons and shirts and roast chickens.

Outside a church a wedding party posed for the photographer, a skinny groom with well-oiled hair in a bright blue suit, loose and flared at the ankle, holding hands with his teenage bride, flanked by bridesmaids in pink and green taffeta and a page boy, very small and nervous, fiddling with his bouquet of plastic flowers. All but the groom wore white gloves.

The cab tried a short cut down a narrow alley, only to find its way blocked by a tethered mule with a wooden saddle.

'Do you never miss the old life?' Joe asked

'Not a lot. I miss friends, once in a while I miss London. Living in the tropics may seem exotic at first glance, but it's really not that glamorous. The climate's stifling, the diet's monotonous, the company can get claustrophobic. Nothing works. Every day you're surrounded by poverty and disease, corruption and inertia. But there are plenty of compensations. An English guy was in here last year, kept looking at me across the bar, finally came over and asked me if I used to be Mike Osborne, he remembered me off the telly. That sort of summed up it – I used to be Mike Osborne. Now I'm just me. If that makes sense. I'm much happier with things the way they are now.'

Joe believed him. He liked the new Mike. He missed some of the old flippancy, some of the old abandon, but the thoughtfulness and commitment helped fill a void that had always been below the surface, filled it with something you couldn't but respect.

The cab finally dropped them off outside a dirty downtown office block strangled by power lines. They pushed their way through the crowds to the entrance and climbed the stairs to the third floor.

Rikki Dack's white-walled office smelled of wax polish and aftershave. The room was calm and cool, in contrast to the street outside. The windows were closed, and an air-conditioning unit rattled in the corner.

Rikki acted as shipping agent for St Andrews, responsible for the import of drugs and materials from outside the country. He looked expensive and ill, a thin man in a well-pressed linen suit with a gold watch and a silk handkerchief in his top pocket. A panama hat hung on the stand by the door. Joe guessed him at around fifty, although he could have been ten years either side. His manner was quiet, and slightly formal.

He got up as they entered, shook hands, gestured to two leather chairs, and offered them coffee.

'How are you, Rikki?' asked Mike.

Dack shrugged his shoulders.

'I can't complain.'

Mike grinned.

'Ah, go on.'

Dack allowed himself a wry smile, took out a lacquer cigarette case and offered it across the desk.

'Very well. I have failed to win the National Lottery. My doctor says I need two new lungs. My wife complains I don't find her attractive any more. It's true, but what can I do? The plain fact is that she is no longer an attractive woman. Business is quiet, and there is new competition all the time.'

'But you get by,' said Mike.

Dack inhaled on his cigarette and blew the smoke at the ceiling fan.

'I get by. And you?'

'We're still looking for Willie.'

'So I gather.'

There was a knock on the door and an overweight woman with technicolour make-up teetered in on high heels carrying a tray of coffees. Dack watched her hand round the cups in silence, and waited until she had left the room before he spoke again.

'You've heard nothing?'

Mike shook his head.

'Nope.'

Dack took out a leather phial of saccharin with his initials monogrammed on the side and dropped two pills carefully into his cup.

'As I told you, he came through here on the 8th to check on a couple of shipments from the States.'

'Anything special?' asked Joe.

Dack threw Mike a questioning look.

'Joe's a friend,' said Mike.

Rikki put down his cup and wiped his lips on his handkerchief.

'There was a problem with customs.'

'We bribe, you have to,' Mike explained to Joe.

'And Willie delivers the cash?'

'On occasion.'

Willie as bagman was a new image to Joe.

'What was in the shipment?' asked Mike. He sounded surprised.

'Nothing very special,' said Rikki. He got out a ledger and turned the pages. 'Antibiotics, sterilizers, IUDs, some water purifying equipment. The customs wanted more than usual, too much. We talked about it. Willie wanted to be sure everything was in order, he spent an hour checking the papers.'

Mike frowned.

'I thought we'd sorted that problem. Send it back through Mexico, down through Guatemala.'

'I'd already made the arrangements,' said the lawyer. 'He was just checking.' He turned to Joe. 'Sometimes there are problems with the customs. This is a poor country, government employees are not well paid, it's necessary to buy their co-operation. Not a lot, a few hundred dollars once in a while. We're presently engaged in a new round of wage negotiations with our friends in the Ministry.'

'You have to pay duty on medical supplies?' Joe asked.

'Not duty. Sweeteners.'

Mike asked if he could make a phone call. Dack told him to help himself in the outer office. Once he'd gone Joe sat for a while, looking at his feet, neither of the two men speaking.

'How did Willie seem?' Joe asked eventually.

Dack closed the ledger.

'As English as ever.' He smiled. 'Forgive me, I don't wish to appear rude, I have a great affection for your country. And for your father.'

'Did he say where he was going?'

'Copán, to look at the ruins. He asked my advice on buses and places to stay. I told him the Hotel Mirabelle. The best of a bad bunch, Copán is not famous for its creature comforts.'

Joe wondered what a man like Rikki Dack thought of this circus, of Mike and Willie and Frank, why these people should choose to come to his country, what motives he assigned to them. He reached into his shoulder bag and got out Willie's map.

'Could I run through a few more dates with you?'

Dack smiled.

'Of course.'

He read out the dates of Willie's three previous visits to

San Pedro. Rikki noted them down neatly with a gold fountain pen on a virgin legal pad, then checked them one by one against his diary. Two fitted; one, six weeks before, was a blank.

'You're sure?' asked Joe.

Rikki clipped his pen carefully into the inside pocket of his jacket and leaned back in his seat.

'Positive.'

Mike came back into the room, and took his pocket diary out. Joe asked Dack if Willie might have had any other business in town.

'Not that I can think of.' He flicked through the pages until he found the date. 'According to this he was in Tegoose.'

A fly rattled at the window. Rikki took a steel ruler out of the drawer of his desk, walked across the room and with craftsman's precision squashed it against the glass. He wiped the ruler on a tissue, put it back in his desk and sat down.

'Maybe he made a mistake. People do at his age. Where did you find the map?'

'Under his bed,' said Joe.

'Strange that he didn't take it with him this time.'

'It had slipped down between the mattress and the wall, I expect he couldn't find it.'

'May I see?' asked Dack.

'Of course.'

Rikki spread the map out on the desk, tracing Willie's lines one by one with his finger, at first casually, then with more concentration. Joe and Mike came over to join him.

When he'd finished he shook his head.

'You'd know better than I would what he was up to,' he said to Mike.

At that moment Joe's eyes spotted a familiar name on the map.

'Cedros,' he said, pointing at a dot near the end on one of Willie's lines, fifty miles north of Tegucigalpa.

'What about it?' asked Mike.

It took Joe a moment to remember.

'Bunty Burgess. She said she and Bobby worked there before they came to the Cay. Before that they were at La Entrada. Wherever the hell that is.'

Rikki pointed with his fountain pen to a point midway along the line that followed the road from San Pedro Sula to Copán.

'It's where you change buses,' said Dack. 'The Lina line *rapidos* take you from here to La Entrada, continue on to Santo Rosso. You switch at La Entrada and take the *regulares* to Copán.'

Rikki looked at Mike, Mike looked at Joe, Joe folded up the map and put back in his bag.

'Bobby Burgess,' said Mike thoughtfully. 'Well well well. And he came to San Pedro first but he didn't come to see you?'

'Not that time,' said Rikki.

'Then why?' asked Joe.

'San Pedro,' Mike explained, 'is the regional headquarters of The Good Book Union of the Americas. Three blocks from here.'

'First catch your preacher,' said Dack. 'Enjoy your trip. And good luck.'

12

At the bus station in San Pedro Mike and Joe showed round Mike's beach photo of Willie. The first man they showed it to had seen the old man two days before in Tegoose. The second identified him as a well-known Mexican opera singer. Two women had spotted him boarding a boat for New Orleans a week ago; a bunch of teenagers swore he was staying in town at the Hotel Fernandes recruiting workers for an oil rig.

Joe started off writing down the details, but after twenty minutes he gave up.

'You remember a guy called John Stonehouse?' he asked Mike as they boarded the Calin Line *rapido* for La Entrada, from where a *locale* would take them on into the mountains and Copán. 'Used to be a Labour party minister, got into money trouble, left his clothes in a heap on the beach and took off to Australia. The only reason they caught him was someone mistook him for Lord Lucan. The only way he could prove he wasn't Lucan was to prove he was John Stonehouse. They didn't even look the same.'

The coach was crowded with people and luggage, the windscreen hung with plastic saints and football flags. The radio played loud salsa music through cheap speakers. Children pushed down the aisle selling melon slices and paper cups of ice dripping with hideously dyed red syrup.

'Hepatitis-In-A-Basket,' warned Mike. 'Stick to *Agua Cristal*.'

The road ran up the long valley away from the city, past

cement works and fruit warehouses, out into open country. The eighty miles to La Entrada would take two hours; at La Entrada they'd have another three hours to wait for a connection to Copán. Joe planned to spend the time looking for traces of Bobby Burgess's ministry.

'There used to be two main fundamentalist outfits,' Mike explained: 'the New Tribes Mission and the Summer Institute of Linguistics. Both set up after the Second World War, both well funded out of the Southern States. Serious Old Testament headbangers, chiefly interested in native tribes. They believe anyone who isn't baptized goes to hell for eternity. Not just pagans, Catholics and Anglicans and Orthodox too. But mostly they went for pagans. Find a tribe someplace, round them up like cattle, put them in camps. A lot of them died, spiritually and physically. They don't give a flying fuck about the material welfare of their converts so long as their souls are saved. The ones who don't die are persuaded to get rid of their old beliefs and ceremonial, and taught to recite the Bible like parrots. The convenient bits, that is – Old Testament, mostly, plus a verse or two from St Paul. No Sermon on the Mount, no love-your-neighbour, strictly Armageddon stuff.'

He shifted his buttocks. The narrow plastic-covered seats were designed for the Latino build and leg-length. The temperature was in the mid nineties, and both men were sweating.

'Bobby Burgess was with the New Tribes?' Joe asked.

'Used to be. The Tribes were very big for a while, plenty of funding, they had what amounted to their own airline. In parts of Asia and South America they ran districts the size of small countries. There was a conspiracy of interest between the Mission and right-wing dictators. The evangelists sorted out troublesome tribes much more effectively than the military could. And at no expense to the government.'

'But not any more?'

'Things aren't quite as bad as they used to be. Journalists got in and started writing articles in the Western press, the Catholics started kicking up, there was a fuss at the UN.

The guys are still out there, but they keep a lower profile these days. I think Bobby moved on when he began to feel the heat, signed on with the Good Book Union. The GBU are far more careful, they employ PR guys and lobbyists back in Washington. The Acceptable Face of Fundamentalism. Some people think they're just the New Tribes under a new name, you wouldn't know.'

Out of the window Joe could see a white wall of rain approaching across the flat valley bottom. Passengers stood up to close the windows, and the driver turned on the wipers. A minute later the full force of the deluge hit the bus.

'Summertime . . .' Mike sang tunelessly, '. . . and the living . . .'

A chrome-encrusted truck emerged from the mist, headlights on, horn blaring. The bus swerved to the right, two wheels on the red mud embankment, the driver fighting the steering wheel like a ship's captain at the tiller. A suitcase fell from the rack on to Joe's shoulder. By the time he'd recovered they were back on the tarmac again.

'We going to make it to Copán in this?' he asked nervously.

Mike gave a cheerful shrug.

'Maybe, maybe not. The road's okay as far as La Entrada, maybe a bit dodgy from there on.'

There was no way of telling what countryside lay beyond the mist. Occasionally Joe glimpsed a watercourse or a thatched hut and what might have been tobacco leaves drying in a barn.

It was still raining when they reached La Entrada. Mike and Joe collected their bags and ran through the downpour towards a neon hotel sign. A line of impassive Indians in plastic pack-a-macks sheltered on the front porch.

'Is closed,' said one of the Indians.

Mike gave him a big grin.

'Not for long.'

He walked up to the door and pushed it open. They found themselves in a low-ceilinged room with a rough wooden floor, half a dozen tables, a silent juke box, a dead pot-plant in a tin bucket and a defunct ceiling fan. The place smelled of damp and mould, old food and stale tobacco and kerosene.

'You fancy a drink?' asked Mike.

'Badly.'

'Hold on a sec.'

He vanished into the shadows. Joe sat down and lit a cigarette. He heard voices from the back of the building, and then Mike returned with a tiny old woman, so old that she looked to Joe like a faded paper flower. She shuffled across the room and turned on the lights and the overhead fan.

'Carmel, this Joe Wilde. An old friend from England.'

'How you doing, Joe?' Carmel asked in a voice deep enough to be male and unmistakably American. She wore a nylon housecoat which ended at her knees and fluffy white slippers tied with pink bows. Joe guessed she must be about eighty.

Carmel opened the door of the fridge.

'You fancy a beer?'

'Please.'

'Nationale or Salva Vida? They sell two brands of beer in this country,' she explained to Joe, 'Nationale and Salva Vida, and for some reason people who drink one never touch the other, though I'm damned if I can tell the difference and I'm damned sure they can't either. You got a preference?'

Joe didn't. He knew bars and clubs in London where people drank Venezuelan cactus beer and Angolan yam-stout and authentic Albanian lager at five quid a glass, but as far as he was concerned beer was beer. Apart from Harp lager, he didn't know how anyone could drink Harp.

Carmel took three bottles of beer from the fridge, put them on a tray, shuffled over to the bar and collected a bottle of Flor de Cana Extra Seco and three glasses.

'Best rum in the world,' she growled, 'only folks can't buy it in the States on account it's Cuban. The price of ideological purity.' She grinned. 'Pleased to meet you.'

She held out her hand, so deformed by arthritis that it seemed all knuckle and claw. Joe was still wondering what an octogenarian American was doing running a hotel in a place like La Entrada.

'Where did you two meet?' he asked.

Mike poured the rum.

'You tell him, Carmel.'

'It's too long a story and my name ain't Carmel, it's Marie-Louise.'

'She's a friend of Amos Lipstein,' said Mike. 'She got ill one time down on the coast, Amos fixed her up.'

Carmel came from Texas, where she'd been a primary school teacher. Late in life she'd married a Honduran called Carlos O'Leary. Carlos ran a trucking business in Fort Worth. After they married he sold up the house and the business and bought a 1,000-acre tobacco plantation midway between La Entrada and Copan. For five years they lived like colonial barons, ran the business, improved the land, kept a yacht on the coast at Puerto Cortes, took holidays in Europe and the States. Then Carlos got cancer. By the time he died the estate was in bits. Two bad harvests and a tax bill finished it off.

Carmel could have cut and run, but she felt obliged to the creditors and workers. She sold up, paid off the debts, and used what little was left to buy the hotel and a small annuity.

Joe asked her why she didn't move back to the States.

'You ever been to Fort Worth?' She grinned and refilled the rum glasses. There were footsteps upstairs, a door closing, the sound of a cistern flushing. Joe wondered who was keeping Carmel company.

'Excuse me one moment,' said Carmel. 'I have a drunk upstairs stayed over last night, sounds like he's alive at last. A friend of my late husband.'

She disappeared upstairs, and Joe heard English voices, quietly at first, then Carmel shouting in mock-indignation.

'You ain't comin' downstairs dressed like that, not with company.'

And then a male voice laughing. A moment later Carmel was back, alone.

'You ever seen a seventy-year-old Florida widower dressed up in a lady's nightshirt with his teeth out? One upstairs if you care to look.'

'You've no shame, Carmel,' said Mike. 'A woman of your age.'

'Ah, but he's got the body of a sixty-five-year old.' Carmel gave Joe a wink. 'Talking of bodies that have seen better days, have you seen Amos lately?' she asked Mike.

'Not in a couple of months.'

'I heard he ain't been too well.'

'He was fine last time I saw him. His heart's not great, eyes are bad, but he's off the cigs and booze. Good for a few years yet.'

'I'm glad to hear it. So what brings you to this hole in the road?'

'We're looking for my father,' Joe explained.

Carmel threw him a sceptical glance.

'In La Entrada?'

Mike told her the story. When he'd finished Joe took out Willie's photograph and passed it across to Carmel. She took a pair of glasses out of the pocket of her housecoat and held the picture at arm's length, first upside down then the right way up.

'He's a judge?'

'Ex,' said Joe.

'You ever been up in court?'

'No.'

'Me neither. Except the tax people. I'm told it gives you a thing about judges.'

'Try having one for a father,' said Joe.

Carmel laughed, gums gleaming.

'Then how come you're looking?'

'Things I want to say to him.'

'Three weeks ago, this was?'

'About that.'

'Three weeks ago I was in bed, six days I didn't get up at

127

all except to go to the bathroom. You get like that sometimes when you're old, you ain't ill but you don't want to get up. Sleep all day, stay awake all night, listen to the radio, mind racing round like a rat in a cage.' She studied the picture again. 'But I can ask around. Where'll I find you if I get news?'

Mike was sitting astride his chair, elbows on the back, fingers playing with a twist of paper. He looked up.

'I'm not sure. We'll probably stay over in Copán tonight. We haven't got any definite plans beyond that.'

'I'll find you if I need to,' said Carmel. 'This country ain't as big as it seems.'

Outside the rain had cleared. Joe looked at his watch. They still had three hours until their bus left.

Carmel asked Mike about St Andrews. He told her about the bomb, making a joke of it. It was Joe who brought up Bobby Burgess.

'The preacher? He on the Cay now?'

'I'm afraid so,' said Mike. 'Didn't he used to have a mission here?'

'Sure did.' She was massaging her knuckles, kneading them between her fingers. 'They rode him out of town, torched the church. Bits of it still standing, up by the post office, some guy from Canoa bought it, plans to turn it into a pool hall.'

Joe asked what had happened.

'He moved in around five years ago, bought a plot of land, started spending money and preaching the Word. Had a wife and a couple of fellows with him, young kids from the States, they called them the Smilers round here because whatever you said to them they just smiled at you, like they were on some sort of chemicals. It was the Indians they were after, didn't seem to give a shit for the rest of us. Except government people, they were always well behaved when there were government people around. But mostly it was Indians they wanted. Got 'em some, too, started handing out new clothes to the women and scaring the men with tales of hell fire. You didn't see what's left of the church yet?'

Joe shook his head.

'Some place,' Carmel continued. 'They had a book of church designs, chose one they thought would appeal to the natives. Sort of Mayan looking, at least I think that must have been the idea – built like a pyramid at the base with stone steps round it, only the stone in these parts is soft as cow shit so they used cinder-block instead.'

'There are still Mayans here?' Joe asked.

'Mayan-Quiché. You don't get a lot of the real McCoy any more, most of them are mongrels, go to the Catholic churches and hang around the bars when they got money, brew up a pot of *boj* when they don't. You ever drunk *boj*? Smells foul but it don't taste that bad. Made up of sugar cane and some kind of roots. Once in a while the *brujos* organize a festival. Everyone dresses up in capes and jaguar skins and eagle feathers and antlers and those queer winged hats they copied off the conquistadores. Dance around for days on end, nobody gets to sleep for a week. Dull stuff once you've taken your photos. Burgess took a lot of photos.'

'Then he started sweet-talking them. Bought new frocks for the women, told the men to cut down on the drink and start worrying about the hereafter. Indians'll try anything new just for something to do. Also the Catholics still charge for weddings and funerals, Bobby did them for free. The Catholic clergy didn't like it, trespassing on their territory, not to mention their pocket books. But the government people couldn't get enough, helped Burgess all the way. You ready for more beer yet?'

'Sure,' said Mike. Carmel collected more bottles from the fridge.

'The government don't give a toss about religion but they give more than a toss about politics. Catholic clergy got a bad name for encouraging radical politics in this country. Not the bishops, you don't make bishop if your politics don't fit. But the priests are apt to get mixed up in radical causes. There's no danger Bobby Burgess is going to start recruiting for the Revolution. Plus there seemed to be money changing hands.'

'So what went wrong?' Joe asked.

'The weather. Two years the harvest was bad. The river burst its banks, carried away half the *barrio*. Happened to coincide with when Bobby arrived. Bobby got sore, said it was the people's fault for sinning. No big deal, but there were arguments, police got involved. Then there was the fire, place started to go up like a tinder box, would have been worse only the weather was still bad.'

'Did they find out who did it?' Joe asked.

'Police said it was an accident, candle fell over.' Carmel took a sip of rum and put down her glass. 'Only they don't have no candles in that kind of church. Bobby done it himself, a couple of Indians saw him out with the kerosene can just before she blew.'

They talked on for a while, but Joe could see the talk was beginning to tire Carmel. After half an hour they finished their drinks and said their goodbyes.

'You been to Copán before?' Carmel asked Joe as they were leaving.

'No.'

'Two kinds of folks go to Copán. There's tourists go for the ruins, and there's people want to get in and out of Guatemala without too much trouble. Enjoy Copán, stay out of Guatemala. Kill you for your socks in Guatemala.'

'Thanks for the advice,' said Joe.

Mike turned off the lights on the way out.

There was a market in the town square. Indian women in red patchwork dresses squatted in front of baskets of onions and peppers and sisal sacks of beans rolled back at the neck, two men unloaded branches of plantains and finger bananas from a flat-back truck, a group of teenagers gathered round a stall selling pirated music cassettes and videos. More stalls sold tortillas, bean stew and *atole*, the sweet cornflower gruel that was the staple of the inland diet.

'What's with the Marie-Louise?' Joe asked as they walked on up the slope towards the post office.

'Carlos couldn't take it, wouldn't marry her unless she changed it. What did you make of her?'

'I'd love to have met her fifty years ago.'

'Wouldn't we all,' said Mike.

The ruins of Bobby Burgess's church were much as Carmel had described them. The cinder-block steps were overgrown with weeds, and creepers stretched out over the concrete floor inside. Overhead bats darted in and out of the charred rafters, and the air smelled of bird shit. On the end wall someone had spray-painted 'Bye Bye Bobby' in four-foot letters. Mike climbed over the rubble and eased himself into the remains of the pulpit.

'Brethren in Christ!' he bellowed. 'What shall it profit a man if he know God but know not the delights of Bunty Burgess?'

'Amen!' Joe shouted back.

A macaw flew off in fright, crimson and blue against the clouds.

Later, they called in at the police barracks to ask about Willie. They found the sergeant in a back office, feet on the desk, watching American wrestling on an old black and white portable TV.

Mike greeted him in Spanish, raising his voice to make himself heard over the television. The policeman looked up. Mike reached into his pocket and produced the photograph of Willie and Sarah on the beach. The image of Sarah and his father together confused Joe. He felt a sense of danger, but also a sense of excitement.

The sergeant took the photo.

'This him?'

Mike nodded.

'Name is Wilde?'

'Yes.'

The policeman tossed the photograph back on to the desk.

'Never seen any Mr Wilde, but I seen the photo. You the second people been in here looking for him this week.'

Joe looked at Mike.

'You're sure?'

'Sure.'

'What did he look like?' Joe asked.

'Yankee. All Yankees look the same to me. A man, maybe thirty, maybe a little older.'

'Did he have a name?'

The sergeant smiled.

'Nixon, called himself Richard Milhous Nixon.'

13

The afternoon *locale* to Copán negotiated the hairpin on the weary sighs of a dying clutch. The rust-red, mud-washed road, new but already showing signs of erosion, ran diagonally up the steep slope, so that Joe's view was level with the treetops, looking down on terraced fields of tobacco, a river, then out across the valley to low wooded hills. Once in a while they passed a wattle hut with a coconut-palm thatch. There were naked children in the doorways. Overhead buzzards circled.

'Frank Carreras,' said Mike.

'What about him?' asked Joe.

'He's the only American I know who'd tell a policeman he was called Richard Milhous Nixon.'

Joe looked at him.

'Are you serious?'

'I don't know. Probably not. I was just running through the options. Frank was on the mainland last week.'

'I thought he was down at Jiuba.'

'He was. At least he said he was. We can easily check.'

'Can you think of a reason why he would be looking for Willie?'

Mike thought for a while, then shook his head.

'No. There are three things that motivate Frank. Food, sex, and dislike of authority.'

'And medicine?'

'Yes, that too.'

'Money?'

'Not at all.'

'Do you trust him?'

Mike hesitated again.

'I don't know – it never occurred to me not to. He's always been dead straight with me.'

'What the hell,' said Joe. 'It's Richard Nixon we're looking for.'

They were among low hills now: miniature tree-clad peaks, like green crystals, swamped by low cloud. The driver slowed up as they approached a village, then stopped. An army jeep blocked the road ahead.

All conversation had stopped. The driver turned off the radio, the bus door opened and a sergeant climbed in. He stood for a moment, eyeing the passengers, then walked slowly down the aisle, checking the luggage. Finally he barked two words in Spanish.

Joe looked at Mike.

'He wants us out. Bring your passport.'

Only the young men got out, leaving the women and children inside. They assembled in a line on the side of the road, supervised by two armed conscripts.

The sergeant walked slowly down the line, inspecting papers. He looked to Joe like something out of a movie, heavy set, face half-obscured by his hat and dark glasses, a submachine gun hanging from his shoulder. His dignity was somewhat impaired by the fact that he clearly couldn't read, passing the identity cards to a subordinate for checking. When he reached Joe and Mike he paused, looking them up and down.

'*Americanos?*' he asked.

'English,' said Mike.

'Doing what?'

Mike nodded at Joe.

'He's a tourist. I work on Cow Cay. We're going to Copán, to see the ruins.'

The sergeant handed their passports to his assistant, and waited while the conscript read through the pages. All was in order.

'You have luggage?'

Joe collected their bags from the bus, laid them out on the ground and undid the zipper. The sergeant bent down and poked through the contents, lifting out the clothing, feeling the pockets. When he got to Joe's grip he pulled out an electric razor, tested it, then slipped it into his pocket.

Joe looked at Mike, and said nothing. Three years since they'd seen each other, and yet they could still say all they needed with a single glance. It was at Cambridge that Mike had taught Joe to be bold by stealth, to know more than you show, although they hid nothing from each other, or nothing that mattered.

Of the nine men who had got off the bus, three had been taken away to the jeep. They were all still in their teens; one was in tears. The other male passengers stayed where they were, studying their feet. No one was arguing.

When the sergeant had finished going through the luggage Mike spoke to him briefly in Spanish. The soldier listened, nodded, shook his head. Mike then took Willie's photo from his wallet, and showed it first to the sergeant, then to the conscripts. There was no reaction.

They climbed back on the bus, leaving the three youths to the mercy of the army. Joe was chilled by the whole experience.

'Are they going to shoot them?' he asked Mike.

'Not at all. Military recruitment, Honduras style. They'll do four years guarding banks and cleaning latrines. I'm sorry about your razor, claim it on insurance. The military here are not well paid.'

The bus stopped again half a mile down the road in the village. A gasket was leaking, acrid grey smoke pouring from the engine. While the driver went off to get a mechanic Joe and Mike got out to stretch their legs and look around. There wasn't much to look at: a thatched cantina, a few shacks, a dead dog lying in a pool of black water beside the road. The air was thin and damp and full of flies. The cantina had half a dozen roughly made chairs, a fridge and a bleached-out poster of Madonna on the wall. An Indian woman in a dirty grey dress came out from the back, a cigar in her mouth. Mike ordered coffee.

'What about you?' he asked Joe. Joe opted for Coke.

This is a God-forsaken country, Joe reflected: beautiful but God-forsaken. For most Westerners poor countries are either a recreation ground or a guilt-fest, nothing to do with their own emotions or experience. Exotic landscapes, hot climates, colourful natives look great on the telly, but the reality's anything but.

What the hell was Willie up to in a place like this? Willie who complained about the climate and hygiene in countries like Italy and Spain.

He came to the Cay because he was bored out of his skull. He met a woman. He probably quite enjoyed shouting at the natives and bending B. J. MacIntyre's ear on the veranda over a mug of scotch. And he couldn't face going home to stare at the embers of a none-too-pretty life.

Then something must have happened, something he stumbled across, someone he met. And from then on he'd been operating on his own. He'd made trips to the mainland, and hidden them from Mike and Frank and B.J., even Sarah. Although there didn't have to be anything significant in that: Willie was always his own man, a firm believer in the Need To Know principle.

There are things going on here in Honduras that are either miraculous, criminal or insane. Letter follows.

Letter follows. He'd been so hypnotized by the first sentence that he'd forgotten the second.

Maybe he never sent it, maybe someone sent it for him, posthumously. The writer Romain Gary's mother, separated from him in France and dying during the war, wrote two years of letters to her son to be posted to him weekly after her death, which they were, to his subsequent confusion. But if Willie wrote and sent it then it must be somewhere, most probably sitting on the hall table in Harvist

Road amongst the supermarket vouchers and minicab fliers.

And there was the card itself. He reached down and opened his grip, took the card out of an inside pocket and put it face-up on the table.

The photograph of the heroic general on his bird-shit-coated marble horse looked a lot less exotic here than it had in London. By the look of the chrome-bumpered Fords and Volkswagen beetles it had been taken some years before.

Mike brought the drinks. Joe lifted a lump of ice out of his Coke and crunched it between his teeth. He passed Mike the card.

'You any idea where that is?'

Mike picked it up and put on his glasses.

'Tegoose,' he said. 'Circa 1968. Guy on the horse is in fact Napoleon III, part of a job lot brought over when France had no further need of them. You get them all over the place rechristened as various local despots. That one's just across the square from the Presidential Palace, I forget who they pretend it's of. Some general.'

'What's the longest a card could have taken to get to London?'

Mike took a sip of coffee and put down his cup.

'Two or three weeks, I'd guess. Could be less, could be longer, but the mails are better than they used to be.'

'And how long would a letter take?'

'About the same.' He paused. 'Shit, of course. He'd have sent it to the flat?'

'I assume so.'

'You have a mail forwarding service?'

'Of sorts. He's called Eddie Scargill, lives in a wheelchair on the ground floor.'

'Phone him.'

'He'll be drunk.'

'Phone him anyway.'

'I will,' said Joe. 'Soon as I get to a phone.'

The bus sounded its horn. Joe tossed back the last of his

Coke, crunching the ice between his teeth as they ran across the road and climbed on board.

It was dark by the time the bus groaned painfully up the hill into Copán. Copán is a small town, hardly more than a village, part market, part base camp for the Mayan ruins, narrow cobbled streets running off a grassed park fringed with palms, surrounded by low pantiled stucco buildings. You could tell it rained a lot: the square straddles a ridge, and stone gutters and concrete culverts border the pavements. They parked under a dim street light outside the church, and got out into the thin damp mountain air. It was still warm by English standards, but cool compared to the coast.

The Hotel Ritz was a simple affair. Their rooms were on the first floor, reached by an open staircase and a balcony which ran round three sides of a small courtyard. The sound of a radio came from downstairs. Joe dumped his bag on the iron bedstead and opened the shutters on to the street. He felt awful, a cold sweat beading his forehead, a deep nausea seeping through his gut.

At that moment he farted, and felt it liquid. The ice, he realized: they put fucking ice in my Coke at the cantina. Ice made with tap water, tap water taken from God knows where.

The first cramps hit him, and he made a dash out the door and down the balcony, following a hand-painted sign that said WC. The door was locked. He ran downstairs.

'Are you okay?' Mike shouted from the balustrade.

Joe didn't answer. Everything outside his own physical discomfort was like a dream. The hotel, the woman behind the desk, the American backpackers asking about bus times all seemed part of another world, glimpsed through the window of a runaway train. He desperately wanted to be alone.

By the time he reached the downstairs toilet he was no longer able to think clearly about anything. He stumbled into the windowless closet and squatted over the hole in the floor, his trousers round his ankles, trying to get his mind back into focus. The contents of his stomach were attacking him at both ends, and he was unsure which orifice to present to the pan. He tightened his stomach muscles, and promptly vomited over his feet.

Mike was calling to him from outside the door, but he was past conversation. Twice more he vomited, four times his bowels opened. For what seemed like an eternity he squatted under the bare light bulb, watching the mosquitos, smelling the drains, unable to move. Eventually he pulled on his trousers, got to his feet, leaning against the damp plaster walls to steady himself, and opened the door.

Mike was sitting crosslegged on the floor outside, reading a paperback. He was smiling sympathetically.

'Welcome to Honduras, kid.'

Mike helped him back upstairs, put him to bed, disappeared for a minute and returned with the bucket and a bottle of Agua Cristal.

'You got any blockers?' Joe asked.

'No use, you'll just have to let it run its course. If it doesn't clear up in a couple of days we'll see about a doctor.' Mike passed him the bottle of water. 'Drink as much as you can. I'll get some salt. Dehydration's the problem.'

He sat on the end of the bed, hands on his knees, watching Joe drink. The liquid passed through him like flood-water down a storm drain. He levered himself out of bed just in time to reach the bucket.

'Do you know,' Mike grinned, 'that the British Standard test for a toilet U-bend is a copy of the *Daily Telegraph* rolled up and cut in half – flush that away and you're in business. Would be the bloody *Telegraph*, wouldn't it. I'll leave you to rest for a while. Give me a shout if you need anything.'

'What if I can't shout?'

'Break a window.'

Joe drifted in and out of sleep. The single threadbare sheet was laid straight on top of the mattress so that each time he tossed it wrapped itself around him. Every twenty minutes or so he got up and visited the bucket. Twice he was too weak to walk. On thy belly shalt thou go, he decided, and crawled, the ancient linoleum cool and soothing on his skin. Eventually he fell into a deeper sleep.

His dreams were delirious but not unpleasant, weightless clear-sky summer days in the Hebrides drifting into winter evenings in warm bars in Camden Town, meandering journeys with some woman who was fond of him, sometimes Marian, sometimes a girl he used to know at Cambridge and had never had the courage to date.

He woke with his gut aching, in urgent need of the bucket. At some point Mike must have been back and left a jug of salt water on the wooden chair beside the bed and put a blanket over him. He staggered across the room and bared his buttocks to the galvanized steel.

Sweat dripped from his face, his limbs seemed to move independently of his brain. He went across to the window, which gave on to a thin lane lit by a dim orange street light. A dog worried at a refuse bin, but otherwise the town seemed deserted. He looked at his watch: it was past midnight. The air was still warm, but a cool breeze rustled the cheap cotton curtains. He cursed his own folly, cursed himself for being 5,000 miles from home. Sickness is best endured at home, in privacy, with familiar comforts to hand.

Back in bed he drank a glass of water, and lay for a while looking at the ceiling, listening as the liquid guttered its way towards his stomach. Another wave of nausea swept over him, his muscles went into spasm again. Back to the bucket.

Oh Willie, if you only knew the lengths I'm going to. Why? Part mercy mission, he conceded; but also part challenge, the young bull come to show the old bull he can't cope on his own any more. Only the young bull's fucked before he's started, shitting his heart out in a doss-house in the middle of nowhere.

Think of a motive for Frank, he told himself, just to pass the time. Think of a motive for anyone, come to that.

Willie found something out but needed evidence to prove it. Something he couldn't trust anyone with, not even Mike.

Why wouldn't he trust Mike?

Because Willie never trusted anyone. Not now, not ever. He never delegated anything, apart from cooking and typing. The rest he kept to himself until he was ready. Joe wondered if it was a habit he'd picked up in court, or if he'd always been that way. Joe was the same, never delegated, hid what he was doing or feeling until he was satisfied it was ready.

Around two he drifted off to sleep again. It was light when he woke, sounds of Spanish voices coming from the lane, the insistent beep of a truck reversing somewhere, a radio, more voices from the balcony, American this time. He tried sitting up, but the energy evaded him.

Mike must have been listening out for sounds of movement, because a moment later there was a knock on the door.

'Enter,' said Joe wearily.

Mike had a jam jar of flowers in one hand and two paperbacks in the other.

'Whatever you do don't try eating them,' he said, putting the flowers on the windowsill.

'How did you know I was hungry?'

'Personal experience. I'll bring you some glucose later, but in the meantime stick to water.'

Joe looked at the books, both much travelled: *My Life and Loves* by Errol Flynn, and an Ed McBain.

'They don't have a great library here,' Mike apologized. 'Errol's dirty bits are on page 167, or that's where it falls open. He wallops her with a stiff hair brush at the crucial moment. I don't own a hairbrush, but I tried it with a comb once. She hit me back with a bedside light. Quite a night.'

He came back at lunchtime with a flask of hot water and a packet of glucose crystals which he mixed in a plastic beaker.

'Willie was here okay, I checked the hotel registers. Spent two nights at the Maya Inn, flash bastard, they have baths up there, soft toilet tissue, all that shit. He checked in on the Thursday night, spent Friday at the ruins, registered his next destination as San Pedro Sula, took the bus out to La Entrada on the Saturday morning.'

Joe tried drinking the glucose, but ended up back on the bucket. Mike looked out the window until he'd finished.

'How far away are the ruins?'

'A mile or so, out by the air strip. We'll take a look before we move out, it's worth the trip. They reckon they cover a hundred square miles, the stuff here is only the tip of the iceberg.'

'Did anyone talk to him?'

'The hotel manager remembers him because of his age. He says Willie made some phone calls, mostly inside the country, one to the UK. Bought postcards, cashed a traveller's cheque, complained he couldn't find English cigarettes. Ate alone at the hotel the first night, went out somewhere on the Friday night. The manager thinks he may have been meeting someone, but it might just have been other tourists. You know how it happens, you get talking with someone out at the sites, arrange to meet up for supper. I don't know where he ate, but I'll ask around this afternoon.'

'How far are we off the Guatemalan border here?'

'No distance at all.'

'Who runs the smuggling?'

Mike shrugged his shoulders.

'Rikki fixes all that, via the army.'

'The army?'

'The army. How did you get on with Errol?'

'Dull stuff,' said Joe wearily.

By the end of the day he'd finished the McBain too, and was reduced to *The Good News Bible*. Mike brought him more glucose, and this time it stayed inside him for almost an hour.

'Give it a couple of days,' Mike consoled him.

Joe pushed himself up on to his pillows.

'Willie said on his hotel form he was going back to San Pedro, and took the bus to La Entrada?'

'Right.'

'Where else could he have got a connection to from La Entrada?'

'Tegoose.'

'So if he wanted to muddy the trail he'd say he was going back to San Pedro, but take the other bus.'

'That's what I figure too,' said Mike. 'I'll tell you what else I figure. Your old man's alive and up to something.'

14

EDDIE SCARGILL BOUGHT a 500 cc Suzuki motorbike in his first year at Hornsey College of Art, scarlet with metallic blue trim, took it for a spin on the M25, skidded under a Dutch vegetable truck, broke forty-three bones and wound up in hospital for eighteen months, spreadeagled on the bed like an upside-down spider with weights wired to his legs and arms. Friends had to hold his cigarettes to his mouth for him, a puff at a time, posting look-outs for prowling nurses. The same friends also brought him whisky in Lucozade bottles and amphetamines hidden in boxes of Tic-Tac mints. Eddie wasn't about to let hospitalization get in the way of his hobbies.

Eddie talked like George Formby. He had buck teeth and big skinny hands with dirty nails and a crew-cut. When he went back to college in his wheelchair he switched from painting to graphic design, which he could do sitting at a desk, and got straight back in to raising hell. When he graduated he signed on as a lecturer, and he'd been there ever since, the best part of ten years. Art school lecturers know better than to go looking for work in the outside world, particularly if they're in a wheelchair.

People went out of their way to call him partially abled, or physically disadvantaged, but he always corrected them.

'Crippled,' he'd grin, 'crippled says it just right. And a pint of Websters, since you ask.'

He had a mate called Mick who pushed him around town. Eddie and Mick had a party trick: they'd split up,

Eddie would go into a pub, three minutes later Mick would come in, storm up to Eddie screaming abuse, tell him to stop fooling around with his wife, kick over his wheelchair and start putting the boot in. Wonderful outrage on all sides, until one afternoon when Mick was midway through the performance and looked down to discover he'd chosen the wrong cripple. He got three months suspended. Eddie nearly died laughing.

Eddie lived downstairs from Joe in Harvist Road. He complained constantly about answering Joe's calls on the pay-phone in the hall, and Joe complained he never got the messages Eddie took when he did answer the phone. Apart from that they got on fine. Joe was teaching Eddie to play the piano. They drank together every Sunday lunchtime in the Mason's Arms in Salisbury Road, went to see Arsenal once in a while, took it in turns to write to the landlord complaining about the plumbing. Joe called Eddie Ironside, and got a gift-wrapped Perry Como album each Christmas in revenge.

Wednesday was Eddie's film night. Didn't matter what was on, Eddie and Mick – and Joe if he was around – went to the Odeon at Swiss Cottage and sat in the front row dropping speed, sipping lager and improvising new dialogue for the movie. People used to come every week just to listen to them. Afterwards they ate at the Pizza Express in Finchley Road, then adjourned to the Mason's Arms until closing time, when Mick pushed Eddie back home to the flat.

Eddie had been back ten minutes when the phone rang in the hall.

'Is that Eddie Scargill?' asked a distant voice.

'I'm terribly sorry,' Eddie said politely, 'Eddie's is Spain,' and hung up.

Five minutes later it rang again. Same far away voice, but more determined this time. No question, just a statement.

'Ironside don't hang up my name's Mike Osborne I'm a friend of Joe Wilde's I'm phoning from Honduras Joe's upstairs with amoebic dysentery there's something he wants you to do for him.'

'Why the fuck didn't you say so in the first place?' said Eddie. 'Hold on while I get a pen.'

It was mid-afternoon in Copán. Bright sunlight shafted down between the overhanging eves of the narrow streets, pigeons and sparrows pecked at the dust. On the narrow stone pavement outside the hotel small clumps of American tourists obstructed the townspeople. Across the street a German with a long-lensed Nikon photographed an old Indian woman in a poncho and bowler hat who sat smoking a cigar against a wall. Dedicated travellers, unphased by the discomforts of the journey and the rudimentary accommodation.

Mike paid for the call and went back upstairs. Joe was sitting up in bed, pale-skinned and sweating.

'The letter's there okay,' Mike told him.

'What does it say?'

'He doesn't know. It's in Latin.'

'It's in what?'

'Bloody Latin. Eddie says he doesn't have much Latin beyond *post coitum omne animal triste est*. He's going to courier it to Cow Cay.'

'You have a courier service to Cow Cay?'

'Believe it or not we do. The daft buggers guarantee worldwide delivery. Which means they fly it to Tegoose and bribe a TAL pilot to take it on to Morgan's Hole. Takes four or five days. How's your Latin, incidentally?'

'About the same as yours, I suspect. "Caesar being about to enter Winter Quarters first commanded the cohorts to take stock of their undergarments", not a lot more.'

They'd had the same teacher at Glenalmond, a fat bachelor called Willenkin who wore a bow tie and overpolished his shoes.

'Why the hell would he write in Latin?' asked Mike.

'Habit, I suppose. Fifty years of *res ipse loquitur* in the courts. Why did you tell him to send it to the Cay?'

Mike perched himself on the windowsill, hands in the pockets of his jeans.

'Because I know it'll get there. I could have told him to send it to Tegoose, I suppose. If necessary Frank can bring it over to us when it arrives.'

'We're trusting Frank again?'

'I was joking about Frank,' said Mike. 'At least I hope I was.'

It was two more days before Joe was fit to get up. He felt a fool, lying there 5,000 miles from home shitting his guts out, wasting Mike's time, looking for a man who he now suspected had no desire to be traced.

He slept a lot, started work on a lyric for a tune he had in his head, lay for long periods watching the ceiling and listening to the sounds outside, trying to picture a town and landscape he'd only glimpsed briefly in the darkness the evening they arrived. Every few hours Mike came and fed him, first more glucose, then a little maize porridge or a soft-boiled egg. While, he ate Mike would sit in the window drinking beer by the neck and talking about old times.

'What were you meant to be doing this week?' Mike asked him.

'You really want to know? Monday I had a gig in Belfast.' Joe spooned his way suspiciously through a bowl of porridge. 'Wednesday I promised to talk to a man about a charity concert in aid of "Help The Aged". A session on Thursday, some guy used to play bass with a famous rock band, got blown out in an argument, they bought him off with a solo record contract, gave him a studio for a month and fifty grand to hire musicians. In return for which he's meant to come up with an album of his own material. Only he doesn't have any material. He's been sitting in there for three weeks, or he had when I left. Every morning he rings up and books some guys, gets them over, they jam all day in the hope that a tune will emerge. All they get is twelve-bar blues. Meanwhile he's going nuts. I think I was meant to be his last hope.'

'Do you feel bad about it?'

'I feel bad about missing the cheque, not a lot else.'

'Do you still enjoy the music, Joe?'

'Sure.'

'You never want to do anything else?'

'Not really. More of the same will do me fine.'

'Then what do you worry about these days? Apart from Willie.'

Joe put down his porridge.

'Not being able to play as well as Earl Hines. Getting replaced by computers. All my friends settling down and moving out of town. Hearing my voice sometimes and it sounds like Willie. Not just the accent, the intonation, the phrases. And you?'

'I worry about the Cay, and Jiuba, and what we're doing to the planet and each other. I worry about the first Lord Leverhulme.'

'The Sunlight Soap man?'

'Soap, margarine, model factories, all that stuff. Company's called Unilever now, before that it was Lever Brothers, though to the best of my knowledge there was never a brother.'

'Same with Faber & Faber,' said Joe. 'There was only ever one Mr Faber, but he thought two sounded more substantial.'

Mike sucked at his beer bottle and put it down on the sill.

'When Leverhulme got to seventy he retired from the business. Hugely rich, still in reasonable health, decided he wanted to do Something Good before he died. So he bought the Outer Hebrides, or most of them. This would be, what, 1920 something I suppose. Someone he met in a hotel had told him how wretched life was for the islanders, no work, terrible housing, unspeakable climate.

'Leverhulme decided to use all his business experience and some of his wealth to turn the islands into a Model Estate. Looked at the problem, decided the answer was Fish. So he went up to Harris, erected a brand new port on the south coast, filled it with brand new trawlers, called it Leverburgh. Then he started to build a railway fifty miles across the bog from Leverburgh to Stornaway, where he established a canning factory. That was the plan: catch the fish, can them on the island, give the islanders as many jobs as possible. Pure philanthropy, nothing in it for Leverhulme at all.'

He took another sip of beer.

'To copper-bottom the whole operation,' he continued, 'his Lordship set up a chain of shops all over the UK just to sell Hebridean fish – Mac Fisheries, gone now but you used to see them everywhere.'

'And what happened?' asked Joe.

'Bloody islanders screwed him, all the way. Tore up his railway lines, squatted in his sheds, refused to let anyone touch a fish on the Sabbath so the whole lot rotted on the quay. He kept trying for a couple of years, then sold up, left them to their own devices, cleared off the way he'd come.'

'You reckon that's what'll happen to you?'

'It's possible. Sometimes I think people can't cope with altruism, they think it's unnatural.'

'But the islanders are on your side, aren't they?'

'I think so. Sometimes I wonder.'

'Do you ever think of jacking it in?'

Mike smiled.

'Good God no.'

On the afternoon of the third day Joe was well enough to get out of bed. He took it gently, an hour or two at a time, still eating little and resting between walks around the town. He explored the municipal market, dark and dirty and labyrinthine and black with flies, reeking of cooking and the sweet smell of raw meat; where Indian women sold white cheese and vegetables and prescription drugs out of shoeboxes, asked for by colour – the red and black, the pink, the green and blue, fished out by the handful and wrapped in twists of old newspaper.

Willie was here, he told himself. Doing what?

Buses rattled through the narrow alleys, horns blowing. Children with no shoes and outstretched hands called *'denero'* from wide eyes. Pairs of soldiers, young and small, leaned against the walls, smoking and stroking their automatic rifles. A mule with a wooden saddle was tethered to a lamp post.

Joe visited the church, Spanish-fronted and cool and poor, decorated with photographs of saints dressed up in modern clothes like tailors' dummies. St Catherine's ruptured bones stuck out through her wounds, clearly visible beneath her nylon petticoats. Above the altar Christ hung like a jaundiced haemophiliac, bleeding copiously over his towelling loin-cloth.

This was the Land of Death, where revolutionaries wore plastic skull masks and painted 'O Morir!' in six-foot letters on the walls, where funerals engulfed the towns in black crêpe for days on end and coffin-sellers competed for business on the pavements with bicycle repairmen and shoeshines and lottery sellers.

Beside the sad little confessional of boxwood and torn and faded curtains a list of times had been written up on a cardboard sheet tacked to the wall. There was no sign of a priest, only a bent old man dusting under the benches with a straw broom.

Corn grew through the cracks in steps. From its low ridge the church looked out over terraced fields of maize to a muddy river, then low green jungle hills, so green that the air seemed opaque. Every so often the crumbling apex of an overgrown pyramid erupted among the trees. The ruins covered over a hundred square miles, of which perhaps a third had been surveyed and a mere half a dozen excavated and restored.

'Did Willie like this sort of stuff?' Mike asked Joe the next morning as they walked past the air strip towards the high chain-linked fence which surrounded the site. Two light aircraft sat in the grass beside the control hut, a third was taxiing out. Oleander and flame trees bordered the unpaved runway, and a wind sock hung limply in the warm air.

'In his own way, yes. When I was a kid in Hexham he was always taking visitors up to the Roman Wall.'

Bleak November afternoons, rain-lashed spring days, whatever the weather, shivering in the north wind on the escarpment at Housesteads, Willie lecturing the unfortunate guests on Roman bath houses and Mithraic temples: though Joe always suspected that the expeditions had more to do with punishing the guests than the pursuit of archaeology. Willie hated having people to stay, could never think of anything to talk to them about, just as he always detested staying in other people's houses.

A chain-smoking teenage conscript in a gaucho hat slouched against a tree by the entrance selling tickets from a roll, a machete hanging by a string from his neck. Above him a brightly coloured macaw sat on the gate post, tethered by a steel chain, preening itself for the tourist lenses. A distressed American woman was complaining to the youth about the absence of toilets. He gestured her towards the trees and lit another cigarette.

Inside the fence the jungle had been pruned and grassed to parkland. They walked down a wide avenue between the trees to a clearing, where stone stelae carved with grotesque figures stood around a sacrificial altar shaped into a giant tortoise. Red and green parrots called from the branches, butterflies the size of a man's hand sunned themselves on the stones. Beyond lay a restored ball court with terraced seating on two sides. Satellite TV would have paid top dollar to cover Mayan ball games, in which the losing side suffered ritual execution.

At every turn statues and carvings stared out at the thin straggle of tourists: grinning hags, cartoon jaguars, dragons and demons with bulging eyes and Ken Dodd teeth, and Indian faces, the same faces that still stared at you in the streets of the town.

They reached the great staircase, fifty feet high, each step carved with hieroglyphs recording the history and learning of the Mayans, a civilization whose scientific skills far predated those of Europe. It climbed a precipitous slope crowned with tall trees: in places their roots had worked through the slabs and formed knots, holding the edifice together.

Joe was tired, and sat down head in hands.

'Do you know the irony of this shit?' Mike asked, pointing at the hieroglyphs. 'The Mayans knew they were doomed, this was meant to be their time capsule, everything they knew about anything. It's all there, immaculately carved in stone. But no one can read it. The Americans have been at it for fifty years, but most of what they've managed to decipher is just Filofax, names and dates, and even they don't make a lot of sense. You're sitting on the Complete Meaning of Life, but it's unintelligible.' He looked down at Joe. 'God, you look awful kid.'

He was right. Joe felt completely gutted.

'I'm sorry, I have this jinx on high art. Every time I've been to Florence the Uffizi was closed, every time I've been to Chartres they had the scaffolding up on the windows. I twisted an ankle in the Hermitage, I got sunstroke the day I was meant to go to the Taj Mahal.'

And now the shits at Copán. He wasn't even sure he could make it back to the village, stopping every couple of hundred yards. Waves of nausea swept over him, but mostly it was just weakness, a refusal of the body to do what he told it.

They passed through the gates and were skirting the air strip when a two-engined Piper taxied out to the runway, turned and revved its engine for take-off.

Mike stopped.

'Good God.'

By the time Joe looked up the plane was halfway down the runway, nose up, wheels off the ground. All he could see was the silhouette of the pilot, headset on, struggling to gain enough height to clear the trees.

'What?'

'Beside the pilot.'

As the Piper banked away to the north Joe strained his eyes. He could just see a second figure in the co-pilot's seat.

'Who is it?'

'Bobby Burgess,' said Mike. 'Well well well.'

15

THREE MALE FIGURES, one black, two white, called up from the road to Sarah. She was sitting cross-legged in the shade inside the hut, braiding her hair, listening to British Forces Radio from Belize. You got a lot of Brit crap and stuff you didn't understand on BFR, but they played good music, old rock songs mostly, unlike the salsa shit and screaming ads that came out of Honduran stations. She wrote down the names of the English bands sometimes, save them up to drop into the conversation with Mike Osborne or Frank or Joe. Trick was to name a band and say you used to like their early stuff before the smooth-out-the-bumps producers got their hands on them.

'Heh, Sarah!' a voice shouted from the road. 'You up there?'

She leaned forward and parted the bead curtain with one finger of her splayed hand.

Beach bums. A Canadian, Rod The Diver, short and muscled. Beside him a black islander, Larry Murphy from up at Parson's Creek, wore a lot of neck and wrist jewellery; and behind Larry a young dope-head Swiss in dusty bleached denim shirt and loose white cotton trousers tied with a drawstring, no shoes. An embroidered Greek-island bag hung from the Swiss's shoulder.

'You boys buying or selling?' she asked.

'Ain't doing neither,' Larry shouted back. 'Got something to show you. Poems.'

'What kind of poems? The rhyming kind or the kind got no full stops in them?'

'Swiss poems,' said Rod. 'Only in English. You're going to like 'em. A lot.'

'I bet,' said Sarah. 'Come on up.'

What the hell, she wasn't doing anything much. And she liked Rod, liked his innocence, never hurt a fly in his life. The Canadian lived on a none-too-new yacht moored over in Morgan's Hole, used to have a wife called Sylvia and a seven-year-old daughter called Daisy.

Rod and Sylvia ran a Dive shop in Windsor, Ontario, the Lunch-Pail City. Then one year the federal budget told Canadians they had no money, and for four months the shop didn't sell a single item. They tried for another year, then handed their mortgage deeds in to the bank, took Daisy out of school, packed up their yacht and set off to sail down the Mississippi. A rough trip, in mid-winter: the boat frosted some nights, the cabin was uninsulated, and the river rarely touched the towns, days on end you saw nothing but mud-flats and levees and scrub woods.

From New Orleans they headed down to Mexico, Yucatán, Belize where they were hassled by drug-peddling rastas, until they finally reached the Cay. Rod took a job teaching diving outside Morgan's Hole, but after two months he fell out with the manager and got fired. He found another job the following day working on yacht charters out of Spanish Harbour, across the island. They lived on the boat, still anchored off Morgan's Hole, Sylvia teaching Daisy to read and write in the same cabin they slept and cooked and lived in. Then a storm busted the boat. Sylvia decided she'd had enough, missed her friends and creature comforts, cleared off back to Canada with Daisy.

Rod stayed. He found himself a local girl, patched up the boat. When the charter company folded, he took any work he was offered, taught tourists to dive, did a bit of carpentry, fixed other people's yachts. He was a gentle, innocent boy, confused by life. The only thing that had decided Sarah to keep her distance from Rod was that he had no prospects, or none that she could figure.

'You got any water, Sarah?' he asked her now.

'Sure. You boys headed any place particular?'
'Just getting out of town a while.'

They'd walked from Morgan's Hole to Reef's End, eaten nothing, drunk nothing. Sarah called out to Omangatu, below with her herbs, to get them some food and water, then settled back to look at the poems and the dilated eyes of the Swiss. Swiss and hippy didn't seem to her much of a mix: he had the eyes but his body looked dry-cleaned. He also looked as though he hadn't eaten in a month. Give him another few weeks and he'd be cabling home to daddy for his air ticket, like most of that kind.

The Swiss reached into his shoulder bag, took out a poem, handwritten on some kind of parchment, and passed it across to her.

> Change
> Everything that is the same
> Must change
> To become
> Different
> Must all be different
> Stone to water.

It was signed at the bottom 'PT, Mexico', then a date three months before.

'That's it?'

The Swiss smiled.

'I have more.'

'I bet you have.'

'Thought maybe you like to sell 'em in the gift shop,' Larry suggested. 'A business opportunity. Sell 'em for a dollar, you keep twenty cents.'

'You know something, Larry? You just the man I been looking for. I got a coachload of American tourists due in half an hour, stayed awake all night worrying what I goin' to sell 'em.'

The Swiss looked at her with wide eyes, trying to figure what was going on. Rod managed a smile.

'Take a couple anyway, just in case.'

Sarah didn't give a shit about the doped-out poet but she didn't want to hurt Rod, who was only being kind to the stranger.

'Maybe. Sale or return.'

She got up and went down the ladder, returning with a cane tray with a bottle of water and four plastic beakers and a plate of biscuits.

Larry took out a pack of cigarettes and offered them round.

'So how you keeping, Sarah? Seems to me your life gone kinda quiet since Willie Wilde wandered off, I figure you could use some excitement. I was you I'd be looking for a replacement, 'stead of wasting time hanging on.'

'You volunteering, boy?'

'You offering?'

'No.'

Larry laughed and inhaled on his cigarette.

'You could try Frank, I suppose, I reckon he's available. Unless you got your eyes on Willie's boy.' He gave her a look. Sarah wasn't biting. 'But if I was you I'd have a go for Frank. Great thing about doctors is they never short of money, same as lawyers. Quieten him down some, get him to lose some weight, ease up on the dope. Only he gone away for a couple of days, and he got plenty shit waiting for him when he gets back.'

'What shit?'

'All kinds of shit down at St Andrews, some kind of epidemic breakin' loose. Mike Osborne away, Frank away.'

Sarah looked across at Rod.

'They really got an epidemic up there?'

'They've got some sick people.'

'What kind of sick?'

The Canadian shrugged his shoulders.

'No one seems too sure. A couple of patients got ill with fever sometime yesterday, this morning there's four more down with it. Tommy Willis, Mick Jones, Ali Corona, I don't know the others.'

Larry stubbed his cigarette on the Empire State ashtray.

'Bunty Burgess been up see if she can save any souls, Bobby's away some place. Like one of those women goes to take a look round an auction house day before the sale.'

'Where'd Frank go?' asked Sarah.

'Took off yesterday,' said Larry. 'Jiuba, I guess.'

'Mike Osborne still away too?'

'Yup. Seems like the holiday season round here.'

'This epidemic serious?'

'Seems so,' said Rod.

Sarah kept two poems, 'Stone and Water' and a short piece about a crow called 'black/no colour'. The Swiss said he had plenty more if she needed them. Sarah said she'd let him know.

That afternoon she took a ride into Morgan's Hole with the Chinaman, got him to drop her off at the hardware store and wandered across the street to the chemist's to buy nail varnish. She walked tall, the way she always did, head in the air, hands in the back pockets of her jeans.

The first thing she saw inside the chemist was Esther Manley's arse. Esther had her back to the door; her feet were on the floor, but her stomach was balanced across the counter while she stretched across to where the pharmacist was running his finger down the pages of a drug catalogue. The pharmacist was a tall sallow bespectacled Spaniard called Pedro Ambrona, a former left-wing university activist who'd done time for agitation and on his release had opted for a quiet life far from Tegucigalpa. The other reason he'd wound up on the Cay, it was rumoured, was that he'd failed his pharmacist's exams.

His finger had reached the bottom of the page.

'You're the medic, Esther, you tell me. You sure it's not malaria?'

Esther straightened.

'Malaria don't come in batches. One mosquito per patient. You ask me this feels like virus.'

'Or allergy?' Pedro suggested.

'To what?'

'You people got problems?' Sarah interrupted.

Esther turned.

'No jokes, Sarah. This one's serious.'

'What you got?'

'Eight cases. Fever, muscle aches, bone aches, headaches, vomiting, dehydration.'

'They goin' to pull through?'

Esther said she thought so, but she didn't look convinced.

'You want me to get the *brujo* in?' asked Sarah. She knew Esther wouldn't, but she enjoyed asking.

'It's worth a try,' said the nurse. 'Least until Frank gets back.'

Sarah looked at her in astonishment.

'It's that bad?'

'It's worth a try,' Esther repeated. 'You think she'd come?'

'Who – Omangatu? You payin'?'

'I guess.'

'Then she'll come. You got wheels?'

'Sure.'

As they were leaving a thought crossed Sarah's mind. She turned to Pedro.

'You like poems?'

The chemist looked at her over his glasses.

'Long as they're not Swiss.'

'Ah shit,' said Sarah. 'Let's go.'

Esther drove hard, spectacles on, pudgy hands gripping the wheel, throwing the jeep to and fro across the road to avoid the ruts, back along the coast road to Reef's End. A spume of red dust trailed behind them.

'So where's Frank got to?' asked Sarah.

Esther wiped her brown face with her forearm.

'Gone to Jiuba, see about some construction business on the new place. Least that's what he told us.'

'He got a woman there?'

'Don't care if he have or he don't, so long as he come back quick. Radio phone ain't working but we sent word. Don't know what's the matter with that boy these days, jumpin' round like a nut in hot fat, prickly as a puffer fish.

Never stays the same place two days running. Playing loud music all the time, smokin' ganja.'

'Reason he do that,' said Sarah, 'is so he seem like a black man. At least I figure that's what he tryin' to do. Why the shit would a white man want to be black? Makes no sense to me, not the way things organized at the moment.'

'They reckon we know things they don't know, they reckon deep down we noble and pure, plus they feel bad about us poor folks.'

'What the hell that got to do with playin' music loud and smokin' grass?'

'You want my advice, don't try figuring it out. And don't go asking them, they apt to come on sincere. Don't know about you but I can't stand white people when they come on sincere.'

'You know something, Esther? I reckon you could do Frank Carrera's job, go to college for a few years, you got the brains.'

Esther laughed.

'Some days seems like I do it anyway, college or no college.'

'They asked you to move to Jiuba yet?'

'Nope. And if they did I wouldn't go. They got thousands of Indians don't speak English or Spanish, they got insects big as rats, they got malaria, they got rain, they got no road and no shops and no TV. Plus they got Mike Osborne and Frank Carreras.' She laughed again. 'Job's yours if you want it. I ain't goin'.'

'Not even for Virginia's sake?'

'Not even for Virginia, God rest her.'

They'd reached Reef's End. Esther stayed in the jeep while Sarah disappeared inside to get her mother. Omangatu was laughing when she emerged from the shadows under the hut. Her expression didn't change when she laughed: all that happened was that the thin leathery slit in her tortoise face opened and closed and a hiss of air escaped.

She shuffled up the bank in her ancient black pleated dress and straw hat and bare feet, hissing uncontrollably,

Sarah following with a wicker basket tied over with a piece of sacking.

Once in the jeep Omangatu stopped laughing, settled herself into the front passenger seat, nodded at Esther, and then farted, same way she always greeted anyone medical. It drove Sarah nuts but Omangatu said she couldn't help it, it was her body's way of adjusting, same way dust made you sneeze or ice made you shiver: medics made her fart.

The *brujo* pulled a cheroot out of the pocket of her dress, stuck it between her teeth, and grinned at the countryside.

They parked outside the clinic, and Esther led them across the grass to a low concrete building with steel window-frames. Inside twelve beds were arranged in a line under a circling ceiling fan. The ward smelled of soap and iodine and flowers: someone had put a jar of sweet-scented stock on a windowsill.

The patients were all male, all black, none of them younger than forty. There were three other visitors in the room. An orderly was taking temperatures, a nurse comforted an old man vomiting into an enamel bowl, and beside the end bed Bunty Burgess sat on a wooden chair, leaning forward and whispering into a patient's ear.

'This started yesterday?' asked Sarah.

'Uh huh,' said Esther. 'Ain't nothing I ever seen before. Morning, Mrs Burgess.'

The preacher's wife looked up, eyes blinking.

'Good morning, sister.'

'Any miracles you got to spare we'd appreciate it you send them our way.'

'Ain't how it works,' Bunty said politely but a little sourly. 'If I could I would.'

'She ain't here for miracles, she's here for the harvest,' said Sarah cheerfully.

'Hush,' said Esther.

Omangatu still hadn't spoken since the time she left the hut. She advanced slowly into the middle of the room, hesitated for a moment, sniffing the air, her cheroot still clenched between her teeth.

Sarah looked first at her mother, then at the patients. They looked pale and empty-headed, lying on their beds in striped pyjamas that didn't fit them, heads back, eyes on the ceiling, twisting their limbs once in a while to ease the pain. Tommy Willis raised his forearm in greeting when he saw her watching him, then let it fall back across his chest.

'How you doin', Tommy?' she asked.

'To be honest with you Sarah I doin' shit.'

Sweat was running down his face and neck, gathering in a pool above his breastbone.

'Same as ever?'

He smiled.

'Same as ever.'

Omangatu coughed, then shuffled forward to the next bed, where Ali Corona, white-haired and toothless, lay with his knees to his chest, eyes flicking nervously around his sunken sockets like dogs pacing a pen. The *brujo* placed her forefinger and thumb on each side of his windpipe and squeezed hard. Ali let out a cry. Omangatu let go, then whispered something to Sarah.

'She says he smokes too much,' Sarah explained. 'All his life. But that's not the trouble now.'

Outside there was the sound of a car drawing up, a door slamming.

The *brujo*'s hands moved on to Ali's stomach, her fingers forming two claws as she pushed into his abdomen. Again she whispered to Sarah, again Sarah broadcast the news.

'Drinks too much also, but that ain't the trouble either.'

Omangatu picked up a plastic pill bottle off the chair beside Ali's bed, lifted the lid and sniffed.

No one was watching her. All eyes were on the door, where Frank Carreras stood with his hands in the back pockets of his denim shorts.

'What the fuck is going on here?' he said, very quietly.

Esther looked at him, then across at Omangatu, then back to Frank again.

'We got problems, Frank.'

'So I hear. Tell me about them.'

Frank went over to Tommy Willis, felt his pulse, then put his hand on Tommy's forehead. Esther hovered behind him, waiting for instructions.

'Get syringes,' he said. 'Party's over, folks.'

Bunty Burgess was the first to leave. Omangatu and Sarah followed her out into the sunlight. A moment later Frank and Esther emerged and headed across the clearing towards the Rectory.

Sarah's first problem was how to get herself and her mother back to Reef's End. She toyed with the idea of asking Bobby Burgess for a lift back into Morgan's Hole, but thought better of it. Hang on a while, she decided, then get Esther to run us over. Esther was a conscientious woman, at the back of her head she'd have a message to herself to make sure they got home all right.

Frank was coming back across the grass, on his own now, a small cardboard box under his arm with medical symbols on the side. He took a slight detour to avoid the two women standing in the shade of the mango tree, but Sarah headed him off. In the distance she could hear a phone ringing.

'Hi,' she said when he was ten paces away. 'You going to tell us what's up with those people in there?'

Frank looked upset, the way you look when you've left someone else in charge of a simple task and get back to find they'd screwed up.

'Nothing much,' he said, trying to be matter-of-fact about it but sounding a little tetchy. 'Allergic reaction. Couple of days and they'll be fine.'

'Allergic to what?' she asked, but she never got an answer. Esther was on the steps of the Rectory, looking urgent.

'Phone for you, Frank,' she shouted.

Frank turned.

'Take a message.'

'I think you better take it,' she called back. 'It's Mike. He's in Tegoose.'

Sarah watched him run back across the grass to the Rectory, like some African animal – rhino, hippo, the kind with centres of gravity below their bellies. Tegoose, eh? How come these boys get to do all the travelling round here?

A minute later Frank was back.

'More problems?' she asked.

'His post,' Frank said. 'I got twelve patients in high fever and Mike Osborne wants his fucking post hand-carrying to Tegucigalpa.'

'I could do that,' said Sarah, staring him straight in the eyes.

'I bet you could,' said Frank. 'Only the post in question ain't got here yet. Oh yeh,' he added, 'and they found Willie.'

'You serious?'

'No, just tired. But they've found someone who's seen him.'

'In Tegoose?'

'In Tegoose.'

16

MIKE OSBORNE KNEW all Central America's capital cities, and despite some fairly gruesome competition he reckoned Tegucigalpa was the pits. On a scale of one to ten Tegucigalpa came out at minus twelve, just above Belize City.

It's a hill town surrounded by sharp green mountains: at times its steep lanes are awash with flash floods and overrunning storm drains, coating the city in a slurry of red mud sediment; at others, when hot sun replaces the unforgiving rain, the mud turns to dust and hot winds blow head-high garbage through the streets. Whatever the weather the air reeks of garbage and dead dog.

Downtown Tegoose is tiny, hardly more than five or six blocks surrounding an undistinguished Spanish Colonial cathedral and a tiny pink presidential palace, baroque-cum-Alhambra with a roof of shingle tiles like fish scales and a modest garden eaten bare by four pet deer. Outside the palace gates the presidential guard, in B-movie battle fatigues and sinister black helmets, smoke and fondle their guns and gossip with friends among the passers by.

Beyond the palace is the ineptly named Rio Grande, an empty river course full of rubbish and urchins, and beyond the Rio Grande a fly-blown open market rank with the smell of raw meat, and stalls selling old Bee Gees tapes and posters of Barry Manilow and the Blessed Virgin Mary. Away from the river a few crowded acres of steep stone streets climbs the muddy hillsides towards the sprawling squalor of the shanties.

Around the cathedral precinct people sit on low stone walls, sell lottery tickets and watches and sunglasses, wait for buses, queue for a phone. In the squares newspaper vendors hawk *La Presa*, fat matrons scratch at their corsetry, businessmen with bare arms and gold bracelets meet and talk, nodding, scratching their noses; giggling schoolgirls gather at a fountain, school books in a circle beside them.

A block from the palace there's a Burger King, where the manager chases off loose-fingered six-year-olds with the same fly swat he uses on the cockroaches. Bloody ironic, as Mike had pointed out as they walked from the bus depot to the hotel: the Third World's taking over the capitals of the West, the West's doing the same to the Third World. Shepherd's Bush looks more and more like Cairo, meanwhile Cairo is screaming for more McDonalds and Pizza Huts.

The Hotel O'Higgins was cheap and central, and had a working phone in the lobby, a cool damp paint-flaking stairwell which smelled of cooking fat and coffee, among other things. A rack of keys tied with wire to wooden tags hung on the wall behind the desk, where an old man sat stock still listening to what sounded like a baseball match on the radio.

Mike called the old man Juan and Juan called Mike Mister Osborne and they seemed to have known each other a long time. Juan had told them as soon as they arrived that he'd seen Willie, but not for a while, maybe two weeks ago, the judge had stayed two nights. He was happy to talk more but first he wanted to listen to the game.

So in the meantime Mike was making phone calls. Joe sat against the opposite wall on a metal chair with a torn plastic seat, leaning back with his hands behind his neck. His lunch was still inside him and he was wondering if it was safe to eat again.

The sports commentary gave way to a commercial break. Mike stopped dialling, replaced the old Bakelite receiver on its cradle, and stubbed out his cigarette.

'Old man Wilde, he just stayed two nights?'

Juan nodded.

'Sí.'

'Did he tell you where he'd been or where he was going?'

'Why would he? The same every time, he comes from the Cay, he goes back to the Cay. Something happened to him?'

'Maybe,' said Mike.

'Did he have any phone calls?' asked Joe.

The radio had switched back to the game.

'Two weeks ago – it's hard to remember,' said Juan. 'The girl is on during the day, I can ask her, it's possible she may remember.'

Mike took a banknote out of the top pocket of his shirt and put it on the counter.

'Gracias,' he said, picking up his bag.

'Very welcome,' said Juan, pocketing the note. 'Enjoy your stay.'

'What news from the Cay?' Joe asked Mike as they carried their bags to the first-floor landing.

'No sign of Willie's letter, Frank'll bring it up when it arrives. He seemed a bit distracted, there's a bug at the clinic.'

'Did you ask him what Richard Nixon was doing in La Entrada?'

Mike laughed.

'Go to hell.'

'Who else did you talk to?'

'I spoke to a guy called Bernard Wiggins at the embassy, he says he'll meet us for a drink at six.'

'What's he like?'

'Bernard? Cavalry twill and stout brogues, very keen on cricket. Personally I think he's a pain in the arse, but your father seemed to like him. They knew each other years back, in England – Wiggins started out life as a lawyer.'

Wiggins. The name was vaguely familiar, but he couldn't put a face to it.

'Did you tell him why we wanted to see him?'

'Of course not. You know what bloody embassies are like. Missing persons reports are the junk mail of the consular service. I thought we'd catch him off duty, make it personal.'

Joe's room was dusty and damp but not unpleasant, tall and narrow, painted medicinal pink, with a door at one end and a thin vertical window at the other, opening on to a tiny balcony. The cheap double divan was covered in a quilted nylon spread, orange with large brown flowers and yellow leaves. The mirror above the sink was cracked and there was no soap. A bare light bulb hung from the ceiling.

Joe, like most touring musicians, was a connoisseur of cheap hotels – the Regency in Whitehaven, the Bull in Doncaster, the Waverley in Southampton, the Saracen in Aberdeen, damp sheets and cigarette burns on the woodwork, brewery ashtrays and cracked sinks, cornflakes and white toast and tea the texture of molasses. He felt utterly at home at the O'Higgins, more at home than he'd ever feel in the perfumed anonymity of a Holiday Inn or a Hilton.

He put his bag on the bed and went over to the balcony and looked out on to the narrow canyon of the street. The noise was mighty, battered buses and Fresco trucks and scooters battling down the steep green hills of the *barrios* into the city centre, a violent bedlam of car horns and radios and shouting children.

Piles of cement and breeze blocks littered the pavements, men with wheelbarrows and shovels competed for space with urchins and women laden with shopping bags. Up the slope, through the tangle of electric cables, he could see a tumbling shanty hillside of wooden houses and flowering shrubs, washing and water tanks and aerials, climbing steeply to pines, the green gashed red with mud erosion. A helicopter flew over, lights flashing, then a Hercules transport heading for the airport.

He lit a cigarette and tossed the match down into the street.

Willie was here. The bugger has a plan, he's on a scent.

San Pedro Sula, La Entrada, Copán, then here.

Criminal, miraculous or insane.

Frank Carrera was in La Entrada – maybe.

Mike saw Bobby Burgess at Copán.

An Aid project, an evangelist, a hippy doctor, a bomb

under a Land-Rover, someone running medical supplies from Guatemala. An old man with a young lover, playing the amateur detective, pursued and pursuing. Too stubborn (or thoughtless) to let his son or his lover know what he's doing. Old enough to drop dead any minute. Temperamentally incapable of asking for help.

Everyone's looking for the judge. And he's out there somewhere.

He wondered what Willie would do in a town like Tegoose. Quick tour of the sites: the church of San Francisco Antigua and its celebrated altar ornaments; the Cathedral of San Miguel, more altar ornaments, fine font in the native manner; the Mint, wooden ceilings in the Mudejar tradition: and that's about it, maybe two hours, even a zimmer frame could do it in a morning.

People didn't come to Tegoose for the sites; they came on business, or to buy things they couldn't buy elsewhere, though God knows there was little enough to buy in this city.

They came because there was an airport with flights out of the country. An airport, but no railroad, the only capital city in the Americas that didn't have a railway.

They came because the government was here, and the military, and the hospitals; to be treated by dentists who used anaesthetics and doctors who read medical journals.

They came to bribe and be bribed. To visit embassies, and bishops, and lawyers, and the hooker bazaars of Belén across the river in Comayguela.

Joe wondered if Willie would go to a brothel. He might, he just might: he came from an age and class where sons were sent to brothels to be educated, where a naughty trip to the whorehouse was the logical end to an evening on the town. But it didn't feel Willie's style, and he had Sarah these days. Again it struck Joe as odd that Willie had vanished and told Sarah nothing. If that was indeed the case.

If not the brothel, then the bar. Somewhere which spoke English and sold whisky. Real whisky, not Mexican bourbon or Twelve-Year-Old Sporran frae Bonnie Taiwan or whatever other shit they sold in the local watering holes. Somewhere with English newspapers and clean bogs and bored ex-pats.

In Tegucigalpa the ex-pats gravitated to the big hotels, the Holiday Inn Plaza, the La Ronda or the Honduras Maya, where UN statisticians and Elmer Gantry missionaries camped out in the coffee shops, and shit-head mercenaries and deodorized US embassy counsellors propped up the air-conditioned bars, eating roasted cashews out of glass bowls, picking their teeth with their cocktail sticks, lining up the imported beers.

The Maya was where they found Bernard Wiggins, sitting on his own at a table away from the bar reading a five-day-old copy of the *Sunday Telegraph*, open at the sports page.

The diplomat put down the paper and stood up as they approached. He was a skinny, well-intentioned man in his mid-forties, with short hair, a long neck and Prince Charles ears: a Real Brit.

Joe didn't have much time for Real Brits, though he'd been raised among them and knew how to pass himself off as a member of the Establishment. Which in a way, he supposed sadly, he was, part of that dissenting but tolerated fringe which provides a cultural conduit between the middle classes and the dangerous waters of Art and Radical Politics.

'Did you see Willie Wilde's son on television the other night? Really rather entertaining.' Not Joe Wilde: Willie Wilde's son, One Of Us.

Mike knew all about that stuff too.

'Bernard, thanks so much for coming.'

'Not at all. How are you, Mike?'

'Fine. I'm sorry we're late.'

'You're not, I was early, ha ha.'

'Bernard, this is Joe Wilde, Willie's son.'

'Hallo Joe, pleased to meet you. I've heard a lot about you.'

The English can keep these games going for hours. Mike offers to buy drinks, Bernard insists, Mike overrules him,

Bernard accepts reluctantly provided he's let buy the second. Acres and acres of this nicely phrased shit, which was the sort of thing Joe wrote songs about when he first started writing songs.

'How's your father?' Wiggins asked him when they finally sat down.

'Ah,' said Mike. 'That's what we wanted to talk to you about.'

'He's missing,' said Joe.

Wiggins raised an eyebrow, wiped the froth of beer off his lip with the back of his hand and put down his glass.

'Since when?'

'Three weeks ago. He went to Copán to look at the ruins and dropped out of sight. All we know is that he came on to Tegoose afterwards. Mike thought you might have run into him.'

'By missing you mean . . .'

'He hasn't been in touch.'

Wiggins took another sip of beer.

'He was here, what, about a fortnight ago. He wanted to make a Will. Phoned up one morning, arranged to come in. He had it all written out, he just needed a witness. It's not uncommon at his age, people feel the need to get their affairs in order.'

Joe and Mike exchanged a glance.

'Do you have a copy?' Joe asked.

'No, he took it away with him.'

'How did he seem?'

'Best of spirits. The arthritis was bugging him a little, but nothing serious. He said the mountain air got into his joints, the coast suited him better. He wanted to know if I had any contacts at the American Hospital. We went out to lunch afterwards at the Nan King – it was rather amusing, he'd assumed that Chinese restaurants were an English phenomenon, he was quite shaken to discover Chinese waiters who only spoke Spanish.'

'Mike says you knew him of old,' said Joe, watching the diplomat's face.

'Yes, small world. I started life as a lawyer, in Manchester, we used to run into each other from time to time. We didn't know each other well – he's a lot older than me. The bugger tied me in knots in court a couple of times – he was a QC then, I was defending. Around the time I decided I wasn't cut out for the law and signed up with the FO. A formidable opponent was Willie.'

Joe had rarely seen his father in action. Partly because Willie never encouraged his wife or son to take an interest in his work, partly because he was a fraud lawyer, working on cases of stifling tedium that often ran for years at a time.

'The Crown versus Hennessey and Hennessey and others,' Wiggins recalled. 'Misuse of Beef Intervention subsidies, among other things. Two Irish brothers from County Kilkenny who had a scam running, packaging up bones and offal and passing it off to the intervention boys as Grade A steak. No one ever ate the stuff, it all went into refrigerated stores. Still there, for all I know. The odd thing was that the Hennesseys were up on two sets of charges. Halfway through the case Willie announced that he was dropping the heavier charges. None of us could understand it, you knew in your gut that they were guilty. I shouldn't say that, but they were. I thought he must be angling for us to plead guilty on the lesser counts, but he wasn't. He didn't even consult the Director of Public Prosecutions, he just got up in court and announced it. The DPP's office was furious at the time. Willie still got his convictions, but the brothers got off lightly. Do you remember the case?'

Joe shook his head.

'I asked him about it the other week,' Wiggins continued. 'He said he didn't trust the police evidence. He knew the court would buy it, but he couldn't. So he just withdrew the charges, off his own bat. Could have been professional suicide, I'm surprised he never talked to you about it.'

'He never talked about cases.'

Never. Sometimes after the conclusion of a trial he'd come home in slightly better spirits, open a bottle of wine, and you knew he'd won. But that was all. He never talked about his cases, or his colleagues. There were other times when he was so absorbed in a trial that he hardly spoke at all: he'd come back late from the office, eat in silence while he read his papers, propped up on a book in front of him on the dining table, making notes as he chewed. The books and notes looked so dull that Joe could never think of a question to ask. Very occasionally, when other lawyers came to the house socially, they'd mock something Willie had done in court, or comment on a judgement, but Willie never rose to the bait. Joe knew from their tone of voice that they admired his father, and for a teenager that was enough.

'How did you first meet him again?' he asked Wiggins.

'He came up in April for the St George's Day party at the embassy – he had a CBE, as you know, the embassy has a list of ex-pats and sent him down an invite.' Wiggins smiled. 'Willie feels more strongly about these things than you do, Mike. The first I knew was when he walked into the room, looking for the drink.'

Mike was sitting back in his chair, relaxed and casual, arms folded, one foot resting on the opposite knee. He smiled and lit a cigarette.

'Not difficult. Did you suggest anyone at the American Hospital?'

'I put him on to a fellow called Dick Sinclair. I don't know if he did anything about it, it didn't seem urgent. Wretched business, arthritis. There isn't a lot you can do about it in my experience, not unless you let the surgeons put you on the table – not always a wise option in this country. I told him he'd be better off going back to UK and getting it seen to there.'

'I don't suppose you can remember what was in the Will, can you?' Joe asked cautiously.

'To be honest with you I didn't read it. The man's a lawyer, I assumed he knew what he was doing. All he needed was a couple of witnesses. I was one, we got my secretary to sign as well just to be on the safe side. Two weeks, eh? I wonder where he could have got to. You've checked the hospitals and so on? But then they would have got in touch with us anyway.'

He leaves the Cay without telling anyone, Joe told himself. Copán may have been a blind, a cover story. Then he comes here and sorts out his Will, which means he thinks his life's at risk. But he wouldn't come to Tegoose just to write his Will, there must have been another reason.

Then he vanishes.

Either he was looking for something, or he was running away. Or both. Fuck him, why didn't he tell anyone? He could have talked to Mike, or Sarah, or Frank. But Willie was never a team man, he had to do everything himself, sniff around and do his groundwork and present the results as a *fait accompli*. The moment a lawyer loves best is the moment he lures the accused into a trap, then produces the surprise witness, the fatal flaw, the smoking gun. But who the hell is the accused? And what is the crime?

Most legal work, Willie had told him once, is dull stuff. Talk to everyone, exclude nothing. What distinguishes a great criminal lawyer is his attention to detail, his willingness to read small print, to keep asking questions, to treat everything as potentially relevant, to avoid assumptions. The only assumption he should make is that no virtuous man is without sin, and no sinner without virtue.

Mike phoned Dr Sinclair from the hotel reception, but the doctor was out of town, attending a conference in Miami, not expected back until the weekend. His secretary declined to give out a number where he could be reached. Mike asked if there was a William Wilde undergoing treatment anywhere in the hospital. There wasn't.

They rang the other hospitals, and the police stations, and showed Willie's photo round the airline offices. No one remembered him. The next morning they visited the Department of Immigration, nine storeys of steel and glass, guarded by soldiers and a chain-link fence; wandered down endless corridors, in and out of bare-walled rooms with metal furniture and air-conditioning units that dribbled like old men, talked to secretaries in high heels and inch-thick make-up, interrupted men in shirt sleeves eating mid-morning cream cakes at their desks, Mike using his Spanish, Joe smiling politely.

'You have records of everyone who comes in and out of the country,' Mike would insist politely.

'Perhaps.'

'Those green forms we fill in at passport control.'

'Yes, I know the green forms.'

'Do you file them?'

'Of course.'

'Is it possible . . .'

'Sadly, no. I am not authorized.'

'Could you tell me who would grant such authorization?'

'That depends.'

He is at lunch, she is in San Pedro, they have a meeting, all the conjugations of bureaucracy. Come back tomorrow, in a month, you must write a letter, please have these forms signed by a priest.

'Tell them we work for the CIA,' Joe suggested.

'Everyone in this fucking building works for the ClA.'

By the time the Department closed for lunch they'd given up. They were back at the Hotel O'Higgins when Frank phoned. Mike took the call in the lobby. The news didn't look good to Joe, watching him from the iron chair across the stairwell. For a full minute Mike didn't speak, just stood there eyes down, pinching at the bridge of his nose.

'We'll get the afternoon flight,' Mike said finally, and put down the phone.

'Problems?' Joe asked.

'We lost three patients, Frank's in a state. He doesn't know what they died of. We'd better pack, there's a flight at four.'

'Do you need me?'

'Need you for what?'

'Would I be any use to you back there?'

Mike scratched at the back of his head.

'No, I suppose not. Why?'

'I thought I'd stay in town for a couple more days, if that's okay.'

He didn't know why he said it, there was no reason to stay, no one else he could think of to see or to talk to. But

175

for some reason Tegoose felt unfinished business, perhaps because a lukewarm trail was marginally hotter here. Mike was looking worried.

'What for?'

'Just to look around.'

Mike shrugged.

'Sure. This is a rough town, though. Be careful.'

'I will.'

They walked up the stairs together, not talking. When Joe reached the door of his room he stopped and turned.

'Mike, is there something you're not telling me?'

Mike looked surprised.

'Like what?'

'Nothing, it doesn't matter. I just get the feeling you're frightened of something and I don't know what it is.'

'Failure,' said Mike, straight out. 'I'm scared of losing what I've built. We live on the cliff's edge all the time down there, anything could blow us over. That's all.'

'You're sure you don't want me to come with you?'

'Sure, thanks. I'll be fine. Willie's still the main thing.' He reached over and gripped Joe on the shoulder. 'Don't worry. We'll find the bugger.'

'If he wants us to,' said Joe.

17

THE REASON SARAH went into the airline office in Morgan's Hole was to avoid getting into conversation with B. J. MacIntyre. Not that she didn't like B.J., but once he had you that was the morning gone, he could talk all day about shit all and whenever you made a move to get away he put his paw on your shoulder to make sure you didn't, and when he had something private to say he leaned right in to your ear and the smell of onion off his breath poured over you like fog seeping down a hillside.

B.J. was walking down the street towards the post office, Sarah was coming out of the grocers with a brown paper bag of fresh bread and a packet of Mr Delicious Qwik-Fry Rice. Two more paces and he'd have had her.

The office, like most of the premises on the main street, was deep in dust from the road outside. It contained two chairs, a wooden counter with an empty perspex brochure-holder, a telephone, a desk-fan and an old poster of Acapulco, Playland of the Western World. Also against the back wall were some industrial-size scales and a small table piled with papers and packages.

Beatrice behind the counter was looking out the side window into the alley, thinking about something other than the airline business. She looked up as Sarah came through the door.

'Hi,' said Sarah. 'Robert Redford just called up and told me to meet him for lunch, I'd like to arrange a charter. You got one of those seaplanes they used in *Hell In the*

Pacific? Bobby has a big pool, I thought it might be a kind of stylish way to arrive.'

Beatrice studied her nails, bit at the varnish, studied them again.

'Where's he live?'

'Some place in the Rockies, I'm sure the pilot'll be able to find it, if not we can always stop and ask.'

'They hellish slow, those seaplanes. What time's the lunch?'

'He just said lunch, didn't give a time. Anyhow, I figure on being a little late. That's what Jackie Onassis' father advised her: always keep them guessing, I read that in a magazine. Or maybe it was Liz Taylor, I forget.'

Beatrice sat up straight and yawned.

'How you doin', Sarah?'

'Fine, or I will be once that fat preacher gets off the pavement. You got a cigarette?'

Beatrice offered her a pack. Sarah put the cigarette in the palm of her hand and tossed it up towards her mouth. It missed. She tried and missed again. The third time she accidentally snapped the cigarette in two.

'I saw a French guy in a movie once could do that any time.' She took a second cigarette, gripped it between her teeth and settled herself on the counter, legs dangling. 'So who's travelling round here?'

'Same as ever. Men, mostly. Tax inspectors, soldiers, fishery agents, preachers, road engineers, usual shit. Your man Wilde ever show up?'

'Nope.'

'Got a package here for his son, came in on the morning flight.'

'I was about to ask,' said Sarah. 'Mike Osborne phoned up saying there's a package coming for Joe. Joe's in Tegoose, he wants Frank to carry it up there for him. Only Frank's busy at the moment so I got to take it for him.'

'Frank wants you to take it to Tegoose?'

'Well it was my idea really, but he said I could, yea.'

Or words to that effect. What Sarah had said was 'I

could take that', and what Frank had said was 'I bet you could'.

What the hell.

'You got a ticket?' asked Beatrice.

'No, but you about to give me one. Charge it to Frank.'

'You sure about this, Sarah?'

'Frankly no, but I'm prepared to take a risk on it. All the good things I ever did I never thought about them before I did them. Things I puzzle over always work out bad. Make it First Class, I reckon Mike Osborne would want me to travel First on a job like this.'

'Ain't no First Class.'

'Oh dear oh dear what is the world coming to. What's the in-flight movie?'

'Ain't no movie. When you planning on coming back?'

'I have to tell you now?'

'No, not unless you want to save Mike some money.'

'It sort of depends on my next assignment, we're not really meant to talk about these things.'

'You got any luggage?'

'How much you allowed?'

'Twenty kilograms. Half a hog or thereabouts.'

'I don't own twenty kilograms of anythin'. Maybe take a hat, change of underclothes. This a direct flight?'

'Change in Tela and San Pedro. Get you in to Tegoose maybe eight this evening.'

Beatrice wrote out the ticket, put it in a folder, and handed it across together with Joe's package. The package looked important, a padded envelope covered in plastic-wrapped courier company dockets and 'Urgent, By Air' stickers and customs forms and stamps, but it didn't feel important, it felt to Sarah like a letter, or maybe a document of some kind.

She phoned St Andrews from the air strip, sounding she hoped English and far away, spoke to a woman she suspected was Esther and explained she was a friend of Joe Wilde's, was it possible to speak to him? And when it wasn't, she asked if they knew where he was, and the voice said, 'Hold on, I'll check', and then told her Hotel O'Higgins, Calle Santa Lucia.

'Thank you so much, madam,' Sarah said politely, writing the address on her wrist. 'I do appreciate your help.'

'That's okay, Sarah,' said Esther. 'Don't worry, I won't tell a soul.'

Joe put Mike in a taxi, and then headed down the hill into town.

He had no very definite plan. He started by walking across the river into Comayaguela, once a separate town in its own right, long since absorbed into the capital. If Tegucigalpa was impoverisned, Comayaguela had even less. The shops sold cheap hardware and mountains of greying corsetry. Trees sprouted from the pantiled roofs of the houses, dogs prowled the gutters, the half-paved streets were peopled by cripples of every shape and form: outside the vegetable market two fought each other with crutches.

'*Somos haraganes*,' muttered a man in the watching crowd: We are good for nothing.

At first Joe thought that the two young men in cheap leather jackets leaning against the wall of the cantina were looking at him because he was a tourist, a rare European in a quarter which attracted few foreigners. He saw them again as he recrossed the river, thirty yards behind him, and instinctively slipped his wallet from his inside pocket and stuffed it down the front of his jeans. But when he looked again they'd vanished.

Outside the cathedral a Moonie approached him and asked if he'd like One World. Joe said it depended on the World. An evangelist with a loud hailer harangued the lottery sellers.

He headed for a mall of boutiques and craft shops with Visa signs cut from magazines, the wares inside crudely made and expensive, rough wood carving and bad embroidery. He found a bar, sat down at a table, ordered a beer and lit up a cigarette. Just as Willie would have done.

His fellow customers were Tegucigalpa's bourgeoisie, fat

fussy women and strutting, diminutive men. In Honduras, he decided, not even the rich are rich. The waiter brought his beer on a tin tray and stuck the bill neatly in the empty tooth-pick stand.

To find him I've got to understand him, Joe told himself.

But I don't want to understand him. *Tout comprendre c'est tout pardonner* is a recipe for the nut-house.

We live inside different ideas of the world. In Willie's world there are Great Certainties, the Greatest of which is that seductive old whore, The System. Preserve, value, defend, know who you are and where you come from.

That was Joe's problem: he knew exactly where he came from, and he wanted no part of it.

Whenever he was in danger of adopting a firm position on anything he undercut himself, or took refuge in humour. He had no ideology, just a wry acceptance of human imperfection, to the point where Marian, now house-hunting in Wiltshire in her wedding-gift Golf GTi, had once described him as an equal opportunity cynic.

She was right: an equal opportunity cynic with a thin, protective veneer of humanitarian compassion.

Willie couldn't stand folly or fools, Joe enjoyed both. Willie had strong views on Right and Wrong: Joe saw himself as nonjudgemental, tolerant, easy-going, amenable, interested in other people's points of view. He found it hard to think of a cause he'd risk his life for. Willie appeared to have found one. Not money, not power, not politics: it had to be a moral question.

Morality was a dirty word in Joe's generation, with largely sexual connotations. He was on the side of Good against Evil, the poor against the rich, the weak against the strong, generosity against meanness, all that shit. He was also careful to avoid the demonologies of the modern age – masculinity, race, Englishness, capitalism, authority, the state. He admired individuals but with reservations, he had no heroes, no causes. You can paddle in causes but don't jump in, we all know what happens to people who get carried away by causes.

But then that, he suddenly realized, was of course exactly what he was doing. The cause was Willie.

Outside in the square the evangelist had given up and was storing his megaphone away in a canvas grip. The sun was low on the horizon, throwing long shadows across the cobbles, bathing the white stucco of the buildings in soft red light. He paid for his beer and bought a four-day-old *Sunday Times* from the kiosk outside the Hotel La Ronda. The mortgage rate was up, England had lost a one-day match against Sri Lanka, skirts were above the knee again. London fiddles while the world burns.

There were two ways back to the hotel, a long detour back down to the Presidential Palace, or a short cut through the alleys that ran up the steep hillside to his right. He opted for the latter, folded the paper under his arm, and headed up the steps.

The lane was narrow and cobbled, so steep that at times it gave way to steps. Old bedding hung from the overhead windows and a trickle of grey water ran down the gutter.

He was halfway up the hill when he heard footsteps behind him. The two men were on him before he had time to turn. The first blow hit him on the neck, and he stumbled, raising one hand to shield his face, stretching out with the other arm to break his fall. As he hit the ground a boot caught him in the stomach. He groped out and caught an ankle and held tight. Someone cursed in Spanish, and a fist landed on the side of his neck. Joe had both hands on the ankle now. He pulled, and a body sprawled on to the cobbles beside him. The fist hit him again, in the chest this time, so hard that he felt his lungs about to burst. After that he passed out.

When he came to he was alone. His wallet was still in the front of his pants, but his bag had been ransacked, the contents strewn across the alley. The two men from Comayaguela had vanished.

He lay for a while nursing his bruises. Waves of nausea passed over him, and his head ached. Slowly he got to his feet, collected the contents of his shoulder bag, limped over to the wall, and sat down on a step. If robbery was the motive, his assailants had drawn a blank. His passport was back at the hotel, his cash in the wallet. The only damage was to his person: bruised ribs, bruised neck, a graze on his knee where he'd fallen on the cobbles.

Back at the O'Higgins he showered and bathed his wounds, wondering whether to bother going to the police. It hardly seemed worth it: nothing had been stolen, all he had was a vague description of the two men. What puzzled him was why they'd followed him all the way back from Comayaguela, waited until he'd drunk his beers and read his paper. Two hours' work for the sake of what they must have hoped was at best a tourist wallet. Pickings must be hard to come by in this town.

He ate Chinese at the Nan King, where Willie and Bernard Wiggins had adjourned after the signing of the Will: toothpicks in bottles on formica tables, a neon light flickered by overhead fans, a bottle labelled Heavenly Sauce, Glasgow, England; a trio of young Hondurans at the bar in cowboy boots and jeans with improbable brand names, Lavi, Pepay, King George. None of the Chinese spoke any English. He ate a bowl of soup and started on a plate of noodles but gave up. He felt awful.

Afterwards he found a bar with a TV. He drank four bottles of beer while he watched an ancient edition of *The Love Boat*, changed to Tequila for *Johnny Carson*, then switched to whisky for *Celebrity Squares*. He'd never heard of any of the celebrities, apart from a woman with too few wrinkles for her age who he thought might have been one of the wives in *Dallas*, or possibly *Falcon Crest*.

I could go mad here, he decided. I know no one, I don't speak the language, I've been mugged, I'm looking for someone who doesn't wish to be looked for. He felt disconnected from any recognizable reality.

Think Willie, he kept reminding himself. Get inside the head.

He went to bed at ten, still looking for the key. What would motivate the bastard? At home it might be some monstrous illegality, but the word had little meaning here, people did what was necessary to survive, not even Willie would judge Hondurans in that way.

It could be Bobby Burgess. Bobby belonged to a Western culture, and could be judged by Western values. It could, hypothetically, be Frank Carreras, if Frank was up to mischief: loose-living, dope-smoking, anti-establishment Frank would be a red rag to the old bull, and American to boot. Willie could be extraordinarily pompous about Americans.

Or it could be none of the above. The Willie Joe knew, the ossified self-obsessed brogues-and-claret lawyer, had clearly mutated into someone else during his time on the Cay. Mutated, or reverted.

He'd found a woman, apart from anything else. Joe wondered what had happened. Lying naked under his single sheet watching the thin shaft of street light seeping through the crack of the brown and orange curtains, listening to the sounds from the street outside, he found himself thinking about Sarah, still wondering what had happened between her and Willie.

Maybe he asked her out on a date, showered and shaved and put on a tie and took her into Morgan's Hole for a candle-lit meal. Sarah would be a sucker for all that, but it wasn't Willie's style.

Then again he might have used alcohol, tanked himself up on Dutch courage and then taken her for a walk along the beach in the moonlight, except that drink made Willie anything but intimate. In drink he became declamatory, shouted at waiters or hunted around for someone to harangue on the shortcomings of the Crown Prosecution Service. The more nervous he'd get the more he'd drink, the more he drank the more nervous he'd become.

There was a sound in the corridor, footsteps approaching.

That's it, Joe realized. Sarah would have decided to act, played him along all day like a fish on a line, sent him away confused and love-struck, then waited until he was back home and asleep. The first thing Willie would have known would have been a body slipping into bed beside him, soft hands caressing him out of sleep. No words, no embarrassing preambles, just tender hands and a friendly conch.

The footsteps had reached the door. Joe lay very still under the single sheet, watching the door in the darkness. There was a knock. Joe said nothing, turned silently on to his side and closed his eyes.

There was another knock, louder this time.

'Mister Wilde?'

The voice was male. Joe reached down and grabbed his underpants off the floor and turned on the bed light.

'Come in.'

The door opened. It was Juan, the desk clerk. The old man wore a cheap leather jacket over a white cotton vest and brown synthetic trousers. He had bedroom slippers on his feet.

His manner was formal, almost shy, even when he saw the bruise on the side of Joe's neck.

'You had an accident?'

'Looks worse than it feels,' said Joe. 'Two guys in the wealth-distribution business had a go for my wallet.'

'You need a doctor?'

'No, I'll be fine. What can I do for you?'

'I spoke with the girl, she says there was one visitor the second day he was here, a minister.'

'American?' said Joe.

The clerk nodded.

'There was an argument, in the lobby. He stayed maybe ten minutes.'

'Did she gather what the argument was about?'

'She's here now, you can ask her.'

Joe reached out for his shirt and carefully pulled on his trousers. He was sore, but only in the way you feel sore after a bad game of Rugby. Nothing was broken.

Juan waited until he was dressed and out of bed, then turned and spoke briefly. A woman of around twenty appeared round the door jamb, plump, with a round Spanish face and thick dark hair tied in a braid.

The argument, she said, was none of her business and she had been trying not to listen, anyway she did not understand much English, but Señor Wilde had a loud voice, and it seemed to her that the American gentleman was refusing a request, or had failed to do something. It was difficult to follow the preacher because he had some trouble with his speech.

'A lisp?' Joe suggested.

The woman looked at him.

'Lithp.'

She smiled.

'Sí.'

'Did they leave together?'

No, the preacher had left alone, Willie had gone back up to his room, then five minutes later he'd come down and checked out.

After they'd left Joe sat on the bed smoking a cigarette.

Bobby Burgess. Bobby who'd been in La Entrada, and Copán, Bobby who had a thing about St Andrews. He'd talk to Bunty Burgess first, Bunty had a certain innocence about her. He got back into bed and lay for a while reading. Around eleven he turned out the light and started drifting into sleep.

This time he heard no footsteps in the corridor. The first sound that alerted him was the quiet click of the door opening.

For a moment Sarah wondered if she'd come to the wrong room, she had a chronic fear of such disasters, but the smell reassured her. Not a strong smell, not unpleasant, but male and familiar. It was dark, she could hear steady breathing, then a movement from the bed, someone turning in their sleep, then silence. She waited a moment, then closed the door as gently as she could.

Willie used to cough in his sleep, a smoker's cough, heaving the phlegm back up from his lungs into his throat. Sometimes he used to pretend he was asleep even when he wasn't, as if in celebration of the first time. But this isn't Willie, forget Willie.

Her eyes adjusted to the darkness. She took off her blouse, unbuttoned her bra and put them both on the chair, listening to the breathing, not entirely sure what would happen, excited by the danger. She unzipped her jeans, steadying herself with one arm against the wall as she stepped out of them.

She knew as soon as she lifted the sheet that he was awake. His arm reached over and touched her side just above the waist.

'You have to be gentle,' he said softly. 'I've just been mugged.'

18

Dawn was breaking, the first morning sounds starting up in the street, a man spitting, metal shutters opening, the first buses straining up the hill towards the *barrio*.

Sarah lay on her back, slack-jawed and snoring. Joe heaved himself up on to his elbow and looked around the room. He felt stiff, and there was a violent bruise across his chest. The air smelled of cigarette smoke and sweat. He slipped out of bed, splashed his face with cold water from the sink, and looked at himself in the mirror.

'There's something you ought to know,' said a voice from the bed. 'I'm married.'

'Me too,' said Joe.

Sarah sat up and helped herself to a Marlboro.

'Bullshit, you ain't married, ain't the marrying kind, that's what the judge said.'

'In England "not the marrying kind" means "gay".'

'Doesn't seem to me that's your problem.'

Joe got back into bed and took a cigarette.

'Did you really call him the judge?'

'Sure. That's what he is, isn't it?'

'I suppose so. Is that who you're married to?'

'Who, Willie?' She laughed. 'Shit no. I married at fourteen, fellow named Fat-nose Parsons, worked on a banana ship out of Mobile, said he'd take me back to Texas with him. Only he didn't, end of the week he was gone, home to the other Mrs Parsons. I still got the ring some place.'

They breakfasted at what claimed to be a French-Style

Pâtisserie across from the Presidential Palace, four marble-topped tables roped in off the pavement and a red and white PVC awning which needed a clean.

Sarah wore the clothes she had arrived in: tight denim jeans and a floral blouse in pale blues and reds, the top buttons undone to reveal the tops of her breasts. She smiled a lot as she ate her way through the cakes, a smile of big capped teeth latticed with braces.

'You know a lot of rich people in the music business?' she asked Joe. 'I mean really rich.'

Joe pondered the question. Anyone in England was rich by Honduran standards.

'A couple,' he decided. 'Rock stars, agents.'

Sarah was leaning forward, stirring her coffee, licking the froth off her spoon.

'Is it true the rich are unhappy?'

'Not at all, we just want them to be. And it suits them to be thought miserable, takes the curse off inequality, lessens the jealousy factor. I mean they have problems, but no worse than the rest of us, just different. Where to get the Aston Martin serviced, what colour to paint the murals in the bathroom, what to talk to their accountant about at lunch once they've finished talking business. But no, in my experience the rich have a good time. Their personalities go to shit, but they're happy.'

'That's what I reckon too,' said Sarah. 'You got a woman back in England?'

'No.'

'What about the radio girl?'

Joe choked on his pastry.

'Willie told you about Marion?'

'Mmm.'

'Did he tell you she got married?'

'Not that I remember. Why did she do that?'

Joe wiped his mouth with his napkin.

'I was driving her nuts. She said I wouldn't take anything seriously, the moment anything got serious, I made a joke of it.'

'What's wrong with that?'

'It gets wearying, I'm told.'

'Was she rich?'

'Not particularly. She has a good enough job, she produces radio documentaries for the BBC. Owns her own flat, buys nice clothes.'

'Did you pay for her treats – dinners and so on?'

I hardly know this woman, Joe reminded himself. Twelve hours ago she was no more than a witness to the case, a clue to Willie.

Put it down to research, he decided.

'You want an honest answer?'

'Whatever suits you.'

'When Marion let me pay for dinner, I knew she was going to let me fuck her. If she went Dutch, that was that.' He laughed to hide his embarrassment. 'Tell me what's the sexual politics in that.'

Sarah licked cream off her thumb.

'Maybe she thought you had a hooker fantasy, maybe she thought that stuff turned you on.'

'But it doesn't. Hookers don't love you, I'm funny about that sort of thing.'

'I'm not saying you had a fantasy, I'm saying maybe she thought you did. Anyhow, the reason I'm asking is I don't have any money.'

Joe smiled and paid the bill off the shrinking wad of notes Mike had left him. Sarah looked away until the waiter had gone, then took a flower out of the vase on the table, sniffed it and stuck it behind her hair.

'What's next?'

'Bunty Burgess,' said Joe. 'I'm getting into religion.'

'She in town?'

'Not so far as I know. Have you got plans?'

'I thought I might put in some window shopping, maybe a movie. If you've got things to do . . .'

And then she remembered.

'Shit, I got a present for you.'

*

The package was back at the hotel, wrapped in a polythene shopping bag under a clean set of underwear, two oranges and a cloth bag of toiletries and hair-slides. Joe opened it with a pocket knife and slipped out the contents.

There were two envelopes. One contained a brief note scribbled in thick black felt tip on the back of a gas bill.

'Dear fellow Perry Como fan,' Eddie had written. 'Some fucker called up asking for your mail. You have some untrustworthy acquaintances so I told him it was in Latin, herewith for your own eyes. Rent due next Thursday.'

The other envelope was marked Air Mail, with a raft of exotic stamps along the top. It was already open. Inside was a single sheet of cheap blue paper torn from a pad covered in Willie's bold italic script.

'*JW*,' it began: no endearments.

This is a strange country, as you know. Good climate, execrable food, creature comforts a very mixed bag. I am not sure what people make of me, nor I of them. There is kindness in some quarters, but also great inertia and an irritating acceptance of Fate. Religion is truly an opiate here, a curse which in time will I think destroy much of the charm of the islands. Cf Samoa, Fiji et al. Mercifully it plays little part in the working of St Andrews, which is a remarkable institution, and a tribute to your friend Osborne's dedication and ingenuity. It is refreshing in this day and age to find a man motivated by something other than self-interest or political dogma.

I have I hope been able to contribute a little in return for my board and keep. My work is largely administrative although I have been instrumental in introducing self-filtering water works for the settlement: three interconnected ponds lined with a rubber sheet to prevent leakage into the subsoil, then partially filled with local soil, stones and gravel. We plant a species of reed, Phragmites australis, *in the beds. The sewage waste is led through the roots of these reeds, and during its passage through the root-zone is cleansed by microbiological degradation and physical/chemical processes. Nitrogen is removed by denitrification and heavy metals are bound in the soil. A sampling hole allows the water to be analysed before it is returned to open water course. Can process water for 60 adults. Clean water is a problem everywhere, as is dysentery and unwanted pregnancy, also the usual tropical diseases.*

I had planned to return in a few weeks, but have become involved in an investigation which may take a little longer. There may be nothing in it but you know how it is with lawyers in the heat of the chase. At least it occupies what remains of my intellect. Don't worry if I'm out of touch for a while. I am not as yet in any apparent danger.

I would rather you didn't mention any of this abroad. If someone is obsessed by an investigation people eventually become bored, finally irritated and antagonistic. There may be nothing in it, and I do not wish to be thought a bore for nothing.

There is some research I need doing in London. I'll phone when I can, which is not always easy here.

W.W.

Joe tossed the letter on to the bed.

Fuck the man. A page of eco-chemistry, a request to be left alone. The bastard's enjoying himself, he doesn't want to be found. I might as well have stayed home in Kilburn.

'He write anything about me?' asked Sarah, picking up the letter.

'Not a word. But he wouldn't, he'd be shy about that sort of thing.'

She read through the first page.

'The water stuff, Willie put it in but it was Frank's idea, he read about it some place, got a fellow in the States to ship him down the plants, had to come in the back door, you ain't meant to go moving living plants from one country to another, government people get upset.'

'What's the back door?' asked Joe.

'Two or three of them. Put them on a shrimp boat up in the Gulf someplace, walk them across from Guatemala or Belize or Nicaragua. Same way the guns come and go. Guns and illegals.'

She turned the page.

'So he ain't missing.'

'Apparently not.'

'Only if he meant to go someplace and got into trouble he could be, only you'd still think he wasn't.'

She was right: once he'd taken off anything could have happened. And things had been happening: someone had blown up Mike's jeep, David Vaz had hanged himself, the old man had made a Will, all was not tranquil.

'You still going after him?' asked Sarah.

'I'm not sure.' He thought for a moment, conscious of her eyes watching him. Big eyes, very open, full of mischief. 'If he needs help, I'd help him.'

'Only way we goin' to know the answer to that is ask the man.'

Joe laughed nervously and lit a cigarette.

'How the hell do you propose doing that?'

'Same way you catch any animal. Set a bait.'

He looked at her.

'What's the bait?'

'I am.'

'What happens if he bites?'

Sarah grinned.

'Worry about that when it happens.'

'And if he doesn't bite?'

'Then we go find him.'

Joe didn't know whether to take her seriously. He sucked on his cigarette and blew the smoke in a long column towards the morning sky.

'If you're the bait, what's the trap?'

'Jealousy,' said Sarah. Big grin. 'Old bulls got a thing about the next generation messing with their women.'

'And how do the women feel about it?'

Sarah sat back on the bed, shoulders, against the wall, hands behind her neck.

'The thing in this country is you take each day as it comes. Meanwhile you take any fun that's on the street.'

'You really believe that?'

'No, I just testing you, that's all. We got a lot of acquaintin' to do, Joe Wilde. I thought we might as well get started.' She swung her legs up off the floor and laid them across Joe's lap. 'You got any plans worked out for today yet?'

Joe reached across and kissed her.

'Bunty Burgess, I told you.'

'I got an idea,' said Sarah, slipping her hand inside his shirt, palm down on his stomach to avoid the bruise. 'Close your eyes and think of Bunty.'

At that moment the fat Bakelite phone on the bedside table gave out a single ring. Joe reached out and lifted the receiver.

It was Bernard Wiggins.

'He's in the United States,' the diplomat announced. 'Or at least he was. Lost his passport in Houston, the consulate issued him with a temporary replacement.'

'When was this?' asked Joe, signalling Sarah to get him a pen and paper.

'Eight days ago. He said he needed it in a hurry. Which means he may have moved on by now. Or back. I talked to the vice-consul. He seemed in fine spirits.'

'What the hell happens in Houston?' Joe wondered out loud.

'Not a clue, I'm afraid,' said Wiggins. 'How are things otherwise?'

'I got mugged.'

'Oh dear. Are you okay?'

'Fine,' said Joe. Sarah had her hand on his thigh. 'Just a little confused. Listen, could you do something else for me? Find out what you can about an agency called Third Aid, they're based in the States. In particular if they've any connection with religious fundamentalists.'

'What kind of connection?'

'Any kind. Good or bad. Oh, and if there's any way of checking on a Dr Frank Carreras who works for them. US citizen, must be around thirty-five, currently working at St Andrews.'

The consul sounded dubious, but said he'd do what he could.

It was only after Wiggins had rung off that Joe remembered the last line of Willie's letter. He picked up the receiver again and asked Juan to get him a London number. It rang for three minutes before a voice answered.

'Thank you for calling the Convent of the Sacred Heart,' said Eddie Scargill. 'I'm afraid there's no one in to take your call –'

'Fuck off, Ironside,' Joe interrupted.

'Joe? Where the hell are you? You're meant to be in bloody Belfast.'

'I wish I was. Listen, Eddie, did Willie call?'

'Who's Willie?'

'Ill-tempered old man with a smoker's cough. Long distance.'

'You mean Judge Wilde?'

'That's what he called himself?'

'That's what he called himself.'

'What did you tell him?'

'That you were in Klosters with the Prince of Wales.'

'Did he leave a message?'

'No.'

'Do something for me, Eddie. If he rings again say I'm in Honduras, looking for him.'

'I told him that, too.'

'What did he say?'

'"Well that's a fat lot of good." Or words to that effect.'

'When was this?'

'Couple of days ago, or thereabouts.'

'He didn't say where he was ringing from?'

'No. He said "This is Judge Wilde, is Joe there?" I said "No, he's in Klosters." He said "bugger". Then I said you were in Honduras, and he said "fat lot of good", and I said "up yours too, vicar", and then for some reason he hung up.'

'You're all charm, Eddie.'

'I love you too.'

They checked out of the Hotel O'Higgins at noon. On their way to the airport they stopped off at the American Hospital, where Wiggins had sent Willie to have his arthritis looked at. Sarah waited downstairs in the cab. Joe went inside, told the receptionist he had a message for Dr Sinclair's office and took the lift to the third floor. Sinclair's secretary was on a call. He stood with his back to her, studying the medical registers on the shelf while he waited for her to finish.

'There's a public library at the embassy,' she said sourly as she put down the phone.

'Read them all,' Joe said sadly. 'You get desperate in this town. I wanted to leave a personal message for Dr Sinclair.'

'What's the message?'

Joe picked up a pad and scribbled his name and the number at St Andrews.

'Could he call Joe Wilde, Willie Wilde's son. As soon as he can. It's important.'

'Important to whom?' said the secretary.

'The human race.'

Sarah was chatting up the cab driver when he got back downstairs, telling him they had to catch a flight to New York, they'd be spending a few days there on business. Via Miami, she added, in case there weren't any flights from Tegoose to the Big Apple.

They drove out through the edges of town. It was warm, the damp green countryside steaming in the afternoon sun. There were hawks overhead, riding the thermals.

'Do you miss him?' asked Joe.

'Who, Willie? Yeah, I suppose I do. You get used to people, changes your rhythms when they ain't around. I'm fairly mad at him too. He should have told me he was goin' away, no way I was about to stop him.'

Joe had been wondering about that too, wondered if it should make him suspicious. Except that Willie saw women and work as very separate: women were to do with your left-over time. It wouldn't occur to his father to put a woman before his job.

'How about you?' asked Sarah.

'It's not about missing. I only see the bugger two or three times a year. But I worry about him, yes.'

'Worry about what?'

'That he'll make a mess of his old age, I suppose.'

Sarah reached back and scratched between her shoulder blades.

'We all got a right to mess things up, so long as we don't go blaming it on other people. Old folk no different from the rest of us in that respect. He ever talk to you about growing old?'

'Not a lot,' said Joe. 'He has a sort of rule about personal things, you only talk about them in metaphors. He'll complain about the neighbours, or the young, or the state of the country. You dig down a bit and you can sometimes work out what it is that's really bugging him. He moans about the young because he hasn't got the energy or imagination to cope with other ways of thinking or doing things. You get very defensive about your certainties at his time of life. My mother hated the whole Women's Movement thing because it came too late to help her, she realized that if they were right her life needn't have turned out the way it did, they made her feel inadequate because she never had a job, let herself be fucked around by Willie. You ever talk to your mother about things?'

Sarah laughed.

'Sure. She tells me she don't like what I'm doin' with my life, I tell her that's tough, she's the one raised me. Omangatu's an embarrassing woman to have for a mother, that used to get to me. Then one day I suddenly thought – why should I be embarrassed by my mother? She's the one they think's mad, it's not my fault, there's nothing I can do about it. Things been okay since then.'

The airport lay on a shallow plateau ten miles from the city: a Mayan concrete block, flat roofed, with a railed balcony for spectators and a glass control booth. On the far side of the single runway the old terminal, a green hangar embroidered with Italianate towers and concrete colonnades, had been taken over by the military, the surrounding scrub strewn with camouflaged DC3s, helicopters and air force personnel doing PT. Beyond lay a junk yard of dead planes, a watch tower, thirty-year-old fire tenders and pickups, rusting aircraft steps, luggage trolleys abandoned in the weeds.

The flight to the coast was delayed, and they waited for two hours in the terminal, browsing the dusty craft shop and news stands selling *Time* and the *Miami Herald* and drinking beers. Sullen soldiers in battle fatigues sat around on plastic chairs smoking cigarettes and stroking their carbines. Joe was hungry but there was nothing to eat except biscuits and chocolate bars.

A party of American Christians arrived off a flight from Houston, eager young men and women with shampooed hair and wide-open eyes and sincere handshakes, lightweight pullovers over their shoulders, lean and hard and well-fed.

'What I can't figure,' Sarah said to Joe, 'is what all you well-off people doin' in this shit-hole in the first place. I mean – what you all looking for? The Spaniards were different, the Spaniards came here looking for gold. But there ain't no gold any more, there's nothing. Mike Osborne, he had a good job back in the States, kind of job people here give their tits to get their hands on. There ain't no good jobs in this country. None at all.'

'I think it's simple,' said Joe. 'Mike's trying to help. I can't see what's so wrong if he gets to feel better about himself along the way.'

'You reckon.'

'I reckon.'

'And how about Willie?'

Joe was beginning to wonder what he'd let himself in for with Sarah. Incest, for starters, or it felt that way. But his hormones were up and running: he kept glancing at her when he thought she wasn't looking, and sometimes when she was.

Be careful, he warned himself. They play by different rules round here.

'You tell me.'

'Man's running away from himself.'

'That's possible too. Only you can't, it's a contradiction in terms. Did he change a lot on the Cay?'

'Oh yeah, he changed.' She smiled, pink gums and braced teeth, and swallowed a mouthful of beer. 'At least he did and he didn't. One moment he's bawling everyone out same as ever, next he's smoking dope and goin' to bed with women young enough be his granddaughter.'

'Did he do a lot of bawling out?'

'Plenty. That man got something he's angry about deep down inside himself. Never could figure what it is.'

'Human imperfection,' said Joe. 'His own in particular.'

'You get angry like that?' she asked him.

'I used to, I had a terrible temper as a kid. I was the resident cabaret at school, when people got bored they'd bate the shit out of me until I blew my top.'

'You still get that way?'

'Not a lot.'

'Willie make you mad?'

'Yes, he still does, sometimes. Right now I could strangle him.'

They changed planes in San Pedro Sula, another hour of cold beers and cigarettes in a humid departures hall filled with well-fed priests and government officials. Joe noticed that Sarah didn't drink as much as she looked as though she was drinking, and did more thinking than she let on.

'You goin' to tell Mike about the letter?' she asked as they made their way across the tarmac to the waiting DC3.

'Is there some reason I shouldn't?'

'I guess Mike's okay, it's who he might tell could be a problem.'

'Like who?'

'Sounds like you getting interested in Frank all of a sudden.'

'I'll tell Mike, I have to.'

'Okay. Second question. If Bobby Burgess is up to something what the hell was he doing having arguments with Willie in Tegoose?'

'You tell me.'

'Only reason I can come up with is that he ain't the hare Willie was chasing. You know that saying, my enemy's enemy is my friend. Maybe they both chasing the same hare, only for different reasons.'

'Maybe we better ask him,' said Joe. 'Him or his wife.'

It was almost dark when they landed at Cow Cay, the sun disappearing into the clouds over the mainland hills thirty miles to the west.

'First thing you goin' to do when you get back,' said Sarah as they walked over towards the line of taxis under the palms, 'is play me one of your songs. Been waiting days to hear what you sound like.'

19

THE WAY JOE learned to cope with the bating and bullying at Glenalmond was through music. It happened in his third year, when he shared a study with a fat, bespectacled, acne'd red-head from Bearsden called Porky Fisher. Porky was bad at everything schoolboys are meant to be good at: games, jokes, deceit. His father was dead and his mother spoiled him, which made matters even worse. But along with the tinned Dundee cakes and soft-leather wool-lined gloves and magazine subscriptions she gave him a Dancette record player and an allowance which paid for all the albums he wanted.

What he wanted was the Blues. Everyone else was listening to Abba and Gary Glitter and the Bay City Rollers: Porky spent his evenings playing Big Bill Broonzy and Sonny Terry, Memphis Slim and B. B. King and Muddy Waters.

Joe couldn't believe what he was hearing. His own mother liked musicals and light opera: he'd been raised on a diet of Rodgers and Hammerstein and Franz Lehar and Julian Slade. Willie was more or less tone deaf. Piano lessons, which Joe suffered from the age of eight, had been agony: he could play the notes, but his heart was never into 'Men of Harlech' or *Rondo alla Turca*.

A week of Memphis Slim changed all that. He learned to improvise, his left hand thumping out a twelve-bar boogie while his right played around with chords and runs that never made it into *Golden Hours of the Piano* or *Fifty Waltzes from the Masters*. Ever since then the Blues had been his real love.

He often wondered what happened to Porky. Not a lot, probably: a plump wife and plump kids and a life of chartered accountancy in the Glasgow suburbs, probably, his record collection stored in the rafters of the two-car garage. But Joe loved him still.

The piano in the Old Rectory at St Andrews was a missionary legacy, upright and ornate under inches of dust and piles of old newspapers and magazines. It stood below a framed map of Honduras in the dining room, much neglected and as far as Joe knew unused since his last visit three years before.

He played it now because Sarah asked him to, and because when he refused her Mike insisted. The mood at St Andrews was grim. No radios played in the compound, no one sat around on the grass under the mango trees, even the guinea fowl had lost their voices. Five had died before Frank and the pharmacy got the outbreak under control.

Five dead, two missing: the other news waiting for Joe and Sarah was that Bobby and Bunty had upped sticks and moved out. Two nights ago they were here, the next morning they were gone, without explanation, leaving only their furniture and fittings crated up on the quay waiting for shipment.

Mike was sitting across the room on an ancient leather armchair with horse-hair coming out the arms, his feet on a stool, a glass of whisky in one hand and a joint in the other. Sarah stood with her back straight against the door jamb. Next door in the kitchen Frank was making supper. Outside a dying shell-pink sunset burned the hem of the pale evening sky. Bats flickered around the trees.

Joe gave them 'Harlem Moon' first, then a couple of pieces of his own, 'Kick-em When They're Down' and 'Painful as Falling Off a Log', allowing himself a quick glance across to Sarah once in a while. She was playing it cool but he could see she was impressed.

Mike refilled Joe's whisky glass.

'Give me "Keep the Coal in the Jacuzzi", or "Cathcart Ceilidh".'

'Later,' said Joe, closing the piano.

Sarah went through to help Frank. Joe helped himself to his drink and sat back down on the stool.

'Meanwhile tell me about Bobby.'

'He just moved out. No warning, the first anyone knew was when Bobby and Bunty turned up at the air strip with a heap of suitcases. There's hell in town, he owed money all over the place. I expect he'll pay up in the end, or the Church will.'

'Bobby saw Willie the day after he got to Tegoose,' said Joe.

Mike looked up.

'He what?'

'Juan got hold of the girl, she said Willie and Bobby had an argument, she doesn't know what about, except that Bobby hadn't done something Willie wanted him to. Or was refusing to do something, she wasn't sure which. Bobby left, Willie checked out shortly afterwards.'

Mike held the butt of his joint carefully between two fingers and took a final puff before flicking it out of the window.

'I'm glad in a lot of ways, good riddance. Those people are a bloody cancer. But I wish I knew why he'd gone. Feels like rats leaving the ship. What the fuck could he and Willie have been up to?'

'"My enemy's enemy is my friend", according to Sarah. She could be right.'

'But who the hell's the enemy?'

He got up and walked over to the window.

'You want the rest of the news?' asked Joe. He told him about Willie's letter, and his phone call to Eddie, and what Wiggins had found out. Mike listened in silence, eyes on the sunset, his back to the room.

'It sounds to me as though he'll be back of his own accord before too long,' he said when Joe had finished talking. 'How are the bruises?'

'I'll live,' said Joe. But he still hurt, and he was tired from the journey.

*

They ate in the kitchen, Mike at one end of the scrubbed pine table, Frank at the other, Joe and Sarah facing each other in between, Joe wondering whether she'd eaten here often when Willie was around, if this was a familiar scene to her.

Probably, he decided. She certainly seemed to know her way around, what lived in which cupboard, where the whisky was kept.

'It's the fucking funerals I'm dreading,' said Frank. 'The whole bloody island'll be there.'

'What's the problem,' said Sarah brightly. 'You got nothing to wear?'

Frank had given her a hard time over her airline ticket.

'It's not your fault, Frank,' said Mike. He picked at his teeth with a fingernail. 'You can't take these things personally. If you start taking them seriously you end up doing nothing.'

'Yeah, I know the theory. But I never lost five patients like that before.'

'What did they die of?' asked Joe.

'A parasite. Easy enough to treat if you get to it in time. Only I didn't.'

'Who'll take the service?' he asked.

'B.J.,' said Mike. 'It may be a little unorthodox, but it'll be fine.' He took a drink and put down his glass. 'God, what a mess.'

For a minute no one spoke. Joe felt a foot on his ankle. He reached down, rested his hand on it, and looked across the table. Sarah was staring straight at him, chewing a slice of pie.

'How's the new clinic coming on,' he asked Frank vacuously.

'Jiuba? Fine. Or it will be. We're still recruiting staff, there are a couple of Aid workers coming down from the States next week but we still need paramedics. The health thing's a lot worse over there than it is here, malaria mostly.'

'I'd like to see it some time,' said Joe, watching Frank's face.

Frank said nothing.

'Sure,' said Mike. 'Time I went down again too. Next week, maybe. You taking malaria tablets, by the way?'

Joe shook his head.

'Frank'll fix you up in the morning. You ought to have typhoid and the other jabs while you're at it.'

The general atmosphere of depression was getting to Joe. No one ate much, no one had much to say. He badly wanted to be alone with Sarah, do what Willie had done, rent a cabin out at B.J.'s, lie out in the sun, get in some swimming. It was a long time since he'd had a real holiday.

Around ten Frank went off to check the patients. Sarah got up too and collected her bag from the hall.

'Been a long day, jet-lag's getting to me.'

'How are you getting home?' asked Mike.

Joe wondered what to do. He hadn't planned anything. He looked at her, but she wasn't going to help.

'Reckon I'll walk back. Exercise'll do me good.'

'You're welcome to stay over.'

'Thanks but no thanks,' she smiled.

Joe was on his feet, but too late.

'Be seeing you,' said Sarah, and she was gone.

After they'd washed up Mike suggested a walk by the shore. The moon was up, the black hills silhouetted against a sky pricked by a thousand stars. Land crabs scuttled underfoot as they made their way through the trees down to the beach. It was a setting that encouraged intimacy.

'Could the deaths have been prevented?' asked Joe.

'I don't know, I'm not a doctor. I don't think so. It wasn't his fault he was away when it happened. Very few of the towns and villages in this country have doctors, things like this happen all the time, no one's surprised. They expect better from us, that's all.'

Mike's voice was weary, shoulders hunched, hands deep in the pockets of his jeans. Joe was tired too.

'Will there be trouble?'

'I doubt it. It's just a cumulative thing – Willie, Vaz, now this. And Bobby Burgess, I wish to hell I knew why Bobby cleared out.'

'Do you think he's the full shilling?' asked Joe.

'Who, Bobby? No, of course not. I'd worry less if he was. What the hell could he and Willie have been up to?'

'They didn't have to be up to anything, or not together. Willie didn't have to be in love with the guy, he might just have been asking questions.'

'Maybe,' said Mike doubtfully.

He bent down, took off his plimsoles and rolled his trousers up to the knee. Joe did the same, and they walked together along the edge of the beach, feet in the blood-warm water, listening to the waves wash over the reef.

They reached a point where a line of rocks jutted out beyond the beach into the lagoon.

'You fancy a swim?' Mike asked suddenly.

They stripped naked and waded out into the sea, hands dangling, eyes watching the streaks of phosphorescence on the ripples. Joe waited until the water was up to his waist then toppled slowly forward and swam for twenty yards towards the reef. Mike followed in a lazy crawl, overtook him, then turned on to his back and floated, his face just visible in the moonlight, blue as a corpse.

They used to swim together like this at Glenalmond twenty years ago, on June days, in deep black pools in burns that tumbled down rowan-clad canyons in the Perthshire hills, both of them hot and sweating from the climb and glad of the icy brown peat water.

'You ever get sharks in here?' Joe asked a little nervously.

'Not inside the reef. There's an old hammerhead cruises further out sometimes. In the lagoon you only have to worry about the odd barracuda. He'd take a bite out of you but he wouldn't kill you.'

'How about sting rays?'

'Yup, we get them. Sting rays, electric rays, Moray eels, scorpionfish, Portuguese men-of-war, bristle-worms, long-spined sea urchins. Float or swim, just don't put your feet down unless you can see where you're putting them.'

Joe's nerve was going.

'I can't bloody float.'

Mike laughed.

'Then swim in a circle.'

Back on land they dried themselves on their T-shirts and walked briskly on towards the headland to get warm again. This was where they'd caught David Vaz, Joe suddenly remembered. Poor fucking David.

Mike sat down on a rock and took out a pack of Marlboro.

'This is the first place I've ever lived where I felt part of the landscape. Cities are different, you don't really notice the details in cities, but I've walked down this beach more or less every day for four years now.' He passed Joe a cigarette. 'You get to understand the rhythms, the tides and currents, what lives where and why, patterns of migration, all the little ecosystems. It's terribly liberating to realize your mortality is so insignificant, so mundane. You realize there's nowhere to arrive at – this is it, here and now.'

'Do you ever get lonely here?'

'I feel very alone sometimes. I'm not sure if that's the same thing. You never need to feel socially lonely, it's a very sociable society. The same applies to sex, sex is a casual business, a way of being affectionate but without all the emotional shit we lay on it in England. Two people feel like going to bed together, then they go to bed. Half the time I can't work out which children belong to who. The key to parenthood isn't who conceived you but who raised you. There's justice in that: conception takes seconds, child rearing goes on for bloody years.'

Joe lit a cigarette.

'I was thinking this evening how strange it would be if Sarah had got pregnant by Willie.'

'Maybe she is. She's quite capable of it. You need to be careful with that girl, Joe. She's a charming and resourceful woman and she's looking for ways to get on in life. I don't blame her, but if I was you I'd be wary.'

He could have said it in a way that was no more than advice from a friend, but something in his tone grated on Joe.

'I'm over twenty-one, Mike.'

'So is she.'

'What does that mean?'

'It means she plays games. She tried it on Willie and now that he's offside I suspect she may be about to try it on you.'

Joe didn't want to talk about himself and Sarah because he didn't know what there was to talk about. A night and a day in a strange city, that was all. So far. But he felt defensive about her. And about Willie, too.

'Try what on?'

'Grab you by the cock and lead you where she wants to go.'

'Jesus,' said Joe. 'I don't believe this. What the hell have you got against her?'

Mike's voice was getting louder.

'She's a fucking fantasist, Joe. She doesn't know what's real and what isn't.'

Joe got up.

'This is personal, isn't it. What happened, she kick you out of bed or something?'

'As a matter of fact I've never had the pleasure. Which probably makes me unique on this island.'

Joe couldn't believe what was happening. Couldn't believe it, couldn't stop it. He rarely lost his temper, but when he did he was a man possessed, he and Willie both.

'So what's she done to you? Pissed on your bloody halo?'

Mike was standing too now, the two men a yard apart.

'First, I don't pretend to have a fucking halo. Second, I don't give a shit who does or doesn't bed her. But I've got better things to do with my time here than sort out Sarah's bloody wreckage.'

'You seem to have plenty of time for Frank Carreras' wreckage.'

'What the hell's Frank got to do with it?'

'He's been struck off,' Joe said quietly.

Mike hesitated. Joe wanted to see his face, but it was lost in the darkness.

'What do you mean, struck off?'

'He's not on the US medical register. I checked in Sinclair's office at the American Hospital, there was a raft of registers on the shelf. He was in three years ago, he's not in it now.'

There was another silence.

'I know,' Mike said eventually.

'Why the hell didn't you tell me?'

'It didn't seem relevant. It happened a couple of years ago, he was involved in a row with a colleague in Thailand, the thing got personal and the other guy reported him for sleeping with one of the patients.'

'Of course it's bloody relevant,' said Joe. 'Everything's relevant.'

'You sound like a sodding lawyer.'

'Jesus,' said Joe. 'What the hell else have you been keeping back from me?'

He got up and stood looking out to sea, his back to Mike, watching the fishing boats. Mike stayed where he was, pulling hard on his cigarette.

'This isn't a fucking Missing Persons agency, in case you hadn't noticed. I'm trying to run a project. It's not bloody perfect and we may have made mistakes, but we've achieved a lot. I've got a second project due to start up which will do the same on a much larger scale to communities which routinely endure illness and death on a scale which most Westerners find literally unimaginable. And we do it on no resources, in the face of considerable hostility and suspicion from the authorities.'

He threw his cigarette butt on the sand and screwed it under his heel.

'Frank Carreras is a good doctor, on the register or off it. You get a lot of young interns coming out to places like this, they look on it as a sort of holiday, six months somewhere exotic, then they go home and get on with the medical rat-race. There's a sort of machismo about working in the Third World, provided you don't do it for too long. But Frank's in for the long haul. Sometimes you get the motivation, sometimes you get the skills, it's rare to get the two together.'

'If Frank fucked someone he shouldn't have,' he went on, 'that's between him and his maker, as far as I'm concerned. He's a good doctor, you've seen him at work. Anyway, you're a right one to bring up sexual ethics – you come on all noble about helping your poor old geriatric father, but it didn't take you long to get your hand inside his girlfriend's jeans once the opportunity came up.'

Across the bay in Morgan's Hole two trawlers were moving out through the gap in the reef towards the open sea. Floodlights illuminated the decks, and miniature figures moved among the nets, preparing for the night's fishing.

For a moment Joe thought he was going to hit Mike, felt his muscles tighten, a blinding wall of white rage enveloping his brain. At the last instant he held back and walked away down the beach, away from St Andrews, moving fast, not knowing where he was going. After fifty yards he looked back, but Mike was lost in the darkness.

The trawlers were far out to sea now, their lights playing on the waters. He followed the shoreline, shoulders hunched, still alive with anger. He didn't give a shit about Frank Carreras' Thai philandering. Maybe Frank was a charlatan, maybe he wasn't; maybe Frank had a role in what was happening, maybe he was just a superannuated hippy with a healthy disrespect for establishment values. What he minded was Mike.

He remembered a rhetorical question from one of Graham Greene's novels, he couldn't remember which: why is it only our friends whom we betray? It was a small thing, a fact which Mike had chosen to keep to himself, at worst a sin of omission. But there had never been any sins of omission between him and Mike.

That was the thing about Mike: he was entirely direct in everything he did. He didn't lie, he didn't scheme, he didn't play games. People like that are rare, and according to conventional wisdom wither on the vine at an early age. The fact that Mike played straight and yet flourished had always been a wonderful thing to Joe, living proof that honesty and integrity were practical skills. Not just admirable: practical. And if that was true there was hope for all of us. If it wasn't then there was no hope at all.

Why? He kept asking himself – why would Mike lie about Frank? Why would he lecture him about Sarah? Mike, of all people?

He'd been walking for almost an hour before it occurred to him to wonder where he was going. It was past midnight. The lights of St Andrews had long since vanished to the east: ahead the landscape was lost in darkness. He tried to cut inland and find the main road, but the undergrowth running down to the beach was by now impenetrable, and after a brief incursion he returned to the shoreline and resumed his original path.

The same path, he realized, that Willie would have taken every day from St Andrews to Reef's End. Rounding a corner he found himself on the edge of B.J. MacIntyre's compound. To his left a long thin jetty projected out into the lagoon, to his right he could see a dim light in B.J.'s curtained window.

Not B.J., he couldn't face B.J. He skirted round the perimeter of the compound until he reached the road. A hundred yards further on he saw a second light coming from Chris Long's veranda and heard the sound of a radio, and admitted to himself for the first time where he was heading.

Sarah was still up, sitting on the edge of the balcony, legs dangling, a cigarette in one hand, a bottle of Seven-Up in the other.

'What kept you?' she asked, tossing the cigarette down into the shadows. And then she saw his face. 'Christ, you look like you just met a shark.'

They sat for over an hour, three feet apart on the narrow wooden balcony, not touching, Joe doing most of the talking. The night was black, fireflies hovering among the bushes. Once in a while fowl shifted in the lean-to.

'What you arguin' about ain't what you think you arguin' about,' said Sarah when Joe had finished. 'Ain't about me, ain't about Frank Carreras. What's happenin' is you each arguin' inside yourselves, cos you guys got this thing where you can't ever think things, through on your own, you have to find someone else to be the other side of whatever it is you unsure about. Never could figure out why.'

'Socrates,' said Joe. 'So what are we really arguing about?'

'Mike looks at you,' said Sarah, 'sees how level you are, remembers the way he used to be, wonders if he ain't goin' a bit over the top on all this stuff down at St Andrews, maybe misses the old life, maybe wonders if he ain't gettin' carried away, cutting the odd corner. Like not checking out Frank Carreras, for example. Plus he gone celibate, don't like to see other people having a good time in the sack. Not you, not me, not the judge.'

'And me?' asked Joe.

'You got things you don't like in yourself. You can't figure what you feelin' about Willie, things you ought to be feelin' but you ain't. Also you look at Mike and what he's doin' and you feel guilty you ain't doin' the same.' She got to her feet. 'Last thing is you ain't used to arguin' and shoutin'. Most folks argue all the time, no big deal. You run a mile to avoid arguin', you get into a fight you think it's the end of the world. Man and woman if they get into a fight they wind up in bed, fuck some sense into each other. Mike ain't about to fuck any sense into you, but I'm willing to try.'

'Because you're mad at me?'

'No clues,' said Sarah.

20

THE FUNERALS BEGAN with a service at the tin-roofed Methodist chapel on the hillside above Reef's End. Shortly before ten Sarah and Joe joined the long procession of mourners climbing the steep concrete steps behind B.J.'s Fried Chicken shack.

Below on the road, where the jeeps and minibuses from Morgan's Hole were lined up in the shade, a toothless old Spaniard, barefoot, with his trousers rolled just beneath the knee, herded three cows and a calf towards the shore, while men in ill-fitting Sunday suits dusted their lapels and women in dark frocks adjusted their hats. The air was sweet with the smell of hibiscus, humming birds hovered at the blooms, a pair of guinea fowl scratched in the dust beneath the trees.

The chapel when they reached it was little more than a hut, with a white tin tower and a single clanging bell, doors and windows open so that once inside you could almost reach out and touch the banana and breadfruit trees. The walls were stone, painted a fading custard wash. Three light bulbs hung from the ceiling, their flexes thick with cobwebs.

Five coffins lay in a line along the length of the aisle. There were ten pews on either side of the aisle, then a low wooden rail hung with far-from-new purple cloth, and then the pulpit, backed by a faded mural of an Edwardian English youth at the tiller of a sailing ship in a storm, watched over by a bearded white Christ. Below, hand-printed on card and drawing-pinned to the wall, were the words 'God Is The Pilot'. On one side of the altar stood a worm-eaten wooden table piled with tracts and hymnals. On the other an old woman with tortoise skin and claw hands, her head wrapped in a blue turban, sat at an ancient piano, its veneer peeling like the bark on a eucalyptus tree.

Half Morgan's Hole and all Reef's End had turned out for the service, the elderly and the bereaved crammed six to a pew, the rest standing at the rear, spilling out into the porch. Mike and Frank had arrived early, and stood with a line of St Andrews workers against a side wall, studying their prayer sheets. Captain Mendes was there too, impassive behind his reflective glasses, and Larry, and Doug The Diver, but not the Swiss poet.

Mike acknowledged Joe with a tight-lipped nod, the kind civil service colleagues offer each other at State Occasions. The two men were thirty feet apart, separated by hats and bare heads and the line of plain pine coffins. Joe managed a formal smile, then looked away. He was embarrassed: embarrassed at what had happened, embarrassed at what was happening now, embarrassed about what might happen afterwards. And he was angry with his own anger, angry at the mess of it all. He looked at the coffins, and the faces of the bereaved, their peasant dignity, their resignation. Death matters, reconciliation matters, the love of those you love matters. The rest doesn't matter a fuck.

The tortoise coughed loudly and launched into 'The Lord's My Shepherd'. Those with seats stood up, and B.J. made his entrance through a side door. The preacher wore an immaculate short-sleeved blue shirt and well-pressed black trousers, and carried his head high, peering through bottle-glass spectacles at the mourners to see who was missing.

The piano was untuned beyond redemption, but the congregation sang as vigorously and with as little restraint as a primary school assembly. Even Sarah, who changed key with every line, gave it her all. Only Mike and Frank, with

Anglo-Saxon restraint, appeared self-conscious, their voices lost in the general cacophony.

B.J. took as his text the story of Noah, in a loose contemporary translation, berating times present. Godless days, he informed them: if the people before the flood had had preachers they would have been saved. Yet we have so many preachers and still are not saved. The world could end tomorrow, Nicaraguans and communists and unbelievers come and destroy the island. And yet in death there was hope for those who knew God.

He then illustrated the fate of the ungodly trying to get into the ark, turning his back to the congregation and scratching at the wall with outstretched hands, like an animal trying to escape from a well.

They carried the coffins back down the hill, six men to a coffin to take the weight down the steep steps; placed them on the backs of three pick-up trucks draped in crêpe and purple ribbons, and formed up in a loose cortège for the journey to the cemetery.

Four elderly musicians in black top hats led the way: two trumpeters, a tuba, a saxophonist, their instruments tarnished, the last survivors of some long-ago missionary band, quivering through the harmonies of 'The Fight Is O'er, the Battle Won'. Behind them the women had put up black umbrellas to shade themselves from the sun. In the distance, through the gently rustling palms, the silver waters of the lagoon shimmered in the heat. A solitary pelican flew low over the water and landed on the jetty.

Joe and Sarah stood under the trees watching, waiting to take their places in the procession. Joe knew people were looking at them, sensed the disapproving eyes of the married women under the shaded protection of their hats, saw the raised eyebrows of their husbands.

'You feel shy being seen with me?' asked Sarah under her breath. She was looking almost demure in a long black cotton skirt and a cream blouse, her straw hat pulled low over her forehead.

'Of course I'm fucking shy.'

'So was Willie.'

'Thanks a million.'

He'd have moved away except that she had her hand hooked over his arm, the way women do. It struck Joe that you never saw a man with his hand hooked over a woman's arm. It also struck him that there just might be someone watching who might let Willie know.

He'd also decided that this was something between him and Sarah and Willie and no one else's business, nothing to do with any of the other present shit that was going on. If it ever came to a decision it would be up to Sarah to do the deciding. One thing that the past week had proved to him was that his father was a man in full control of his faculties, well able to fight his own corner.

It had even occurred to him to go home and leave him to it. What stopped him as much as anything else was curiosity: curiosity at the spectacle of Willie dusting off his old skills and instincts, revisiting the ghosts of his youth.

Sarah mystified him. He'd never met a woman like her before. Her chronic unpredictability excited him, but it also scared him: scared him because almost everything she did challenged convention and common sense.

Sarah had no common sense at all. Which wasn't to say she had no sense: most of what she said and did contained its own logic. But it was a different, uncommon logic, based on premises that were strange and at times shocking. She had no inhibitions, she cheerfully helped herself to other people's possessions and emotions, and she didn't give a shit about what people thought. And yet she did it all with a smile, that teasing defiant cap-toothed smile that dared the world to take offence, knowing that it wouldn't.

The only other person he knew who utterly disregarded the opinions – and feelings – of others was Willie. But there was a fundamental difference between Willie and Sarah: Sarah knew how to have fun.

It was Mike who made the first move. On the walk to the

cemetery they were separated by the long procession of mourners, and it was only when they were among the tombstones, watching the pall bearers lowering the five coffins into their shallow graves in the sandy soil, that Joe felt a hand on his shoulder. He turned his head. Mike was standing a pace behind him. As the two men looked at each other the tension between them was almost unbearable. They said nothing, but Joe sensed that things would be all right. Different, but all right. He was also shocked by how tired Mike looked, at the grey stains under his eyes.

After the ceremony ended they lost each other in the crowds. The next time Joe saw him Mike was further down the slope, talking to Captain Mendes. They stood a little off the path, and as Joe watched a woman separated from the tide of mourners flowing past them towards the road and spat deliberately on the ground at Mike's feet. Mendes turned to say something, but Mike held him back.

'You two goin' to make up now, or do we have to wait all day?' asked Sarah.

'We already did,' said Joe. 'Who's the crone?'

'Woman that spat at him? Name's Gloria, she do that all the time. Kind of woman got her knitting out when they hanged the King of Spain.'

'France,' he corrected her. 'And he wasn't hanged, he was guillotined.'

'Maybe we talking about different kings,' said Sarah. 'You reckon B.J.'s goin' to open up the Chicken shack? I'm starving. Maybe talk to the man about renting his chalet at the same time.'

'I've already got a place to stay,' Joe objected.

'You do but I don't. Nothin' but single beds at the Rectory.'

'I have to talk to Mike.'

Up to that moment it hadn't occurred to Joe to move out of the Rectory permanently, but now that it did he found the idea tempting. The reason he hesitated was Frank. He wanted to know more about the American, and Reef's End didn't seem the place to find it out.

'Tell me what you want to know,' Sarah offered. 'I'll find it out for you.'

'Not yet,' said Joe. 'Not yet.'

Mike was waiting by the Toyota when they reached the road. Frank was inside at the wheel, engine running.

'Joe wants to ask you for lunch,' said Sarah, 'only he shy to ask.'

Mike smiled.

'Sure.'

B.J. still had his blue preacher's shirt on under his apron. Business was good, and a dozen diners sat at open-air wooden tables beside the shack while the big black man scurried up and down the steps to his kitchen, hands full of plates, lecturing his customers on hell-fire and the shortcomings of Mexican mayonnaise.

The warm wind rained mangos on to the sandy soil. Everything ate the mangos: pigs, hens, blackbirds, crabs, even the dogs, rib-thin and bare-toothed, cruising like sharks among the trees.

Mike looked like death, but he was doing his best, taking care to talk to the other customers, a smile here, a handshake there. He'd always been good with people, remembering their children's names, and to ask about relatives overseas. Sometimes he was treated coolly, but mostly people were kind to him and seemed to bear him no ill-will.

They sat on wooden benches at a table some distance from the hut and ate fried chicken and plantain and tinned sweet corn washed down with ice-cool Cola.

'Bobby Burgess', Mike announced, 'cleared out because he was threatened.'

Joe looked up.

'Who by?'

'Someone who knew his business. Bobby has a kid at school in the States, horrid little bugger with red hair and bad skin, name of Ezekiel, would you believe, Zeek for short. Comes down here on his vacations. Ask Sarah about him, she rubbed toothpaste on him one time and told him it was sun cream, the poor brat burned like a burger, he was in bed for a week.'

Sarah giggled.

'I know about Zeek,' said Joe. 'Bunty told me at Vaz's funeral. She said it was the worst thing about being a missionary's wife, you had to leave the children behind. I said she was in good company, I seemed to remember that Jesus told the disciples to abandon their kith and kin, all this shit about The Family got written in afterwards when the church got into social engineering. She wasn't amused. So tell us about Bobby.'

'Two nights ago someone rang his door bell. When he answered it there was an envelope on the mat, with a note inside telling him his beloved Zeek was in danger unless he got off the island. Whoever it was knew the address of the kid's school.'

'This is according to who?' asked Sarah.

'Mendes. He thinks it may have been a joke, someone took a dislike to Bobby and slipped him the note to see what would happen. Only Bobby took it seriously.'

'Did he have any suggestions as to who that might be?'

'Not really. But by the way he watched my face while he was telling me I think he has his suspicions.'

Mike gave them a half-smile.

'Did you do it?' asked Joe.

'Good God no. I told Mendes that Bobby probably set it up himself, same way he burned down his own church in La Entrada. His kind need to be persecuted, if they can't find someone to persecute them they have to do it to themselves.'

It wasn't until Sarah went over to talk to friends and Mike and Joe were left alone that they raised the subject of the previous evening.

'I'm sorry,' Mike said quietly. 'I have no excuses. I'm just sorry.'

'Me too,' said Joe.

'It's daft, really. I spent half the night trying to work out why I didn't tell you about Frank, and I still don't know.'

'Let's forget it,' said Joe.

Mike leaned forward to take a sip of Cola, but his eyes stayed on Joe.

'I haven't told you everything yet. You remember at Copán, at the air strip, I said I'd seen Bobby Burgess. It wasn't Bobby, it was Frank.'

Joe just sat there, cutlery in hand, looking back at Mike. He didn't know what to say.

'I'm sorry about that too,' said Mike. 'We need to talk, Joe. You moving back to the Rectory tonight?'

Joe lifted a plantain on his fork and put it in his mouth.

'Sarah wants me to move out here, rent a chalet off B.J.'

'Same thing she suggested to Willie,' said Mike, without a hint of malice.

'The thing about history repeating itself,' Joe joked back, 'is you only need one story, you don't have to keep learning new plots.'

A kid in his early twenties drove slowly along the beach on a second-hand Kawasaki, a girl of seventeen in a swimsuit laughing on the pillion, turned once he was sure everyone had had a chance to see, and drove back towards Morgan's Hole.

'Maybe it's not such a dumb idea,' said Mike. 'If Willie got to hear about it he'd get back in touch soon enough.'

'That's what Sarah reckoned. Only I'm not sure I'm looking for Willie any more. What I'm looking for now is whatever or whoever he went after in the first place.'

'Isn't that the same thing?'

'Possibly,' said Joe. 'Are you going to tell me why you lied about Bobby and Copán?'

'I guess I was protecting him.'

'What was he doing there?'

Sarah was coming back through the tables carrying three bottles of beer by the neck.

'I asked him. He said he needed that drugs consignment

in a hurry so he flew up and collected it in person.'

'Which drugs consignment?'

'The stuff Willie went to see Rikki Dack about. The customs at San Pedro Sula wouldn't let it in, they diverted it through Guatemala.'

'Do you know what was in it?'

'I know what it says on the boxes. Antibiotics, mostly, seemed fairly routine to me. But I'm not a doctor, Joe, I rely on Frank for all that stuff.'

Sarah sat down with her legs astride the bench.

'You two still friends?' she asked, helping herself to a cigarette.

'Afraid so,' said Joe.

Mike left at three. There was no problem renting the chalet: fifty dollars' deposit, fifteen a day for rent, fresh laundry twice a week, go easy on the water, generator goes off at ten.

'Send the bill to Mike,' said Sarah. 'Same as last time.'

B.J. wiped his hands on his apron.

'Last time was double occupancy, cost a little more.'

'I told you, same deal as before.'

B.J. looked doubtful.

'That mean you want the same chalet?'

'Perhaps not,' said Joe, feeling very English.

The preacher collected a key and an armful of linen and led them across the compound and through the trees to a faded green wooden cabin with a rust red roof. An old rope hammock hung on the veranda beside a cane armchair.

B.J. stripped the bed and Joe helped him with the sheets. Sarah tried the tap on the sink, then ran her finger along the wooden shelf on the wall and inspected it for dust.

'Get it cleaned up soon as we can,' said the preacher a little testily. He took out a handkerchief and wiped a windowsill. 'No use dusting places when they got no one in them.'

'A little decoration wouldn't go amiss neither,' said Sarah. 'Fresh curtains, there's some French cottons I saw up in Tegoose, go nicely in here if you got the rugs to match. And lampshades, lampshades all the rage these days.'

B.J. put the handkerchief back in his pocket.

'You the kind of woman if God made the world in seven days you'd take a look and say, I'm not sure about the blue.' He handed Joe the key. 'You want to eat tonight, let me know.'

'Not tonight,' said Joe. 'I've got a date in town.'

21

At seven Joe hitched a lift into Morgan's Hole, and by half past was sitting alone at the bar of The Gable hotel drinking beer and thinking of England, of Kilburn pubs and Camden Town kebab houses, of Tesco's and TV and the Rottweilers tearing up the muddy turf of Queen's Park, of ordinary life. Ordinary life was what he liked best, more of the same, getting drunk and playing music and abusing Eddie Scargill. What the hell would Sarah make of all that?

She'd like it fine, he decided, once she'd got over the shock of not living in Belgravia and shopping in Bond Street. Take her a little while to get used to, but she'd settle for it. Until something else came along.

There was no sign of Mike. The only other customer in The Gable was a gloomy white man in his fifties, ruggedly dressed in a safari jacket and desert boots, seated at the far end of the bar under a stuffed shark, smoking untipped cigarettes and reading a dog-eared paperback. From his bearing Joe guessed he'd been a soldier once.

He had. He was Belgian, and his name was Jean-Louis Cocteau. He bought Joe a drink, and moved his stool along the counter, and sat looking straight in front of him at the bottles behind the bar, talking in short enigmatic sentences which Joe suspected were designed to make a messy life sound more eventful than it had been. Joe wasn't in the mood for this kind of conversation but he had nothing else to do, and until Mike arrived he had nowhere else to go.

Jean-Louis had fought in the Congo, whether as conscript

or mercenary wasn't clear. When that ended he stayed on in Africa, drifting from country to country, running small hotels and cafés, running foul of revolutions and getting into trouble with corrupt regimes. He hadn't been home to Belgium in thirty years.

'What brings you here?' asked Joe.

The Belgian held his cigarette away from his mouth.

'Money, politics. Africa is finished now. The time came to move on. I have an interest in a hotel project along the coast, for divers. It has possibilities, but I don't know if anything will come of it. What the hell, the whole world's going to change soon,' he added. 'The storm will come. Europe should stand firm, but it won't.'

Joe asked if he himself would run before the storm, or stand and meet it. It was a while before the Belgian answered.

'Face it and walk away backwards,' he said eventually. He poured more beer into his glass. 'You're the judge's son, aren't you?'

'You know him?' asked Joe.

'Everyone knows everyone here. Particularly the whites. But yes, I know your father. Drunk with him, cracked jokes with him, argued with him.'

'Argued about what?'

'Politics, religion, women – the usual. He's a bit crazy, but then you know that.'

'What kind of crazy?'

'The kind of crazy that thinks humanity should be perfect. Which is crazy because no one is. Not me, not you, not Bobby Burgess, not Frank Carreras.'

Joe took a sip of beer and put down his glass.

'What did he say about Frank?'

'That he takes too much dope, which is true. That he talks too loud, which is also true. That he doesn't listen to what other people say. And that he leads Mike Osborne astray sometimes. Like a bulldozer.'

'Does he?'

'I've no idea, it's not my business. I'm just telling you

what your father said. He's a man of strong opinions. Are you like him?'

Joe lit a cigarette and inhaled.

'We're all like our parents, aren't we? Whether we like it or not. Either like them, or exactly the opposite, their footprint in the sand.'

'Which are you?'

'The footprint, I suppose.'

'Are you close to him?'

'In a way. I don't think I knew him very well, but yes, I suppose we're close.'

'You know where he's gone?' asked Jean-Louis.

'No.'

'Think of a possibility. If you can come up with a theory that satisfies you, keep it. It may be the truth, it may not be: the important thing is whether you can live with it.' He finished his drink. 'And be careful.'

It was then that Joe noticed the packet of Senior Service on the bar.

'Can I ask you a question?'

'Sure.'

'Where do you get your cigarettes?'

'In Tela, there's a man imports them from England.' He smiled. 'A doctor.'

Before he had time to say the name, Joe knew which doctor. Amos Lipstein. The man who first brought Mike Osborne to Cow Cay.

Jean Louis looked at his watch and stood up.

'I must be going. But remember what I said: find an explanation that suits you and go home. You'll be doing yourself a favour.'

Mike walked in five minutes later.

'I'd forgotten you knew Amos,' he said as they settled into a table far from the door. The place was still empty but neither of them wanted company if it showed up. 'I'd forgotten but I remember now. That must have been before he moved back over to the coast. His eyes are fucked, poor bastard.'

Joe could still see the little Jewish doctor, with his Shakespeare beard and balding dome: sad-eyed hypochondriac little Amos who'd come to dinner one evening the last time Joe was here, forked over his plate of food as though checking a scalp for head lice, eaten nothing and talked passionately about international conspiracies and frailties of the human body. Amos was the man who told Joe that the tapeworm has no anus and no brain, and that rabbit fleas synchronize their breeding so that their young are born at the same time as the rabbit's, hop straight on. Joe tended to remember such things.

Lipstein's eyes had been bad even then, but there'd been nothing wrong with his brain.

'You're right,' said Mike. 'Amos smoked Senior Service, same as Willie. For what it's worth.'

'You know those nights when you realize there are no fags in the house? Normally happens around two in the morning, you'd drive fifty miles to get some. Even if you don't want one at that moment, the panic of being without when you do destroys your reason. Did Willie know Amos?'

'Sure. They argued. Not about anything in particular. I think it was jealousy, they were both used to wearing the crown of Wise Old Buzzard and resented the competition.' Mike took off his denim jacket and draped it over a chair. 'You're not suggesting Willie fucked off because he'd run out of fags?'

'It was just a thought. Is Amos on the phone?'

'Not any more. He says if people can phone you they never come to see you,' said Mike. 'He gets lonely. Have you forgiven me for last night yet?'

'There's nothing to forgive. I behaved like a fourteen-year-old.'

'No you didn't, you had every right, and I've got a lot of explaining to do. I'll start at the beginning. Yes, I knew about Frank. He's barred from practising in the United States, but he's not barred from practising in Honduras, provided he doesn't advertise himself as a doctor. I don't give a shit about his sex life, and nor do his patients here.'

'You knew when you hired him?'

'I didn't ask. I've done business with Third Aid before, I trust them. I also need them. I have no money of my own, Joe. It all has to come from somewhere. And there are always snags, wherever the money comes from. Always, always, always.' He tapped the table for emphasis. 'Governments, aid agencies, churches, private philanthropists, they all have their own methods and motives. You shop around and find the one that causes you the least pain. Third Aid suits us.'

'Because?'

'Because they're straight about their motives. Unashamedly so. They're in the guilt business. The money comes from drug companies. Drug companies get a terrible press, they're seen as pariahs, cashing in on other people's misfortunes. That's not how they see themselves, but they know it's how they're perceived. Most of the do-good aid agencies won't touch them with a barge pole. I can't see what difference it makes where the money comes from, what matters is what you do with it.'

'That doesn't explain why they send you defrocked doctors.'

'They gave me Frank because they think he's good, which he is. They knew about the business in Thailand, but they thought he deserved a second chance. He's worked for them for years. He's also a malaria expert, which is what we need for Jiuba. And he speaks good Spanish. Third Aid are funding Jiuba, they thought Frank was the man to run it, but they were honest with me about his past.'

He signalled to the bar for more drinks.

'So how come you didn't tell me all this before?' asked Joe.

'Because I'm paranoid about it. If word got out that I'm using drug company money it could cause all sorts of problems. And because I didn't think it had anything to do with Willie. I thought if Willie was after anyone he was after Bobby. I still think he may be. Also the Jiuba thing is at a crucial stage. We need government permits and we need local good will. If I lost Frank now the whole thing could go away. These things are fragile, it only takes a puff of wind to blow them away. I've spent three years getting it this far.' He ran his hand back over his brow. 'It's become something of an obsession, Joe. It has to be if it's going to happen. And obsessives get paranoid, they trust no one. It scares me sometimes. It scared me last night.'

'All because someone screwed a patient in Thailand?'

'All because someone screwed a patient in Thailand. And because that same someone was sitting in the cockpit of a Cessna in Copán when they should have been supervising peons putting in drainage ditches in Jiuba. It wasn't a premeditated lie, it was a reflex. And once I'd done it I couldn't undo it – I literally didn't know how. I said it before, Joe: this thing has taken over my life.' He paused, and drained his whisky. 'I'm in a mess, Joe. I need help.'

Public schoolboys don't ask for help, it's the ultimate treason. You ask someone to help you put up a greenhouse, or organize a shoot or a charity function, you discuss a business project or moan about your marriage. But if you have a personal problem, it's up to you to solve it.

Asking for help was admitting defeat: people who asked for help became beholden, social invalids, twisted wheels, objects of pity. In that class a cry for help represented a Rubicon beyond which lay perpetual failure. You'd get the help but the respect would be gone for ever. Joe was the same: he'd never asked anyone for help in his life, nor Willie before him.

The barman brought more drinks.

'Keep talking,' said Joe, 'and I'll see what I can do'.

'Do you remember a woman called Virginia?'

'You told me she died.'

'Malaria,' said Mike. 'That was the start of it.'

Virginia was an inheritance from the Anglicans, for whom she had acted as housekeeper. Everyone loved Virginia. She looked like a turtle, short and round, with a head that seemed to project straight out of her chest and a laugh that broke crockery. She came from Jamaica, where a curate's wife had found her in an orphanage. For fifteen years she had kept house for the curate and his family. The curate became a vicar, and was appointed to St Andrews. Virginia moved with him. By the time St Andrews closed she was well past retirement age, somewhere in her late sixties.

Mike met her the day he moved in to the Rectory. She came dressed in her church best, carrying an armful of flowers that would have graced a royal funeral. She never left. She didn't want money, though he agreed to pay her. He didn't want a housekeeper, either, but Virginia said that didn't matter, lots of people thought they didn't need housekeepers until they got one. She kept the house spotless, tended the garden, washed and ironed, helped with the cooking. But the real reason he kept her was her laughter, and her sense of joy. Whatever problem you had it was unlikely to survive Virginia.

Like everyone else working at St Andrews, she'd taken precautions against malaria. Had she been at St Andrews when she was infected, there would not have been a problem. But she'd gone to stay with friends on the mainland. The friends were old and living alone in a remote area of the coastal plain: Virginia called it a holiday, but in fact she'd gone to nurse. The nearest town was sixty miles away, almost a day's journey on bad roads if anyone had been able to go for help. Her deterioration was rapid, and by the time her host and hostess realized what was up it was too late.

Mike didn't know a lot about malaria at that time, but he soon learned. The disease is carried by a minute animal parasite which breeds in the stomach of a single genus of mosquito, *Anopheles*. After a period of roughly ten days the parasite's young hatch out, and from that point on, the mosquito itself becomes the carrier. Once a victim has been bitten, the parasites travel through the bloodstream to the vital organs, in particular the liver. There they lie dormant, often for a fortnight or more, before returning to the bloodstream and attacking the red blood cells. At this point they also multiply at a rapid rate. Each time the parasites breed, the victim suffers fever, headaches and violent shivering. Sometimes these attacks recur daily, sometimes every three or four days. By now the red blood cells are much depleted, leading to anaemia and a wide range of other symptoms.

The parasite that attacked Virginia is known in the trade as *Plasmodium falciparum*, which causes malignant tertian fever. It's most common in Africa, but is now spreading into the American tropics and parts of Asia. Secondary symptoms include dysentery and cerebral malaria and a wide range of other acute problems due to congestion of the organs by huge quantities of damaged blood cells.

There are two ways in which health authorities cope with the disease. Ideally you attack the breeding grounds of the mosquito with insecticides, but the scale of the task is Herculean. How do you begin to spray an area the size of south-east Asia, or Africa, or Latin America? And even where it's been tried the mosquitos have become resistant.

'The alternative is to treat the victim with drugs,' Mike explained. 'Only the drugs aren't effective any more either, because the parasites have become resistant to them too. The health industry has more or less given up. Three hundred million people a year are infected, and at least a million and a half of them die. Malaria is the world's number one killer. And it's out of control.'

'But you reckon you can beat it?'

'Of course not. But I can keep fighting it. Someone has to. The US Army used to have a major programme, but they're cutting back. Most of the pharmaceutical companies can't see the point of developing new drugs if they're going to be out of date inside a year or eighteen months. And most of the people who die are poor and black, there's more money in cosmetic surgery or cold cures.'

'Let me get this straight,' said Joe. 'You and Frank and a few friends are going to succeed in tackling a problem which the combined forces of the US Government and the world pharmaceutical industry have failed to crack.'

Mike shook his head violently.

'No no no. You're missing the point. It isn't a question of

either/or, cure it or give up. It's a question of alleviation. Cure when you can, minimize the suffering when you can't. No glamour, no revolutionary solutions, just try and do your best to help the poor fuckers.'

'And this is because of Virginia.'

'Virginia was the start of it, but once you get an idea like that in your head it sticks there, it seems so obvious.'

'So what's the problem?'

'The problem is that no one else sees it that way, or precious few. And the more obstruction I come up against, the more obsessed I get. I hadn't realized how deep I was in until Willie went missing, the way I reacted. Of course I was worried about him, worried sick. But I wasn't going to let it screw up the main thing. I didn't even think it through, the response was automatic.'

'You still haven't told me what you want me to do.'

'Watch my balance, Joe. Tell me when I go too far, the way you did last night. A lot of the time I feel out of control, I scare myself. A couple of months ago I nearly punched a guy in Tegoose, some poor sodding bureaucrat in a cheap suit who wanted me to put down a bond on stuff we were bringing in from the States. When I saw Frank in Copán I panicked. The same thing happened last night. Madness, both times. I realized I didn't trust *anyone* any more, not even you. Madness.'

They were drinking hard, whisky with beer chasers, and the effects were beginning to show. Joe could hear it in Mike's speech, the way he was speeding, drumming his fingers on the edge of the table. Partly nerves, and maybe he'd dropped something before he came out, but mostly it was drink. Joe wasn't in much better shape himself, and had to steady himself on the back of the chair when he got up to go for a leak.

Shortly after he got back the power failed, and they sat on by candlelight while the barman went looking for paraffin for the oil lamps. The drink had washed away any lingering tension between the two men. Not just the drink: it was as if Mike's *mea culpa* had forged a new bond between them. But it didn't stop him continuing to apologize.

'I'm a rat, Joe.' He put down his glass. 'A self-pitying egocentric rat.'

'For fuck's sake,' Joe said. 'Stop.'

'I can't.' Then he managed a wry smile. 'Okay, I'll try. So you met Jean-Louis.'

'I'm afraid so.'

'Arsehole,' said Mike. 'But harmless.'

'He thinks the end of the world is nigh.'

'So do a lot of people round here. Great ones for omens and portents. It doesn't rain for a couple of months they think Armageddon's round the corner. If it rains too hard they think the same. You should hear Omangatu on the subject. You been introduced yet?'

'After a fashion.'

'She has a serious body odour problem. Willie used to call her The Skunk, when he was talking to her you could see him shuffling round to get up-wind.'

There was something Joe knew he'd meant to ask Mike, but he couldn't remember.

'Did she disapprove of Willie and Sarah?'

'I haven't a clue. Probably, she's a great disapprover. But they seemed to get on okay, in a grunting sort of way.'

Joe remembered.

'Dr Sinclair didn't phone, did he? The guy from the American Hospital? I left your number with his office.'

Mike shook his head.

'But don't worry, I'll tell you if he does.' He smiled. 'I promise.'

Joe picked up the packet of Marlboro off the table. It was empty.

'So what do we do next?' he asked.

'I don't know. Nothing, I expect. I have to go to Jiuba for a couple of days. I suggest you hunker down at B.J.'s, get some sun in, explore the reef, keep an eye on Frank, wait for something to happen.' He got to his feet, swaying. 'I'll give you a lift home.'

'Are you sure you're okay to drive?'

'Fine,' said Mike, and walked straight into the door. Joe asked the barman if he could get them a taxi, and they went out on to the pavement to wait.

Mike sat down on a bollard.

'You know what I think Frank's up to? Looking for Willie. And not for the same reason you and I are looking for him.'

'That thought', said Joe, 'had crossed my mind.'

22

GOING TO BED with Sarah was not a dignified business. She laughed a lot, often at moments of the most delicate intimacy. She laughed if Joe said anything romantic, she laughed if he got carried away, she laughed if something didn't fit where it was meant to. If extraneous thoughts came into her head, she talked about them.

They didn't have to be erotic thoughts: it could be anything that came into her head, a fact, a story, a scandal, something she'd read in a magazine. Most of the stuff came from *Reader's Digest*, Chris Long had a stack of them he kept on a shelf above the fridge next to the fly spray.

Lying beneath or astride him, Joe getting his mind on the business, she'd suddenly say, 'Did you know that in Finland they have a measure of distance called a "dog bark"?', or 'I read there's doctors in China can tell from the pulse if a woman's pregnant, even tell you it's a girl or a boy'. Her fingers between his legs, taking him to heaven, and she'd announce, 'You take the letters from "Schoolmaster" and change them around some they spell "The classroom",' or 'Dr Livingstone only made one Christian convert in his entire life, and he lapsed. I read that some place.'

She had a mole between her breasts that people teased her was a third nipple, sign of the witch. Joe came across it with his tongue the first time they went to bed, thought nothing of it until she drew his attention to it.

'Some day I plan to go to the States,' she'd told him, very

matter of fact. 'Get it seen to, maybe fix up my teeth while I'm at it.'

It wasn't that she didn't enjoy herself while all this was going but if she had something to say she said it there and then, the same way she did things the moment they occurred to her, everything in her life was instant.

What she said tonight when Joe bent over the bed and kissed her was:

'You're drunk.'

'I know,' said Joe. 'But I brushed my teeth.'

'Then get in here before you fall over. I don't mind drunks but I mind lifting them.'

She moved over to make room for him.

'How'd it go with Mike?'

'Fine. I think.'

'You fond of him again?'

'Yup.'

'He have anything interesting to say?'

Joe gave her a précis, making it sound more matter-of-fact than Mike had. While he was talking she sat up, switched on the light, collected a packet of skins off the chair and began rolling a joint.

'You believe all that?'

'Yes, I believe him.'

'You're right, he don't lie a lot. Half his problem. Takes a woman to bed he don't give her no love shit, not unless he mean it. He tells you he likes your mouth, or he want to hear your life story, then it's true, he ain't just making sweet talk to get you to open your legs. Says he has to get up in the morning be some place at such 'n such a time, then it's because he has to be there.'

'You know all this first hand?'

She had her tongue out, licking the edge of the cigarette paper.

'No sir, never had that privilege, nor wanted it. Plenty other girls been on that mattress, though, you get to hear stories. Times I toyed with the notion, but I reckon that boy's too straight for me.' She laughed. 'Never was one for the straightforward types. I ain't knocking the man, don't get me wrong, I just like a man who knows how to lie when he need to. I'm funny that way. Besides, he ain't interested in women nowadays.'

'What's the other half of his problem?' Joe asked.

'Hair's blond, or what's left of it. Never fancied blonds,' said Sarah. 'Particularly the kind got freckles. Aside from that I got nothing against the man.'

The room was full of smells, the damp tumble-drier death-rot smell of the tropics, the sharp acrid smell of the smouldering mosquito coils, the sweeter smell of singeing marijuana, plus human sweat, and some perfume Sarah had on her, and the scent of the fistfuls of flowers she'd put in a jar on the chair by the bed. Sarah had a thing about flowers, she was always picking them, sticking them behind her ear or under a hair-slide, or just holding them in her hand pulling the petals off absentmindedly while she was talking to you.

Joe wasn't used to having flowers around, and he rather liked it. At home his mother used to grow the sorts of plants that reminded him of vicarages – things with green variegated leaves, laurels, bloodless hydrangeas, primeval rhubarbs, funereal lilies, waxy things that thrived in damp and darkness and never seemed alive but never seemed entirely dead either. Marion liked florist's cut flowers, neat and tidy and probably irradiated for longer life and preferably enclosed in a cellophane sheath. Sarah's flowers weren't organized and they weren't meant to last, they were there for the moment, get some more tomorrow if it seems a good idea.

'How about Frank Carreras?' he asked her.

Sarah drew on the joint and passed it across to him.

'You mean did I sleep with him? What you want, an inventory?'

'No, just character analysis.'

'You familiar with the phrase, "shit but beautifully cooked"? That's Frank. And no, he ain't my kind either but he's been around too. First thing people tell you about him, he ain't as gross as he wants you to think he is, all that hippy shit, wants you to believe he drives motorcycles through hotel windows when he's not so busy – all that goes away once you got your hand on his cock and his concentration wanders a little. Or so I'm told. Second thing is, he's generally not so drunk as he wants you to think he is, or as stoned, or as stoked up on chemicals.'

'Who told you all this?'

'You ever meet a friend of mine called Larry? Black kid, hangs out in town, friendly with Rod The Diver. Larry's got a sister went with Frank for a while. And there's others.'

'Have you had time to talk to them about me yet?' asked Joe.

'Nothin' to tell,' said Sarah. 'By which I mean I ain't complaining. Or not yet.'

They were lying close, her head on his chest, passing the joint to and fro between them, their bodies beginning to move a little, a foot here, a finger there.

'Story Larry told me today,' said Sarah, turning her head to lick his nipple, then back again for another smoke. 'Kids in La Ceiba, they into sniffing, glue, solvents, all that stuff, does very weird things to you. Four of them out of their heads, went down the docks, caught a couple of dogs, skinned them, then painted them blue. Ain't that weird? I mean, not the skinning them, but the paint. Another guy got a chainsaw, took the legs off a living donkey, police ask him why, he say he want to be famous, that's all, he want people all over the country to go round saying there's a fella in La Ceiba chainsawed the legs off a donkey. You ever tried sniffing that stuff?'

'No.'

'Me neither. Larry say it makes your head feel like frozen stew, thawing round the edges.'

Her hand was on his stomach now, flat and circling.

'Would you do something for me?' asked Joe.

'Sure.'

'Just don't say anything for the next hour.'

'Anything in particular or anything at all?'

'Anything at all.'

'I'll try,' said Sarah, 'but I can't promise'.

Joe put out the joint and turned off the light.

'One last thing,' he whispered as their bodies met. 'I have to be up to see someone in the morning.'

'Who that?'

'Frank Carreras,' said Joe. 'I have an appointment at nine.'

'Liar,' said Sarah, and stubbed out the joint.

The storm came from the north. One moment the sky was clear, a gentle breeze blowing from the sea, grackles and frigate birds and turkey buzzards circling overhead. Two guinea fowl, squabbling and inseparable like spinsters in an English tea room, pecked at the bare earth around St Andrews, their arguments still audible long after they'd gone from sight. The next moment the sky had turned slate grey, and the air was suddenly very still. Lightning flashed offshore, back-lighting tall distant clouds above a flat and oily ocean.

Then came the wind, hard and horizontal, rattling the windows and howling in the rafters like a crew of trapped sailors. It started to rain, in big warm drops, hammering at the corrugated tin roofs, gurgling down the gutters. The scent of wet dust mingled with the antiseptic smells of the clinic.

Joe sat on a plastic chair with the sleeve of his shirt rolled, waiting for his injection.

'I was in a hurricane up the coast in Belize a couple of years ago,' said Frank, checking the catches on the shutters. 'We heard about it on the radio, people keep their radios on all the time over there to listen out for them. She came in from the west first, passed over and turned round and came back, then she switched to the north, all the palms were blown flat, the water was up eight, twelve feet. All the new houses, didn't matter what they were made of, concrete, steel, timber, flattened clean away. You could see the glass in the windows bend like perspex before they shattered.

The odd thing was the old houses, one or two landed up in the bushes, but most of them survived fine.'

He took a swab of cotton wool and smeared a drop of alcohol on Joe's arm.

'You mind needles?'

'Yes,' said Joe.

Frank slid in the syringe.

'You'd mind typhoid a lot more. Did that hurt?'

'Yes.'

'Good.' He picked up a small plastic box. 'These are for malaria. Keep taking them for a month after you get home.'

'Does that mean I'm now parasite-proof?'

'No, but it ups the odds. Though don't knock parasites, we need 'em. Only organisms on earth that don't need parasites are bacteria, the rest of us would die without 'em. Termites don't actually digest wood: they live off the waste of wood-eating protists that flourish in their hindguts. Cows can't digest cellulose, they leave it to the bugs in their rumen-stomachs. We have millions of the fuckers doing us the same favour. Bacteria, fungi. The only thing that makes an organism unique is the way it combines its parasites.' He pulled the needle free. 'Anything else you need fixing while you're here? A quick appendectomy? Circumcision's on special offer this month.'

'You do hair transplants?'

Frank studied Joe's balding scalp.

'Sure. Any particular colour?'

'Red.'

The sound of the rain on the tin roof was so loud that he had to shout to make himself heard.

'We're out of red, I could do you yellow, purple or orange.'

Frank wore shorts and a loose white calico shirt made out of a Mexican coffee sack with the manufacturer's logo still showing on it, flapping open across his drumlin belly, a string of beads round his neck. Joe had on jeans and a pink Dr Pepper sweatshirt Sarah had given.

'How long's the storm going to last?' he asked.

Frank went over to the door and looked out. The rain was like a waterfall, violent and opaque, the trees bent almost horizontal by the gale.

'Doesn't look too bad, give it an hour or so and it'll blow itself over. You want a coffee?'

Joe nursed his arm.

'Why not.'

There wasn't much chance of going anywhere else in that weather even if he'd wanted to.

Frank took a kettle and a tin of Maxwell House out of a cupboard.

'Everywhere you go people peddle you coffee nowadays. You walk into a building with a machete sticking out of your head and they say, have a coffee. I'm here to shoot the Pope, have a seat, he'll be with you shortly, can I get you a coffee. You and Sarah having fun?'

'You're not meant to ask Englishmen questions like that.'

'That's why I do it. Bloody Brits.' He laughed. 'Remarkable lady, I wish you well.'

'You going to warn me to be careful too?'

'Someone did that?'

'Mike.'

'Maybe he just meant don't go getting married to her or having kids. Or not till you've had time to talk it over with your old man.' He spooned Maxwell House into two Mr Smiley mugs. 'Don't take any notice of me, Joe. You had parents like mine you'd understand. It's all in there,' he tapped his head. 'Printed on the genes. Ninety-nine ways not to bring up children. An unhappy childhood's a great contraceptive.'

The American couldn't have been more friendly and straightforward. They talked for a while, about rock music and books, floods and hurricanes, man-eating sharks and 700 lb Jewfish and grouper fish that started life female and ended up male, Joe drinking his coffee and watching for clues, hidden depths, dark secrets, and not finding any. The wind was slackening somewhat but the rain came down as hard as ever.

'How did you like Tegoose?' Frank asked.

'It has a pretty palace.'

'That's about it, isn't it. The truth of the matter is peasants and cities don't mix, they're a disaster. Name me a city that's taken in the peasantry that works.'

'Name me any city that works.'

'Depends what you mean by works, I suppose. Clean sidewalks, public transport, for that stuff I'd vote for Kyoto, Japan, but don't fart in the street or drop a cigarette butt, they put you in a mental home. I know plenty of cities that give you a good time, plenty, but they're all lived in by city people, not country people down on their luck. In Tegoose everyone's down on their luck.' He drained his coffee mug. 'You figured out what your father was up to there?'

'It's all hypothesis.' Joe was watching him, trying not to make it obvious. 'Suppose Burgess and Willie were interested in the same thing for different reasons. Willie goes off, in the meantime Burgess is looking for him, then Willie sends word, tells him to meet him in Tegoose, but when he does they don't see eye to eye.'

'How do you know Bobby was looking for him?'

'I don't,' said Joe. 'But I know someone was. In La Entrada, we walked into the police station with Willie's photo, the guy says to Mike you're the second person to bring that picture in here.'

Frank looked puzzled, or pretended to.

'La Entrada? On the road up to Copán?'

'That's right. Bobby used to have a church there.'

'So who was the first guy?'

'I don't know. The cop thought he was American.'

'So it could have been Bobby?'

'It could,' said Joe. 'Except that if it was Bobby they'd have recognized him.'

'He didn't give a name?'

'Richard Milhous Nixon.'

Frank got halfway through his laugh and then stopped.

'You don't think that was me, do you?'

'Good God no. Anyway, you were 200 miles away in Jiuba.'

'You checked?'

'Sure, wouldn't you? Everyone's guilty unless proved innocent.'

Frank was indignant.

'For fuck's sake. Guilty of what?'

Joe smiled to show he wasn't accusing him of anything.

'I was only joking, Frank. I've no idea where you were. It's Willie I'm looking for, that's all.'

Frank walked over to the door again and lit a cigarette.

'I don't want to be crass about this Joe, but has it occurred to you your father might be dead?'

'It has,' said Joe. 'But I'm not counting on it.'

'He's been gone quite a while. He could have set off to do something and then hit trouble. This can be a dangerous country, healthwise and peoplewise. Two Dutch tourists took a jeep down the Mosquito Coast last year, three months later they found the jeep in the Rio Patuca. Same thing happened to a New York journalist up near Catacamas. In the time of the Contras people went missing all the time. Death comes cheap round here. Doesn't have to be violent, there's no shortage of natural causes – dysentery, malaria, Dengue Fever. Particularly when you get off the beaten track. The life expectancy down round Jiuba is about thirty-five.'

'I know. But I'm assuming he's okay.' Joe got up and buttoned his shirt sleeve. 'Was Willie involved in Jiuba at all?'

Frank shook his head.

'It's no place for old men. I offered to take him down there one time but he wasn't interested. This place is a holiday resort compared to Jiuba. They don't speak English, they don't have much in the way of roads or shops. The makings are there but we've a long way to go. It's another old mission, only this lot weren't Anglicans they were Americans. I guess it was probably okay while they were there – a couple of good bungalows, what used to be a garden. But once you get beyond the bungalow fences it's jungle.'

'And it's bitch to get to,' he continued. 'The road's paved

as far as Trujillo, two hours' east of La Ceiba, but from there on it's seventy miles over rough tracks, take you nine or ten hours on a good day. In weather like this it's impossible, even for four-wheel drives. You can fly in, but anything heavy comes overland, by road or up the river.'

'Why did you chose it?' asked Joe.

'Virginia. Mike tell you about Virginia? That's where she died.'

'And you're sure Willie never went there?'

'Positive,' said Frank.

Mike was down by the shore, machete in hand, gathering coconuts after the storm. He'd spear a nut, lift it up, balance it in his hand and hack off the husk. The islanders did it with astonishing precision, four or five clean cuts and that was that. Mike was hopeless. Sometimes the nut fell off the blade before he managed to palm it: even when he did he cut it too cautiously, a sliver at a time. Each nut took him ten minutes where an islander would do it in seconds. What the hell, he was enjoying himself, utterly self-absorbed, like a man gardening.

Joe sat down on the turf and watched him from a distance, reluctant to intrude, until Mike finally gave up, plunged the machete into the soil and lit himself a cigarette. Joe gave him a slow hand-clap.

'Hopeless.'

Mike looked up.

'I know. The buggers make it look so easy. That's the problem with modern life, I know how to work a computer but I can't even skin a coconut. How did you get on?'

'He's lying. I asked him if Willie had ever been to Jiuba, he said no.' Joe took Willie's map out of his back pocket, spread it out on the ground and pointed to a line running inland from Trujillo. 'He went there, there's even a date. I tried La Entrada on him too, but he played the innocent.'

They walked down the shore. The sky was clear, the hot sun melting the steaming mists off the land. Joe was sweating, dark stains marking his shirt.

'Suppose Frank's up to something. Suppose he's using you, Mike. What for?'

Mike thought for a while.

'It's hard to know. He could be using us as a cover, I suppose. Selfless doctor on philanthropic aid project, nobody's going to ask too many questions. You can come and go, bring things in and out of the country. Could be to do with drugs, I guess, a staging point between Colombia and the States. Or money laundering, but we don't turn over enough cash to make that likely. Ten years ago I'd have said he was working for the Contras, but Nicaragua's not like that any more, the CIA have moved on to the Middle East.'

'Do they grow drugs here?'

'Not really. A bit of marijuana, but not on a significant scale.'

'Could they?'

'You mean set up a plantation in the jungle and ship it out? Yes, I suppose you could. But growing the stuff isn't the problem, it's getting it to market. The DEA and the US customs have the borders pretty well watched. AWACS, ground radar, spotter planes, all manner of electronic gear. You'd have to operate on a scale where you didn't mind losing every third cargo. Expensive business, with a lot of casualties. But it's possible, yes. You'd also need a lot of capital, and some kind of distribution at the far end.'

They'd reached the jetty, a wide stilted boardwalk that projected out forty feet into the clear waters of the lagoon. An old half-deck fishing boat was moored alongside.

'So what do we do next?' asked Joe.

'I'll take him to Jiuba with me. Meanwhile you could go see Amos on the off-chance.'

He bent down and picked up a conch shell.

'Alone, I'd suggest.'

23

The town of Tela lies on the coast midway between La Ceiba and San Pedro Sula. It's a stagnant place, but not without beauty, a decaying banana port built on two sides of a slow-moving river red with silt, bordered by long white beaches and low forested hills. A long pier projects out into the sea, with rail lines on old oily timbers, where stevedores push barrows and unload nets of fruit from box-cars and flat-back trucks. Nostromo country.

Back from the beach, where mules graze and men in straw hats hawk hammocks and sea-washed boulders steam like elephant turds in the humid heat, the front is lined with two-storey houses that have seen better days, secure behind faded white railings and attempted lawns, long since deserted by their Fruit Company tenants. Beyond them lies the real town, a rough grid of rutted roads and concrete pavements above deep storm gutters littered with melon skins and corn husks.

The streets seethe in noisy slow-motion – Toyotas, Datsuns, the Mack trucks of the fruit company, taxis, jeeps, bicycles, lottery sellers, ice cream vendors, pristine school children, shoe shines, soldiers and whores, men selling green oranges and watches and disposable lighters. The faces are Indian and Spanish and mulatto, Chinese, Lebanese, North American, all brands of exiled European, leaning in lines against peeling clapperboard gables, drinking *cervezas* in pool-halls and bordellos, haggling over vegetables, reading the sports papers, sleeping on benches. Cow Cay is a Caribbean island: Tela is Central America.

It was dusk when the bus dropped Joe off outside the crumbling town hall, tall and wooden and half-rotted by termites. Tela was coming alive for the evening. The street lights were on, the bars crowded with boy-soldiers and sailors off the banana boats looking for action. Families sat out on upstairs balconies, enjoying the evening breeze and watching the sun descending towards the fat belly of the water, the sea breathing heavily, rising and falling like a breathing chest at rest. Offshore the lights of a banana boat glistened on the swell. In the distant half-light hanging clouds crept down from the hills.

He walked towards the shore, past a timber church with slatted windows and open doors, a preacher at the pulpit, a fat black lady at the organ, a blue-robed choir chanting. When he reached the front he turned left, counting the street numbers until he reached seventeen. The tarnished copper plaque beside the mail-box said Dr Amos Lipstein, MD.

It had once been a handsome house: two timber storeys under a wide low-pitched roof, stilted against flood and termites and sheltered by palms, and must once have been home to some middle-manager from the Fruit Company. On the street side an upstairs balcony ran the length of the building, curtained behind mosquito nets.

Joe paused for a moment, listening to the ocean, the croaking of frogs, the distant sounds of the town. He could hear a juke-box somewhere, Jagger singing 'Far Away Eyes'. He opened the gate in the low fence, walked up the path, climbed the steps to the screen door and rang the bell.

For a long time no one answered. He rang again, and heard shuffling feet. A light went on in the porch, and a silhouette appeared through the screen.

The woman who opened the door was ancient and bent, legs bowed, all the flesh gone from her limbs, her withered breasts and pouched stomach hanging forward under a silk blouse and pleated skirt, old but well cared for. Her hair was grey and thinning, neither quite combed nor dishevelled, the face pale and almost damp, with a pink mole on her forehead, though her make-up was in place and he could smell scent. She clasped a pack of Stuyvesant in one hand, and a cigarette drooped from her mouth. Joe guessed she must be in her eighties.

'You must be Willie's boy,' she said without removing the cigarette. 'We been expecting you.'

Joe froze. His visit was unannounced: he hadn't called in advance, or sent word he was coming. She stepped aside to let him into the hall.

'Come on in. Amos is resting, he'll be down in a moment. You come on the bus?'

'Yes,' said Joe, and followed her down the corridor.

The old woman's name was Mercedes and she'd been Amos's housekeeper for thirty-seven years.

'Came one day not long after his wife died, he put an ad in the paper for someone to fix his food and look after the house. I signed for a month, been here ever since. Have a seat, I'll fix you something to drink.'

They'd arrived in what Joe assumed was the doctor's study. It occupied a corner of the house, with tall windows on two adjacent walls looking out on to the garden. There were books everywhere, on shelves and heaped in piles on the desk. A cool breeze came from the ceiling fan.

Joe sat down on a leather sofa beside the window while Mercedes unlocked a cabinet and took out two bottles.

'Whisky's all we got, I'm afraid. Scotch or Irish?'

'Irish,' said Joe.

She poured a knuckle of Jameson into a crystal glass and handed it across to him.

'Your father drinks Scotch, if I remember rightly.'

'You've seen him recently?'

'Sure I seen him, a week back. Amos'll tell you all about it.'

Joe fingered his glass. His brain had gone blank.

'How is Amos?'

'You met him before?'

'At St Andrews, a couple of years ago. We had supper with Mike Osborne.'

She poured herself a whisky and sat down opposite him.

'He's not too good, not too bad. Old, is the truth of it, I ain't the only one. His memory comes and goes a bit, forgets things when it suits him.'

'Mike said his eyes were giving him trouble.'

She shifted in her seat, her skirt riding up over her knees, and ran her hand along the arm of the chair in some absent-minded habit of flirtation. She must have been a beauty once, Joe realized. And more than just a housekeeper.

'Trouble?' Mercedes laughed. 'Gone beyond trouble, he's near as damn blind. But he manages, he's got other senses. Blindness does that to you, you learn to smell, learn to listen. Everything has a sound or a smell, clouds have a sound, walls have a sound, I guess you don't notice until you have to. Voices wear expressions, you listen for winces, raised eyebrows, frowns, smiles. I get away with nothing, damn all. He always knows where I am, what I'm doing, who's calling at the door, what's going on in the street.'

'How did you know I was coming?' asked Joe.

'Your old man figured you'd show up in time.' Mercedes smiled. 'He said you wouldn't be able to resist it.'

'How did he know I was in Honduras in the first place?'

'He phoned London one time, someone told him.'

'What was his reaction?'

'He was mad as hell to begin with, went round talking to the furniture about it. Then he calmed down and treated it like a joke. Crossed his mind to get in touch once he knew you were on the Cay, but then he decided he's through telling people what to do.'

'Was this before he went to the States or after?'

'You knew about that?'

'He lost his passport, a friend at the embassy in Tegoose found out. What was he doing there?'

'Checking things out. People, organizations, I don't know the details. Amos will fill you in.' She took out another cigarette and lit it from the butt of the old one. 'Did you eat yet?'

Joe shook his head.

'But don't worry, I'm fine.'

'Not too much in the kitchen right now but I could fix you a sandwich. Ham, cheese, tuna, whatever you fancy.'

Joe hadn't eaten since he left Morgan's Hole that morning.

'Cheese, please.'

Mercedes got up and straightened her skirt.

'Make yourself at home. I'll be right back.'

As soon as she'd left the room he got up and went over to the desk. Someone had been working at it: there were papers, periodicals, a wooden bowl of paper clips, a jar of pens, a full ashtray, an empty packet of Senior Service.

Amos smoked Senior Service too, but he didn't do paperwork any more. Joe picked up an A4 legal pad and flicked through the pages.

The writing was unmistakable.

He picked up a sheet and started reading. Willie used a sort of miniature copper-plate, very precise and tidy, each paragraph with a separate title. Joe was still running his eyes down the headings – Jiuba (finance), Burgess (cases), *Journal of Tropical Medicine* – when he heard movement upstairs, slow footsteps on floorboards, a voice calling for Mercedes. Mercedes called back, and a moment later he heard her climbing the stairs.

He put down the pad, still listening.

The next sound he heard came from the front door, a low click as though someone had lifted the latch. Then there was silence. He put down the pad, wondering what to do.

Mercedes and Amos were talking now, moving around in the room above him. He heard the first gunshot, and then a second.

He was out in the hall by the time the gun fired a third time, running towards the stairs, taking them two at a time.

The landing led to a broad corridor running the length of the house. Fifteen feet away Mercedes was lying face down, her head towards the stairs, arms out, her arthritic claw still grasping a cigarette. Joe hesitated, looking around for a weapon of some kind. He picked up a heavy vase off a table and advanced slowly down the corridor, weighing it in his hand, wondering what on earth he'd do with it if he met a man with a gun.

The door behind Mercedes was shut. He paused again, listening. There was no sound of movement, just the low drone of an electric fan, the ticking of a clock. He braced himself against the opposite wall, raised his foot until it was resting on the door handle, and pushed.

The door swung open.

The room was tall and airy, with a double glass door leading out on to the balcony. The furniture was mahogany: an ornate tallboy, a full-length mirror on a stand, a dressing-table with silver hairbrushes and cologne bottles and an old wedding photograph in a leather frame, two upright chairs and a high-backed bed. The doors to the balcony were open, the curtains flapping in the breeze.

Amos was on the bed, belly up, a little old man, almost bald but with a well-trimmed black beard streaked with grey. He wore a crumpled white linen suit and a white shirt buttoned to the collar, no tie, and purple carpet slippers, one of which had fallen off on to the floor. He'd been shot twice, in the chest and the head. He looked very dead.

There was no one else in the room.

Joe put down the vase and took a step forward. At the last moment he sensed a movement behind the door. And then all was blackness.

The next thing he knew he was dreaming of a Viking funeral pyre, a body on a raised platform ringed with flames, the crackle of burning timber, billows of black smoke.

The body on the pyre, he realized, was Amos. The curtains were alight, the glass in the french windows beginning to crack in the heat.

A dull pain was working its way out from a point just behind his ear. He began to get up, vomited, and sank back to the floor, choking on the smoke.

Keep low, he remembered. Smoke rises. He worked his way on his elbows back out through the door into the corridor.

Apart from the fire the house was in darkness, the electrics burned out. He stood up and started to feel his way along the corridor with his hands, keeping close to the walls to avoid tripping over Mercedes.

Mercedes, Amos, and a killer. As far as anyone outside the house was concerned he had to be the killer. This was a set-up.

Don't panic, think.

There were sounds in the street now, people shouting, animated voices getting closer.

He ran down the stairs, through the kitchen, out the back door and across the yard, keeping low, hoping the house would obscure him from the crowd in the street.

The flames were through the roof now, scattering sparks into the black sky. He turned left and ran on until he reached a gate in the paling fence, pushed through and found himself in a narrow lane, hardly more than a footpath, leading from the beach back into town. Still no one called out, no one came after him.

You're in a strange town, you speak no Spanish, you've no transport, almost no money, hardly enough to pay your bus fare back to La Ceiba. Passport and plane ticket are back at the house. You have two hours, maybe three, maybe less, before people start asking questions about strangers.

I'm not trained for this, said a voice inside his head, these aren't my skills. I'm the kind of guy who spends wars in the Ministry of Information.

He looked at his watch. It was half past eight.

The alley emerged at the back of what sounded like a cinema, a low cement-block building with a tin roof. He remembered Lee Oswald at Dallas, the hour after the assassination, thinking he was safe in the stalls watching a newsreel, except that he'd been seen going in, once in there he was trapped.

Joe walked round to the front of the building and found himself in a well-lit street of bars and cafés. The film was ending, the audience wandering out on to the pavement.

He glanced at the posters, Arnold Schwarzenegger with

what looked like a howitzer tucked under his arm, a helicopter crashing into Capitol Hill.

'I think he's crap,' said a cheerful English voice. Not just English, Liverpool. 'Fucking crap.'

'You're just jealous, Les.' Birmingham this time, with that naive monotone that makes everything Brummies say sound stupid, even when it's not. 'Imagine having a body like that. I bet he wears a bra. Anyone fancy a curry?'

'They don't have fucking curries in Honduras, Terry boy,' said the scouse. 'You'll have to go Mexican. Tortillas, chile con carne, all that crap.'

'Crap's about right,' said Terry. 'You don't buy that stuff, you rent it.'

There were six of them, scald-headed tattooed crewmen off a freighter, tight jeans and denim jackets with the collars turned up, fake Rolexes and shore-leave shirts with crocodiles embroidered on the pockets.

'Did you ever see *Terminator Two*?' asked Les.

'It doesn't work,' Joe interrupted, the way men on neighbouring stools interrupt each other in a bar.

'What do you mean it doesn't work? I thought it was brilliant.'

'If he'd gone back in time,' Joe explained, 'and managed to stop what actually happened happening, then he wouldn't have been around in the future to go back and stop it in the first place.'

'I don't think I follow you.'

'If he came back and stopped himself being born then he wouldn't have been alive to come back.'

'I still don't follow you.' And then Les realized. 'Are you English?'

'Peter Hennessey, how do you do.'

'Hey guys, there's a man from England here. What are you doing here, Peter?'

'I'm an engineer,' said Joe. 'Working on a water purification scheme up the coast.'

'Hey, there's something on fire over there,' said Terry.

The flames were visible over the roof tops now, sirens

sounding in the distance. A thick pall of smoke rose vertically into the night sky.

'Better keep moving, they'll think we started it,' Les laughed. 'Do you know any discos in town, Peter?'

They found a bar opposite the bus station with a barman who spoke English, a fridge full of imported beer and a TV showing poor-quality videos of World Cup soccer, orange grass and purple sky and figures that seemed to move and stay still at the same time.

Joe drank steadily, measuring his pints, pushing his half-drunk bottles back into the raft of empties in the middle of the table. When it came to his turn to buy a round he paid with a five-dollar note, his last. The barman brought him his change. Joe counted it up, shook his head.

'I gave you a fifty.'

'Ten.'

'Fifty,' said Joe. 'I tell you how I know. I've got one of those bill folds where you fold the notes, put a crease lengthways down the middle. Check the till, you'll find it there.'

'You sure?'

'Sure,' said Joe.

The barman looked at him dubiously, went over to the till, picked out the fifty Larry had used to pay for the previous round, examined the crease, frowned, then counted out four tens and a five and handed them over. Joe stuffed them in his pocket.

Where did I learn this stuff? he asked himself. Off Mike Osborne, at Cambridge, he realized. Mike teaching him courage, Mike teaching him to break the rules, Mike doing it as a game, know how to beat the system, in case you ever need to.

By ten o'clock the evening was hotting up. A fat little man from Belfast performed a party trick involving two chairs, a pint of beer, a pack of cigarettes and a plastic pot-plant. Les started the singing with 'Always Look on the Bright Side of Life,' Joe followed with 'The Mayor of Bridgewater', a cook from Cardiff ran through the whole of 'Four and Twenty Virgins.'

Joe glanced across the road at the bus station. The *rapido* from La Ceiba to San Pedro Sula had just drawn in. He excused himself to the gents, slipped out the back door of the bar, and paused for a moment to check the contents of Terry's wallet. Two condoms, a black and white photo-booth snap of a girl with no blouse, an address in Handsworth, sixty pounds sterling, as much again in local currency.

Pay you back someday, Terry. I promise.

24

IT WAS EARLY afternoon in La Entrada, and hot. Nothing moved except the flies and crows pecking at a dead dog in the middle of the street. A man in dungarees lay on his back under the chassis of a truck outside the gas station.

Joe stepped down off the bus and waited for it to drive away up the slope before crossing the road to the hotel. His shirt was soaked in sweat and he was thirsty.

Carmel was asleep on a cane lounger in the shade of the back porch. He sat down on the steps, watching her face, slack-jawed, teeth out, mouth open, breathing steadily. And then he coughed.

She opened one eye, closed it again.

'Bar's closed,' she said, sounding New York and husky.

'I'll wait,' said Joe.

She raised her neck up and looked at him again.

'You been here before, haven't you.'

'Last week, with Mike Osborne. I'm Willie Wilde's son.'

By now Carmel was awake. Her hand reached down on the far side of the lounger, then slid across her mouth as she slipped her dentures back into place.

'So you are. Mike with you this time too?'

Joe shook his head.

'Nope, I'm alone.'

'Go help yourself to a beer, fridge is behind the bar. On second thoughts bring two.'

Joe collected the beers and stood in the doorway pouring them carefully, holding the glasses at an angle. Carmel was sitting up, a cigarette between her teeth, flicking her lighter, trying to get the flint to strike.

'So why'd you come back? We don't get a lot of repeat business round here.'

'I've got a message for Willie. I hoped you might be able to pass it on.'

The lighter finally ignited. She inhaled, coughed, and then looked down at the tip of her cigarette.

'What makes you think that?'

'It's just a hunch I have.'

And her name on the A4 pad in Amos's study.

'I tell you two things,' said Carmel. 'First, this ain't a messenger service. Second, if it was then it would be the kind of messenger service where folk drop in and pick things up, not the kind sends things out.'

Joe put his beer glass to his mouth and kept drinking until it was empty.

'Amos Lipstein's dead, someone shot him yesterday evening. And Mercedes. Shot them and torched the house.'

'Is that a fact,' said Carmel. 'You there when it happened?'

'Yup. A lot of people are going to think I did it.'

'Amos is dead – that's the message?'

'That's the first half. The second half is, it would be nice to see him, if he can spare the time.'

'Any particular time?'

'Whenever it suits him. I'll be back at B.J. MacIntyre's from some time tomorrow.'

She got up, shuffled to the edge of the porch and looked around.

'You sure you're on your own?'

'Yes. What's the matter, don't you trust Mike?'

'Maybe I do, maybe I don't, but I sure as hell don't trust some of the company he keeps.'

'Meaning Frank Carreras?'

'Could be. How'd you get here?'

'I took the bus to San Pedro, spent the night out at the airport, took the morning plane up to Tegoose, spent half an hour checking on flights out of the country. I made a reservation on TAL to Guatemala City.' Making sure people saw him do it, talking loudly like an Englishman in a hurry, sounding as if it was urgent, a real emergency. I'm learning, Mike, I'm learning. 'Then I took a cab into town and caught the bus down here.'

'You should have caught the flight,' said Carmel.

'I toyed with it,' said Joe. 'But I don't have a passport.'

'I'll see what I can do, but I'm not promising. You're right, I've seen him, but not for more than a week. I shouldn't even be telling you that. Is there anything else you need?'

'Another beer,' said Joe, 'and some way to contact Bobby Burgess'.

Carmel waved her hand towards the bar.

'Help yourself to beer, but I don't know about Bobby. He left the Cay?'

'Moved out overnight, lock, stock and Bible, told the police he'd been threatened. Maybe he was. I get the impression Frank Carreras isn't averse to the odd bit of GBH when he's in the mood.'

'You reckon that's who killed the doctor?'

'You got any other ideas?'

'At my age you don't go in much for ideas, I've enough business trying to remember whether I ate breakfast yet.' She held the butt of her cigarette carefully between two fingers and took a final puff before flicking it out into the yard. 'So where's your friend Mike in all this? You told him about Amos yet?'

'He's down in Jiuba, out of touch.'

'They don't have phones down there yet?'

'Only a radio phone, you never know who else is listening on those things.'

'All I can tell you about Bobby is the mission's got some kind of office in San Pedro Sula. You could try there.'

'Thanks.'

'I guess that's where you'd be heading anyway, back down the coast.'

'Probably.'

'You know something?' said Carmel, a hint of a smile finally flickering across her face. 'You're just like your old man.'

'Don't ever say that,' said Joe.

The first thing Joe did when he reached San Pedro Sula was to mail two letters from the post office. One to Sarah on the Cay, one to Bernard Wiggins at the embassy. The second thing he did was to find a hotel with a room off the street and get something to eat. Then he went to bed and slept for ten hours straight.

When he woke it was ten in the morning, grey light filtering through cheap curtains, muffled sounds of the city, an argument going on somewhere. Through the wall someone with a bad cough was spitting into a sink.

He got out of bed, stretched, lit a cigarette and went over and opened the curtains. It was warm, a heavy heat that could bring thunder.

The hotel was built round a central well, roofed in at the bottom to cover what smelled like kitchens. All four walls of the well contained windows into other people's rooms, most of them open to let some breeze in. Small rooms, damp but clean, fifteen dollars a night, four dollars extra if you wanted a shower, checking out time eleven, written in biro on the tourist board card on the back of a door.

An argument was going on in the room directly opposite, but a floor down so that Joe's sightline was restricted, all he could see was part of a bed, an open suitcase on the floor, and anyone who happened to walk past between the bed and the window. The combatants were Americans, a couple in their late twenties, shouting, thumping the furniture, not giving a damn who heard. A man in a white undervest and boxer shorts, pacing a lot, back and forth by the window, a beer bottle in his hand, a woman in a green dress, hair back in a band, not fat but heavily built, sitting on the end of the bed, then standing up, then sitting down again.

The argument was about another woman, the man saying

he's only seen her three or four times, she's the girlfriend of someone called Nick who's a friend of someone called Gary, he's run into her with Nick and Gary, doesn't even know her apart from she's Nick's girlfriend; the woman refusing to believe him. It was like a tennis match, lobs and smashes, long rallies, then silence while they got in shape for the next serve.

'Listen, Fay.'

'Oh shut up, Martin.'

Fay and Martin: they had names.

Joe filled the washbasin and then remembered he didn't have a razor. He brushed his teeth on his finger, dried his face on the towel, and ran his fingers cautiously over the bruise on the side of his head.

Fay didn't believe the story about Nick. Martin said, 'What do you want me to do, ring Larry?'

'Sure.'

'What, now?'

'Now.'

'You're serious?'

'Of course I'm fucking serious.'

'Jesus.'

They kept saying the same things over and over, you wouldn't think it possible that two people could shout so long and so loud without moving the conversation on.

Joe heard a knock at their door, then saw a boy cross the room with a tray of fresh beers and put them down on the table by the window, Fay sitting on the bed with her head in her hands, Martin pulling on his trousers and shirt.

Neither of them spoke while the boy was in the room, all you could hear was the rumble of traffic, a radio somewhere. Then Fay started in again.

'You know that night you said you had to stay over in Daytona?'

'For Christ's sake, I'm not going back over that again.'

Razor, toothpaste, underwear, a bag of some sort, and a map: Joe made a list in his head, then collected Terry's wallet off the chair and counted out his cash. The flight had taken more than half, the bus and hotel most of the rest.

There was a pause in the argument across the well: Martin stuck his head out the window, shaking it, thumping the sill with the side of his fist.

'I hope you get mumps between your legs,' said Fay.

'Go fuck yourself.'

'Up yours too.'

The door slammed and she was gone.

Joe went to his window and leaned out.

'Who needs TV?' he said, loud enough for Martin to hear. 'All the drama you need performed right outside your hotel room.'

The American looked up.

'Jesus. You know what this is about? Premenstrual tensions, fucking PMT, that's all.'

'Divorce her.'

'I can't, I'm a Catholic.'

'I'm sure the Pope would understand. You fancy a drink?'

'How did you guess. Hold on a moment, I have to finish getting dressed.'

'Bar round corner,' said Joe. 'First left, then . . . hold on, what room are you in there? I'll pick you up on my way down.'

'Three one nine. I'm Martin.'

'I'm Alf,' said Joe. 'I'll be down in a tick.'

Martin opened the door first knock.

'You really saw all that?'

'Sure.' Joe walked into the room and looked out the window.

'You didn't see me?'

'I had other things on my mind,' said Martin. 'You know the thing about Fay? She's not like her mother at all.'

Joe let him go out into the corridor first, and slipped the snib on the Yale before closing the door. They took the lift to the lobby, headed for the street, until Joe stopped and patted his pocket.

'Left my wallet upstairs.'

'Don't worry,' said Martin.

Joe insisted.

He took the lift back to the third floor, retraced his steps to room three one nine, knocked to make sure Fay hadn't returned, then pushed open the door.

He selected three shirts from Martin's case, a handful of fresh underwear, grabbed the sponge bag from the shower, went back to the suitcase and felt through the side pockets.

The plastic wallet contained 700 dollars in American Express travellers cheques in the name of Curtis. Joe tore two 100-dollar cheques off the back of the wad, grabbed a laundry bag from the closet, threw in the clothes, ran up to his room and transferred them to a supermarket bag, took the service lift to the basement and walked out of the hotel by the side entrance.

I should feel bad about this, he told himself, but I don't. The fucker's having an affair and he blames it on his wife's period. I should feel guilty?

He caught a cab across town and told the driver when they arrived that he had no change, only travellers cheques. They argued a bit, the guy threatened to call the police, Joe said what's the problem, the only problem I can see is I don't know the exchange rate. The rate's bad, said the cabbie, the dollar's going down all the time, you could see him doing sums. Joe came away with a fistful of lempiras but he didn't have to show a passport.

They were downtown, close to the market, the streets full of women with cages of live chickens on their heads and cigars in their mouths bumping into backpackers and lawyers with plastic briefcases. It took him twenty minutes to buy himself a shoulder bag and find Calle Fernandes.

The Mission offices were on the first floor over a bookshop selling religious tracts. He climbed the staircase and pressed the bell. A white woman in severe glasses opened the door.

'I'm sorry to trouble you,' said Joe, 'but I wonder if you can help me. I'm looking for Bunty Burgess.'

She looked at him over her spectacles.

'You are?'

'Andy Lennox, I'm a friend from England, we met at bible college. I'd fixed to stay with her and Bobby on Cow Cay but she's not there, no one seems to know where she's gone.'

'You'd better come in,' she said cautiously.

The room was like no other he'd seen in Honduras, but plenty he'd seen in the States. Wall to wall grey carpet, new office furniture, iced water dispenser with paper cups, air-conditioning humming quietly in the corner, a second woman tapping at the keyboard of an electric typewriter. Bales of books were stacked against the far wall. There were no pictures, just a calendar with a colour photo of Jerusalem in the snow.

'Reverend Black is out at the moment,' said the woman.

'It seemed like there'd been some trouble at Cow Cay,' said Joe, staying close to the door. 'Is everything all right?'

'It is and it isn't,' said the woman. 'Reverend Burgess had to move out for a while. What did you say your name was?'

'Lennox,' said Joe. 'Andy Lennox.'

'Come on in, Mr Lennox. We'll see what we can do for you.'

Joe put his bag on the floor and sat down while she made a phone call, trying to act eager, hoping whoever she was calling was out.

'Hi,' she said to the phone. 'Could you put me through to the Reverend Burgess please?'

And then a long silence.

'Thank you. I'll call back later.'

She put down the receiver.

'He's not home. Maybe you could come back in an hour or so, I'll let him know you're in town.'

'I'd be very grateful,' said Joe. He picked up his bag, gave her a smile, and headed for the door. Then he stopped.

'I couldn't ask you a small favour, could I?'

'You can try.'

'Could I make a local call?'

'I don't see why not.'

She nodded him towards the telephone and went back to her desk.

Joe kept the line dead with his thumb while he tapped out six digits, then released it and pressed Last Number Redial. Nerve was all you needed for this stuff, just keep your nerve.

'HotelCopantlSulaCanIHelpYou?' a voice sang sweetly, omitting all punctuation.

Joe cut the line again.

'Hello, my name's Lennox, I wanted to confirm a reservation for tonight.' He waited twenty seconds. 'No smoking.' Another twenty, counting it out in his head. 'Thank you.'

Then he put down the phone.

'You want to leave your bag here?' asked the woman.

'No thanks,' said Joe.

The Copantl called itself One of the World's Leading Hotels and had around 200 rooms spread over seven floors looking out on a terrace pool shaded by tall trees. It also had a convention centre, a health spa, three or four tennis courts hand dusted by uniformed peons, and a bar full of Americans in slacks and pastel polo shirts. Joe wondered how much he'd have to be paid to wear clothes like that.

He acted as though he lived in the place, smiled at the porters, went into the gents, shaved himself in hot chlorinated water, dabbed his face with cologne from the free bottle on the mirror-backed marble sink, slipped into a stall and changed into one of Martin's shirts.

Back in the lobby he bought a paper and a copy of *Newsweek* at the news stand and settled down to wait, one eye on the elevators. *Newsweek* in Honduras wasn't like *Newsweek* in England, it was all about prostitutes in Argentina and the state of the Bolivian Trade Union movement, plus a paid-for feature on Brazil, Land of Opportunity, with a lot of pictures of hydroelectric dams and state-of-the-art factory farming.

The paper was in Spanish. He flicked through looking for any mention of Tela, or Dr Lipstein, or photographs of fires, but couldn't find any. People were coming and going from the lifts to the pool, family parties, precocious kids in loud T-shirts, toddlers in bikinis, all the usual shit.

Twenty minutes passed. He wondered whether to try phoning the room, but decided against it. Face to face Bobby or Bunty would have to talk, on the phone they could just hang up.

And then he remembered Dr Sinclair.

He got the number of the American Hospital from the reception desk and walked across to the pay phones. Sinclair answered the phone himself, which was as well because Joe didn't fancy his chances with the secretary. The doctor remembered Willie well, and was surprised and concerned to hear he was missing.

'If you're worried about his health, don't be. He didn't want a check and I didn't offer him one. Mind and body seemed A1 to me, given his age. He smokes too much but then so do I.'

What Willie wanted to talk about was drugs, the medical kind.

'That's what I guessed,' said Joe.

'He told me he was writing an article for the London *Times* on drug companies in the Third World. I asked him if he had a good lawyer.'

'That's what he is,' said Joe, and hung up. Bunty and Bobby Burgess were coming out of the lift, Bobby in a cotton hat and blazer made of what looked like red and white graph paper with a grey shirt and matching tie over lime-green slacks, Bunty in an ankle-length navy blue frock and open sandals, pink flesh bulging up through the openings.

Joe intercepted them halfway across the lobby.

'Small world,' he smiled, 'and getting smaller every day.'

Bobby Burgess looked straight at him, Bunty making a grab for his elbow.

'Don't worry,' said Joe. 'We're on the same side.'

25

It was ten in the morning. St Andrews lay calm and exhausted in the heavy heat.

'I read some place,' said Sarah, 'that if you're up in an airliner and you throw a piece of paper out the window, then the paper don't go the direction you expect it to.'

'Is that a fact,' said Esther Manley from the filing cabinet.

'So it said. But what I don't understand,' Sarah paused to take a sip from her mug of coffee, 'is how you throw a piece of paper out an airplane window in the first place. They ain't the kind of window you can open.'

'Flush it down the john, I guess.'

'But then how you goin' to see what way it goes?'

'Beats me,' said Esther, her eyes on the files. 'How far you want to go back?'

'Maybe a year.'

Esther pulled half a dozen folders out of the cabinet and deposited them on the table.

'And you still ain't told me what you want this stuff for, least not in a way makes any sense.'

'Research,' said Sarah, opening a file. When she got Joe's letter her first reaction had been to throw it in the bin and pretend it never arrived. Then she thought, why not? The man wants me to go burgling and cheating my way through St Andrews, he must have a good reason. 'Medical research. Does Frank sign all the death certificates round here?'

'Who else? He the only doctor on the island, ever since Amos. Shit, I still don't believe what happened to Amos.

Why'd anyone want to kill a man like that? And Mercedes, she never caused no trouble.'

'Is that right?' asked Sarah. 'I mean, I don't want to speak ill of the dead, but she had a tongue could cut stone, that woman.'

'Just her style,' said Esther, 'same way Mike never says anything without making it a joke, same way Frank tells you you wearing the ugliest dress he ever saw, he don't mean it, just a way of talking. You heard anything from Joe?'

'Not so's you'd notice. I reckon he got plenty on his mind at present. Be in touch when he got space for some affection in his life again. What the hell is Quatrone B?'

Esther reached over for the file.

'Brand name for codeine phosphate, painkiller. Apt to make you drowsy but apart from that there ain't no harm in it. You still ain't tell me who this is for.'

'Mike Osborne.'

'Is it hell,' said Esther. 'Mike wants to know anything, he calls me himself. And he never calls about nothin' medical, that's Frank's department.'

'Well he did now.'

Esther shook her head.

'I sure as hell hope you know what you're doing, girl.'

'Haven't a clue, and that's the truth.' Sarah closed the file. 'You mind if I take these away?'

'Of course I mind, those are medical records, how'd you feel if someone walked off with a file listing all the things ever went wrong with you.'

'File'd be too heavy to carry,' said Sarah. 'That photocopier over at the house still working?'

'Far as I know.'

Sarah drained her coffee and put the mug on the table.

'I'll be back.'

The Rectory was unlocked. People used to tell Mike he should watch his doors and windows more closely but he never bothered. No one thieved much on the Cay, the place was too small, anyone turned up in town with something they didn't have yesterday it was apt to get noticed.

Sarah went through to the study and switched on the photocopier, listening to the hum of the machine warming up, watching for the green light to go on, studying the moron-proof diagram on the side. She took two copies of everything until the paper ran out, tried to reload, ended up with a wad jammed in the feeder, red lights flashing, problems beyond her technical grasp. What the hell, she was doing her best.

She wondered where Joe was, what he was up to. She'd burned his letter the moment she'd read it, told everyone it was from a guy she'd met in Tegoose. Even lied to Esther about it. Esther was okay but the woman was apt to talk, abhorred a silence.

She looked around the study, opened a few drawers, checked the other papers on the desk, but there was nothing there, just a load of bills and brochures and the usual shit you found in offices, old book matches, paper clips, batteries, plastic knobs or screws off some machine they got rid of years ago.

The brochures were about machines and construction, not medicine. Esther was right – the man knows nothing about medicine, has to rely on Frank.

There were no personal letters she could find, but then Mike never seemed to get much personal mail, the only personal thing in the place was an old snapshot with frayed edges of a bunch of students on a stone bridge over a little river, old buildings in the background. It took her a while to pick out Mike and Joe, Mike smoking, Joe with his arm on Mike's shoulder. She also found three hundred dollars in an envelope, put them in her back pocket, and replaced them in the envelope with a hand-written IOU.

Fuck Mike, it was Frank Joe was after. She went upstairs and tried the door of his room, but it was locked. She found a bucket and sponge in the kitchen, went outside, started cleaning windows. After five minutes she collected a step ladder from the outhouse and began cleaning upstairs, leaving Frank's window until second, just in case anyone was watching.

The sash pushed up easily. She kept working with the sponge, rubbed at the glass, went inside, polished it from there until the whole window was clean. She emptied the bucket of water onto the grass below her, gave a wave towards the clinic as though she'd seen someone she knew there, then popped back in through the window.

Joe wanted papers but he hadn't specified what papers, all the letter said was take anything that looked interesting. Documents, letters: if in doubt lift it.

She started with the chest of drawers: T-shirts, underwear, a couple of volumes of airport porn tucked in under a pile of jeans. Next she opened the cupboards and ran through the coat hangers, checking jacket pockets and the insides of shoes. There was swimming gear in there too, flippers and a mask and snorkel and a harpoon gun, all innocent enough. But then she didn't really know what she was looking for, Joe had just told her to look round if she got the chance, see if Frank left any clues.

There was a cardboard shoebox among the flippers. She put it on the bed, slipped off the rubber band and lifted the lid. More office junk, restaurant bills and taxi receipts and old airline tickets and a pocket book full of figures. Telephone call, three dollars, postage stamps, eight lempiras – the man's expenses. Who'd he submit expenses to?

Under the receipts was a smaller box, not much bigger than a cigarette pack, full of bullets. No gun, just ammunition.

Fancy that.

She placed the whole shoebox inside the bucket, gave the windows a last polish and climbed back out the window and down the ladder.

She walked back into Morgan's Hole along the coast road, her photocopies and the box swinging from her wrist in a plastic shopping bag, telling herself she was getting bored with this whole business. Not with Joe, but with Mike Osborne and Frank Carreras. At the same time she felt that something was about to happen that might shake up this fucking half-asleep drunk-breeding island, toss everything up in the air like knuckle jacks; maybe when they all came down again things might arrange themselves better. Maybe she'd really get to New York next time. Or London.

She was on the outskirts of town now, passing the first line of bleached-out tin-roof shacks, hogs asleep in the shadows, dogs unwrapping the garbage, flies everywhere. A voice came from the darkness inside a hut:

'How come you say you love God, you love God you go to church.'

A tall black man came out of the door, toothless, barefooted, trousers rolled to the knee, a stained shirt buttoned to the neck and knotted at the waist, a filthy yellow trucker's cap squashed over his concertina'd face. He sat down on the step, saying nothing. Not much to choose between him and the hogs.

She found Larry and Rod leaning against the rail outside the post office, looking across the street at Bobby Burgess's half-built concrete hall. The sign was still hanging from the scaffolding, 'Coming Soon, Praise The Lord, The Good Book Union of the Americas', except that someone had painted out 'Coming Soon' and written 'Gone Fishing' instead.

'You do that?' Sarah asked Larry.

'I ain't got the education do a thing like that,' Larry grinned.

Sarah put her elbows on the rail and shook her head.

'I don't know what's happened to young people these days, got no respect. What happened to the Swiss?'

'He cabled home for an airline ticket,' said Rod. 'Says he's going back to college. His father says if he finishes his studies he'll give him a car.'

'They have cars in Switzerland?' asked Sarah. 'I thought that place was all snow and mountains. So what's new?'

'What's new', said Larry, 'is you got a visitor.'

Joe was sitting crosslegged on the balcony at the top of the ladder, balancing a copy of *Reader's Digest* on his knee.

'That's private property,' Sarah called up from the road. 'You going to go quietly or do I have to call the police?'

'"All Property Is Theft",' said Joe, still looking at the magazine.

'Says who?'

'Pierre Joseph Proudhon.'

'Who the hell is he?'

'A Frenchman. Dead. Born 1809, died 1865, it says here.'

Joe closed the *Reader's Digest* and swung his legs over the edge of the balcony.

'Where'd you get the shirt?'

'Fell off the back of a Yank.'

'You bring anything back for me?'

'Another shirt, only pink,' said Joe. His was beige. 'You pleased to see me?'

'Maybe. You going to tell me what the fuck's going on round here?'

Joe told her what had happened at Tela, about Mercedes and Amos and the sailors, about Carmel and Martin and Fay and Dr Sinclair and Bobby and Bunty Burgess, Sarah taking it all in, deciding that maybe it wasn't such a boring business after all, not boring but scary and she couldn't make her mind up what to make of it.

They walked down towards the shore, through the palms and breadfruit trees, Joe talking while his eyes were on the birds, a carpenter woodpecker, humming birds, black and white pigeons, crows and crab-catchers. Joe had a thing about birds, needed to know what they were called, same way Willie used to, and she'd make up names for the ones she didn't know.

When they reached B.J.'s Joe went into the chalet and changed while Sarah waited outside, and when he came out again she asked him to show her the bruise on the side of his head, but he wouldn't, and she said 'Fuck You', and he said 'What, here?' They went back inside and stayed there for a little over two hours, naked on top of B.J.'s single white sheet, Joe sweating a lot in the heat, Sarah teasing him but laying off the Amazing Facts, drinking whisky straight from the bottle.

'You believe in God?' she asked him, head on his chest, sharing a cigarette between them.

'I believe man makes God in his own image,' said Joe.

'What the hell does that mean?'

'It means I think the Irish are Catholics because they're Irish and the Scots are Protestants because they're Scots, people chose a God that suits their temperament. The English don't believe in extremes so they come up with the Church of England. The Church of England is so theologically flexible you don't really have to believe in God at all.'

She passed him the cigarette.

'Do you believe in God?'

'I believe we come from the timeless shapeless individualless extragalactic mess, and for three score years and ten plus whatever the doctors inflict on us we're made individuals, and the purpose of this is to teach us that it's better to be part of the anonymous mess, grateful to be able to sink back into the eternal blob again. How about you?'

'I tell you what I think,' said Sarah. 'I think Bobby Burgess is probably gay.'

There was a knock at the door. Sarah got under the sheet while Joe pulled on a pair of shorts.

'Anyone in there?' B.J. shouted.

'Coming,' said Joe.

The preacher handed him a telegram.

'When did this come?' asked Joe.

'Fellow brought it over from the post office, just got in. You two eatin' tonight? Got shark steak comin' in if you interested.'

Joe said he'd let him know, went back into the chalet and ripped open the envelope, and read the message. It was dated that morning from Santa Julia.

JIUBA IT IS STOP E.T.A. THURSDAY STOP SUGGEST
YOU MAKE TRACKS STOP WW

Joe handed it across to Sarah.

'Where the hell's Santa Julia?'

'On the coast, twenty miles downstream from Jiuba. You goin'?'

'Yup. You want to come?'

Sarah thought for a full minute. It was the first time he'd ever seen her think about something that long.

'Sure,' she said eventually.

They got up, and walked on down to the thin pier which ran out into the lagoon. On the sand a little puffer-fish, caught in a net, had inflated itself, self-important and still confident of its invincibility as it suffocated. A dug-out was moored at the far end of the pier, a young black man in torn-off jeans worrying over the old Seagull motor bolted to its stern.

'You ever been down to Bull Strand?' asked Sarah.

'There's a Bull Strand on Cow Cay?'

'Best beach on the island. Only no one goes there because there's no road. Only people go down there are from the dive resorts, once a week the resorts pump out their shit tanks into the ocean, pile their people into boats and take them down to Bull Strand for a barbecue while the water clears.'

The boatman was called Moses and had lobster pots to check along the coast. It was a real dug-out, twenty feet long, three feet wide, with short planks nailed sideways to make seats.

They stayed a hundred yards out from the shore. The dug-out moved surprisingly fast as long as you didn't move around too much in her. The tree-line became jungle, running right down to the water: every once in a while they'd pass a clearing with a thatched hut built up on piles. The people here were Caribs, indigenous Indians, dirt poor and despised by the islanders. The huts were bamboo caked with dry red mud, the people mud-coloured too.

Sarah called Moses The Sprinkler. Joe asked why.

'Because I's a Methodist,' he explained. 'Methodists they's like Catholics, both Sprinklers. Baptists –' he pushed down the air with his open hand – 'they do the whole head.'

Moses' father owned forty acres along the bay, and Moses

had started to build what he called a hotel, an unclad timber frame set back from the sea, with a wooden staircase, leading nowhere. But he didn't plan to bring the road in.

'Too many people come, come for the day, go home to Morgan's Hole, spend no money.'

Those he wanted he'd bring in by boat. It was a real project, but he spoke of it with a distant vagueness that made it sound less concrete than it probably was. Maybe he'd just sell up and be done with it. He was sick of being poor. Tourists, he said, always disapproved of islanders trying to sell land, even on ninety-nine-year leases; but it was easy for them, they had money already.

Bull Strand was clean and wide, and stretched a full mile out to the eastern tip of the island. Inland it was screened by palms, and an area of jungle had been cleared for cattle, the ground red and dry, the cattle all bones. A low hill rose behind; Moses said the native Indians used to have a settlement there, and offered to take them up and show them where to dig for pottery shards. Joe said another time.

Moses left them off by a makeshift shelter built by the dive people, and said he'd pick them up again in a couple of hours when he'd finished with his pots. They stepped from the boat straight into the shallow water and waded ashore.

This is it, this is the idyll, Joe told himself, the day you get early in every affair when the world stops and you forget what's been before and what may come after.

As soon as The Sprinkler was gone they stripped off and walked into the warm sea, and swam out to the reef. The water was very clear, tinged the lightest green, the sky cloudless. Thin, translucent syringefish flew across the surface, and under the surface there were multicoloured butterfly fish, angelfish, damselfish, parrotfish, grunts, gobies, wrasses, moving in shoals or feeding singly and in pairs among the corals. Sarah said imagine they're birds. Joe dived, forcing his eyes open, wishing he'd brought a snorkel.

They found the turtle moving slowly through a deep trench in the coral, and followed it for ten minutes, sensing its loneliness.

'"Like a pelican in the wilderness,"' Joe recited afterwards, as they lay with their bodies in the shallow water at the edge of the beach, propped on their elbows, watching the hermit crabs.

> and like an owl that is in the desert,
> I have watched, and am even as it were a sparrow:
> that sitteth alone upon the house-top.

'That one of your songs?' asked Sarah.
'I wish it was.'
They ate dinner at B.J.'s, Sarah complaining about the coleslaw to get the preacher going, Joe watching her, drinking beer and playing footsie under the rough pine table. After they'd eaten they climbed the hill to the chapel, and Joe sat down at the old upright piano and asked her what she'd like him to play.
'Anything but modern jazz,' said Sarah. 'Never understood what people see in modern jazz.'
He played her Jelly Roll Morton instead, and some Bessie Smith, plus a couple of things of his own, and she stood with her chin on the piano watching him, tapping the lid with her fingers. It was almost midnight when they went to bed.

The next morning they got up at six and swam again, ate breakfast at the Chicken Shack, then walked up the slope and collected clothes from Sarah's hut for the trip to Jiuba. Omangatu stayed downstairs among her pots. It was only when they were leaving that she called Sarah over and spoke to her briefly.
'She says be careful,' Sarah explained as they set off up the hill towards Morgan's Hole, looking for a lift into town.
'Did she say what of?'
'Foreigners.'
'She mean me?'
Sarah laughed.
'I didn't ask.'

'Tell me something. Is she often right about things?'

'Sometimes,' said Sarah. 'But then who isn't.'

There was no traffic on the unpaved earth road. They'd walked about a mile before Joe got the sense they were being followed. At first it was no more than that, a sense of someone keeping track of them, holding back among the trees. Then when he'd stopped to light a cigarette he saw a figure some distance away.

'Don't look now,' he said quietly, flicking the match on to the road. 'We have company.'

Sarah looked straight away.

'The guy in the blue shirt?' she asked. 'Just ducked in behind the bank?'

'He's following us,' said Joe. 'Did you recognize him?'

'Nope,' said Sarah. 'My eyes ain't too good for that sort of thing. You want to stop and ask him what he wants?'

'Not yet. Just keep walking.'

Two minutes later a jeep came along, heading for Morgan's Hole. Sarah waved it down.

'You take the ride,' said Joe, 'I'll hold back and see who our friend is.'

Sarah climbed aboard. Joe bent down as if to follow her, then slipped into the ditch, keeping the vehicle between his body and the road back to Reef's End.

'See you at The Gable,' he said, and crept into the bushes.

'What the hell he doing?' the driver asked Sarah.

'Expanding his life experience. He ain't never been bitten by a snake before.'

Joe lay flat for a while, then crawled towards a tree and cautiously pulled himself upright, trying to keep out of sight while allowing himself a quick glance back down the road. Blueshirt had given up on the subterfuge and was jogging up the hill. In his right hand he carried a walkie-talkie.

Joe waited until he could hear footsteps, the heavy breathing as the man drew almost level with the tree. Then he jumped, a rugby tackle, pulling them both to the ground. He had no confidence in his wrestling skills, so the next thing he did was to hit the man full on the mouth with his fist. He didn't know how the mouth felt about it but his hand felt as if it had been run over by a tank. The scream of pain didn't come from Blueshirt, it came from Joe.

He got to his feet, shaking his hand, nursing it with his mouth. Blueshirt was still on the ground, conscious but not looking too happy. He was a big man, black, with broad boxer's shoulders and very short hair. The moment Joe looked at him he knew he was a cop. When he heard a vehicle approaching from the direction of town, he knew who'd be in it.

'Oh dear,' said Captain Mendes. 'Oh dear oh dear oh dear.'

26

It was the same office they'd sat in the day David Vaz hanged himself, the same blue and white Honduran flag hanging limp on the pole outside the door, the same view of shanties leading down to the shore through the square window, the same clip-board and ring of keys hanging on the nail above the desk. Even Mendes didn't seemed to have changed, still talking in short sentences, still keeping his own council.

He sat behind the desk, hands in prayer.

'You can have whatever lawyer you want. You can have consuls. You can have attorneys, clergymen, psychiatrists, as many as you need. Or can afford.' He lowered his hands and dropped them face-down on the desk. 'I think you will need them.'

Joe said nothing, his eyes on the floor. Keep your mouth shut, avoid eye contact. Mendes stood up and walked over to the window.

'There are formalities,' he said. 'Questions. I don't know why I need to ask them, we already know the answers. You were in Tela on Thursday night?'

Joe didn't answer.

'You went to see Dr Amos and his housekeeper. By the time you left they were both dead, the house was on fire.'

To Mendes' left a uniformed sergeant sat in an upright chair taking notes, writing down the Captain's questions, then waiting with his pen on the paper for Joe to reply.

'We know because you left your bag in the study, we have your passport.'

Joe scratched the back of his neck.

'Tell me, how much are you getting paid for this?' he asked. 'A hundred dollars? A thousand?'

'Tut tut,' said Mendes.

'Are you getting this?' Joe asked the sergeant. 'This is my statement, the one I want read in court. You see the trouble is that Frank Carreras works on expenses. It isn't his money, he has to keep a record. Everything he spends – tips, drinks, tropical clothing allowance, bribes to policemen, all written down and stored away in a locked closet in his room. In a shoebox. At least they were.'

Mendes didn't flicker.

'Facts are facts, Mr Wilde.'

'It's Joe,' Joe corrected him. 'At least it was last week.'

'That was then and this is now,' said the Captain.

'The Vaz business was cheap,' Joe continued. 'Fifty dollars, but he was only an islander, people always bump up the rates for tourists.'

Mendes sat down again and lit a cigarette.

'I'll keep you here tonight,' he said. 'Tomorrow we'll move you to San Pedro. The sergeant will bring you food.'

He began to tidy his papers.

It was Vaz's cell, too, twelve feet square, a bare concrete floor, a wooden bed-frame with a foam mattress, an upright chair, a sink, a meshed-in bulkhead light above the door. A parliament of small insects occupied the ceiling.

'Aren't you meant to take away my belt and shoe-laces?' he asked the sergeant.

The policeman gave him a Look.

'I don't figure you the hanging kind.'

As he locked the door a lizard scampered up the wall and vanished behind a beam. Joe sat down on the chair and gently massaged his knuckle. Nothing was broken, but the skin was badly bruised and painful to touch.

He started to sing, a piece of tartan pastiche he'd written twenty years ago, at Glenalmond – the same song Mike had asked for, the night Vaz hanged himself:

> There's a song that I keep in ma hearrrt,
> And a kilt that I keep in ma carrrr,
> There's a ceilidh tonight in Cathcart
> Yous'll be welcome whoever yous are –
> There'll be young folks and old folks a-plenty
> An' middle-aged people, perhaps,
> An' if they've had a drink they've had twenty
> They'll be throwing up into their laps
> An' pretending Fort William is pretty
> An' that Skye is nae owned by the Dutch
> That the weather on Mull is nae shitty
> An' the midgies don't worry them much . . .

He got up from the chair, went over to the sink and ran the tap over his hand.

> Och, ma daddy's in Lochmaddy
> An' ma wife is in Portree
> But ma pussie's in Kingussie
> So that's where I want tae be . . .

The trouble with Western man, as someone once said, is that he's incapable of being at peace alone in an empty room.

He sang his way through 'Route Sixty-Six', 'Save the Last Dance for Me', 'On the Street Where You Live', 'Tell Me Who's Been Polishing the Sun', 'There's a Kind of Hush', 'The Lord's My Shepherd', 'Proud To Be an Okie from Muskogee', 'For Those in Peril on the Sea' and 'Itsy Bitsy Teeny Weeny Yellow Polka-dot Bikini', at which point he launched into Desert Island Discs, doing the Sue Lawley bits all simpery, Sue asking the questions. Not questions – statements with a question-mark on the end, the same way Roy Plumley used to do it.

'Your father was a judge?'
'You went to school in Scotland?'
'Music was always important to you?'
'You never got married?'

The trick was to give a one-word answer, then Sue had to ask a real question.

'No.'

'Why not?'

'I've always been scared of permanence. That was what Dylan Thomas's drunken wife Caitlin said, I read it in *The Guardian* years ago and I can still remember every word: "It was, I think, the panic of vistas of dull permanence we fought so dementedly against. Permanence is the wet blanket that gives the deadly quality to marriages."'

Sue hitching up her bra strap – this is radio, no one's watching, not even the Studio Manager.

'What exactly do you mean by that?'

Six times a show she asked that, every time anyone said anything interesting.

'I mean I'm scared of getting it wrong. If you're scared of getting it wrong you play safe, if you play safe you wind up with the vistas of dull permanence again. I act radical but deep down I'm deadly cautious. No, that's not true, I'm not cautious but I think I ought to be.'

'You never fell in love?'

'All the time. There's no problem falling in love, it's finding someone to do it back that's the problem.'

'Maybe they all did and you didn't notice.'

'Maybe.'

'Your parents had a difficult marriage.'

'Difficult for whom?'

'You tell me.'

Difficult for everyone. Difficult for me, difficult for Margaret, difficult for Willie. Poor bugger didn't know anything about women or relationships, he never had a chance.

To understand everything is to forgive everything. Very true, not very helpful. It's not understanding which is the key, it's knowing what to do about it. Marx understood what was wrong with capitalism, but he hadn't a bloody clue how to fix it, people thought that because his analysis was right then his solution must be right too. A right lot of tears that all ended in. Then they assumed that because Marxism was a fuck-up, capitalism must be okay. Plenty more tears to come before they wise up to that one too.

Willie should never have married Margaret, Margaret should never have married Willie. But then where would I be?

'Your next record.'

'Anything by Randy Newman.'

'Anything?'

'Anything.'

At two o'clock he got lunch, a tin plate of refried beans, a piece of dead fish, type unknown, a plastic beaker and a jug of water.

After he'd eaten he played hide and seek with the gecko for a while, poking it out from under the beam with his shoe, closing his eyes so as not to see where it went next. Everyone likes playing hide and seek, even lizards.

Supper was guava stew and pigeon peas, plantain for afters. At seven it got dark, someone switched the light on, the mosquitos got worse. Shortly after eight the door opened and Mendes walked in.

The first thing he did was to throw Joe a pack of cigarettes.

'How long do you need?' he asked.

'A week,' said Joe. 'Maybe less.'

'You can have four days, more would be too risky. I can tell San Pedro Sula you're ill and unable to travel. The shoe box, where is it?'

Joe opened the pack and took out a cigarette. Mendes held out a light for him.

'Omangatu has it.'

Mendes smiled.

'You trust her?'

'Why not? Willie does. There's a whole hunk of stuff out there – affidavits, depositions, photocopies, everything a prosecuting counsel needs. Or almost.'

'When did she tell you?'

'When she heard about Amos. Willie said only hand it over if she heard he was dead, she decided she'd hand it before someone killed him.'

'You're sure he's still alive?'

'No. But I'm counting on it.'

Mendes let him out by the back door. The two men stood together on the step for a moment.

'To understand why I need the money,' Mendes said quietly, 'you would need to know my wife'. He smiled sadly. 'Sarah will meet you on the road to Reef's End, outside town. Be a little discreet until you're clear of the houses. Four days.'

'Four days it is,' said Joe.

The sky was watery and full of stars, a ghostly rice-paper moon hanging low over the black silhouette of the hills. He made his way along the shore until he reached the edge of town, and then cut up to the road. There were no street lights, the cabin doors were closed. Sounds of television came from inside, an argument, someone chopping food in a kitchen. The yellow eyes of a dog watched from the darkness, an unlit cyclist swerved to avoid him, blue land crabs scuttled in the undergrowth.

Sarah was waiting at a bend in the road. He saw her cigarette first, a single red dot in the darkness. She had on a thick fisherman's jumper that Joe recognized as one of Willie's, and carried a green nylon grip from which she extracted a second jumper, also Willie's. Who but Willie would take two sweaters to the Caribbean? But then Willie wasn't coming to the Caribbean, he was coming to Mexico. It could be cold at night in the sierras.

'Gonna be cool out there till the sun gets up,' she said.

'Out where?' asked Joe.

'Out there.'

She pointed at the sea.

Larry was waiting for them on the beach beside a small rubber inflatable, the kind that lets water in if you sit on the side. There was scarcely room for the three of them, Joe and Sarah squashed thigh to thigh in one end, Larry working the paddles.

'Would it be rude to ask where we're going?' asked Joe.

'I thought you wanted to go to Jiuba.'

'In this?'

'I'm beginning to think,' said Sarah, 'that you ain't as bright as I thought you was.'

It took them ten minutes to reach the yacht, riding on the swell beyond the reef. The boat was showing no lights. Larry helped Rod haul up the anchor while Joe and Sarah climbed into the cabin. The *Canada Goose* was thirty-two feet long, structurally sound but battered and bruised by her long trip down the Mississippi and the storm that had demasted her in Morgan's Hole the year before. Rod had taken care with the repairs but he'd lacked the right materials. You could also tell from the state of the galley that a bachelor had been living alone on her, and living simply.

But the *Goose* moved fast through the water, the engine throbbing on full power. The sea was calm and black. Sarah found a bottle of whisky in the galley, and the four of them sat together in the cockpit, smoking and talking. Joe was glad of his sweater. He found the mechanics and rituals of sailing incomprehensible, but he didn't mind boats as long as they were someone else's responsibility.

'We should make landfall around six in the morning,' said Rod. 'All things being equal.'

'Which landfall?' Joe asked.

'Santa Julia, I hope.'

He took out a laminated map showing the channels and reefs along the north coast and pointed to a settlement forty miles east of Trujillo.

'God knows what's there, but the fishermen say the anchorage is manageable. Jiuba's twenty miles upriver. I doubt the *Goose* will be able to manage it, but we'll see when we get there.'

Joe liked the Canadian, liked his eagerness, his enthusiasms, his uncomplaining nature, even his naïveté, but there was something sad about him, a sense that his life was drifting away, would never deliver what he wanted. Ten years from now he'd be old enough to be an eccentric exile, but in the meantime he was little more than a lost child. Joe also guessed that Rod was in love with Sarah, in a hopeless, private sort of way: that he'd do anything she asked.

At midnight Sarah went below to sleep. Joe stayed with Rod and Larry for a while, asking them about the boat, trips they'd made, storms they'd survived: small talk, but none the worse for that. Shortly after one he turned in too. Sarah was curled up diagonally across the thin double bed in the prow under a blanket, her gentle snores just audible against the slapping of the waves against the hull. She opened one eye as he crawled in beside her, then went back to sleep.

Larry woke them at five with mugs of coffee and toast, and they went up on deck, stiff-limbed and bleary. The sails were up, the sun was just rising to the east, the long flat coast of Honduras just visible in the distance. Two frigate birds were following them, wings beating lazily in the breeze. Further along the coast a trawler was fishing.

It was two in the afternoon by the time they reached Santa Julia. The village was built on an archipelago of small islands at the mouth of the river estuary, backed by low jungle hills, the houses on stilts, some thatched, some with tin roofs, the paint gone and the rotting woodwork bleached the colour of cigarette ash, lining inlets awash with rotting trash and tree fronds, the surface of the water bubbling with mosquitos and crabs.

A narrow canal separated the islands from the mainland, with shacks on either side and a through traffic of canoes, dug-outs and launches, leading to a ramshackle harbour. On the shore side of the canal, behind a shrimp processing plant, a cluster of modern buildings climbed the hillside – a manager's bungalow with a lawn and yelling American children playing outside it, a Seventh Day Adventist church, a police station. A black man in a white T-shirt was mowing the bungalow lawn, sprinklers watered the flowerbeds, black birds squabbled in the palms.

A mud-coloured dredger, riding high out of the water, motored through the canal and docked by two shrimpers alongside the pier. Rod followed it at a distance, waiting for the swell of its wash to subside, cut the *Goose*'s engine and tied up at the deck of a two-storey clapboard building splattered with advertising signs for Lombardini diesel and Champion spark plugs and a hand-painted notice that said 'Gift Shop Offers You General Merchandise And A Very Good Line In Hardware, Our Pleasure Is To Order It Let Us Know'. Above it a second sign said 'Property For Sale'. A stack of green soft-drink crates was piled against the wall.

Inside the shelves were bare, except for half a dozen relabelled rum bottles full of honey, cigarettes, soap, some rusting tins of peas and a refrigerator full of Frescos. A tired, thin, elderly Spaniard with the look of a man whose lungs had gone sat behind the counter reading a magazine.

'How you doing?' asked Rod.

The Spaniard looked up.

'Not so good. You need diesel? Help yourself, pay when you finished.'

Rod went outside to fill up. Joe stayed in the shop.

'We need to get to Jiuba. Is the river navigable?'

'Depends,' said the Spaniard.

'On what?'

'How much water in the river, how big your boat.' He glanced out of the door. 'What you draw in that?'

Joe hadn't a clue, it was like asking him how many horse-power a car had.

The Spaniard was shaking his head, something Joe suspected he did a lot.

'In that, not a chance.'

Joe offered him a cigarette. The Spaniard looked at the pack, took out a Marlboro, snapped off the filter and put it in his mouth.

'You want a boat?'

'Yes.'

He tapped his finger on the counter, thinking of possibilities, rejecting them.

'How long you need him for?'

'Two or three days,' said Joe.

The Spaniard was shaking his head again.

Sarah came through the door, went over to the freezer,

took out a bottle of Seven-Up, and bit off the cap. When Joe turned to look at her she made a gesture with her thumb and forefinger.

'Fifty dollars?' Joe mouthed.

'Fifty dollars'd buy this whole fucking town,' she said out loud, and passed him the bottle. 'But then who the hell'd want to buy it?'

The Spaniard was looking at Joe.

'You not Mr Wilde by any chance?'

'Joe Wilde, yes.'

'Why didn't you say?'

'You never asked.'

'Been expecting you, Mike Osborne sent word you might show up. You know how to work an outboard?'

'More or less.'

'Come back in an hour.'

Sarah paid for her drink, and they walked back out on to the deck. Joe felt exhausted: his hand hurt, the sweat ran down him in torrents, all the way down his back to his buttocks.

'So what's the plan?' Sarah asked.

'I guess Rod and Larry can stay here with the *Goose* and I'll go on upriver. If I'm not back by tomorrow he can come looking, maybe bring along a policeman or two.'

'You want me along?'

'It's up to you.'

She bit her nail.

'You planning on shooting anyone, torching their houses?'

'Maybe,' said Joe.

'Then I'll come. Willie goin' to be there too?'

'That's what I'm counting on.'

'You lookin' forward to seeing him?'

'In a way. How about you?'

Sarah bit her lip.

'Depends what kind of mood the man's in.'

He looked her in the eye, but there were no clues, none at all.

'Meanwhile', she added, 'we got an hour for the sights. Bright lights, big city. You fancy the shrimp plant or the Adventists?'

'The post office,' said Joe. 'At least I assume this place has a post office.'

They found it half a mile away, a tin hut between two banana trees, with a girl of fifteen behind the wooden counter listening to a pocket radio.

'Good afternoon,' said Joe, putting down a five-dollar bill. 'I wonder if you could help me. I'm trying to trace a telegram.'

The girl remembered the telegram, of course she did, you didn't get a lot of telegrams coming and going in Santa Julia.

The man who sent it was American, long hair, midthirties, big as a bear.

'Answering to the name of Richard Milhous Nixon, by any chance?' asked Joe.

The girl looked at him.

'I don't understand.'

'It's not important,' said Joe.

The Spaniard was standing on the quay when they got back, filling the twin outboards on a well-dented fifteen-foot aluminium riverboat. Joe looked at it suspiciously.

'How come she's flat-bottomed?'

The Spaniard screwed the top back on the fuel tank.

'Sandbanks. You feel her touching, get the engine out the water.'

He demonstrated, pulling a pin and swivelling the motor until the propellers were clear of the water. 'There's spare gas in front, alongside of the anchor. Flashlight in there too, but you shouldn't need him.'

'How much do I owe you?' asked Joe, reaching into his shirt pocket.

'You don't,' said the Spaniard. 'It's paid.'

For the first half hour the river was wide and slow and green, running like a wide road through the jungle. Joe steered cautiously, one hand on the outboard. Sarah sat in the prow, watching the water for submerged logs and hazards while he kept his eyes on the shore. They passed a village, half a dozen straw huts set back from the river edge, and a dug-out filled with Indians passed them on its way downstream. Apart from that they saw no humans, only wildlife: parrots cawed in the trees, monkeys barked, egrets and herons fished on the slobs. The heat was oppressive and Joe longed to swim, but he knew it would be madness. There were pin-sized fish in there that swam up your cock and then extended their barbs and stayed there: penisectomy was the only known cure.

The land began to rise on both sides to low jungle hills, and the river twisted west into a wide horseshoe bend. Silted beaches appeared on the outside of the arc. Half a dozen crocodiles slid down the sandbanks into the water as they approached. Shortly afterwards, beyond a point where a small tributary joined, the river narrowed again. Joe was watching the currents when he caught a glimpse of metal through the trees. Someone was waiting in the tributary.

He had just enough time to pull the arm of the outboard as hard as he could towards him. The boat lurched violently and turned through ninety degrees. At the same moment he heard the roar of another engine. He looked to his right. Two things happened. A steel rope laid diagonally across the river suddenly cleared the surface, at the precise spot the boat would have been if he'd kept heading upstream — ten feet further and they'd have capsized. Simultaneously a launch emerged at speed from the tributary. For a frozen moment he could see the whole length of the hawser. On the right-hand bank it was attached to a tall hardwood tree; on the opposite side it ran around a second tree and on to the back of the launch.

Joe steadied the boat and steered it back upstream against the current. The launch was thirty yards away, and in trouble: the force of the hawser had sheered off the mounting of the outboard, leaving the engine hanging loose by its safety cord. Frank Carreras had abandoned the wheel, and picked up a shotgun. Sarah screamed. Joe shouted at her to get down, and inched the boat towards the hawser. Frank hesitated, uncertain whether to use the gun or rescue the outboard.

'Grab the rope!' Joe shouted.

Sarah leaned forwards and took it in both hands, straining to lift it clear of the aluminium hull. The first time it slipped from her hands. Joe slowed the engine and glided with the current. A shot rang out, peppering the water to their left. He waited until Sarah had regained her balance, and pushed upstream again. There was a second shot, also wide. Frank didn't bother to reload: the launch was listing badly astern, and his hands were back at the wheel, struggling for control.

This time Sarah caught the rope, ducked down and let it pass over her. There was a clang as it sprang down against the hull. Joe kept the boat moving, and at the last second let go the outboard and grabbed. The metal hawser tore at his hands, and it took all his strength to hold it over his head. A moment later they were clear. Joe opened the throttle and they surged on upriver.

'He gonna follow us?' Sarah shouted.

Joe looked back. Frank had managed to beach the launch in the shallows and was reloading the shotgun, but he was already out of useful range.

'Not in that he isn't,' said Joe.

An English tourist and his West Indian companion drowned in a tragic boating accident. His father, a retired judge, missing presumed dead on a trip to see – what would Frank have planned? Mayan ruins? An aid project run by a friend of his son? The sort of story that makes five lines on an inside page in the British papers – what a tragedy, what a coincidence, how awful – and then vanishes.

Who cares?

27

JIUBA, BEFORE THE missionaries came, was no more than a general store and a cluster of stilted shacks strung out in a line between the mud road and banks of the Rio Paulaya, a sluggish slow-moving brown river which drained the jungle flatlands between the mountains and the sea, twenty miles to the south. It had an indigenous Indian population – not the hat-and-blanket Indians of Copán, but blow-pipe loincloth Indians, hardly out of the Stone Age, peoples who had lived undisturbed for centuries in the inhospitable swamps and jungles of Eastern Honduras and Nicaragua, terrain which held no riches for outsiders.

By the time the missionaries left, Jiuba looked more like a refugee camp. Five thousand or more Indians, lured from the woods by an astute cocktail of bribery and menace, had set up camp beside the river, given up their traditional way of life, put on cheap acrylic clothes and been taught to chant hymns.

Abandoned by the incomers, they had since learned to drink liquor and sell their daughters to the traders and fugitives who from time to time passed up and down the river; had learned to use the generator and video recorder on which they'd been made to watch Christian homilies, and acquired a library of badly duplicated pornography and cheap horror movies to fill in the long dark evenings. They'd also taken to wearing each other's clothes, so that the men often dressed in ankle-length paisley frocks and the women in white boxer shorts and nothing else. They died of malaria, they died of drink, they died of dysentery, they died because there didn't seem much point in doing anything else. Stone Age man had hit the Junk Age in a period of a little under ten years. Of the five thousand who had come out of the jungles slightly less than one third were still alive.

Whenever Mike Osborne thought about the place he had to remind himself of what he believed he could achieve there. Aside from the human crisis the place was fraught with practical problems. There was electricity when the generators were running, but they often broke down. Fuel had to be brought up the river by boat, or trucked in over unpaved and often impassible roads from Trujillo. The climate was unspeakable: Frank Carreras compared it to standing under a hot shower in a cage full of insects. There were snakes, too, and scorpions, and jaguars, and rodents with teeth that could cut through steel mesh.

It was rough country, by any standards. Those native Indians who had refused the missionaries and stayed in the jungle were elusive and often hostile. The Honduran incomers were violent and lawless – traders and slash-burning farmers, often drunken, always violent and utterly without scruple.

Every few years a new wave of intruders would arrive – missionaries, government officials, mineral prospectors, political refugees from across the Nicaraguan border – and try to carve out enclaves for themselves. Few lasted more than a year: disease, climate, and physical violence dealt with the weak, and the strong soon packed their bags and headed back to the relative security of the settled lands to the north and west. You found the ruins of their ambitions on the river banks, or up tracks off the road, tin buildings abandoned to the jungle, parrots inhabiting the eaves, termites eating away at the timbers, every one a reminder of the scale of the task ahead, and its probable conclusion.

And yet Mike believed it could be done. He wasn't here to steal the jungle's natural resources, or collect taxes, or preach hell-fire religion; he didn't want to civilize, or convert, or build a legend for himself. He just wanted to treat the sick, period.

He'd bought Jiuba for 50,000 dollars from the missionaries the year they were flung out by the Honduran government for mistreating the Indians. Not because the Hondurans gave a shit about how anyone treated the Indians, but because Peace Corps workers who had seen what was going on made a fuss in Washington, and Washington demanded action. Kicking out half a dozen biblical nuts was exactly the sort of token action that suited both sides. The missionaries moved on to Peru, Tegucigalpa got its military aid, everyone was happy.

Mike was happy too. What he got for his money was an all-American hamlet on the banks of a navigable river, with an air strip and a bunch of buildings constructed to standards which would not have been out of place in small-town America.

At the heart of the settlement, on a low rise a hundred yards back from the river, were three well-built bungalows, with concrete walls and tiled roofs and air-conditioning, white-painted storm shutters and window frames, galvanized water tanks, washing lines, dog kennels, children's swings and sand-pits, and septic tanks, all enclosed behind low paling fences.

There were screwmarks on the walls where the satellite TV dishes had been, but the dishes and TVs had gone back to Oklahoma. The rest of the fixtures and fittings came with the houses as a job lot. They included the furniture, generators, fridges, cookers, gingham curtains, even showers and flush toilets.

The missionaries and their families had left in a hurry, and in the months before Mike took possession nature had begun to reclaim the small suburban gardens. Ant-hills had appeared in the overgrown lawns, and the flowerbeds were already strangled by creepers and vines. But Mike wasn't worried about the gardens: what he needed was the buildings.

Apart from the bungalows these included a schoolhouse, a chapel and a small multi-purpose shed which the Godsquad had used as a storehouse. Mike had hired local labour to clean up and clear the vegetation, and appointed a foreman to oversee the maintenance of the existing structures and the erection of two long wards on the edge of the jungle, close to the Indian settlement.

Between them, he and Frank had already found most of the staff. The ancillary workers they'd hired locally, where possible. Trained workers – two paramedics and six nurses, all recruited and paid for by Third Aid – were due to fly in at the end of the week.

Meanwhile, Mike was the only white man in Jiuba that afternoon. He sat on a tree stump at the edge of the clearing, dressed in shorts and canvas boots and a white cotton hat, sweat pouring down his face, thinking about the long road that had brought him to Jiuba; about the places he'd lived, Perthshire, Cambridge, London, Boston, the flats and houses, the countries he'd visited as a reporter, Afghanistan, Alaska, the Yemen, Tibet, dry deserts and the champagne air of the Alps.

But mostly he thought of his childhood in the Scottish borders: of Dryburgh, Smailholm, Duns and St Boswells, rain-washed reiver towns tamed by John Knox; of red sandstone bridges and peel towers and gothic villas, the Clydesdale Bank and the Carnegie Library; of shepherds and sheepdog trials, bare hills, the cold black River Tweed running smooth over salmon weirs, of sedgegrass, bog-cotton and solitary pines; of seven-asides and shearing contests, of whisky and oatcakes and flasks of hot tea.

And now Jiuba.

He thought too of friendships and lovers, of people he'd worked with and people he'd loved. Only Joe knew it all, only Joe would understand.

There were times in his life that he looked back on with pleasure, times when the luck was running, times when he had known harmony with the world, excitement at the start of each day. Times too that were wasted, empty, spent alone with no purpose, tiresome to remember because they meant so little.

All that was gone, the good and the bad, there was no

thought in his head of going back. He felt a different excitement now. If he died in this place, if his body rotted in this soil, he'd die happy. Whatever happened to Mike Osborne? He found himself, he found his purpose, he found the bliss of solitude.

A figure was climbing the bank from the river. At first he thought it as one of the construction workers – Juan, perhaps, who had two wives and seventeen children and kept a pet snake in his lunchbox; or Franco with three fingers on his left hand who liked to joke about the Indian women. He took off his hat and wiped the sweat from his eyes and looked again.

'Joe!'

He got up and started walking across the clearing. Joe had seen him, and waved back.

How the hell did he get there? The night rains had washed away the track to Trujillo, it would be days before they had it cleared. The radio had been dead for three days: Frank had fixed for a replacement to be brought in but there was no sign of it arriving.

The river: he must have come up the river from Santa Julia.

Wherever he'd come from Mike was pleased to see him.

The two men were twenty yards apart now, Mike stopped, and waited for Joe to reach him.

'What kept you?'

'Leaves on the line at Morden,' said Joe. 'That, and your friend Frank Carreras.'

'Slow down,' said Mike. 'What are you talking about?'

Joe was unshaven, the skin beneath his eyes pouched with grey. His arms and legs were red with sunburn.

'I got a cable from Willie telling me he'd meet me here. Someone had fixed a boat for us at Santa Julia. And a couple of miles upstream Frank Carreras was waiting with a shotgun and fifty metres of steel hawser.'

'Oh God,' said Mike. He sounded vague, his eyes defocused. 'Where is he now?'

'Last time I saw him he was beached on the river bank reloading a shotgun.'

'Did he follow you?'

'Not yet, but I expect he will. You got any firearms here?'

'There's a pistol somewhere, I think. Back at the bungalow.'

'Are you all right, Mike?' Joe asked.

Mike didn't answer. Joe tried again.

'Is Willie here?'

'Willie?'

'My father.'

Mike stared at the jungle for a moment. Joe could see him trying to concentrate.

'No, he isn't. Should he be?'

'I hoped you could tell me. We'd better get moving. Does this place have any police?'

Mike laughed.

'Good God no. Why would we need the police?'

Joe grabbed him by the shoulders.

'For God's sake, Mike.'

Mike's eyes came back in focus.

'I'm sorry, Joe. It's just tiredness. Don't worry about Frank, I can handle him.'

'You reckon,' said Joe.

They set off across the clearing. There were parrots in the trees, vain argumentative birds. A mule was tied to the railings. The sounds of carpentry came from the new wards. Joe wasn't saying much, just looking around, taking it all in. So this was Jiuba, memorial to the late housekeeper Virginia. Also to twentieth-century evangelism; and in years to come to Mike Osborne.

Looking at it you knew it was hopeless: blink and the jungle would cover it all again.

It was cool inside the bungalow, air conditioning units rattling in the windows. Frank and Mike had a bedroom each; the living room was stacked with crates, the kitchen doubled as an office, with papers and supplies piled up around the furniture, a sideboard, a formica-topped table, half a dozen plastic-seated upright chairs, a standard lamp with a raffia shade. The sink was full of unwashed dishes.

Mike went into one of the bedrooms and came back with the pistol and a box of shells, counted out five, loaded them into the magazine and tucked the gun into his waistband. Joe got beers from the fridge.

There was an open folder on the table, embossed with the name Masson-Pohl, and a half-written letter in a portable typewriter. Mike cleared them away and they both sat down. Joe kept his eyes on the window, watching the clearing, listening.

'Someone tried to kill me, Mike. In Tela. They shot Amos and Mercedes. I was downstairs, I don't know if they knew I was there, they may have been hoping to get rid of the other two before I arrived. I heard the shots, ran upstairs, and got sandbagged. Next thing I knew the place was on fire. I got out just in time.'

'Jesus,' said Mike. He thought for a while. 'You're sure it was you they were after?'

'Sure. I wondered myself for a while, wondered if it could just have been a burglary, something I stumbled across. But whoever it was then rang the police and fingered me for shooting Amos. Mendes arrested me when I got back to the Cay.'

'Then how come you're here?'

'I paid him off,' said Joe. 'Same way that Frank did.'

He watched Mike's face, saw the focus go from his eyes.

'It's more complicated than you think,' Mike said eventually.

Joe put down his glass.

'I don't think so, Mike. I think it's all very simple. The only complication is Willie.'

28

'How much do you know?' asked Mike.

'Most of it' said Joe. He got up and collected another beer from the fridge. 'I know about Masson-Pohl and Quadrone B, I know Masson-Pohl control Third Aid, I know about David Vaz, and the other poor bastards. I know how much it costs to develop a new drug, and how much it costs to test it in Europe or the States, and what the restrictions are. I know it's a great deal cheaper to try the bloody thing out on black men and brown men in a place like Honduras than it is to do it in New York or Sydney or Dublin or wherever else drug companies normally do their tests. And I don't know but I can guess the sort of sums you've done in your head and the deals you've made with your conscience to justify the whole thing. I also know you think what you're doing is a noble thing to do. Stop me if I'm boring you.'

'You're not,' said Mike. 'Keep talking.'

'I've talked to Bobby Burgess. He told me about the complications with Quadrone A, which he suspected was what finally fucked David Vaz's health. He was suspicious about David, but when the others went down he was more than suspicious. But he didn't want to get involved. Willie wanted him to make a statement, but he wouldn't, he had enough problems of his own.'

'The rest is mostly guesswork. Willie smelled a rat, but he didn't know if the rat was you or Frank Carreras, so he set about finding out. He's a lawyer, he set about it the same way any lawyer would. He looked for witnesses, he researched the background, he talked to Sinclair and Amos and I don't know who else. Amos already had his suspicions, but he couldn't do anything about it, he was old and blind and his memory was cracking up. They worked on it together. The drugs were coming in through Copán, Frank picked them up and brought them to the Cay and stored them in the fridge in the clinic, alongside all the anti-malarial stuff. And they got mixed up. Someone – I don't know who, could have been Frank, could have been Esther, it doesn't really matter – gave the wrong injections. First to Vaz, then to the other five.'

'Meanwhile Willie's out there some place sniffing around, and I've landed in looking for Willie. David Vaz came to the Rectory looking for help, and wound up in the wrong place at the wrong time. He didn't blow up the jeep, you did that, placed the charge and timed it so you knew we were safe inside the house, make it look as though someone was out to get you. You couldn't think who that was supposed to be so you fingered poor old Bobby Burgess. The man's a nerd but he's not the killing kind, he even gets Bunty to squash his cockroaches for him. Not that I think you killed David, he did that for you, by then he was so ill he couldn't think straight. Is this making sense?'

Mike was sitting down again, legs stretched out in front of him, inspecting his feet. He didn't look up.

'There are 300 million cases of malaria in the world at the moment. A million and a half people will die of it this year. No one's doing anything about it, they've given up.'

'I know that,' said Joe. 'You already told me.'

They sat in silence, listening to the air-conditioning, the hum of the fridge, Joe still watching the clearing. Mike ran his hand back through his hair.

'You remember I was talking to you about the Great War, about the need to discover the hidden idiocies of our own generation. Our sin is the same as the men and women who let the Somme happen, it's the sin of doing nothing, pretending the suffering of others doesn't exist, cultivating our gardens and not looking over the fence to see what's happening on the other side. I came down here from Boston and looked at what was going on, but I looked at it with different eyes, I looked on it as though it was the Somme, and decided to do something. Not a lot, but something. That's all.'

'It doesn't work like that, Mike,' said Joe. 'Where do you stop? You make your tryst with the devil, you take money from pharmaceutical companies. Forget for the moment that Masson-Pohl aren't in this for love of the human race, that they're simply looking for ways to make more money. That's not important, it's simply the way capitalism works. What matters is what it does to you. At least that's what matters to me.'

The boat was moored a mile downstream, hidden from view by an overhanging branch. Sarah wanted to go ashore, but she felt safer where she was, out of reach of the snakes and jaguars she was convinced lurked in the undergrowth. She wished Joe would get back, she wished she was home on Cow Cay reading a magazine, she wished they had sea breezes up here, instead of this heavy, heavy heat.

The hull was aluminium and hot to the touch, fifteen feet of open boat with two well-used Yamaha outboards bolted to the stern, a can of spare fuel down in the bilge and a cool-box of beer and Seven-Up, no longer cool. She couldn't understand why anyone would own an aluminium boat in this climate.

She slapped her neck. There were insects everywhere. Not just mosquitos, all manner of flying insects, black, brown and red, purple and yellow, all of them hungry. Butterflies, too, big fuckers, keeping low over the water.

In winter, in Ontario, Rod had told her, it was so cold you didn't go out at all, you got in your car in the garage, drove it to work, parked underground, took the elevator to your job, shopped in heated malls full of things you don't need, bought your food precooked in the supermarket, went home and watched TV, called your friends up on the phone.

Rod told her about it to explain why he never wanted to go home again, but it sounded like heaven to her, she couldn't figure the catch.

She looked at her watch. Joe had been gone an hour.

'What Third Aid give me', said Mike, 'is the money to save lives. They pay for the running of St Andrews, they've financed this place. You've seen the results. They have a drug which they think can control malaria. This way they can get it to market in half the time. Every month it's available saves more lives.'

'It takes lives too.'

'I know, that upsets me too, believe me. Someone screwed up, it shouldn't have happened, the doses are meant to go to patients who are already terminal. Quadrone A had side effects, but they've sorted that now, we're on to Quadrone B.'

'How long are you going to keep going?' asked Joe. 'C? D? Right through the alphabet? What happens when they ask you to start testing cosmetics or sun-creams?'

'The preliminary results are good.'

'You killed those people, Mike.'

'You could look at it that way. But you have to take the broader view. It sounds corny, but you *have* to. For every patient I've lost we'll save dozens, maybe hundreds, maybe thousands. Anyway, we kill people every day by neglect and indifference. No one makes much of a fuss about it.

'We get excited by a major famine, a TV documentary, the odd charity concert. But those things only scratch the surface. The basic problem is that whole continents are undernourished and racked by disease while the developed world puts on weight and worries about plastic surgery. Hour by hour people die who don't need to die, but we're still looking for some miracle fix which will solve the problem without anyone getting hurt and without touching the West's standard of living. We're kidding ourselves, it doesn't exist. We have to break the taboo.'

Joe looked at his friend, looked at the battered steel

pistol butt sticking out of his trousers. He wondered what he was going to do. Wondered too how long it would take Frank to fix his boat. And where Willie was. Tell Joe Willie's coming to Jiuba, tell Willie Joe's coming to Jiuba, bait the trap both ways.

'Where do you stop?' he asked. 'Malthus had a perfectly good theory for all this, he said let nature run its course. You think Quadrone B's okay, but you don't know. Masson-Pohl aren't in this game to save mankind, they're in it to make money for their shareholders. It's cheaper for them to use brown men to test their investment on, that's all.'

'I don't give a shit what their motives are. What matters is finding a way to beat malaria.'

'What matters,' said Joe, 'is how we behave as individuals, that's all. The moment we start cutting moral corners on one thing, we start cutting them on others.'

'That's a handy excuse.' Mike put down his beer. 'I'm sorry, that was unfair. It's just that this bloody cult of the individual drives me nuts. Look at the time and money that the West puts into freeing a single Middle East hostage or tracking down a one-off killer in the Home Counties. Some guy kills someone in a pub, we'll put 200 policemen on the case. Millions of pounds, all the resources of the state. How much did the bankruptcy people pay themselves for looking over Robert Maxwell's books? All that matters is that the bastard's dead. You try raising that kind of money to build a hospital in Somalia or Bolivia or wherever, listen to the answers you get.'

'You still haven't told me where you draw the line,' said Joe. 'What about Amos and Mercedes?'

Mike looked away.

'They wouldn't have died if it wasn't for Willie.'

'Are you going to kill him too?'

'I didn't kill them. That was Frank.'

'Do you know where Willie is?'

'On his way. That was the plan, get both of you here, find out what you knew, explain what I'm doing. I thought you'd understand.'

'Your plan, but not Frank's. Frank had a different idea.'

'I knew nothing about it, Joe. I swear.'

'And what were you going to do if Willie and I listened to your story and decided not to buy it, to go public?'

'I hadn't thought that far ahead,' said Mike.

'Then you'd better start thinking now. Because I've listened, and I don't buy it.'

'You'd destroy St Andrews? You'd destroy what we're about to do here?'

'It doesn't have to be like that,' said Joe. 'You need help, Mike. You said it yourself, only I didn't understand what you meant.'

Joe was still watching the clearing, still listening. At first he thought the sound of the outboard coming from the river was something else, a distant chain-saw, a generator. But as it got closer he knew.

'Company coming,' he said quietly to Mike, eyes scanning the jungle. 'I've told you what side I'm on, it's your turn now.'

But Mike had already decided. When Joe looked back into the room his oldest friend, the man whom he'd known and loved for all his adult life, was standing there expressionless, holding the pistol, pointing it at Joe.

'I don't want to, Joe,' Mike said. 'But if I have to, I will.'

When Sarah heard the engine, she changed her mind about the jaguars. Maybe he wouldn't see the boat, maybe he would. She wasn't about to stick around and find out which. She grabbed a branch and swung herself ashore, grazing her leg as she stumbled among the roots. The undergrowth was dense and treacherous. Thorns tore at her legs and arms, but she pushed on, trying not to disturb the foliage. By the time Frank's launch passed she had a three-foot-thick hardwood tree trunk between her and the river. She waited until he was upstream before risking a look. Frank was in the stern, one hand on the outboard, the shotgun crooked under his shoulder. As she watched she heard him slow the engine as he approached the jetty.

Her first instinct was to get away from the river. She struck inland, fighting her way through the vines and lianas, clambering over the ghoulish roots of the hardwoods, watching in horror as fallen leaves sprouted wings and dead twigs scrambled away from her footfall. This whole fucking place was alive.

She'd gone maybe fifty yards when she hit the path, a narrow mud canyon three feet wide which twisted through the jungle towards the mission. She stopped and listened, looked both ways, and then set off. God knew what she'd find at the end of it, but she wasn't going back into the jungle. Not now, not never.

Gradually the path widened. She walked cautiously, jumping at every sound, every time a branch brushed against her or an insect landed on her arm. But despite her caution the Indian must have been there a full thirty seconds before she noticed him.

He was standing still as a stone, wearing only a pair of ill-fitting jeans and a necklace of feathers. A cigarette hung from his mouth. The moment Sarah saw him he vanished. She turned to run back the way she had come. Two other Indians blocked her way. One wore a loose cotton dress over his jeans, the other a pair of what looked to her like golfing shorts, yellow with a purple check, and a trucking cap. Both carried bows and arrows. Their faces were painted in alternate stripes of white and ochre. She turned again. Feather Necklace was back, and he had company, maybe a dozen males, dressed as though they'd run at speed through the garment rails of a charity shop. They carried arms, machetes and bows and blowpipes, and one of them had a ghetto-blaster suspended on a long strap from his neck.

Her first instinct was to take off her T-shirt and use it as a white flag. She picked up a stick, took off her shirt and passed the pole through the armholes, and held it aloft.

Instantly the Indians raised their weapons and began to jabber excitedly. Sarah thought of the statue of St Sebastian in the cathedral in La Ceiba, the saint in a nice modern three-piece suit and polished black shoes and a nylon hairpiece, with a white shirt and tie, soaked in blood and hedgehogged with arrows, two of which stuck out of his hat like a cowboy in a cartoon, Seb looking up at the ceiling delighted with himself despite the arrows. Must have been on something, you couldn't feel like that with a chest full of arrows unless your brain was getting chemical help from somewhere.

They don't put those bows down soon, she told herself, I'm going to shit myself.

As she watched the Indian with the ghetto-blaster reached down and pushed a button. The sound hit her like a disco machine.

> Jesus Loves Me, This I Know,
> For The Good Lord Told Me So

A full choir, organ, trumpets, the works.

I'm going back in the jungle, she decided. Now.

She had one foot back in the jungle when she saw the snake.

At that point Sarah screamed.

29

It was fifty years since Willie Wilde had ridden a motorcycle. They'd changed, but not much. Same principles, just a lot of new gizmos he didn't understand and soon discovered he didn't need. Fellow he bought it off in La Ceiba showed him the whys and wherefores, tried to fiddle him on the exchange rate, laughed when Willie pulled him up. No hard feelings, that was the trick to this country. And no soft ones either.

He was sick of travelling. Tegoose, Houston, New Orleans, Tegoose, San Pedro, La Entrada, Tegoose again, San Pedro again, buses and string-tied aeroplanes, cheap hotels, even a brothel once, in error. And now Jiuba. Why the hell did Joe want to meet him in Jiuba?

Sick of travelling, but elated by the bike, the warm air rushing past, the excitement of a downhill run after a long climb.

The first twenty miles from Trujillo were easy enough. The road to Jiuba ran a straight line through banana and pineapple plantations, unpaved but in reasonable order. Willie was stiff as a board on the bike, but not too uncomfortably so: the problem arose when he got off and tried to straighten his rusted-over joints. His skin by now was the colour of blotched redwood. He wore shorts, a battered panama and what had once been a white shirt. His kit was in a canvas bag.

Once the road left the plain the going deteriorated. There were watercourses with no bridges, fords where the only way across was to drive straight through, avoiding the rocks as best you could. There was little habitation along the way, just the odd Carib settlement and Indian village. He didn't talk to anyone as he drove through, just smiled, gave them a wave, headed on into the jungle.

Bloody Joe, the boy could have messed up everything. Maybe he has. But rather to his surprise Willie looked forward to seeing him. And to being seen.

He spent much of the journey thinking about food, planning menus, all week he'd been planning the meal he'd have when he got home. Mixed antipasto with fried haloumi, then bouillabaisse, heavy on the garlic, then Châteaubriand, the kind they used to do in the Green Dragon at Hereford, rare and tender, with crunchy roast potatoes, horseradish, asparagus, maybe a light side-salad. And for pudding Ambrosia creamed rice with home-made strawberry jam. In fact when he got as far as the pudding he wondered if he wouldn't be better off settling for nursery food right through, start with sardines on white toast, steak and kidney pie and mash and frozen peas, maybe even ketchup.

The going got worse, the ruts deeper, the fords more hazardous. Three hours into the journey he reached a village on the banks of a deep river, and had to bribe a ferryman to take him across. Thereafter progress was slow, the land beginning to rise towards low hills, until finally he reached a point where the road had been washed away entirely. A crew with an old bulldozer was trying to make good the damage. They carried the motorbike by hand through the boulders, used ropes to haul it up the slope, Willie standing watching, saying 'Thank You, Thank You, You're Most Kind', over and over again in loud English, slipping them ten dollars when they'd finished.

Just as he was leaving he turned to the foreman.

'Anyone else been up this way today?'

The foreman shook his head.

'Only Indians.'

'Aeroplanes?' asked Willie, pointing at the sky.

'No aeroplanes.'

Odd, that.

Jiuba wasn't the sort of place you could drop in on incognito. But he knew all the ways in and out, where the flights came from and what they carried, which boats came up the river, who ran them, what they were paid. Amos had good contacts, once you knew the questions to ask the old idiot.

Carmel said Amos was dead now, Amos and Mercedes both. Two murder counts to add to the list. But the problem here wasn't finding out who'd done what, the problem was finding who you could trust to tell about it. Not the police, the police were anyone's for half a crown. If there were going to be charges they would be filed in the States. At first, when he knew Frank was involved but before he knew for sure Mike was, it occurred to him to talk to someone. But they'd think he was mad, this old Englishman with a bee in his bonnet.

Say nothing until you can prove it. Do nothing until you're sure.

His body ached, the skin on his face and arms was raw and burned, the heat and humidity were intolerable, but he felt fitter than he'd felt in years. His spirits were high too. Once he'd got the menu fixed he started whistling Gilbert and Sullivan, all the way through *HMS Pinafore* and *The Gondoliers*, then he started singing hymns, tuneless but *fortissimo*.

He'd bought Coca-Cola and biscuits and a tin of tuna in Trujillo, and helped himself to a bunch of bananas along the way. Around midday he stopped at a clearing, propped the bike against a tree and ate lunch. Not a soul around, just the clamour of parrots and the screeching of monkeys. After he'd eaten he lit a cigarette and sat on a stump, massaging his joints and smearing barrier cream on his face and arms.

He wondered who or what was waiting for him at Jiuba.

It doesn't matter now, he said out loud. *Wilde v Osborne*

and others is a foregone conclusion. It doesn't matter what happens to me. The evidence is all there with or without me now. If I live I live, if I die I die. He wouldn't mind a bit longer, though, given the choice.

Which is why he decided to approach Jiuba with a certain circumspection.

Mike Osborne was still holding the gun.

'You'll have to kill us both, you know that,' Joe said, looking him straight in the eyes. There was nothing there.

Keep talking, he told himself.

'I met a guy once, a journalist, he was out in Australia doing a film about the Australian army. The military took him out on manoeuvres one day, one side pretending to be Russians, the others the good guys. Blanks going off left right and centre, choppers flying around. And in the middle of it the good guys ran out of ammunition. The colonel sent up a flare, called a temporary truce, told them that for the rest of the exercise they'd have to fight without ammo. If they saw one of the other side they had to point their guns and then shout "bang!" as loud as they could. If someone shouted bang at you you were dead. And then he told them to get on with it again, they spent the rest of the day running round the countryside hiding behind trees and shouting "bang".'

Mike had told him the story.

'You don't understand,' said Mike. 'I'm the good guy, you're the Russian.'

'Bullshit.'

Mike said nothing.

'A BBC radio reporter was sent down to Plymouth to welcome Sir Francis Chichester back from sailing round the world,' Joe continued. 'When he got back he submitted his expenses for the day, including a claim for a hundred pounds for the hire of a cabin cruiser to go out and greet the flotilla. His editor accused him to his face of lying, he said he'd seen Chichester's return on TV, seen the flotilla, seen your man in a little rowing boat doing his commentary. Your man says oh, how stupid of me, took back the claim and wrote in a new line: to hire of rowing boat to reach cabin cruiser, ten pounds.'

Mike went over to the table, picked up the pack of Marlboro with his free hand, tapped out a cigarette and put it in his mouth, holding it between his teeth without lighting it. The gun was still pointed at Joe.

Joe was looking over Mike's shoulder, out the window, wondering what Frank Carreras was up to. It didn't take him long to find out.

Frank may have skirted the clearing stealthily, but he came in the back door of the bungalow like a truck at full speed: kicked the door clean out of its frame and kept going, shotgun raised, just to make sure he was welcome.

'Mike?' he bellowed.

'In here,' said Mike, not moving. 'We've got a caller.'

'Well well well,' said the American. He stood in the kitchen doorway, unshaven, his sixteen corn-fed stone sweating freely, a red bandanna tied round his neck. 'Just the one? What happened to your lady friend, Joe? And your father, come to that – Willie didn't show yet?'

They have a problem, Joe realized. They need all three of us, because Willie knows, and Sarah knows, and all it needs is one to talk. They need to kill us all.

And they need the accident, because there are too many people here, too many potential witnesses. Workmen, Indians, paramedics. That's why Frank hit us downriver. That's why he'll be planning to get to Willie before he gets here too.

He wondered too where Sarah was, if she was still on the boat, if Frank had seen her.

Frank collected a beer from the fridge and sat down, shotgun across his knees.

'So how you doing, Joe? Mike been filling you in on current developments in the medical world?'

'I'm fine,' said Joe. 'It's Mike I'm worried about.'

'Mike? What about me? Shit, has he been telling you all

this is my idea? No no no – I'm just a jobbing actor, Mike's the director. That's right, isn't it Mike?'

Mike nodded.

'He's the one who does the hiring round here,' Frank went on, 'Just in case you have any illusions. I'd hate to think you had the impression he was being used. He called us, not vice-versa. Not that it matters much.'

'Don't worry, I know', said Joe. 'Illusions aren't a problem to me any more. I also know you killed Amos and Mercedes on your own initiative, and I know you've already tried to kill me twice, and I've a shrewd suspicion you haven't finished yet.'

Frank looked at his watch.

'The old boy left Trujillo this morning. He shouldn't be long. How we going to handle this, Mike?'

Joe watched Mike's face, saw him wince, but only for a moment. It was like looking at a house you once lived in, a car you used to own, so familiar that you have to work hard to remind yourself that they're not part of your life any more.

'Seems to me we need another accident or two,' Frank suggested.

Joe realized Mike wasn't listening.

'What?' he asked.

'I was suggesting an accident.'

'Sure,' said Mike. He was still staring at Joe, but it was a blind stare, his mind somewhere else entirely. 'What had you in mind?'

'What I have in mind', said Frank, 'is that someone is going to have to go meet Willie and someone is going to have to wait here with our friend Joe, and at the risk of sounding selfish I think whoever it is stays with Joe shouldn't be his childhood buddy because he might get overtaken by a sudden rush of sentiment.'

No one said anything for a full minute.

'I'll take care of Willie,' Mike said finally. He got to his feet, still holding the pistol.

'Go for the tyres,' said Frank. 'Meanwhile Joe and I'll go

for a little walk down to the river, see if we can find Sarah, send them back downriver. In one way or another.'

Mike hesitated.

'I'm not sure I can do it,' he said.

'Okay,' said Frank. 'You stay, I'll go look after Willie, we'll sort the rest later. That pistol of yours loaded?'

'Yes.'

Frank was at the door now, checking the safety on the shotgun.

'You screw up for me, you screw up for yourself too.'

'I know,' said Mike.

'See y'all,' said Frank. And then he was gone.

'What's in all this for him?' Joe asked as he watched the big American walk across the clearing.

'I don't know and I don't really care,' said Mike. 'Excitement, I suppose. And money. And maybe a bit of idealism too.'

Joe was watching the gun.

'I suppose a cigarette's out of the question?'

Mike reached into his shirt pocket, fumbling for the pack single-handed, eyes still on Joe. He pulled out a Marlboro and pushed it across the table; followed by a box of matches.

Joe leaned forward, put the cigarette in his mouth, and lit up, and then lowered the still-burning match and dropped it carefully into the waste-paper basket under the table.

Burn, damn you.

'Bunty Burgess has a theory about you,' he said, drawing on the cigarette. 'She says you're short of a mother-figure. That was what Virginia was, that was why her death got to you so badly.'

'Crap,' said Mike, leaning back on two legs of the chair.

'That's what I said too.'

The papers were burning now, slowly, but with enough smoke to draw Mike's eye.

'What the hell . . .'

Joe didn't wait. He caught the underside of the table and

lifted it as hard and fast as he could, then dived sideways. The table caught Mike full in the stomach, knocking him backwards off the chair, spilling crockery and mugs over the floor. Joe was on the ground now. He had just enough time to grab a cast-iron skillet and bring it down on Mike's wrist before Mike had time to use the pistol. The gun rattled as it skidded away across the linoleum.

Joe was on his feet again. He picked up a chair and raised it above his head, but Mike saw it coming, ducked to one side and caught Joe's ankle with his good arm, pulling hard. Joe went down again. They fought in silence, breathlessly. Even with a broken hand Mike was more than a match for him, always had been. But he was fighting clean, muscle and bone, like a sportsman, trying to get him in a head hold. Joe scrambled for an implement, any implement.

His hand found the skillet again. This time he aimed it into Mike's stomach. Mike gasped and loosened his hold. Joe hit him again. Mike let go altogether, and raised his arms to protect his face.

'Pax,' he said softly.

'Fuck pax,' said Joe. The pistol was five feet away. He got to his feet and edged towards it, the skillet raised in one hand, ready to come down on Mike's skull if he made a move. He kicked the pistol away across the floor towards the open door.

It came to rest at Frank Carreras' feet. The American had been running: sweat poured from his temples. For a moment he looked at Mike, then at Joe. Then he raised the shotgun, so that Joe could see straight down the polished barrels.

'You're both mad!' Joe shouted.

Frank shook his head.

'No such luck.'

Joe heard him slip the safety catch.

There was a single shot. For a moment nothing happened, then Frank fell forward.

It was only when he was lying face down that Joe saw the red patch between Frank's shoulder blades. There was less blood than he'd expected, just a stain the size of a half-crown, pulsing slowly.

Willie was standing in the doorway, both hands holding a pistol. He looked at Mike, then at Joe, then tossed the gun on to the table.

'We know when we deceive others,' he said, 'but not when we deceive ourselves.'

'Who said that?' Joe asked.

'I did,' said Willie. 'Christ, you look a mess.'

Joe remembered very little of the next hour. He remembered his father helping him into the bathroom and propping him up on the WC, bathing his face with cold water, disappearing for a while, returning with a bottle of Jameson's and a first-aid kit. Then nothing, then finding himself stretched out on a sofa, Willie taking two cigarettes out of a pack of Senior Service, lighting them both and handing him one.

Joe inhaled, coughed, then took another puff, trying to piece together some kind of chronology.

'Where's Mike?'

'I locked him in the shower.'

'Is he okay?'

'Given the circumstances.'

The two men looked at each other, not knowing what to say next. In the stillness Joe could hear a generator, and then someone whistling. Willie went over to the window.

Joe got up from the sofa, moving carefully across the room until he was standing shoulder to shoulder with his father, looking out at the clearing.

Sarah was naked to the waist. In her left hand she carried a white T-shirt attached to a stick. Her right hand was swinging a dead snake by its tail. Ten feet behind her was a loose gaggle of Indians, talking excitedly among themselves.

'Hide the bloody whisky,' said Willie.

Joe didn't move.

'What about Sarah?'

'What about her?'

'Three into two won't go,' said Joe, still watching Sarah. She was maybe twenty yards away, still swinging the snake.

Judge Wilde scratched the back of his neck, sucked on his cigarette and stubbed it out . . .

'I suppose we'd better bloody ask her.'

DOC

'Don't make the mistake of falling for his masculine charms at first sight.' Not much chance of that happening, Miranda Lewis thought ruefully after her first encounter with Dr Alex Emmerson. It was unfortunate that her work as the only dietitian at Lenchester General was bound to bring her into contact with the arrogant paediatrician!

Lee Stafford was born and educated in Sheffield, where she worked as a secretary and also in Public Relations. She now lives in Herefordshire with her husband, who is in hospital catering management, and her two young daughters. The household is completed by two goldfish and a tortoiseshell cat.

Doctor Off Limits is Lee Stafford's third Doctor Nurse Romance.

DOCTOR OFF LIMITS

BY
LEE STAFFORD

MILLS & BOON LIMITED
15–16 BROOK'S MEWS
LONDON W1A 1DR

All the characters in this book have no existence outside the imagination of the Author, and have no relation whatsoever to anyone bearing the same name or names. They are not even distantly inspired by any individual known or unknown to the Author, and all the incidents are pure invention.

The text of this publication or any part thereof may not be reproduced or transmitted in any form or by any means, electronic or mechanical, including photocopying, recording, storage in an information retrieval system, or otherwise, without the written permission of the publisher.

This book is sold subject to the condition that it shall not, by way of trade or otherwise, be lent, resold, hired out or otherwise circulated without the prior consent of the publisher in any form of binding or cover other than that in which it is published and without a similar condition including this condition being imposed on the subsequent purchaser.

*First published in Great Britain 1986
by Mills & Boon Limited*

© Lee Stafford 1986

*Australian copyright 1986
Philippine copyright 1986*

ISBN 0 263 75540 1

Set in 10 on 11½ pt Linotron Times
03–1086–54,300

*Photoset by Rowland Phototypesetting Ltd
Bury St Edmunds, Suffolk
Made and printed in Great Britain by
William Collins Sons & Co. Ltd, Glasgow*

CHAPTER ONE

MIRANDA LEWIS locked the door of her small office at the end of another satisfyingly busy day, and thought, not for the first time that week, how fortunate she had been to land the job as dietitian at Lenchester General Hospital.

It did not seem possible that only a short time ago she had been stuck in London—stuck in every way, fretting and uncertain of her future, worrying about the next step in her career, and her deteriorating relationship with Tony, and how she could possibly reconcile the two.

And now, here she was, with her own office, the only dietitian at this medium-sized hospital in the bustling, attractive little market town. At the end of the day, she faced nothing more onerous than a cycle ride home along the lanes, through the blossoming Herefordshire countryside, to her father's house in the peaceful black and white timbered village of Ibsey. As for Tony, it was as if he inhabited another world, and the only emotion she now felt with regard to their long-impending split was an almost light-headed, overwhelming relief. The decision had been hard, and she had dithered over it for a long while—after all, it isn't easy to break with someone who has been an important part of one's life for more than two years—but she had finally made it, and everything else had fallen miraculously into place.

Miranda almost skipped down the steps to the car-park, bidding a cheery good night to the girl on the reception desk in the foyer, and walked briskly to where she had parked her bicycle, unobtrusively in a corner, where she thought it would not usurp any of the space reserved for staff cars. Doctors, particularly, were known to become most irate if anyone took their regular plot, and not without reason, since their time was valuable, and in this largely rural area a car was a lifeline.

She felt the rubbery softness of her back tyre just in time, before mounting, and groaned softly. Just when she had been congratulating herself on how well everything was going! Still, it was only a minor problem, and one she could remedy herself in a matter of minutes.

'Into each life a little rain must fall,' Miranda murmured ruefully, as she took her puncture kit out of her saddle bag, and started on the repair. It would, annoyingly, be the case that the kit was right at the bottom of her bag, underneath a collection of tissues, assorted tools, two library books she had offered to return for her father, but not had the opportunity, and sundry other odds and ends, but never mind. She would be finished soon, and then she could tidy up and put everything away. It was fortunate that there was no one about at the moment . . .

She was so engrossed in endeavouring to complete the repair quickly, that she never heard the man's steps approaching, and her first awareness of his presence was the shadow falling across her kneeling form.

'Are you proposing to litter the car-park with your impedimenta for much longer?' asked a cool, deep, sarcastic voice. 'I realise that if one is about to be run over, a hospital forecourt is the best place to be, but I really don't want to be responsible for mowing you down. On the other hand, I do have several appointments to keep.'

Miranda looked up, flustered and disturbed by the unexplained hostility in the voice which accosted her.

The man was standing between her and the sun, so she was unable to discern his features clearly, but she had a swift impression of height and breadth of shoulder. A tall man, to begin with, and looking down at her from a commanding position, which left her at a disadvantage.

She was of a reasonably equable temperament, not given to rudeness, but something about his manner made her hackles rise. There was a sense in which one could say she had travelled two hundred miles to escape male arrogance, and here it was, rearing its ugly head once again! And she did not even know this supercilious individual.

'I might be able to finish sooner if you were to move out of my light,' she suggested frostily.

'Certainly.' He shifted his position, and now that she could see him better she saw a dark, lean, unsmiling face beneath a thatch of tousled black hair. Surprisingly, his eyes were not dark, but a clear, silvery grey, and his mouth, which had a full lower lip which might, in other circumstances be described as sensual, was drawn into a hard, uncompromising line. There was something nineteenth century and Byronic about his particular brand of good looks, and Miranda briefly and wickedly imagined him in tight trousers and a romantically ruffled shirt. She secretly christened him 'Heathcliff', and was unaware that a faint smile turned up the corners of her mouth.

'I fail to see what you find so amusing. The fact is that you're not a particularly tidy worker, are you?' he said scathingly.

This was, as a general statement, way off course. Miranda's wardrobe, her bedroom, and her desk top all bore witness to a meticulous and organised personality. Only her saddle bag, its contents liberally strewn around her, hinted at a buried streak of anarchy. But although his remark made her gasp at its patent unfairness, there was little she could do to redress the impression she was making.

'Nor are you noticeably patient,' she retorted. 'There. I've done, now.'

She began to gather up her belongings and replace them in the bag with studied and deliberate carefulness, but he didn't pay her any further attention as he opened the door of his car and slid behind the wheel. Only as he started the engine and let in the clutch did he wind down the window and remark, almost conversationally,

'I've been wondering to whom that heap of antiquarian junk belonged. Do yourself, and the rest of Lenchester General a favour, and get a decent set of wheels.'

Miranda watched the car glide smoothly across the car-park and edge out into the road.

'Well, really!' she said disgustedly. What did he think gave him the right to talk to her as if she were some scatterbrained schoolgirl? To accuse her of being an incompetent litter-lout, and to refer to her bicycle in such derogatory terms!

Miranda glanced down at the vehicle in question, her beloved Bessy, which she had owned when, one must face it, she *was* a schoolgirl, and which she had dug out of an honourable retirement at the back of her father's garden shed to tide her over until she managed to find a car. Well, maybe Bessy's paintwork was a trifle faded and scratched, and she certainly wasn't the acme of gleaming modernity, but all the same!

She rode out into the road, signalling carefully before easing into the flow of traffic, well aware that to a certain kind of motorist, bikes are as good as invisible. Whereas to others, she thought wryly, they are all too noticeable, even when they are only parked. This brought her back to the acid little encounter outside the hospital, which, to be honest, had not really left her thoughts, and as she cleared the last set of traffic lights and headed out of town an awful suspicion began to grow in her mind.

'Miranda, my girl,' she chided herself, 'you might just have made the most unfortunate gaffe, getting cross with that man!' Only a person sufficiently high up in the hospital hierarchy would have the natural hauteur to berate anyone so freely. A higher administrative officer, for instance—but she had met all the admin staff. Well, then, he had to be a senior doctor or, horrors, possibly a consultant! She had not, in a little under a week, had the chance to meet all of them yet.

On her very first day at Lenchester, Miranda had struck up a friendship with one of the staff nurses. Julie Morris was about Miranda's own age, single, and devoted to her work, but she was also a lively and outgoing personality. Miranda was quieter, more reflective, but the two young women, although trained in different disciplines, shared a bond in their thoroughly professional attitude towards their jobs, and they quickly found that they had quite a lot in common.

'On the whole,' Julie had said, as they had coffee together in the staff dining-room, 'you couldn't wish for a nicer place to work. Almost everyone is pleasant and helpful, and most of the doctors are fine, so long as you're doing your work competently. There are a couple of things to watch out for, though.'

Miranda smiled. 'There are always pitfalls,' she said. 'Nowhere is perfect, but I take people as I find them.'

'Me, too. Everyone can't get on like a house on fire, and often it's no one's fault. "I do not like thee, Dr Fell—the reason why, I cannot tell" and all that. But *some* people are just difficult, full stop.'

'Lenchester has some of those?' Miranda grinned.

'One or two. Our charming lady administrator, Miss Carmichael . . . you've met her, of course?'

Miranda nodded carefully, not wanting to say too much. Aline Carmichael was her direct superior, and she would have to see more of her in the course of her duties than would any of the nursing staff below the rank of sister. She was a glossy, impeccably turned out lady in her early thirties, the epitome of an efficient career-woman, neat, professionally-styled hair, tailored suit, deliberately brisk manner, and yes, maybe her smile had struck Miranda as somewhat clipped, but it was too early to say definitely that it was insincere.

'The word is, watch her, and don't turn your back unless you want a knife in it,' Julie said warningly. 'Sister Price is an old battleaxe, but believe me, I'd sooner have her breathing down my neck than La Carmichael!'

'I've met Sister Price. She sniffs condescendingly at my reducing menus, and calls me "gel".'

'Anyone female and under fifty is a "gel" to Sister Price,' Julie laughed feelingly. 'And where food is concerned, she's still living in the era of porridge and tapioca pud. *All* her patients need "building up", even if they're fifteen stone!'

'I know what you mean.' Miranda's smile was wry. A high proportion of her work was, to put it in a single word, education, and not only of patients. The trouble was, she thought, that nurses were only just beginning to be taught about nutrition. And even some doctors took the attitude that food had little to do with the healing process, and were either indifferent or actively hostile towards new ideas and innovations as regards hospital diet. 'I have a suspicion Mr Meredith shares her opinions about what he calls "new-fangled notions".'

Julie giggled. 'The Welsh Wizard!' she said. 'He's a lamb really, even if he is a mite set in his ways. He must be almost coming up to retirement though. It's the next generation of medics who'll have all our fates in their hands, so to speak. Which brings me round to Lenchester Handicap Number Two—Dr Alex Emmerson.'

Miranda frowned. 'I don't believe I've met him, yet.'

'You'd remember, if you had,' Julie assured her. 'Don't make the fatal mistake of falling for his masculine charms at first sight. For one thing, he's a confirmed misogynist. In fact, he really only likes little people—say under twelve.'

Miranda raised her eyebrows questioningly, and Julie supplied the answer.

'He's the consultant paediatrician.'

At the time, Miranda had been too busy assuring her new friend that there was not the slightest possibility of her falling for anyone's masculine charms at first, second or subsequent sights. After two years of Tony, and the disappointments and indignities of the last few months, she considered she had acquired a healthy immunity to that disease.

Only now, riding along the narrow country lanes between fields of budding hops and white-blossoming fruit trees, did the pieces of the jigsaw slot neatly and unpleasantly together in her mind. An attractive man . . . a man of undoubted presence and authority . . . a man who, according to hospital gossip, had an ingrained resentment of women . . . Could it be that this was the man with whom she had shared that acrimonious exchange of words? The more she thought about it, the more she inclined to that conclusion, and she realised that it was not exactly the brightest of starts to her career at Lenchester General. It was sheer bad luck that she had not previously met Alex Emmerson in the day to day business of her work, because undoubtedly, since many dietary problems involved children, and illnesses specifically concerning them, she would come into contact with him a good deal.

Miranda sighed. What could she have done? Could she have acted otherwise? *Reacted* otherwise to his provocation? Although she was not the kind of girl to go out of her way to seek a confrontation with anyone, neither was she one of nature's doormats, and she would have found it virtually impossible to let him verbally walk all over her, without offering any retaliation.

Her shoulders lifted in a philosophical little shrug as she freewheeled down the gentle incline and round the corner into the village. You couldn't win them all, and if she had succeeded, inadvertently, in putting Dr Emmerson's back up, there was very little she could do right now to remedy the offence. She would just have to be doubly polite and careful when they next met. Surely the man could not be so unreasonable as to hold it against her for the rest of her time at Lenchester? Miranda's natural optimism reasserted itself, and she determined not to let the incident cast a blight over her newly rediscovered pleasure in life.

Approaching it from the north, one came upon Ibsey almost without warning. There was a sign, of course, but that did little to mitigate the surprise of rounding a sharp bend and finding oneself abruptly in the High Street, where fourteenth-century black and white, cruck-timbered houses jostled squat tudor cottages and symmetrical Georgian facades in a happy, uncritical admixture of style and period. Forsythia exploded brilliantly against the white walls of the old houses, daffodils tossed their trumpeted heads merrily in window boxes, and the first, early tendrils of honeysuckle had begun to climb round the door of the tiny post office. At the Green Dragon Inn, the hopeful proprietor had set out his tables and umbrellas in the garden, through which a miniature stream babbled self-importantly, and high above the village soared the church spire, grey against the blue of the sky.

Miranda had come to Herefordshire with the spring, and had been elated by the unspoiled rurality of this green corner of England, tucked up against the harsher uplands of the Welsh Borders. Although the area was all but unknown to her, she was filled with a strange and happy sense of homecoming, a premonition that here, at last, she might put down tentative roots.

In all her twenty-four years there had never been anywhere she could seriously think of as home. Her father, widowed many years ago, had been a regular army officer, and life had been a succession of moves from one posting to another—Cyprus, Germany, Singapore. For a few years, there had been boarding school, which she had endured rather than enjoyed, and after that, college. The four years at the large northern polytechnic had been perhaps the longest period she had ever spent in one place, but she could hardly call her shared room in the hall of residence homely, and the same applied to the bedsit she had occupied, along with two other girls, when she obtained her first job as junior dietitian in a vast London teaching hospital.

Then her father, having retired from the army, had decided that the change from a lifetime of command and responsibility to sudden, total leisure, was not for him, and he had bought a property in the country, which he proceeded to run as a bed and breakfast hotel.

'There's plenty of room for you here, if you ever decide you want to escape from the rat-race of urban life,' he had written to his daughter, very tactfully, not referring to the broken romance she had told him of in a few terse words. 'You could even come into business with me, if you chose to—all that knowledge of diets and nutrition would not be entirely wasted.'

Miranda had hesitated at this. She had known people at college who were bent on going into the hotel and catering industry, but while she was sure it was a fascinating world, it was not quite what she had set her heart on after emerging proudly with her B.Sc. in dietetics. Food was fun, but it was more than that, it was life and health, and she wanted to use her knowledge to help people whose life and health were impaired, imperfect. It seemed to her that the best place to do this was in the hospital service. The advertisement for the vacant post of Senior II dietitian at Lenchester General had been a gift from heaven, at a time when her life was going badly adrift.

Miranda cycled down the High Street, waving casually at the vicar as he passed her, and slowing down to talk to the owner of the all-purpose general shop who was washing his window. Mrs Bright called to her as, resuming her journey, Miranda passed the door of her cottage, telling her to let her father know she had some more of that homemade jam, if he wanted it.

'I'll pass the message on, Mrs Bright. Good afternoon, Mrs Evans.' She raised a hand in greeting to the landlady of the Green Dragon, who was outside, wiping the tables.

'Afternoon, Miss Lewis. Tell the Major I've reserved the snug for the cricket club meeting tonight.'

Meadowlands, the house her father had bought, stood a short distance outside the village, and as its name indicated, was set amidst fields, gentle farming country, with the tilled red soil and lush grass lapping its boundaries. Peaceful black and white cattle leaned over the fence at one end of the garden, their large, bovine eyes regarding the world serenely, and on the other side of the property was a field of grazing sheep and frisky young lambs.

The house was not old by Ibsey's standards. It had been built in the seventeenth century, the successor to a small, cruck-built cottage which still stood at the far end of the garden and was part of the property. This small house, whose eaves and joists all seemed to learn tipsily in towards each other, was known as Cruck Cottage, and Major Lewis had occasionally rented it out as a holiday let during the previous summer.

Meadowlands was more squarely and sturdily built, but its walls were washed white, and its paintwork gleamed black, in keeping with the fourteenth-century motif. Its dormer windows winked brightly in the sun, and the shrubs in the garden were already in vibrant leaf.

She put her bike away, and let herself into the hall, thinking gratefully of a quick shower, a change from her neat skirt and blouse into something more casual, and then a cup of tea. There was no sign of her father, but a note addressed to her was propped up against a bowl of flowers on the shiningly polished hall table, and she supposed she had better read it before going any further. 'The Major' as he was universally known in Ibsey, had very quickly inveigled himself into the heart of village life, and despite running a business, was involved in so many activities that this was often their only method of communicating.

> 'Miranda—had to go out unexpectedly. A prospective tenant rang up about Cruck Cottage and wants to look over it this afternoon. He's coming at 5.45, so be a brick, and show him round.' [she read].

A glance at her watch revealed that it was five-forty already, so bang went her shower and cup of tea, she thought with a smile. Only this morning she had reproved her hyperactive parent that he really didn't have enough time to spare for work, and he should think twice before joining any more societies or sitting on any more committees. He had merely laughed, and said that village people had the sense to know that if you wanted anything done, the right way to go about it was to ask the busiest person you knew. An excess of leisure meant a lazy mind, and vice versa.

Miranda took a quick look at herself in the hall mirror to make sure she was tolerably presentable, and ran a comb swiftly through her short, windblown crop of light chestnut brown curls.

She was not given to spending a lot of time looking in mirrors, and if asked to describe herself, would have found it difficult to put a precise label on her appearance.

'I'm a medium sort of person,' she had once observed dispiritedly to Tony, and regarding her, he had ungallantly agreed, 'Yes, I suppose you are.' Neither short nor tall, slim, but not excessively so, trimly-curved, but not what one would call voluptuous, with eyes that were not blue, or grey, or green, but hovered indecisively somewhere on the edge of all three. One striking feature, such as waving, corn-coloured locks, or high-angled cheekbones, would have given her face the drama she felt it lacked, but on the whole, she didn't worry too much about it. She had a very engaging smile, but since the grimace one makes at one's reflection in the mirror is seldom the smile one bestows on others, she was largely unaware of it.

The doorbell jangled loudly, and Miranda tugged the lapels of her shirt, and smoothed down her skirt, which had been freshly pressed that morning, but wasn't improved by two half-hour journeys on the redoubtable Bessy.

'Good afternoon,' she said brightly, opening the door. 'If you've come about the cottage, my father has had to go out, but . . .'

She stopped in mid-flood, and her voice embarrassingly dried up on her. Oh heavens, she thought, it's Heathcliff! Somewhere along the line, without knowing it, maybe in some prior existence, she must have been exceedingly wicked, to have merited this particular punishment!

It seemed to Miranda that she stood looking up at him, dry-throated and unaccountably guilty, for an uncomfortably long period of time, although it must only have been seconds. And the very worst of it was that while she was wallowing in embarrassment, his fine, dark brows were knitting together, as he was apparently having the greatest difficulty in recalling where he had seen her before. A flash of recognition, however hostile, would have been preferable to this slow scrutiny, which told her how unmemorable she must be.

'Wait a minute,' he said after a while, during which she remained at a loss for speech, and there was just a trace of savage amusement in the deep voice she would have known anywhere, even without its owner's distinctive features. 'We've met, haven't we . . . ah, yes, now I remember! Earlier this afternoon. . . it's the girl with the bicycle on loan from the British Museum!'

Miranda found her voice at last, to her own immense relief.

'You do seem to have a grudge against poor Bessy,' she murmured.

'Bessy?'

'My bike. As you hinted, I've had her a long time, and that's what I used to call her when I rode her to school.

She's a very well-travelled bike, is Bessy. She's been all over the world.'

Why, she wondered, aghast at the sound of her own voice, am I talking so much, and such nonsense? Because he made her nervous, she supposed, which was ridiculous. It was her misfortune, not her fault, that she'd been parked nearby him that afternoon and he'd almost had to drive over her. Why couldn't she just forget it and behave as if they had never met at all?

'I'm sure she has.' He cut her off abruptly. 'However, I'm looking for Major Lewis, and I don't have a lot of time. Did I hear you say he was out?'

'I'm afraid so.' Miranda took a hold on herself. 'I'm his daughter. Did you want to see the cottage?'

She had a moment's profound hope that he would say no, he had come to see her father on some quite different matter. Maybe they were both on some rural committee or other. That hope was rudely shattered when he said,

'That's right. I did make an appointment with the Major, and he said it would be convenient to view.'

He looked highly annoyed at the notion of having his arrangements altered, and Miranda was briefly tempted to say that she was sorry, but it wasn't convenient, and would he come another time? Most likely, he would stalk off in disgust, and never return, which would suit her, since she viewed the prospect of his living at such close quarters with some alarm.

But she knew she could not do that. Her father would want to know what had happened, and she could hardly say she had put off his tenant because she didn't like him, on the strength of a few minutes' acquaintance.

'It's perfectly convenient. I can show you the cottage,' she told him. 'If you'd like to come this way.'

She led him along the path that ran alongside

Meadowlands and through the extensive garden and the paddock beyond, drowning in white apple blossom, the grass starred with so many daisies that it, too, seemed almost white. A small stream—the same one which ran through the garden of the Green Dragon—separated the paddock from the garden of Cruck Cottage, which was regrettably overgrown. But there was a venerable quince tree, just beginning to put out bright, blood-red flowers, and a mock-orange which would be fragrant later in the summer.

'The garden has run rather wild, I'm afraid,' she said, sincerely hoping that its condition would put him off. He gave the impression of being a man who demanded perfection.

'That wouldn't worry me,' he said, surprisingly. 'I like gardening, as a matter of fact, and I would quite enjoy tidying this up a little. It certainly needs some attention.'

Miranda bristled at the inferred criticism.

'My father is a busy man,' she said defensively, biting her lip as she thought of the cricket club, the historical society, the parish council. 'Would you like to see inside?'

'Yes, that was the idea,' he said loftily, and she was glad to turn her back on him while she fumbled with the heavy old key in the lock.

The front door opened directly into the living room, and he was obliged to duck in order to enter. There wasn't much clearance between the top of his dark head and the low ceiling, either. In fact, he seemed to dwarf the small room as he stood in the centre, looking slowly around. It was a very simply appointed room, the furniture a mixture of genuine antiques and restored junk-shop finds, and the rest of the house was much the same. Perhaps he would find it not luxurious enough for his taste.

'Nice fireplace,' he observed, eyeing the huge inglenook which occupied most of one wall. 'And there's certainly no need to tart the place up with the fake exposed beams a lot of people are going in for these days.' He ran an admiring hand along the blackened timber nearest him. 'These are obviously the real thing.'

'Yes, it's very old.' Momentarily, Miranda forgot her wariness of him in her enthusiasm for old houses, which he seemed to share. 'My father says someone had boarded up the fireplace and put a dreadful Victorian thing in front, but when they removed it, there was the original, as good as ever.'

'People will tamper. We seem constitutionally unable to leave anything alone.' He wandered through into the minute kitchen. 'The reverse of that coin, of course, is that there would be no progress otherwise. The trick is to know when to meddle, and when to abstain and simply stand back.'

This deep, philosophical vein she had unsuspectingly struck left Miranda at a loss. She thought she heard sadness somewhere in his voice, and was hesitant to press any further along this track, in case he rounded on her with hostile sarcasm once more.

'The kitchen is really terribly cramped,' she said prosaically.

He turned and looked her over slowly, so that the blood rose to her face, and she felt once again as if he had caught her in the process of doing something foolish.

'Yes, Miss Lewis . . .' a quick glance at her left hand . . . 'it is Miss Lewis, isn't it? The kitchen is cramped, the living room is small, the garden is a jungle. And I suppose, when we go upstairs, I shall discover that the bedrooms were designed with the Seven Dwarfs in mind. Why do I have the feeling that you don't really want to let this cottage at all?'

She stared him out, although it took every ounce of nerve she possessed.

'It's no concern of mine. My father wants to let, and I'm sorry if I don't have the makings of an estate agent. Incidentally, what you said about the bedrooms is quite true, and the bathroom is rather primitive. There's no heating in it. But if you would like to see . . .'

'Yes, Miss Lewis, I would,' he said firmly.

Ten minutes later they were back in the living room. He had agreed with everything she said about the first floor. The largest bedroom was barely big enough for a man of his height and reach, and the best that could be said of the bathroom was that it was clean, and the plumbing worked.

'Only sometimes,' Miranda could not resist adding, with relish.

But the view from the upper windows, out over the rolling Herefordshire hills, with the long, hazy shadow of the Black Mountains rising in the distance, more than compensated, in his opinion.

'I'm not so sure you wouldn't make an estate agent,' he said, with just a suggestion of a smile. 'I've decided to take it.'

The smile transformed his face, lifting the brooding darkness which clouded it, but it did not bring any real warmth to the cool, grey eyes. It occurred to Miranda only then that had she wanted to prevent him from moving into Cruck Cottage, she had gone entirely the wrong way about it. This was a man who thrived on overcoming opposition. She should have gushed, praised, oversold the picturesqueness of the place like mad, and maybe he would have been piqued into pointing out its practical drawbacks.

'Well, if you're quite sure,' she said lamely. 'Perhaps you could phone my father and fix up the details.'

She locked the door behind them as they left the cottage, and he stood back to allow her to precede him down the path. He did not speak to her again until they reached the front gate of Meadowlands, where she saw his car parked at the kerb.

'Thank you for showing me round,' he said then, polite but fairly distant. 'Please tell Major Lewis I'll be in touch. Good evening, Miss Lewis.'

'I'll do that,' she agreed. 'Good evening, Mr . . .'

She had mentally shied away from addressing him thus, up to now, reluctant to confirm what she both feared and suspected, but she knew now that there was no escape from the truth.

'Oh, didn't I tell you my name?' he said casually. 'Your father knows, anyhow. I told him when I phoned. It's Emmerson. Alex Emmerson.'

CHAPTER TWO

THE next morning was a Friday, the end of her first week at Lenchester. The week which, Miranda reflected, she had thought was going so well, up until yesterday!

Arriving at her office promptly at nine o'clock, she first of all checked if any messages had been left for her. New patients were being admitted daily, and if any of them had particular problems concerning diet, she would have to go to the wards involved and talk to them, and possibly their families, in addition to conferring with the senior member of nursing staff.

Miranda made a quick note in her diary of which wards she had to visit, and also reminded herself that she had to attend the regular catering staff meeting. In the afternoon she was due at the ante-natal clinic.

By now it was almost nine-thirty, and the daily sheaf of menus had still not arrived from the kitchen for her to check through. Their arrival had become progressively later throughout the week, and she wondered if this were pure coincidence, or whether someone in the catering department was trying her out to see how malleable or otherwise she would prove to be. Miranda grinned, gave it another five minutes, then rang through to the kitchen.

'Ah, it's you, me darling!' the head chef crooned down the phone to her. 'Sure, and the menus are ready, but I was hoping you'd come down here for them yourself, and give me another chance to see your smiling face!'

'You must be joking!' she laughed. 'I don't have the time to come down there and exchange blarney with you! Be a dear and send someone up with them, would you?'

There was a brief pause. Mick Mulligan was a prodigious talker, and incapable of not chatting up anything wearing skirts. He was fond of his own way, but he was a first-rate cook, had been at Lenchester for ten years, and was sure of his place.

'Sure, now, but all me cooks are busy, and I've two missing today. We'll never have lunch ready on time. You just pop down here, and I'll let you have a spoonful of me apple crumble!'

Miranda was very new, but she was fully aware that if she gave in once, Mick would have her trotting down to the kitchen for her menus from now until eternity, and once there, it would take her the best part of half an hour to get away from him.

'Don't give it a thought—I can tell you've got your hands full. I'll phone through to Mr Thompson's office and ask him to send Sally up with the menus,' she said brightly.

Another pause.

'Sure, and there's no need to be bothering the Catering Manager. Himself is up to his collar studs in it this morning. Mrs Dodds will pop upstairs for you . . . it won't take her a minute.'

Five minutes later, the menus for the following day were on Miranda's desk, deposited there by a woman in a white cook's overall and cap.

'Good for you—don't you let him get his own way!' she said with satisfaction. 'There's some that thinks women are only for bossing around or getting their hands on—and Mick Mulligan's one of them!'

No one, Miranda thought grimly, was going to boss her around simply because she was young and female. She had worked through four years of college, gained her qualifications, done her apprenticeship, and was now an expert in her own right, on her own ground. She knew that because dietetics was a relatively young profession, there were those who did not take it seriously, and one frequently had to contend with the kind of prejudiced individual who believed a girl of her age could not possibly have any serious contribution to make. Only time, and her own persuasive persistence and example could counter both those arguments.

As for anyone's getting his hands on her—well, she could cope with the playful lewdness of the Mick Mulligans of this world, which did not have to be taken too seriously. But against anything deeper, more subtle and more purposeful, she was permanently on her guard. She was not about to be confused and belittled and taken for granted by any man—not again. Certainly not so soon.

Miranda went through the general menus, making a note of any points she wanted to bring up with the catering manager, and then she attended to her particular province, the special diet menus—reducing diets for those who were overweight, especially if they had to lose weight before surgery could be performed, diabetic diets, high fibre diets, low cholesterol diets for heart complaints, kidney disease and hypertension. She worked steadily through, and when she was finished, passed the pile on to Maggie, the admin secretary, who smiled up at her from behind her owlish spectacles.

'You've been busy this morning! Have you time for a coffee? I've just boiled the kettle to make Madam's.'

A slight jerk of the head indicated the closed door of Aline Carmichael's office, and Miranda suppressed a smile. She had quickly grown accustomed to the variety of nicknames the staff of Lenchester General applied to their lady administrator. Some referred to her as the

Sphinx, because of the blank stare she could fasten on one from behind her desk, which masked her intentions from the recipient. Others said she was more like a minotaur, waiting in her maze, ready to pounce. To Maggie, she was simply 'Madam'.

'I think I've just time for a cup before I go on the wards,' Miranda said gratefully.

Maggie took Miss Carmichael's coffee into her office, then came out and poured her own and Miranda's.

'What's new, then?' she asked cheerfully. 'Have you managed to find yourself a car yet? Presumably not, since you're still riding the bike.'

'I haven't had much luck. Those I've seen have been too expensive, or else have degenerated too far into the banger category,' Miranda admitted. 'I'll have to keep looking.'

'My cousin's selling his,' Maggie volunteered. 'I only heard about it last night, so I thought I'd tell you and you could have a look, if you're interested. It's a Mini, a few years old, but I know it's been well looked after.'

'Why, thanks, Maggie,' Miranda said. 'I'd be glad to. I must get a car fairly quickly, since I'll need transport for when I have to make community visits. Besides, cycling to and from Ibsey every day is a bit of a bind, and my bike isn't in the first flush of youth.'

Maggie giggled, which made her appear more than ever like a twittery little owl.

'No—you didn't exactly endear yourself to Dr Emmerson last night, did you? I thought he was about to sweep the car-park with you.'

'You saw that, did you? I wonder how many more people were watching?' Miranda groaned, wondering why the thought had not occurred to her before that she had provided an entertaining spectacle for anyone whose window overlooked the car-park.

'Quite a few, I'd say. But never mind. Most of them would be feeling sorry for you. Dr Emmerson can be very scathing when he's a mind to. He had your predecessor in tears on more than one occasion.'

'Is that so? Well, he certainly isn't going to reduce *me* to fits of weeping,' Miranda declared with a determined smile.

Maggie's face wore the smug expression of one who has superior knowledge, and every intention of imparting it.

'Oh, well, Jean had a "thing" about him, you know. That's one reason why she——'

The door to Miss Carmichael's office flew open ominously and the Administrator regarded them both with her basilisk gaze. She wore a smart beige suit, the jacket belted around her waist, but unbuttoned at the neck to reveal a coffee-coloured crêpe de Chine blouse beneath. Her freshly-coiffed hair, artfully streaked blonde and silver, was swept back behind her ears, displaying expensive gold earrings. She looked, as always, as if she had just dispensed with the services of an expert beautician.

How much of the conversation she had overheard, Miranda was not sure, but a hostile, disdainful anger hung about in the atmosphere, which had previously been friendly and chatty.

'Maggie, if you have nothing better to do, I have some letters I'd like to dictate,' she said coldly to her secretary. Glancing back towards Miranda she said distantly, rather as an afterthought, 'Good morning, Miss Lewis.'

'Good morning, Miss Carmichael,' Miranda said steadily. 'I'm sorry for monopolising Maggie's time —she's always so busy. I'll be off round the wards now.'

She smiled back at Maggie. 'Let me know when I can see your cousin's car.'

Walking briskly down the corridor, Miranda fought back her distaste at the woman's manner. She had taken it out on Maggie, who was in less of a position to retaliate, but Miranda was sure Aline Carmichael's anger and dislike had been directed at her. Why? What had she done? In the few days she had been at Lenchester they had met only formally and professionally, and had no overt disagreements. What was it about her that Miss Carmichael objected to?

There were two people who one had to watch out for, Julie had warned, and somehow, quite unintentionally, Miranda had earmarked herself for trouble with both of them!

Try as she might to put it out of her mind, she could not help but wonder what Maggie had been on the verge of telling her about Lenchester's former dietitian, and the 'thing' she'd had for Alex Emmerson. The official version was that Jean Davies had gone home to Cardiff to look after her widowed mother.

I really do *not* want to know, Miranda told herself firmly. She didn't care how many silly women lost their hearts to a man who wasn't worth the trouble. She had been there once, and once was quite sufficient.

She gave herself a mental shake, and proceeded on her way to Ward Three to advise on a reduced-fat diet for a patient admitted with gallstones.

This was Julie's ward, and Miranda found her friend dealing with paperwork in the ward office while Sister Price accompanied Dr Chowdhuri, Mr Meredith's Indian registrar, on his rounds.

'Am I late?' she asked anxiously.

'No. He hasn't seen Mrs Brown yet,' Julie reassured her, and Miranda flashed her a quick smile before making her way down the ward.

Dr Chowdhuri was a quick talker, and the Sister, two medical students and Miranda had to pay strict attention to keep up with him. The patient was, he informed them, a typical example of a cholecystitis sufferer—that is, a woman aged between forty and fifty, who had had several children, and tended to plumpness. She had suffered several acute attacks, with pain and tenderness in the right hypochondrium, radiating to the right shoulder, nausea and vomiting.

Mrs Brown did not seem too happy about hearing herself described as 'tending to plumpness' although it was certainly true, and Miranda, catching her eye, smiled at her with sympathy, to which she responded with a rueful grin. Meanwhile, Dr Chowdhuri had pounced on one of the students.

'And why were we performing the cholecystography, young man?'

'Er . . . so that the dye will outline any stones, sir,' he stammered hopefully.

'Hm. Because most gallstones are radio-translucent, and will not show on a plain X-ray. Kindly try to be more explicit.'

Since the attacks were recurrent, and stones had been shown to be obstructing the neck of the gall-bladder, Mr Meredith was of the opinion that surgical treatment was probably necessary. Miss Lewis would explain about the dietary requirements, Dr Chowdhuri stated, before moving on briskly down the ward, leaving Miranda with Mrs Brown.

'Oh dear! I didn't understand a word of all that!' she sighed. 'All those long words with "ectomy" and "ography" on the end are Greek to me! Is he going to take the stones out, Miss?'

'Don't worry too much about the jargon. It's simply

the way medical people talk to each other,' Miranda consoled her. 'Mr Meredith will see you himself before he decides to operate, or you could have a chat with Sister, or Staff Nurse.'

Mrs Brown brightened. 'That's a good idea. I like Staff Nurse Morris. What are you going to do to me, Miss?'

Miranda sat down on the chair by the bed.

'Nothing very terrible. I'm going to put you on a low-fat, low-calorie diet. I've got a chart here, showing what you're allowed, and the nurses will know all about it too, so that when the meals come they'll know what to do.'

She explained patiently and carefully about the absence of fried foods and fatty meat, fat cheeses, thickened sauces and dressings. All this would be done without the patient having to do a thing about it, while she was in hospital, but Miranda believed the educating process started here, and if she could get through to the person concerned what the diet was for, and how it worked, there was a better chance of him or her sticking to it once the hospital discipline was no longer there.

'I'll come back and have another talk with you about it before you're discharged, and if you have any problems in the meantime talk to the nursing staff, and they'll let me know.'

'Will it help me to lose weight, after I'm out of hospital? I'm always meaning to, but I seemed to put on a stone when each of the kids was born, and never managed to lose it again.'

'It will help, if you keep to it carefully and don't cheat,' Miranda said. 'Well—goodbye for now. I expect the next time I see you, you'll be looking forward to going home.'

She had two or three more such visits to make, after

which a glance at her watch reminded her it was time for the catering meeting. Since it would be the first of these she had attended at Lenchester, it would be impolitic to be late, but she decided she just had time to pop back to her office first and make sure there were no urgent messages. As long as there was nothing outstanding, she could then go on to lunch from the meeting, and straight to the ante-natal clinic after that.

Everything was in order, and Miranda had just picked up her notepad and handbag, ready to leave, when the door of her office opened abruptly, without anyone having knocked, and the tall figure of Alex Emmerson stood framed in the aperture.

She had been expecting a moment like this since she had first realised who he was, but still, it caught her by surprise, so that she just looked blankly at him, saying nothing.

'We meet again,' he said, and she detected an ominous note in the greeting, which hinted that he was not altogether thrilled by the encounter. 'I appear to be running into you in all manner of unexpected places, but what, might I ask, are you doing in the dietitian's office?'

Miranda had taken about as much as she could of this accusatory attitude towards her, and it was to her credit that she managed to say, with only the merest touch of sarcasm, 'I am in the dietitian's office, Dr Emmerson, for the most obvious reason of all. I'm the new dietitian.'

He had a highly expressive face, and in a matter of seconds it registered reactions on a scale from disbelief to disapproval.

'*You* are Jean's replacement?' he queried doubtfully. 'Why on earth didn't you tell me that yesterday when I introduced myself to you?'

It was on the tip of Miranda's tongue to retort that he hadn't exactly introduced himself—he had told her his name, and taken it loftily for granted that she would know who he was. She resisted this impulse, and said reasonably, 'I assumed you would have gathered that I worked here, since I use the car-park every day.'

Litter up the car-park, the thought niggled annoyingly at the back of her mind. She had not liked being referred to as 'Jean's replacement' either. It made her sound like a spare part.

'Yes, obviously, but I supposed you were a clerk or something,' he said dismissively, his manner indicating that this was probably a charitable estimate of Miranda's mental abilities. 'Is this your first job, by any chance?'

'Of course it isn't,' she said quietly, feeling herself teetering on the fine edge of indignation. 'I could hardly come fresh from college to a senior dietitian's post. I worked for two years at a London hospital before I applied for this position.'

'You must excuse my ignorance of the career structure of your profession,' he said with a lordly aloofness. 'Since you are here, I take it you're fully qualified to be so. I have a patient with whom I may need your assistance.'

A variety of glib retorts hovered on Miranda's lips. How could it be that such a lofty being as he might require help from her? Was he sure he didn't wish to check out her qualifications first, before entrusting her with any responsibilities? And so on . . . She swallowed them all firmly, and gave him her serious and undivided attention. They were not acting out some silly game now but discussing a sick person—and, since it was a patient of his, a sick *child*. Personal considerations had to be laid aside while they dealt professionally with the problems involved.

'It's a boy aged nine, a diabetic, who was admitted to Lenchester a couple of months ago and later discharged, with the correct medication and diet prescribed. He was readmitted a few days ago in a hypoglycaemic coma. I've seen him, and I'm satisfied that his daily insulin dosage is adequate. His mother insists that she is maintaining his diet, but I'm convinced that the problem is in this area.'

Surprisingly, his expression softened a little. 'She's a single parent, not much older than you are, at a guess —the husband took off and left them—and there are several younger children. Would you have a word with her about the diet? It's possible she simply doesn't understand it sufficiently.'

Another female idiot, in other words, Miranda thought, and then reproved herself inwardly for being unfair. After all, he could well be right.

'I'll see her as soon as possible,' she said. 'I've got the ante-natal clinic this afternoon, so I'm afraid I shall be tied up at visiting time. Will Monday afternoon's visiting hour be all right?'

'Monday will be fine,' he said surprisingly, and even more surprisingly, he smiled. 'Young Darren can't come to any great harm while he's here, but we must sort out what's causing this before we can allow him home. There's no reason why he shouldn't lead a perfectly normal life, if a few tedious but simple rules are adhered to.'

Miranda did not know what mischievous impulse made her say, 'Life is full of tedious but simple rules, Dr Emmerson.'

'Too true,' he agreed, and for a moment the smile threatened to break into a thorough-going grin. Then he thought better of it and added, 'By the way, I spoke to your father on the phone this morning. I'm moving into Cruck Cottage tomorrow.'

Miranda watched as the door closed firmly behind him. That just makes my day, she thought ironically.

And then, looking once again at her watch, she saw that it was eleven forty-five. The day was not over yet—and she was already fifteen minutes late for the staff meeting!

All in all, Miranda found the ante-natal clinic much easier going than the staff meeting which rounded off her morning, and as she chatted to the expectant mothers, most of whom were cheerful and, this afternoon at least, had no really dire problems, she wished that every aspect of her work could be this pleasant.

Of course, she had started off on the wrong foot by arriving late. That was entirely due to Alex Emmerson and their conversation about the diabetic boy, but she did not think she could hold up the proceedings by explaining this, chapter and verse, to the assembly of catering, administrative and senior nursing staff, so she merely apologised quickly, saying that she had unfortunately been delayed, and slid into an empty seat.

Aline Carmichael flashed her a look of tight-lipped disapproval, but Miranda caught a glimmer of veiled triumph in her eyes—almost as if the hospital administrator would not be unhappy to see her trip over her feet.

She had been only too ready to criticise Miranda's opinions on any subject under discussion, too. A suggestion that greater use of wholemeal flour and spaghetti would be preferable had been met with a curt reminder that these commodities were relatively expensive—did Miss Lewis not realise that the catering department, like any other, had a strict budget to work within?

'That's true,' said Jeff Thompson, the catering manager, 'but I agree with what Miss Lewis says, in principle. Leave it with me, Miranda, and I'll see what I can work out.'

She smiled gratefully at him.

'This is all academic,' Miss Carmichael drawled, glancing pointedly at the clock on the wall. 'I feel we ought to move on to the matter of the vending machines in the staff dining-room. They are forever out of order, and there have been several complaints, particularly from staff on night duty.'

Miranda relaxed a little. Vending machines were Jeff Thompson's problem, not hers. He was young, college-trained, and of a calm temperament, and he took the barrage of criticism from the clutch of sisters present in his stride. The talk had moved on from this to a general session of griping about food in the dining-room.

'Chips,' said Sister Bennett, from Ward Five. 'My nurses are always moaning about the chips!'

'Chips are a very difficult item to keep in good condition, Sister, unless they're freshly prepared for every serving, and I don't have the staff for that. I'm sure Miranda would agree that your nurses would all benefit from eating fewer chips, anyway.'

'Oh, absolutely,' Miranda backed him up. 'Jacket potatoes would be much better, and could be cooked quickly in the microwave oven. What about a buffet-style layout in the dining-room, now summer's coming? Lots of salads, interestingly prepared?'

Sister Price sniffed disparagingly.

'Miss Lewis! Have you any idea how hard nurses have to work? My gels can't get through the day on half a tomato and a lettuce leaf! They need filling up!'

'That wasn't exactly what I had in mind when I suggested salads, Sister Price,' Miranda said placatingly. 'A meal can be nourishing without being full of fat and carbohydrate.' Sticking her head boldly into the lion's mouth, she said, 'How would it be if I had a little talk on nutrition to any of the nurses who were interested?'

Before Sister Price had an opportunity to pooh-pooh

this idea, Miss Carmichael jumped in and did it for her.

'I think one may assume that most nurses are reasonably intelligent beings and don't require lecturing on simple matters like knowing what to eat,' she remarked with a frosty little smile of condescension. 'Miss Davies always had her work cut out coping with *patients*' diets, and when you've been here a little longer, you may find this to be true in your case also.'

There were occasions when it was possible, by being tolerant, by counting to ten, or by simply realising that the matter under discussion was not worth the effort, to avoid conflict, to turn aside argument. This was not one of them. It affected directly the way Miranda saw herself and her role in the life of the hospital. She had no way of knowing whether what the Administrator said about her predecessor was true or not, but she had to speak up for herself.

'If I allowed myself to think that way, Miss Carmichael, I should be failing to do my job properly,' she said quietly. 'Because we all eat, we tend to think food is a simple matter. It isn't. It's a subject bedevilled by misconception and ignorance.'

She emerged from the meeting unpleasantly aware that she had made an enemy. No, that wasn't strictly true. The enemy had been there all the time, she had merely been revealed. Before she had ever crossed swords with her, Aline Carmichael had been prepared —determined—to dislike her. Why? Miranda was at a loss to understand.

'Bravo!' Jeff Thompson said wickedly, as they walked down the corridor together. 'You stood up quite well under fire, all things considered.'

She raised her eyebrows doubtfully. 'I'm not so sure! Is it always like that?'

'More often than not,' he said cheerfully. 'The trouble with nursing staff is that they are so totally wrapped up in things medical, they simply don't see the situation from this end. You, being somewhere in the middle, are the ideal emissary to bridge the gap.' He laughed. 'I loved that bit about "ignorance and misconception".'

Miranda's expression was wry. 'I don't think Miss Carmichael loved it, but I simply couldn't refrain from objecting to what she said! *Of course* hospital dietitians must be concerned with staff. They're the people who keep the hospital running!'

'Aline knows that as well as the next person,' Jeff said easily. 'I don't know what it is with her. A power complex, perhaps? She adores squashing people. She probably sees you as a continuation of poor Jean, and she constantly had her knife into her.'

'But why?' Miranda could not resist asking.

His brown eyes twinkled. 'Don't ask me—I'm a mere male, and not into women's supremacy struggles,' he said jokingly. 'Shall we sample the delights of the dining-room together? I take it you're going to lunch. And before you ask, yes, naturally I eat there—how else would I know what it all tastes like?'

Several hours later, Miranda was seeing the last of the ante-natal patients after the nurse had weighed her and taken her blood pressure, and she had been examined by the doctor on duty. Young Mrs Barnes was five months into her first pregnancy, and already so rotund that she had difficulty lowering herself on to the chair.

'I was just telling Nurse,' she confided chattily, 'I don't know how I'm going to get through the summer, especially if we have a hot one. Look at me—you'd think it was twins I was having, but Doctor says it's definitely only one!'

Miranda consulted the chart in front of her.

'You have put on rather a lot of weight since your last visit,' she agreed.

'Haven't I?' The young woman smiled complacently. 'But it can't be helped, can it? I have to eat for two.'

Miranda wished she had a five pound note for every pregnant woman who had ever said that to her, and for the number of times she had tried to explain that an overweight, unfit mother-to-be made for an uncomfortable pregnancy and greater chances of complications in labour.

'No, Mrs Barnes, you do *not* have to eat for two—that's a fallacy,' she said firmly. 'It's more important you eat the right things—lean meat, fresh fruit and vegetables—rather than vast quantities of whatever takes your fancy. If you give me an idea of what you eat in a day, we'll see if we can work out a diet that will be better for you and your baby.'

It was after half past four when Mrs Barnes waddled out of the clinic, clutching her new diet sheet, and the nurse looked around Miranda's door.

'I've put the kettle on. We could all do with a cup of tea, I think.'

'Lovely.' Miranda stretched, tidied up her desk and went through into the kitchen to join the two nurses, doctor and health visitor. It had been a busy day, satisfying in some respects, although not without difficulties, she reflected. It was at times like this, when they stood around chatting and drinking tea, discussing the occurrences of the afternoon, some amusing, some serious, that the realisation came to her with redoubled force that there was nowhere she would rather be, and no other job she would rather do.

She liked Lenchester General, she enjoyed working as part of this dedicated team of highly professional people. Determined to find and occupy her niche in this tight-knit, hard-working world, she vowed she would not be deterred by the disapproval of Aline Carmichael.

Nor that of Alex Emmerson, either, she added as an afterthought, and wondered why that promise was inexplicably harder to make.

CHAPTER THREE

WHEN Miranda arrived home that evening she saw that all the windows of Cruck Cottage stood wide open to admit the fresh spring air. Two women from the village, who worked regularly for her father, had been through the house from top to bottom, and it was sparklingly clean, waiting in readiness for its new occupant.

'I do believe the old house looks happy at the thought of being lived in again,' Miranda said, gazing across the paddock from the window of their private sitting-room. It may well feel differently when the tenant moves in, she thought, but refrained from making this point to her father.

Major Lewis smiled.

'That's a mite fanciful for a practical old soldier like myself,' he said. 'By the way—I gather you know our new neighbour, or so he told me. Funny, you never mentioned that last night, after you showed him round.'

'I hardly had a chance. You were off out to the cricket club meeting, and when you came in we were busy with the hot drinks for the guests,' she excused herself quickly. 'Besides, I only know him very slightly. He's consultant paediatrician at the hospital.'

'So he told me this morning. I would have thought a doctor of that stature would want something more grand than a rather down at heel, rented cottage, but he says it will suit his needs for the moment. I take it he's single? He said there would only be himself moving in.'

'I wouldn't know,' Miranda said in a tone which

indicated that she had no great interest in Alex Emmerson's marital status.

'Or care, either?' He picked up the hint at once. 'You're not going to be put off men for life, just because that boy in London treated you badly, are you?'

Miranda laughed this off. She had no wish to talk about Tony.

'Why? Are you worried about my ending up a desiccated old maid?'

'I'm not worried in the least, if that's what *you* would prefer,' he replied. 'But somehow, I don't think it is.'

'Maybe not, but it feels that way at the moment,' she said firmly. 'Enjoying my job, and being good at it, are all that matter to me right now. And I'm very happy living here in Ibsey with you.'

'I'll go along with that,' he said easily. 'I suppose it's early days, but it can't harm to have a good-looking young fellow living next door, eh, what?'

It was a joke, but Miranda's head jerked round swiftly, and her expression was one of total rejection, tinged with embarrassment.

'You mean Alex Emmerson?' she gasped. 'You can't be serious! He's the last man on earth I'd choose as light relief to help me over a broken heart . . . assuming that my heart *was* broken,' she added drily.

Major Lewis poured two glasses of sherry from the Bohemian crystal decanter which had, together with the matching glasses, been a parting gift from his fellow officers. He handed one to Miranda.

'Why do you say that? I found him a charming and interesting chap,' he remarked, genuinely surprised by his daughter's vehemence.

'With you, no doubt. He's probably a man's man, but it's common gossip in the hospital that he dislikes women.'

Her father looked at her, his eyes snapping questions over the rim of his glass.

'It's a mistake to pay too much attention to common gossip,' he observed pithily.

'Even when it's reinforced by experience?' she riposted. 'I've been on the receiving end of Dr Emmerson's ire a couple of times, unfortunately, so I'll keep well out of his way unless work is involved.'

It was easier said than done when, on Saturday morning, she saw his car bumping up the unmetalled drive which gave him access to the cottage without having to come through the garden of Meadowlands. Every time Miranda happened to glance out of the window, she saw him coming in or out of his door, fetching suitcases from his car, depositing empty cartons beside his dustbin. And later in the morning she answered the doorbell to a delivery man from an electrical shop in Hereford.

'Is Dr Emmerson in?'

'Yes, but he lives in the cottage at the rear of this house,' she explained.

'Well, see, I got his music centre here, and I can't carry it all that way, can I?'

'You don't need to. If you go down the road a hundred yards, turn left, then right, you'll find the drive leading to the cottage,' she said.

He looked at her blankly, and she sighed and gave in.

'All right, I'll show you.'

Miranda slipped into the passenger seat of the van and gave directions as the man drove. She had intended getting out at the bottom of the drive and walking back to Meadowlands, but he drove right up to the front of the cottage without heeding her requests to stop, and then made so much noise reversing the vehicle so that the rear doors were adjacent to the house, that Alex Emmerson was already standing there as Miranda scrambled inelegantly out.

She was wearing jeans and a sweater this morning, and so, she noted, was he. She had only ever seen him in a dark, professional suit with a crisp shirt and tie, and the effect was odd, as if he were in fancy dress, playing the part of Mr Average at work around the house, for which she felt he was quite unsuited.

His expression as he looked at her was questioning, the steady grey eyes challenging her reason for being there.

'I had to show the man from the shop how to get here,' she said, instantly defensive, not wanting him to think she had come out of curiosity. 'Your music centre has arrived, and they brought it to Meadowlands by mistake.'

'So I see.' He signed the invoice the delivery man held out. 'Bring it through to the living room, will you? I think I'd better give you a hand. The doors are rather awkward.'

'That'd be a help, sir, if you would. Miss! Would you grab them loudspeakers?'

As she could not politely refuse, Miranda found herself carrying the pair of speakers into the living room of Cruck Cottage, and holding them steady as they were plugged into the music centre. She could not help but notice the well-known brand name on the front of the cabinet, and the obvious quality of the merchandise, and wondered, as her father had, why a man who could afford expensive equipment such as this would choose to live in this tiny, rented cottage.

'Will that be all, sir?'

'Yes, thank you.' Alex Emmerson was preoccupied with tuning the dials, but she noted the generous tip he absentmindedly gave the delivery man before he left.

It would have seemed rude simply to follow him out without saying a word, so Miranda remarked casually, 'That's a very handsome piece of hi-fi.'

'Yes, isn't it?' He was squatting, balanced easily on his heels, encouraging the radio to produce an astonishing babble of foreign stations, and did not look up from his task, so Miranda was obliged to look down at the top of his dark head, noting the way his hair waved profusely and almost uncontrollably from his crown. 'I don't like much that's on television, but I enjoy listening to good music.'

'Herefordshire is a great area for music lovers,' she said. It sounded banal, and she wished she had not said it, but he replied,

'Yes, I know. Sir Edward Elgar was born not far from here, wasn't he? And there's the Three Choirs Music Festival. Are you musical, Miss Lewis? Most Herefordians seem to be.'

'Not in the sense of playing an instrument, or singing in a choir,' she admitted. 'But then, I'm not a native Herefordian, either. My father only moved here less than a year ago, and I lived in London before I came to work at Lenchester.'

He looked up then, and she caught a fleeting distress in his eyes before his expression closed.

'So did I.'

'Oh? Which hospital were you at?'

It was merely a casual, almost automatic question, but he frowned deeply, and his reluctance to discuss it further was unmistakable.

'This may be stating the obvious, but London is a big city. We could both have lived there all our lives, without our paths crossing,' he said.

'Yes, of course,' Miranda said lamely. 'I only wondered . . .'

As he said nothing, and the silence grew until it became uncomfortable, she said. 'I'd better be getting back to Meadowlands. You seem to have settled in quite quickly, so I assume everything is all right?'

'You assume correctly.' There was a distinctly chilly gleam in his eyes as he added drily, 'You are wondering about my lack of goods and chattels, I suppose—it's a common female curiosity. I travel light, Miss Lewis. My wife took most of our possessions when she divorced me. I got to keep the suitcases.'

Surprise caused Miranda to suck in her breath sharply. The anger and resentment had been caused by his ex-wife, and should have been directed at her. Perhaps they were, but she was not here to take the force of his bitterness, and it was Miranda, instead, who stood in its path, the cold, remorseless wind whipping around her. She was only a surrogate, but she was a woman, and as a target would serve as well as any member of her sex.

She was perceptive enough to discern the pain which lurked behind this cold, obsessive hatred, but did not see why she should be the victim of it.

'That really has nothing to do with me, Dr Emmerson,' she said coolly.

'No, it hasn't, but sooner or later you're going to want to know the details of my solitary state, since we're going to be neighbours, so we might as well get it out of the way, once and for all,' he stated clearly. 'My wife left me four years ago, and we were finally divorced two years later. It was a considerable relief to me to be single again, and I have every intention of remaining so.'

Miranda was aware of a cold, unpleasant sensation, akin to icy water trickling down one's back, causing her skin to prickle uncomfortably. He was warning her—posting 'keep clear' notices, as if he feared his fatal attractions would be too much to resist, and she would be unable to prevent herself having designs on him!

Her voice was furious, but cold, as she said, 'I should imagine it would be a considerable relief to your wife, too! I'm hardly surprised she left you!'

The exclamation had been torn from her in anger, but she held her breath after delivering it, knowing that this was not a sensible way of talking to a man one hardly knew, who was nonetheless a senior member of hospital staff. With every encounter, with every exchange of words between them, she was driving herself deeper into a mire from which it grew increasingly difficult to clamber out. He would never like, respect or trust her, and all her working life at Lenchester would have the shadow of his hostility clouding it.

She looked up into his face, almost hopelessly, expecting to see a furious emnity there, but to her further astonishment, he was gazing down at her with the puzzled, faintly lost expression of one who seeks definite guidelines and points of unchanging reference on an indecipherable map.

'If it's so obvious to a virtual stranger what a highly unsatisfactory husband I was, then I expect you're right,' he said wryly.

The sudden evaporation of his anger deflated the bubble of her own, and left her wishing she could retract the hurtful words.

'I shouldn't be the one to throw stones,' she said quietly, on a note of self-disparagement. 'Having recently emerged from a broken relationship, I'm not exactly an expert on what makes these things work. However, you and I have one thing in common—for now, we're hell-bent on maintaining our independence.'

It was an olive branch of considerable proportions, and she expected him to accept it with grace. Had he done so, they could perhaps have salvaged enough mutual respect to enable them to be, if not friends, at least friendly colleagues.

But Alex Emmerson merely laughed—scathing, sarcastic laughter, which left her in no doubt of how he regarded her statement of intention, even had he not had the gall to say, with cool amusement,

'I have learned from experience never to believe a woman when she expresses a preference for the single state. It's usually a clever ploy behind which she hides her true purpose.'

Miranda gasped at this open and unashamed effrontery, and she never knew from where she dredged up the courage to face him squarely.

'I never said I wanted to remain single all my life,' she declared. 'Although I can't envision it right now, there may come a time when I meet someone I wish to marry. However, you can be assured that person won't have an ego a mile high, and a poor track record! Good morning, Dr Emmerson!'

She turned and stalked indignantly from the cottage, not waiting to see what impression, if any, her words had made, and kept up a spanking pace all the way down the drive, so that she was red-faced and breathless when she arrived back at Meadowlands.

Her father was checking his accounts at his desk in the corner of the lounge, and he looked up, surprised, as his daughter flounced into the room, positively quivering with nervous energy and with a face the colour of a beetroot.

'Good Lord!' he said mildly. 'I haven't seen you that colour since you won the junior sprint when you were ten years old! Whatever's the matter?'

Miranda pointed furiously out of the window at the cottage.

'That man is the matter!' she exploded. 'How long has he taken the cottage for? Can't you tell him we need it ourselves after all?'

'Steady on!' He eyed her curiously. 'He's only just moved in. I can't ask him to leave, particularly as he's paid a month's rent in advance. Says he wants to use it as a base while he looks for a place to buy.'

'Let's hope he finds one very soon,' Miranda said fervently. 'Because I, for one, do not find the prospect of living in such close proximity to him unmitigated bliss!'

She stalked out of the room again, obviously too agitated to settle anywhere, closing the door behind her so firmly that the walls vibrated.

Major Lewis tapped his teeth with the end of his pen, and permitted himself a faint smile of satisfaction. He had seen his daughter in all manner of odd moods since she broke off with that young man in London whom he had never really liked. He had seen her arrive home defeated and dispirited, silent and uncommunicative about the cause of the split, he had seen her pick up the threads of her life with admirable determination, and throw herself with real, unfeigned enthusiasm into her work. Then he had seen her quietly content, only occasionally brooding on her imagined personal failure, busy, occupied, helpful . . . but somehow impossible to reach, in the inner sanctum, where she hid her secret self. But never, until this moment, had he seen her blazingly, unashamedly angry, with her dander up so high she could not conceal it, a furious sparkle in her eyes, and a fighting tilt to her chin. Something, or someone, had given her back the verve which had been knocked out of her by the London years, and whatever the reason, he was glad of it.

*   *   *

On Monday afternoon, Miranda went down to the children's ward in time to see Darren Saunders' mother during visiting.

In spite of the fact that there was something inherently heart-rending about sick children, there was an air of cheerfulness about the ward. Although ill, the patients were still children, and the atmosphere was lifted by their incessant curiosity and interest, their zest for the minutiae of living. There was chatter and laughter, toys, books and crayons were much in evidence, the children's own drawings and paper collages decorating the walls. Now, at visiting time, there were small brothers and sisters, too young to be at school, who had been brought along, and there was a greater volume of noise than one usually associated with a hospital ward.

Sister Robertson was a small, calm, wiry woman in her mid-thirties, who gave the impression of swimming with the tide, of going along with the chaotic ambiance around her. It was only an impression, as was the chaos, which was intended to make the children feel at home and allay their natural fear of this strange environment. In reality, Sister had everything well under control, missed little, and loved every one of her charges, even the awkward ones. Especially the awkward ones.

'So you're the young lady who took over from Jean Davies,' she said, looking Miranda up and down in a friendly, if appraising manner. 'Either I'm getting old, or the new staff are getting younger all the time!'

'You certainly don't look old to me, Sister,' Miranda laughed, 'and I'm pushing twenty-five myself!'

'Gracious! Positively in the sere and yellow,' Sister teased gently. 'What can we do for you, Miss Lewis? We have visiting right now, as you see, but that's almost finished.'

'Actually, that's why I came,' Miranda said quickly,

anxious to dispel the notion that she had thoughtlessly chosen a bad time. 'Dr Emmerson asked me to have a word with Darren Saunders' mother.'

'Oh well, if Dr Emmerson says so, that's fine with me,' Sister said firmly, and Miranda suppressed a curious urge to ask this calm, cheerful woman how on earth she managed not only to survive, but to appear so content with her lot, when she had to work so closely with that dreadful man. 'That's Darren in the third bed down on the left, and Mrs Saunders with him.'

'Heavens!' Miranda exclaimed. 'She looks more like his elder sister!' She looked down the room at the young woman with the long, pale straight hair and the small, pinched face, who was trying to control two awkward toddlers. 'Are the other children hers, too?'

'Yes, and there's another one, a girl, just started primary school. You could say she has her hands full, poor girl. It can't be easy, looking after them all on her own, keeping them fed and clothed, and to have the worry of a diabetic child on top of it all!' Sister clucked her tongue sympathetically.

Miranda smiled in accord, and went down the ward to introduce herself to Mrs Saunders. As Alex Emmerson had said, she was not much older than Miranda herself, and must have married virtually straight from school. Close in age, they were worlds apart in experience, Miranda thought, as she chatted to the harassed young woman. Here she was, with her years at college, and her diploma, and her career, the world seemingly at her feet, and yet she admitted to a reluctant admiration for this tired, worried girl. The children were all bright, clean-scrubbed and nicely, if inexpensively dressed, and Darren was as sharp as a knife, full of youthful humour.

After only a few minutes' conversation, Miranda was

reassured that Mrs Saunders was fully aware of the importance of Darren's diet, and his injections, and was adhering to the regimen closely and intelligently. The problem, whatever Alex Emmerson may have thought, did not, in Miranda's opinion, lie with the mother. Maybe, with his low estimation of the female sex, he had veered automatically to that conclusion, or it could be that his autocratic manner had intimidated her, so that she had been unable to answer his questions as clearly and simply as she now answered Miranda's.

'I have been doing it right, haven't I?' she demanded anxiously.

'Absolutely, by the sound of it,' Miranda assured her.

'I'm ever so careful. Not that it's easy, mind, to do a diet for one, with all the rest to cook for.'

'I'm sure it isn't. I don't know how you manage,' Miranda said, quite sincerely, and was rewarded by a look of intense gratitude. 'Don't worry, Mrs Saunders, we'll get to the bottom of it. I'll tell Dr Emmerson all you have just told me. When he's convinced the diet isn't the problem, he'll be able to search for the root of it elsewhere.'

'Oh, he's a good doctor, I'm sure,' Darren's mother said, her tired face lighting up with a touching faith. 'Only, he frightens me to death, see, so my tongue gets all tied up in knots.'

Miranda smiled.

'I know what you mean. It's only his manner,' she said, wondering why she felt impelled to interpret Alex Emmerson to others.

'Yes, I know. He's marvellous with the kids—all of them here adore him. Darren thinks there's no one like Dr Emmerson. His own children are very lucky. I wish mine had a father like that,' she said, with faint regret.

Miranda found herself wondering if he had children of

his own. He had not mentioned them, and she did not feel inclined to ask him anything of a personal nature, not after the encounter she'd had with him on Saturday.

'He only likes little people,' Julie Morris had said, and from what Miranda had heard, it would seem that little people liked him, too. An odd, contradictory man.

She watched Mrs Saunders gather up her offspring, pull up their socks, fasten their cardigan buttons, and leave the ward, holding one protesting child firmly by each hand.

I shall never be a young mother, Miranda thought, with fleeting self-pity. The years Tony had strung her along had robbed her of that chance. Maybe she would never be a mother at all. At least Mrs Saunders had her children, whatever other troubles life had brought her.

She did not like the pang of unbidden envy this thought provoked, and banished it swiftly, turning back to the boy. It would do no harm to have a few words with Darren himself.

There was often more to be learned from talking generally to the patients about their lives and interests than by direct interrogation on the subject causing the trouble. Miranda had learned this early in her career, and it proved itself true yet again.

Darren was only too happy to chat on about his school, and his likes and dislikes concerning the teachers and the lessons. It appeared that what he really liked was sport.

'Football—that's brill!' he enthused. 'When we go up to secondary school, we can do rugby as well. I watch that on the telly—it's great!' His expression became concerned as he asked, 'It doesn't mean I can't do sport, just because I'm like this, does it, Miss?'

'Certainly not, Darren,' Miranda assured him. 'Lots of diabetics lead very active lives. As long as you keep up with your injections, and watch your diet. You could help your mum with that—she must have lots to do, looking after your brother and sisters.'

'Yeah—our little 'uns are a right nuisance,' he agreed cheerfully. 'I could help Mum cook—cooking's great, and it's not sissy, is it?'

'Not at all. A lot of professional cooks are men, like the head chef here, for instance.'

He grimaced.

'We could do with some more of them to cook our school dinners!'

Miranda joined in his laughter.

'I'm sure they aren't that bad!' she smiled.

'Not really, I s'pose. I don't half get hungry by dinner time, and sometimes I come over all dozy and funny . . . you know, like I'm going to pass out.'

'Your body is telling you it needs help—you must learn to watch out for that,' she told him. 'But surely, your mid-morning snack helps you get through until lunch?'

The snack, usually a bar of special diabetic chocolate, was one of the requirements of Darren's diet, and according to his mother, it went to school in his tuck box every day. But watching the shutters suddenly come down on the boy's lively face, Miranda experienced a pang of doubt and an accompanying tingle of excitement such as a detective might feel on unearthing a vital clue.

'Darren—you are eating your snack, aren't you?' she probed. 'It's most important, and if you miss it out, it could result in your being brought back into hospital in a coma—like you were the other day.'

He regarded her with disbelief.

'Just for a bit of chocolate—naw!' he exclaimed.

'It could be—particularly on the days when you've had PE, and your energy is running low,' she insisted.

The boy looked at her thoughtfully.

'We did have football the day I flaked out,' he said slowly. 'But, Miss—we aren't allowed to eat sweets at break. A lady came round and talked to us about teeth, and fillings, and all that stuff, so Mr Collins—that's the headmaster—made a new rule about it.'

Miranda nodded.

'That would be the health visitor, I expect. But that rule doesn't apply to you, Darren. Your teacher knows it's vital you have your snack.'

He looked down, picking at the counterpane with one hand. Miranda could see he was troubled, and she pressed on gently.

'You haven't been eating your chocolate, have you? Won't you tell me why not?'

His voice sank to a whisper as he said, 'I gave it to Johnny Wilkes. He said I'd get done if I was caught eating sweets in the playground. He said he'd see I got caught!'

Miranda was torn between indignation and amusement. But her exasperation came out on top, because, owing to the activities of some playground bully, this plucky boy was jeopardising his recovery.

He sneaked a glance at her from the corner of his eye.

'What's going to happen, Miss?'

'It's going to be all right, Darren,' she told him firmly. 'I'll speak to Mr Collins, and I'm sure he'll sort out Johnny Wilkes! And in future, be sure to eat your snack. We want you out on the football field, not lying in bed here!'

On the way out, she stopped to have a word with Sister Robertson.

'I think I might have solved Darren's problem,' she said, and explained briefly the end result of her chat with the boy. 'Will Dr Emmerson be in today?'

'I doubt it. He's generally in Ross-on-Wye on Mondays. But he has a round tomorrow—you might catch him then. Shall I give him a message to contact you?'

'If you would,' Miranda replied. She could, of course, see Alex Emmerson sooner than that, simply by walking across the paddock to the cottage. But she had no desire to seek him out, and thought it better if her dealings with him were confined to on duty hours in the safe, clinical environment of the hospital.

But her spirits were buoyant as she returned to her office to phone Darren's school. It was always deeply satisfying to have helped solve a patient's problem—that, after all, was what her job was about. But in this case, a spring of triumph welled up within her, from a less altruistic source.

Over to you, Dr High and Mighty Emmerson, she thought wickedly. This scatterbrained female, whom you don't think capable of repairing a puncture properly, let alone holding down a responsible job, might just have done something right, in your opinion, for once! Let's see you put *that* in your pipe and smoke it!

CHAPTER FOUR

As it happened, Miranda did not see Dr Emmerson on Tuesday. She was detained in Miss Carmichael's office while the Administrator repeatedly went over some point in the small print of Miranda's contract of employment, over which she claimed to be unclear, and Miranda, determinedly trying not to fidget with impatience, endeavoured to dredge up from her memory details of her career to date.

'This may all seem very mundane to you, Miss Lewis,' Aline Carmichael said sharply, sensing Miranda's ill-concealed desire to be off about her work, 'but it affects your future grading and your salary, and therefore it's in your own interest to iron out these small discrepancies.'

'I'm sure that's so, Miss Carmichael, but no doubt they will have all this information on file somewhere at my previous place of employment. If you don't mind, I really ought to go down to the children's ward. There's something I should see Dr Emmerson about.'

The angle of the perfectly coiffed blonde head shifted, and a perceptible alertness tautened the neat features, but Aline Carmichael's eyes were as blankly inscrutable as ever as she said, 'I don't doubt that for one moment, Miss Lewis. There generally is. Your predecessor found it necessary to consult Dr Emmerson with surprising frequency, and I see you are all set to follow in her footsteps.'

Miranda seethed inwardly, and fought hard to maintain a composed exterior.

'I'm not sure what you're suggesting, Miss

Carmichael. If there was some . . . relationship other than a professional one between Miss Davies and Dr Emmerson, then surely that was no one's business but their own.'

'It became mine, as her superior, when it interfered with her duties,' the Administrator rapped back smartly. 'What "relationship" there was existed only in Miss Davies' mind. As *your* superior, I am merely pointing out that it would hardly help your career if you were to make the same mistake. Alex Emmerson is not interested in the romantic adoration of young women.'

Miranda could hardly believe that she was sitting in the Administrator's office, actually taking part in this bizarre conversation. There was a quality of unreality about it, and yet it was not possible to mistake the nature of the message. Miss Carmichael was warning her off. Because she genuinely had Miranda's career prospects at heart, and did not want her to be hurt? She was not naive enough to believe that—her short acquaintance with Aline Carmichael had convinced her that this lady was a consummate exponent of the art of looking after number one.

She recalled the odd snide remarks Miss Carmichael liked to let drop about Jean Davies, and unbidden, she heard Jeff Thompson's voice saying 'She constantly had her knife into poor Jean.' Was it just possible that this clever, attractive, devious woman had made her predecessor's life a misery to deter her from pursuing her infatuation for Alex Emmerson, because she herself had a vested interest there? And was all set to repeat the process with Miranda, to ensure that she did not follow suit?

She took a deep breath. This had to be straightened out here and now, and perhaps only then could the two of them achieve an amicable working relationship that was not distorted by undercurrents of a personal nature.

'Miss Carmichael, I'm not Jean Davies, and her problems, whatever they were, are not mine. What is certain is that I'm not about to go overboard for any man right now, and if I were, I would most assuredly not be foolish enough to lose my head over Dr Emmerson. However, I do have to see him about a patient, so if you don't mind, perhaps we could discuss the contract details some other time.'

Aline Carmichael smiled her dazzlingly false and very unnerving smile, while her eyes remained expressionless.

'Oh yes, do hurry along, Miss Lewis. I wouldn't wish to detain you,' she said airily, as though she had not spent the last half an hour doing exactly that. 'Don't worry about the contract—I'll get Maggie to ring up and get the details.'

As Miranda reached the door, about to make a thankful exit, she called out softly, 'Oh, Miss Lewis—I'm highly gratified to hear you express such sentiments. If we women are to take our place in the professional world alongside men, it does not help when members of our sex lose their ability to think rationally, simply because a man smiles at them. Does it?'

Very clever, Miranda thought, as she hurried along the corridor. *Appealing to my feminist principles, when I'm pretty sure she doesn't give a hoot for the advancement of any woman except Aline Carmichael!*

On a more sober note, she mused thoughtfully that working in the professional world alongside men did not confer on one an immunity from the hazards and pleasures of falling in love—on the contrary. Today's women, as they struggled to equate the complex demands of jobs, emotions, families and homes, were exposed to those perils as never before. Men were everywhere, and there was no avoiding contact with them. And most of the time, she thought, remembering Tony, they gave one no quarter.

Miranda reached the children's ward to discover that Dr Emmerson had finished his round and left five minutes earlier.

'He was very pleased about Darren Saunders,' Sister Robertson said encouragingly. 'He said he was going to a meeting right now, but would ring you later.'

Miranda was in her office for the rest of the morning, working on the diet sheets, but he had not phoned by the time she went to lunch, and she assumed he was still occupied with his meeting.

In the cafeteria, she found Julie Morris just finishing her lunch, and she took her tray over to the other girl's table.

'You look fraught,' Julie said shrewdly. 'Had a particularly rough morning?'

Miranda hesitated, and then decided that she needed to confide in someone who was trustworthy.

'I had a horrendous interview with Miss Carmichael,' she said. 'She actually warned me not to fall for Alex Emmerson—of all people!—and hinted that she thought I was going down the same road as Jean Davies. I gather from the grapevine that she was keen on him?'

'That was fairly common knowledge,' Julie agreed, stirring her coffee. 'Jean made rather a fool of herself really, and I think that was why she finally left, because he never gave her a shred of encouragement—quite the reverse. And of course, La Carmichael was pretty foul to her.'

'She insinuated that Jean was neglecting her work on account of her infatuation,' Miranda said slowly.

'Well, I couldn't say for sure, but I think that's probably a bit of an exaggeration,' Julie said cagily.

'Everyone knew that the Minotaur had it in for Jean.'

'Apparently. And that made me wonder if perhaps . . .'

'If perhaps she has a fancy for the gentleman herself?' Julie finished succinctly. 'There's been a certain amount of speculation about that, but if she has, she's playing her cards close to her chest. But she would, wouldn't she? That's her style. She wouldn't shadow him along the corridors and gaze at him moonstruck, like Jean did. And it is a fact that they have been seen having lunch together in Lenchester. So maybe there's truth in it. But she'll have to angle very carefully for that particular fish, I'd say.'

Miranda thought of the cold anger in Alex Emmerson's eyes as he said, 'It was a considerable relief to me to be single again, and I have every intention of remaining so.' He was a hard, complex, difficult man, embittered by experience, but beneath that brittle exterior she sensed that there was warmth, otherwise how would children, with their instinctive grasp of sincerity, find him sympathetic? Could he be attracted by a cool, calculating woman like Aline Carmichael? And why should I care if he were, Miranda asked herself exasperatedly.

'I just wish she would rid herself of the notion that I'm a continuation of Jean Davies!' she burst out with annoyance. 'Why—Dr Emmerson has made it fairly clear that when he's aware of my existence at all he finds me something of a pest!'

Julie stacked her dirty plate and cup neatly on her tray.

'And you?' she asked curiously. 'How do you feel about Lenchester's most dangerously devastating, infuriatingly elusive unattached male? Doesn't he stir the old heart-strings just a mite?'

Miranda attacked her jacket potato with telling ferocity.

'Not remotely,' she declared. 'In fact, that's exactly what I wish he were—remote. I wish he lived a thousand miles away, instead of at the end of our garden!'

Concentrating furiously on her lunch, she was not aware of the knowing gleam in Staff Nurse Morris' eye as she left the cafeteria to go back on duty.

There was no phone call from Alex Emmerson that afternoon, not even while Miranda was absent from her office, according to Maggie, who took her calls when she was not available. Not that there was any absolute necessity for him to speak to her about Darren Saunders, unless he had some further recommendations to make concerning the boy's diet. But Miranda had somehow gained the impression that when Dr Emmerson expressed an intention of doing something, it would be done, so she was mildly surprised not to hear from him. Disappointed? Of course not—the very notion was ridiculous!

'I did have a phone call from my cousin, though —about the car,' Maggie told Miranda. 'He says tonight would be fine, if you want to take a look at it.'

'Fine. The sooner the better,' Miranda said decisively, and she wrote down the address in Hereford. She had had several requests to give talks on diet to groups of local pensioners and weight-watching clubs, and the question of finding suitable transport was becoming urgent.

On arriving home that afternoon, Miranda parked Bessy and went in search of her father. There were no buses into or out of Ibsey after six p.m., so if she were to go into Hereford that evening, she would need to use his car. A round trip of thirty miles by bicycle, after a day's work, was not an option she seriously considered.

She found him in the paddock at the end of the garden, but not until she was too near to turn back did she become aware that he was talking to Alex Emmerson. The consultant paediatrician, changed once more into cords and sweater, had transformed himself into a gardener and was attacking the proliferation of weedy growth in the cottage garden, which was why she had not seen him at first. He straightened up at her approach and favoured her with a reserved, almost reluctant smile.

Miranda returned it hesitantly.

'Good afternoon, Dr Emmerson.' She turned to her father. 'I don't want to interrupt your conversation, Dad, but I just wanted to check that it will be all right for me to borrow the car this evening.'

Major Lewis frowned.

'Actually, Miranda, it won't, as I shall be needing it myself,' he said apologetically. 'I wish you had mentioned it before, then I could have made different arrangements.'

'I didn't know until this afternoon,' she explained. 'It's Maggie's cousin—the one who's selling the Mini. He wants me to go and see it tonight.'

'Oh dear! I'm sorry, Miranda, but I can't alter my plans now, since they involve . . . other people,' he said, finishing on a vague, evasive note which was totally uncharacteristic of him. However, Miranda did not have time to puzzle over this, for Alex Emmerson, who had been standing, shears in hand, following this conversation, unexpectedly said, 'I'm going into Hereford myself this evening. I could give you a lift, if that's any help.'

Miranda caught her breath. Travel into Hereford, confined in a car with this man, on tenterhooks in case any casual subject of conversation she introduced might provoke a touchy reaction? No thank you, she thought.

'Oh, really, I wouldn't like to put you to any trouble,' she said politely.

'You wouldn't. As I told you, I'm going anyway. I have a business appointment which should not take more than an hour, so I should be able to bring you back.'

The Major beamed brightly at this apparently simple solution to his daughter's problem.

'There you are, Miranda,' he said cheerfully. 'Alex is making you an offer you can't refuse. What could be fairer?'

It was indeed difficult to raise a logical objection to the plan, particularly in front of her father, who, she noted, was already on first name terms with their new neighbour.

'Very well. Thank you,' she said, as graciously as she could.

'That's all right. Seven o'clock suit you?'

Miranda murmured that seven o'clock would be fine, and made herself scarce, leaving the two men to continue their chat. Her father came in five minutes later, and to her enquiry as to what they should have for dinner he said casually, 'Oh, don't bother with anything for me, thanks. I'm eating out.'

Well really, thought Miranda exasperatedly. It was unlike him to be so secretive and mysterious about his activities, leaving it until the last moment to tell her he didn't want dinner, and then saying absolutely nothing about where he was going, or with whom.

Miranda was so rattled, both by her parent's odd behaviour, and the prospect of Alex Emmerson's company, that she committed a cardinal sin against which she was forever warning patients. How many times had she told others that the fact of being alone, and having to trouble to prepare food for one, was *not* an excuse for skimping on proper meals and letting nutrition fly out of the window? Yet that was precisely what she did that evening. She made a cup of tea, and nibbled desultorily on an apple, then spent the rest of the time until seven o'clock wishing vainly that there was some way out of the arrangement she had made.

Short of pleading a sudden attack of migraine, or something equally incapacitating, she could not think of one. Besides, she really did want to see that car, and Maggie would have passed on the message to her cousin that she was coming. This was silly. 'The man can't bite you,' she told herself firmly, sensibly, as she changed from her office outfit of skirt and blouse into a simple, dirndl-skirted summer dress, and draped a knitted jacket over her shoulders.

Alex Emmerson's car was long and streamlined, with a metallic silver finish. He had his window rolled down, one arm leaning on it, the other hand resting negligently on the wheel, and she noted that he had changed yet again, into beige slacks and a short-sleeved, casual shirt. He wore no tie, and the open collar revealed the tanned muscles of his neck. Miranda wondered about the nature of his appointment in Hereford, and expected that he would be about as forthcoming as her father had been about his.

Miranda slipped quickly into the passenger seat. The safety belt was different from the one in her father's car, and silently cursing her own ineptitude, she fumbled vainly with the catch, until he leaned across and fastened it for her, his fingers momentarily brushing against her waist. Fiercely willing her face not to redden, she wondered why she could not be one of those assured females who effortlessly did the right thing on all occasions.

I bet Miss Carmichael doesn't get into a tizz fastening seat belts, she thought ruefully, and this led to a speculation as to how frequently that lady had occupied this place, so that she quite failed to notice that her companion was speaking to her until he repeated what he had said.

'That was a good piece of work you did, finding out what had happened with the Saunders boy. Well done.'

Miranda was terribly afraid that she was blushing; his praise disconcerted her almost as much as his censure.

'Oh, it was nothing very much. You'd have found the answer yourself, once you'd had chance to talk to him at greater length,' she disclaimed quickly.

'Nevertheless, you got there first, and the sooner a problem is diagnosed, the sooner it can be dealt with. Have you spoken to the school?'

'Yes. The staff, of course, had no idea what was going on, and the headmaster promised that whoever was on playground duty would keep a very close eye on the situation in future.'

'You seem to have dealt with the matter very efficiently.' He paused. 'I had thought you would keep me up to date on what action you had taken. I was on the ward this morning.'

Must there always be a sting in the tail, Miranda wondered, even when he was complimenting her on a job well performed?

'I had every intention of so doing,' she told him. 'Unfortunately, I was in with Miss Carmichael, and by the time I got down to children's ward, you had left.'

She vouchsafed this piece of information to make it clear that she had been unable to get away, anxious that he should not think she had merely considered other tasks more pressing. But being only human, she could not resist stealing a covert glance at his profile, to see if the mention of Aline Carmichael produced any reaction. There was none that she could discern.

'I see,' he replied levelly. 'I was in a meeting for the rest of the morning, and although I phoned your office at about a quarter past two, I was informed that you were not back from lunch. Do dietitians always take such leisurely lunch breaks, I wonder?'

The faintly barbed note was there again, and Miranda flushed, this time with indignation.

'Most certainly not! I normally take lunch from half-past twelve to one-thirty,' she informed him. 'By a quarter past two I had been back forty-five minutes, and was, if I remember rightly, on Men's Medical, talking to a patient with a duodenal ulcer. What on earth made Maggie think I was still at lunch . . . and why didn't she give me the message that you had called?'

'I didn't speak to Maggie. The call was put through to Miss Carmichael. I expect she assumed you were not back.'

Miranda was silent. All the admin calls were taken initially by Maggie, who then put them through to the correct extension. Occasionally it happened that Maggie herself was elsewhere on some errand, and if the switchboard considered the caller to be sufficiently important, they would put the call directly through to the Administrator on her private line. This was obviously what had occurred. But for Aline Carmichael to claim that Miranda was not back from lunch, half way through the afternoon, could not be passed off as a mistaken assumption. Miranda had seen and spoken to her, *after* lunch and before she went to Men's Medical.

But she could not tell Alex Emmerson that this morning Miss Carmichael had made sure that she didn't get away in time to see him on his rounds, and that later, she had apparently made a comment designed to suggest that Miranda's attitude towards her hours of work was slapdash and unprofessional. It sounded unbelievable, and furthermore, Miranda would not resort to defending herself by slating someone else. She would have to be content with letting him believe that it was all a mistake.

The subject seemed to die of its own volition, and for a while they both sat in silence as he drove along the winding road, with the countryside green and verdant on either side.

After a while, he said, 'This car you are thinking of buying—are you going to have it professionally checked?'

She frowned. 'I hadn't planned to.'

'It's advisable. With a second-hand car you don't know what problems you are taking on. Of course,' his voice slid easily into an oblique, off-handed mockery —'you might be one of those superwomen who are fully conversant with car engines, in which case I'll retract my suggestion.'

'I haven't a clue what goes on under car bonnets,' Miranda admitted frankly. 'But the person who is selling it is our secretary's cousin, so I'll just have to hope that he's as honest as she is.'

He whistled softly.

'Such trusting innocence will get you taken for a fool one of these days, Miranda,' he said. 'Don't you know the world is full of cowboys and charlatans?'

Her head jerked up at his unexpected use of her name.

'You may say I'm naive if you like,' she asserted defiantly, 'but I trust Maggie, and I don't think her cousin would sell me a load of junk.'

He shrugged.

'Perhaps not, since he knows she will see you every day and be at the receiving end of your complaints,' he conceded. This rather jaundiced conclusion was not in exactly the same vein as her fervent declaration of personal trust, but Miranda had to admit to herself that he had a point.

'Dr Emmerson, you're a cynic,' she accused, half-laughingly.

'The name is Alex, and I'm a realist,' he contradicted. 'However, as my father once owned a garage, I grew up knowing a little about what makes cars work, so why don't I come with you and give this one the once-over?'

The suggestion was almost friendly, and free of his usual high-handedness. He was even smiling, and when he smiled, the Byronic good looks were near-irresistible. Miranda capitulated—after all, she had nothing to lose, she reasoned, and a self-confessed expert's opinion to gain.

'I think . . . Alex . . . you've just made another offer I can't refuse,' she said with a smile.

Maggie's cousin, Arthur, lived with his wife and baby son in a modest semi-detached house on the outskirts of the city. A cheerful, gangling young man with red hair and a lop-sided grin, he was unperturbed by Miranda's arriving with a knowledgeable male in tow, and led them both to the garage. The men had the car bonnet up, and Alex inspected the engine thoroughly, then scrambled underneath with Arthur, after which they spent some time talking in what was, to Miranda, unintelligible technical jargon.

Recognising a fellow enthusiast, Arthur waxed lyrical about all he had done to keep the vehicle in near-pristine condition, and Miranda had to admit that everything looked clean and cared for, from the engine to the gleaming red paintwork.

Alex drew Miranda to one side.

'It's not bad at all—in fair condition for the year and make, and he's certainly looked after it. There's a bit of rust underneath, but what car of that age doesn't have some? Ask him to let you drive it, and don't offer more than £1,000.'

Miranda grinned.

'What makes you think I've got more than £1,000?' she asked.

'Point taken,' said Alex. He glanced at his watch. 'Look, I must go. I'm seeing my accountant, and he's already working late. Where shall I meet you?'

It was a warm, pleasant evening, so Miranda suggested the Cathedral close, and he agreed. She then spent a pleasurable half-hour driving the Mini around while Arthur sat beside her and talked endlessly in his lilting Herefordshire accent, so close to Welsh, about the car's little peculiarities, every bit as if the vehicle were human. Miranda was already fond of the little car, and determined to have it, so it did not take long to clinch the deal.

'I'll have her done up . . . a full service, plugs changed, the lot, and let Maggie know when she'll be ready for you,' he promised. 'Shouldn't take longer than a day or two.'

Miranda was feeling more than satisfied with the results of the venture as she sat on a wooden bench in the Cathedral close, waiting for Alex. The golden evening light slanted beams across the grey-brown stone of the massive Cathedral front, and the sound of the city's traffic, although near, seemed muted and far away. Daisies starred the grass so thickly that the green was overlaid with whiteness, and birds trilled drowsily high up in the trees. The clock in its tower chimed the half-hour, the notes carrying on the clear air. So far away from London that it might be another world, and Miranda felt it all finally slip from her shoulders, and into the past. She knew that at last she could truthfully say she was over it, and the page was closed. An ineffable sense of peacefulness stole over her, and briefly she closed her eyes.

She opened them to see Alex Emmerson striding purposefully towards her. Despite the modern cut of his clothes, the lean, wild darkness about him made him seem a remnant from a past age . . . then she told herself she was being silly and fanciful. The man was a doctor, and a children's doctor, at that!

'Have you been waiting long?' he asked, to all appearances genuinely concerned that she might have been.

'Only five minutes, and it's so pleasant here, I didn't mind at all,' she replied.

There was a hint of devilishness in his smile.

'Content to sit here and gloat over your purchase, I presume,' he remarked astutely, and Miranda could not repress a touch of pique.

'What makes you so sure I bought the car?' she demanded.

'Are you serious? An idiot could see you were intent on buying it, and I'm not an idiot. Was the price right?'

She hesitated, and then decided it was pointless insisting on privacy regarding the transaction. After all, he had helped her.

'I offered £900, he asked £1,000, so we settled for £950.'

'Fair enough, I suppose.'

Not sure where he had parked his own car, she fell into step beside him as he walked along the broad path skirting the Cathedral, and then out the other side of the close. At the end of a quiet street, Miranda became aware of the delicious smell of meat roasting over charcoal, attacking her gastric juices and reminding her of the skipped dinner. Unexpectedly, her companion turned her sharply right through a gate, and into the garden of an inn.

'I have a confession to make,' he said lazily. 'No doubt, as a dietitian, you will castigate me, but I was so busy in the garden I didn't stop to fix a meal for myself.'

'Tut tut,' Miranda said, in mock reproof. She was beginning, surprisingly, to enjoy herself, and wondered why she had found this man so intimidating. Obviously when his mood was relaxed, as it was now, he could be charming company.

'I accept the criticism. I don't usually neglect myself. I'm used to providing my own meals—in fact, I'm quite a good cook,' he said with a disarming lack of modesty. 'I see they've got their barbecue going here, so I'm going to have a steak. You aren't hungry, are you, by any chance?'

'Ravenous,' she confessed, her eyes twinkling. 'I didn't eat either.'

'Really?' The dark eyebrows rose. 'And what's your excuse?'

Miranda could hardly tell him that he was partly responsible, that she had worked herself up into a state which, in retrospect, appeared ridiculous, simply at the prospect of a car ride into Hereford with him. So she fell back on a more plausible reason, which was at least partly true.

'Oh, the oldest in the book . . . my father was going out to dinner and I couldn't be bothered to cook for myself.' She forced a light laugh.

He appeared to accept this at its face value, and they went to the barbecue chef and ordered their steaks. Alex bought two glasses of wine, and they sat at a table in the garden, overlooking the slow, stately progress of the River Wye which flowed past the end.

'He didn't mention earlier that he was dining out . . . your father, that is. Is it a special occasion?'

'I've no idea,' Miranda said, rather aggrievedly. 'He

didn't mention it to me either until five minutes before I was about to start preparing our meal. In fact, he was most mysterious about the whole thing. I can't understand it.'

'Can't you? I can.'

He was laughing, and Miranda's face was upturned to his in complete incomprehension. Frowning slightly, she said, 'I don't know what you mean.'

'Look—our steaks are ready.' He changed the subject. 'Let's go and help ourselves to salad.'

She was so preoccupied by the matter they had been discussing, and his apparent amusement, that she gave only perfunctory attention to the splendid collation of salads, whereas usually, with a professional as well as a consumer's interest in food, she took a close and critical note of whatever was on the menu when eating out.

On returning to the table, Alex said, 'I didn't mean to tease. But truly, Miranda, in a sense the world seems not to have touched you, which is refreshing, if somewhat unusual, in a young woman of your calibre. To me, it would appear from your father's reticence that he has . . . shall we say, a lady-friend?'

Miranda stared at him. She laid down her knife and fork and sat motionless for a few seconds. Then she burst out laughing.

'Dad? A *woman*?' she exclaimed, incredulously. 'I don't believe it!' She shook her head. 'No—it can't be! He has never said anything.'

Alex shrugged.

'Perhaps it isn't serious, or perhaps he doesn't know yet whether it's serious. Men can have their uncertainties too, you know, and maybe he isn't sure how you'd react.'

'I'd react with the greatest of pleasure, so long as it were someone nice,' Miranda affirmed. 'Assuming that there is any basis whatsoever for this notion. I find it hard to take in.'

'Of course you do. To you, he's your father. It's difficult for you to imagine that to some woman he might be simply an attractive, interesting man, still in the prime of life. Eat your steak. It's going cold.'

Appetite reasserted itself, and Miranda realised that she was indeed very hungry. She didn't argue either when Alex suggested fresh strawberries and cream to follow.

'I trust you aren't going to confront your father with this suspicion?' he asked, as they finished the meal with cups of coffee laced with cognac.

'Of course not!' Miranda was highly affronted by the suggestion. 'I won't say a word, unless he tells me himself. I know you think I'm naive and childish, but I'm not such a fool!'

He regarded her thoughtfully.

'I never accused you of being either of those things,' he pointed out. 'Please don't insult me by putting words in my mouth which I haven't used.' He picked up the bill, and pulled three notes from his wallet.

Miranda was once again thrown into mental disarray by his calm, dignified response to her anger. Somehow, whenever they seemed to be getting along pleasantly and equably, she always managed to say the wrong thing, and they were back once more where they started, with contempt on his part and uneasiness on hers.

'Please,' she said wretchedly. 'Let me pay my half of the bill.' And knew at once that she had done it again.

'Absolutely not,' he said, calmly but quite firmly.

'But I insist. You brought me into Hereford, looked over the car for me . . .'

'For neither of which I require recompense,' he said steadily. 'Insist all you wish, it won't make any difference. The only time I consider letting a woman pick up the cheque is if she's a colleague entertaining on business.'

Miranda saw that nothing she said or did would change his attitude, and this determined intransigence filled her with helpless frustration.

'It *is* 1986,' she observed pithily.

'Yes. More's the pity, I sometimes think,' he said. 'It must have been easier for our ancestors. Nowadays, if the women can't beat us, they join us, or they walk out and leave us. Either way, we suffer.'

'Join the club. *We've* been suffering for centuries. Now you know how it feels,' Miranda said spiritedly, and getting up, she swept out of the garden before him.

CHAPTER FIVE

MIRANDA didn't realise that the seed she had endevoured to plant at her first staff meeting had borne fruit until Sister Bennett came to ask her if she would carry out her suggestion to give a talk on nutrition to members of the nursing staff.

'Of course. I'd be delighted,' she said promptly. 'I didn't want to push the idea too hard, as I wasn't sure how much interest there would be.'

'Most of the nurses and sisters are extremely interested—disregarding a few stick in the muds like Sister Price. My guess is that even she'll come along, rather than miss anything, if only to heckle.'

Miranda smiled.

'I don't mind a heckler—so long as I've got the answers. It often helps to get everyone else asking questions, which is good. To say "does anyone want to ask anything?" and be received by a ghastly silence is the ultimate nightmare!'

As soon as she had a chance, Miranda took out the notes she had made for the talks she had already given to slimming clubs and various other groups, and revised them thoroughly. For nursing staff, she could afford to be more far-reaching and technical, discussing diet in relation to specific illnesses, some common ones which nurses would meet regularly on the wards, and rarer ones which still puzzled specialists in medicine and diet. Then she could go on to general principles of nutrition, and their application to everyday life.

The talk was more successful than she had ever

dreamed it would be, and she was highly gratified by the amount of interest it generated.

'I hope you realise,' Jeff Thompson upbraided her, mock-sternly, 'that you have complicated my working life to an unbelievable degree. It's not enough simply to provide food—I now have nurses demanding skimmed milk in their coffee, and stewed fruit without sugar, and I am accosted by sisters conversing knowledgeably about fibre and unsaturated fats! I can't fool anybody any more!'

'Cheer up. There's still Sister Price,' Miranda jested lightly.

'I'm not so sure! Even she was remonstrating with me the other day, to be sure to use less salt because it was bad for her "gels". Seriously, Miranda—it's most encouraging. We need more people to think about what they eat, and be interested in it. Keep up the good work.'

She blushed with pleasure. 'Thank you, kind sir.'

'Not at all.' They were in his office, and he leaned against the door to close it, muffling the noise of the busy kitchen beyond. 'I wonder if you'd care to complicate my personal life as well?'

'What!' Miranda took an involuntary step backwards, looking up at him with startled eyes, and he was surprised by the forcefulness of her reaction.

'Steady on! I only meant perhaps we could see a film or something. I wasn't attempting to recruit you into a seraglio. But I'm not married, or in any way spoken for, and I like you.'

'I'm sorry, Jeff,' Miranda said, embarrassed. 'I suppose I over-reacted. The truth is that having recently emerged from the rough end of a relationship, I'm not ready for complications as yet.'

He considered this thoughtfully.

'Unless they are served up by Alex Emmerson?' he

hinted gently, and Miranda's eyes opened wider than ever. 'Don't you realise it's impossible to keep quiet about anything around here? One of my cooks has a sister who works in that pub by the river you visited.'

Miranda suppressed a groan, wondering just how far around the hospital this titbit of gossip had circulated, and in particular, whether it had reached Miss Carmichael's ears yet.

'That was pure coincidence, our being together that evening,' she said. 'In no way was it a date.'

She could see he was not entirely convinced.

'Hm. Well, I should be careful there, if I were you. You could be hurt—not so much by anything the man might do, but by his indifference.'

'Like Jean Davies was hurt, you mean?' Miranda could not resist asking. 'So you heard about that, too?'

'Oh, sure.' He smiled and shrugged. 'I was the one who had to administer the hot tea and clean handkerchief therapy when she rushed in here, distraught, after he had told her, quite bluntly, that there was no point in anyone trying to replace the woman he had lost.'

Miranda was briefly silent, considering this.

'He must still love his ex-wife terribly,' she said, understanding why he was so bitter, and feeling a pang of sympathy.

Jeff turned to his filing cabinet and began rifling through a folder of reports.

'I wouldn't know anything about that,' he said, with a shudder of relief. 'Fortunately, I'm still heart-whole and relatively fancy-free. And if you ever decide to take me up on that film, just let me know.'

Miranda made her way slowly along the corridor en route to her office, still lost in thought about the repercussions of Alex Emmerson's broken marriage, and her predecessor's unrequited infatuation for him, which seemed to have gripped Lenchester General like a long-running serial. She did not want to be mistakenly cast in the follow-up role, to have people whispering, 'That silly Lewis girl—what a shame! It's happening to her, just as it did to poor Jean!'

She was puzzling over how she could successfully squash this rumour before it got off the ground, when firm male footsteps overtook her, and a deep voice, almost in her ear, said, 'It's the first time I've ever seen you taking these corridors at walking pace! Usually you go at a brisk trot.'

'Alex . . . Dr Emmerson!' Miranda hoped her face did not betray that he was the subject of her guilty thoughts.

Slowing his own pace, he fell into step beside her. It was the first contact she had had with him outside the line of duty since that evening over a fortnight ago, when he had taken her into Hereford, and she was unsure how to address him. Obviously he had to be 'Dr Emmerson' on the ward, and equally obviously, if she met him in Ibsey, it would sound silly if she did not call him Alex. But the present situation seemed to fall between two stools, since they were in the hospital, but not involved in conversation with other staff.

'I'm just on my way from seeing a baby in the maternity ward,' he informed her. 'The poor little mite cries all the time, and although he's hungry, can't keep feeds down, so consequently isn't gaining weight.'

Miranda nodded sympathetically.

'How awful—the mother must be dreadfully worried. Were you able to diagnose the trouble?'

'Yes. He has pyloric stenosis. That means the pyloric sphincter of the stomach is constricted, and food can't pass through. He'll need an operation to enlarge the opening.'

Miranda winced.

'It seems so pathetic, having to operate on such a tiny baby.'

'I know, but it's usually successful, and at least his mother is here with him. The problems are greater with children old enough to suffer from the separation. Ideally, I'd like to accommodate *all* mothers of children under five, but it just isn't always possible.'

She glanced quickly at his dark profile, which always looked softer, less severe, when he was talking about his patients.

'I heard you had introduced a more open system of visiting on the children's ward.'

'That's right. Basically, it means that while we still have official visiting times for friends and other relatives, immediate family may come whenever they like and, within reason, stay as long as they are able. Sister Robertson is coping magnificently. I couldn't hope to run such a system without a person of her temperament and capability in charge.'

'Is it working well, do you think?'

'It's early days, but I have faith in it. Parents can actually be very useful, but staff have to learn a new approach, which involves explaining to them exactly what is needed, and that takes time. But I believe you can't treat a child in isolation . . . he's part of a family, even when he's in hospital.'

They had come to the point where their paths diverged, and oddly, instead of being anxious to escape, Miranda found herself wanting to prolong the encounter.

'It's obvious you love children,' she said. 'Why else would you choose to specialise in paediatrics? Do you have children of your own? I've never heard you mention any.'

His expression darkened, and she wished she had not asked the question—not, she realised, because she feared his anger, but because she regretted causing him pain.

'No, I don't, unfortunately,' he replied shortly, 'and I don't suppose now that I ever shall.'

She watched his retreating form until he disappeared around a bend in the corridor, and wondered why her emotions were so strangely tangled.

During the next few days she thought hard about Lenchester's enigmatic and attractive paediatrician, in relation to herself, her life and her career. She admitted that while she had begun by resenting his initially dubious and sarcastic manner towards her, the 'keep clear' signs he posted around himself, and his arbitrary distrust of all women on the basis of the treatment he had received from one . . . while all this had been true at the start, there had been a definite shift in her feelings towards him.

It had helped, of course, that he had gradually come to accept her in her professional role, to realise that she did know her job, and to seek her advice and assistance where necessary, and this acceptance had overlapped into his attitude towards her as a person. Although his reactions could still be unpredictable, and an unguarded comment from her could still trigger off anger or cynicism, he was less inclined to slice into her at the slightest opportunity.

But over and above the fact that he now treated her less as a potential female hazard, and more as helpful and potentially likeable colleague, Miranda recognised that the change was in herself as much as in him. She had begun to look deeper into the motives and causes beneath his often abrasive manner, to appreciate that his emotions had taken a battering from which they had not yet recovered. She was conscious of an outflow of compassion and sympathy, a desire to understand rather than condemn.

This, in itself, was all very well, but she knew it could be misconstrued, both by him, and by others. She did not want him to form the mistaken impression that she was another Jean, eager to embarrass him with romantic attention while he was still painfully involved with the wife who had left him. Nor did she want such rumours going the rounds of the hospital grapevine.

Unfortunately, that had already begun to happen. First there had been the hint Jeff had dropped. Then Maggie, who had heard from her cousin about the handsome doctor who knew a lot about cars, had been unable to resist making a comment. The same day, Julie had cornered her in the cafeteria, her eyes alight with curiosity.

'Come on, then, tell me all about it! I thought *you* were supposed to be man-proof!'

It had taken a lot for Miranda to convince her that there was absolutely nothing going on in the romance department.

Finally, Miss Carmichael had been pricklier and more dangerous than ever at the staff meeting, lying in wait to trip Miranda up with obscure and devious questions, and pouring mild scorn on every suggestion she made. She had escaped thankfully to the ante-natal clinic, where at least none of the pregnant mums looked askance at her or asked veiled questions about her love-life. For the first time ever, she dodged the subsequent tea and chat with the rest of the staff, on the pretext of having to get home early, and drove back to Ibsey, thanking heaven that it was Friday.

There was only one way she could put a stop to all this nonsense. She had to avoid Alex Emmerson like the plague, except for the occasions when work made their meeting inevitable. She had to be polite and formal and distinctly cool, if necessary, rebuffing any friendly overtures he might make. He was certain to answer coldness with coldness, she thought, suppressing a twinge of regret, and it should eventually become obvious to anyone watching them that the rumours were unfounded.

Saturday afternoons between May and September meant cricket to Major Lewis who, although he no longer played himself, was secretary to Ibsey Cricket Club. This meant that he arranged their fixtures, kept their accounts in order, and acted as general factotum/nursemaid to a group of full-grown men who were quite happy to allow him to do so.

That particular Saturday Ibsey were playing on their home ground, and the Major had pressed Miranda into service to keep score. She didn't mind. The day was warm and sunny and it was quite pleasant to sit on the pavilion verandah, with the bees humming, the click of leather on willow, and the prospect of a cream tea in the interval, and she had no plans other than to relax and unwind.

Today, however, did not promise to be entirely soporific, for they arrived at the field to learn that overnight a member of the team had gone down unexpectedly with summer flu and was unable to play. Several regulars were away on holiday, and even after much frantic telephoning around for a last minute substitute, Ibsey was unable to produce a full team.

'We'll just have to play with ten men,' Major Lewis said gloomily to Ken Digby, the captain.

'Not much else we can do, but I wish it hadn't been Trevor Slaughter who'd caught the blessed bug,' he replied. 'We need old Slogger Slaughter to notch up the runs. With Jim Beale sunning himself in Majorca, we only have one decent fast bowler to our name. Angleton will murder us today, with the greatest of pleasure, since we've beaten them three times in succession!'

'We must battle through to the best of our ability,' Miranda, organising her pen and score-cards on the small, rickety table, heard her father declare stoutly, every bit as though it were Agincourt or Dunkirk, not merely a Saturday friendly match between two village teams. 'Let's hope Mrs Marshall turns up to do the teas, or the day will be a complete disaster. Oh—hello, Alex. Come to watch us do our best to avoid being trounced?'

Miranda looked up sharply, hoping she had misheard, but it was Alex Emmerson who leaned against the verandah.

'Hello, Charles. I hoped I'd come to watch Ibsey win,' he said. He smiled down at Miranda, and she returned his greeting with cool formality, avoiding his eyes and looking down at the empty score-card. 'Are you going to score? Not many women are good at that kind of thing.'

'Oh, Miranda has been keeping cricket scores since she was twelve,' her father said proudly. 'As for winning —we'll certainly pull out all the stops, but we're a man short, and our best bowler is away on holiday. I say!' he hesitated as a sudden thought struck him. 'You don't play, do you?'

'I used to,' Alex confessed, 'but I'm sadly out of practice. Doctors don't get a lot of free time when they're making their way up the promotion ladder. But I can carry a bat, so if you want someone to make up the numbers . . .'

Major Lewis glanced inquiringly at his team captain.

'We'd be grateful. At least it would mean we had a full team. What do you think, Ken?'

Ken Digby held out his hand to shake Alex's.

'I think you've got yourself a game, mate. Come into the pavilion and see if you can find any whites that fit you. Jim Beale's about your height, I'd guess.'

Miranda allowed herself a small sigh as the men disappeared inside. She had envisaged a peaceful afternoon recovering from a couple of trying days at work, and now, here was Alex, whom she had firmly decided to avoid, and she was obliged to spend the afternoon watching him. Nor did he seem inclined to avoid her; while the opposing team arrived and were busy changing, he emerged and sat on the verandah steps in front of her. In his white flannels and shirt, he looked even more devilishly attractive, she admitted reluctantly.

'Why do I have the impression that you think I should not be doing this?' he asked astutely.

This was a little too near the mark, but since he was sitting within touching distance, and looking directly at her, she found it impossible to evade his eyes.

'I never said that. It's kind of you to help out.'

'Always assuming that I do actually help, you mean? Ken Digby has won the toss and elected for Ibsey to bat first, but I'm not sure how far down the order I shall be.'

'Slogger Slaughter bats No. 3 as a rule, but it's usual to send in the highest scorer at that stage, I understand,' Miranda said.

'Not an untried, somewhat decrepit substitute?' Alex said with wry humour, favouring her with a rakish grin, the likes of which she had never seen in the corridors of Lenchester General. He looked far from decrepit. He looked fit and sportsmanlike, and she was glad when he turned and fixed his concentration on the players walking out on to the field. Determinedly, she forced her own wavering attention back to the match and her scorecard, and tried not to look at the broad back and crisply waving dark hair in front of her.

As it happened, Ken sent Alex out at No. 5, when he himself was bowled out for a mere 10 runs, and Ibsey were struggling to make 50. Offering Miranda a nonchalant salute, he strode out to the wicket.

'Well, Charles,' Ken said philosophically, 'I hope your friend hasn't forgotten all he ever learned, because we're well and truly in the soup now.'

Miranda shared that hope. Not only in order that Ibsey should make, at least, a respectable score, but suddenly, ridiculously, she was fearful lest Alex made a fool of himself. He had admitted he had not played for years, whereas everyone else out there was a seasoned player, taking part in a match every Saturday in the summer, and practising regularly. Why it should matter to her if he lost face, she was not prepared to ask herself.

There was a sudden tension around the wicket. Angleton, well aware that their opponents had a new player whose abilities were not known to them, appeared to tighten up and become more alert and watchful. Alex looked quickly but comprehensively around the field, taking note of how the fielders were placed, signalled the umpire to give him leg and middle, and took guard, apparently quite at ease.

Miranda held her breath as he faced the bowler. She watched him play two calm, unhurried, well-timed strokes, testing the pace and direction of the bowling, and then, with only the slightest change in the action of his wrists, drive the third ball firmly through the covers for four.

'Nice shot!' Ken Digby shouted gleefully, joining in the applause. 'Hey—he's not bad! Not bad at all!'

For the next hour Miranda watched, amazed, as Alex picked holes in Angleton's fielding, easily demonstrating every stroke in the book, and finding runs somewhere else whenever the opposing captain dementedly sent fielders scurrying to block him. One by one, the Ibsey players partnering him were dismissed, but whoever shared the wicket with him, Alex batted doggedly on, encouraging them to take runs, increasing his own score all the while. He was still there when the youngest member of the team, Ken Digby's son, Martin, ended Ibsey's innings by sending up an easy catch. When they came back to the pavilion for the tea interval, Alex had made 75 not out, and Ibsey's score had edged up close to 200.

Miranda kept clear of all the approval and adulation surrounding him. Peversely, now that she had ceased worrying that he might not make the grade, she was annoyed with him for having let her worry, for not having reassured her that he was more than capable. Avoiding him, she joined her jubilant parent in the queue for tea, sandwiches and scones.

'Ken has told Alex to be sure to keep Saturdays free for the rest of the summer,' he enthused.

'I shouldn't assume Alex will be able to play regularly. He's a busy man,' Miranda said.

Her father frowned.

'Even busy men need time off,' he observed. 'What's the matter with you, Miranda? I thought you and Alex were getting along well enough lately, but now you seem to be as down on him as you were when you first came to Ibsey.'

'I'm not down on him,' Miranda protested helplessly, and was relieved to be spared from expanding on this, when her father caught sight of the chairman of the parish council, and remembered something he must have a word with him about.

She took her tea and scones, and found a patch of grass in the shade of a tree where she could sit. No sooner had she settled herself than Alex emerged from the tea queue, agilely balancing his cup and plate, and made his way to where she was sitting.

It almost appeared that once she had made a decision to avoid him, he had countered it with a similar one to seek out her company, as if he knew and was being deliberately perverse. She knew that this thought was illogical, but in a deeper sense, there was some basis of truth in it. He had scented her withdrawal, and, perhaps intuitively, reacted against it, out of the confident presumption that he should be the one who set the bounds of any relationship, and decided how close to those bounds the other party dare tread. Miranda's old resentment crept back, and she clung to it, for it was her strongest ally.

'You might have told me how well you played, instead of making yourself out to be a rusty old has-been,' she said reproachfully.

'That would have been tempting providence, Miranda. I know I used to be handy with the bat, but it was so long ago I might just as easily have proved completely useless. Anyhow, at least half of my success was due to the element of surprise—the other side didn't know what to expect from me.'

'You're too modest,' she murmured.

'Do you think so?' He smiled engagingly, quite untroubled by her mild sarcasm. 'Well, one can't go around admitting to being the greatest thing since Sir Gary Sobers, can one? Seriously, though, I enjoyed playing. It made me realise how much I've missed active sport in the last few years.'

'Will you play again, if they ask you?'

'Yes, why not? When I'm free. I wouldn't want to take anyone's place, but Ken says they are always anxious for more members. Can you think of any reason why I should refuse?'

This put Miranda on the spot, and she was grateful for her father's return, which spared her from having to answer.

'Well done, Alex! That really gave Angleton something to think about!' he exulted. 'Now, if we only had Jim Beale, we could soon polish them off.'

'I can't help there, I'm afraid,' Alex said. 'I've told Ken I bowl a bit, but only slow stuff, not the pace, so I can't open the bowling. He said he'd probably give me a few overs.'

Miranda had no doubt in her mind now that he would prove as proficient with the ball as he had earlier with the bat. She was not fooled by his throwaway nonchalance. He was good, and knew it, just as he was good at his work, and knew that, too. The only area where he might be plagued by a shadow of doubt was in his emotional life. In consequence, since he could not achieve perfection there too, had he chosen to close off that side of himself completely?

Alex stretched out his long legs in front of him and leaned back against the tree, perfectly relaxed. Major Lewis, on the other hand, was edgy and unable to remain in one spot for a minute, and finally, noting his constant glances towards the car-park, Miranda said, 'Are you looking for someone, Dad?'

'Yes . . . no. That is . . .' he hesitated, and at that moment Miranda saw a roomy if rather venerable estate car slide into the car-park, and a woman get out of the driving seat. She walked briskly to the rear door, opened it, and two frisky black and white border collies bounded out. 'Excuse me,' the Major said abstractedly, and set off across the field without another word.

Alex allowed his gaze to linger on Miranda's face, but he made no comment, and nor, for the moment, did she. Since that evening when he had suggested that her father might be involved with a woman, she had been particularly attentive to his comings and goings, but he had given away no clues. He was out so often anyway, and involved in so many village activities, it was virtually impossible to keep track of him, and Miranda had adhered to her decision not to pry. She had almost convinced herself that Alex must have been mistaken, but now, here was her father, shepherding the woman towards them as proprietorially as the dogs which frisked at her side.

'Miranda, I'd like you to meet Mrs Carson. This is my daughter, Miranda, and our neighbour, Alex Emmerson, who is consultant paediatrician at Lenchester General Hospital.'

'Margaret Carson, actually, but please call me Peggy,' she said. 'How do you do. I've been looking forward to meeting you, Miranda.'

Somewhat dazed, Miranda returned the greeting. It was disconcerting to meet someone who obviously knew all about you, whereas you had been entirely unaware of their existence.

Peggy Carson was a trim, energetic-looking woman of roughly fifty, with a wide, friendly smile and a mane of silver-grey hair. She wore slacks and a twin-set, her feet encased in brogues, and looked every inch a country-woman.

The dogs sniffed enthusiastically around Miranda.

'Down, Romeo!' Peggy said authoritatively. 'I call them Romeo and Juliet, but they aren't living up to their names,' she laughed. 'I had hoped to breed from them, but unfortunately Romeo isn't interested in Juliet, nor she in him. Nature isn't always obliging, is it?'

Her laughter was infectious, and tension ebbed out of Miranda as she joined in.

'But they're lovely dogs,' she said, patting the head of

Romeo as he subsided obediently, to sit panting at his mistress' side.

'Yes, aren't they? They cover you with hairs, of course. I've given up trying to wear anything decent. Charles, do you think there might be any tea left? I'm gasping for a cup. The visitors who came for lunch stayed on and on, even though I had told them I was going out and I didn't dare put the kettle on, or they'd still be there now!'

She smiled up at him, and he smiled back. Miranda had never seen her father look at a woman so fondly and admiringly, as if everything she said were a source of pleasure to him.

'I dare say I can find you a cup of tea,' he said. 'Would you like to stay here with Miranda while I go and cajole Mrs Marshall?'

'By all means—I wouldn't dream of interrupting that,' she grinned, and they both erupted into laughter —her staid, military-minded father, and this practical, dog-loving, middle-aged woman, laughing like two adolescents sharing a secret joke.

'I have to go. The tea interval is almost over,' Alex observed. 'It was nice meeting you, Mrs Carson.'

'Peggy.'

'Peggy—of course. Miranda? I'll see you after the match.'

She was too confused by the turn of events to do anything other than murmur assent.

'What a charming young man,' Peggy Carson remarked appraisingly. 'Have you known him long?'

'Not really,' Miranda demurred. Mrs Carson was assuming she and Alex were a couple, but surely her father had made it clear he only happened to be renting their cottage? 'We work at the same hospital. I'm dietitian there.'

'Yes, Charles told me. He's extremely proud of you. It must be a fascinating job. When my husband was alive we ran a boarding kennels, which *I* found fascinating, but it was too much for me to manage alone, so I sold out a few years ago. Now I only have these two dogs.'

'Do you live in Ibsey? It's strange that we haven't met.'

'No, I have a house a few miles out on the Brecon road. But I'm on the parish council, which is how I met your father, who, I can see, hasn't so much as mentioned my name in your presence!'

She sounded quite unoffended by this omission, and Miranda warmed to the older woman.

'Actually, no, he hasn't,' she admitted.

'I thought as much. Men can be such secretive creatures, and yet they hate it when we behave in that way. Ah, here's Charles now, with my tea! Bless you, that supplies a long-felt need.'

'Sorry it took so long. I had to persuade Mrs Marshall to boil up some more water.'

'I'm sure you were very persuasive, and I didn't mind waiting at all. Miranda and I were having a lovely little chat.' She winked at Miranda, who laughed.

'No wonder my ears were burning all the while,' he said wryly. 'Back to your scoring, Miranda. The players are coming out.'

For the rest of the afternoon, Miranda tried to concentrate on her score-card and the umpire's signals. It would not do to be distracted by the surprising, if pleasant discovery, that her father had acquired a lady-friend. Or, for that matter, by the disquieting study of Alex's athletic figure out on the field, as he played his part in Ibsey's renaissance and eventual victory by taking three wickets and executing a stunning, one-handed catch.

Mrs Carson came across to Miranda as she was tidying up her table.

'I gather that the custom is for everyone to rendezvous in the Green Dragon after the match,' she said. 'Shall we go on ahead and meet your father there?'

Miranda hesitated.

'I'm sure he'd rather just take you,' she said with a smile. 'Three's a crowd.'

'Not when you get to our age, dear. But there—I'm being silly. I'm sure you'd rather wait for your delightful doctor friend. And I'd better go and settle Romeo and Juliet in the car—the pub will be too busy for two boisterous dogs.'

Miranda had already decided to go straight home. She was sure neither Peggy nor her father would really object to her absence, and in the Green Dragon's tiny, crowded bar it would be impossible to avoid Alex . . . it was becoming obsessively important that she *did* escape from him, and she set off along the lane towards the village.

It was deserted, the spectators having already left, the players still changing in the pavilion. Miranda hurried, scarcely noticing the scene which usually gave her so much quiet pleasure, the spire rising above the gnarled trees round the churchyard, where rooks cawed and circled against the serene blue backdrop of the sky beyond. Automatically, she took the short cut through the churchyard, and was almost out of sight when his voice arrested her.

'Miranda—wait!'

She was not sure what made her obey him, the natural authority in his voice, or the sheer stupidity of running away from him, of which she found herself guilty. But pause she did, and he very quickly caught up with her. He was frowning, displeasure in the dark eyes.

'Why on earth did you dash off like that?'

She bristled at the chiding note in his voice.

'I'm not obliged to wait for you, Alex,' she said, her own voice and her manner chilly.

'Not obliged, no, but I said I would see you after the match, and you agreed, so it's more a question of good manners, isn't it?'

Reluctant to be drawn into an argument with him, she said tersely, 'Yes. I'm sorry. I'm rather tired and I decided to go home. Is that all right with you?'

'That's fine with me,' he said, the irritability in his tone declaring otherwise, 'although I don't see why you couldn't have waited long enough to tell me so. Why are you behaving in this rather strange fashion, Miranda?'

'I don't know what you mean,' she stone-walled desperately, and he cut this short with a snort of contempt.

'Oh, no? Are you trying to make out that it's all in my imagination, that after giving every appearance of wanting to be friendly, you suddenly do a volte-face, and start avoiding or cold-shouldering me?'

Miranda let out her breath in a long sigh. He was too shrewd to fool, and too proud to take her change of behaviour without comment. She might as well level with him, and hope he would see the sense in her reasoning.

'I do want to be friendly. I want to be able to work with you harmoniously, without constantly being in your bad books, and to pass the time of day pleasantly when we happen to meet. But other people seem unable to accept that's all there is to it. There's gossip about us in the hospital. I want it to stop.'

He looked blankly at her for a moment, and then exploded derisively, 'Good grief, is *that* all? Are you frightened by a bit of gossip? You surprise me, Miranda. I thought you were made of stronger stuff!'

She could not explain to him that, other considerations aside, any hint of an attachment between them resulted in her having Miss Carmichael on her back, with all the insidious, nagging unpleasantness that lady was capable of causing.

'It's not very pleasant to think that people are talking about one,' she muttered lamely.

'No, I agree, it isn't, but the only way with gossip is to ignore it,' he said firmly. 'You are listening to an expert on the subject, I assure you. How do you think I felt when I learned that my wife was seeing another man, and that I was the last to know?'

'Perfectly ghastly, I should imagine,' she conceded. 'But that was true, Alex, and one way or another, you *had* to find out. Whereas the gossip about us is quite unfounded.'

'Is that all that's worrying you?' he said, with a soft, short laugh, half humorous, half scornful. 'You don't like—what's the expression—having the name without the game? That can soon be changed, Miranda!'

He drew her into the shadow of the wall where they were isolated and out of sight, and she had time only to protest swiftly, 'No, Alex, that wasn't what I meant . . .' before he stopped her mouth with a kiss.

Miranda had not been kissed since she broke up with Tony, and even then, towards the end, she had avoided occasions which provided opportunity for physical closeness. She honestly thought she had lost all desire to be touched this way, but now, strangely, she was demolished by the strength of his arms, the muscular warmth of his chest, and the sweet but insistent pressure of his mouth on hers, tempting her lips to part.

She forgot how this had begun, her childishness in running from him, and his contemptuous assumption that she would not mind being the subject of gossip which had some basis. She was conscious only of what an amazingly pleasurable experience it was, being kissed by Alex Emmerson, and instinctively, she settled deeper into his arms, allowing her body's softness to relax against his strength.

What on earth am I doing?

Miranda woke up, pulled away, staring up reproachfully into the dark, unworried face of the man she had just kissed with such abandoned enjoyment. She was trembling, and hoped he would interpret that as anger.

'What's wrong, Miranda?' he asked idly. 'That was what you expected me to do, wasn't it? Girls usually do seem to require it of one.'

Now her anger was genuine, fired by a deep humiliation.

'I'm sure they do—girls like Jean Davies, with their heads full of romantic nonsense, who fail to realise you don't give a hoot about their feelings! They expect it, and you oblige them, because it doesn't mean a thing to you. I suppose because one woman hurt you, you think that provides you with a God-given right to take revenge on all the rest. Well not this one, thank you! Not me!'

Dodging past him, she ran down the path through the churchyard, out via the lich-gate, and up the High Street, not stopping until, considerably out of breath, she at last reached the welcome haven of Meadowlands.

CHAPTER SIX

MIRANDA'S talk on nutrition to the nursing staff had repercussions throughout the hospital, as indeed it was intended to, for each ward sister and staff nurse was fired by an enthusiasm not only to re-think her own eating habits along healthy principles, but to educate and convert her patients in so far as it was possible.

'Get them while they are young is the best motto,' Sister Robertson said purposefully. 'Wasn't it the Jesuits who said if you gave them a child till he was seven, he was theirs for life?'

'You want me to indoctrinate your kids—get them hooked on healthy eating?' Miranda mused. 'Good idea, but it's not going to be possible to use the same techniques as one uses for adults. They won't want to sit and listen to a lecture. Let me think about it.'

In the end, she enlisted the aid of the hospital play leader, several parents, and the children themselves, and they drew colourful charts depicting different foods, explaining pictorially why they were good for you—or the reverse. Someone's mum brought in a machine which extruded badges, and everyone had fun designing a personal badge relevant to what he or she especially liked to eat.

'We can take this further,' Sister said, with a flash of inspiration. 'All the children adore wearing the badges, so why not make some indicating special diets, or treatment? "Nothing to eat or drink", for example, if a child is due in theatre next morning.'

The idea was enthusiastically adopted, and the ward

began to resemble a production line for badges, the day room littered with discarded prototypes. This was something in which all but the most severely ill could participate, and even they, as always, preferred to have their beds wheeled into the day room, so that they could watch the other children playing.

Miranda, involved in much of this activity, knew that the moment she dreaded must eventually catch up with her, and it did, when Alex's appearance on the ward coincided with her presence there.

She had succeeded in keeping out of his way since the evening after the cricket match, but she had not been so successful in keeping the incident in the churchyard out of her mind. It kept on replaying itself before her eyes with annoying frequency, like a video which refused to be switched off. She saw herself melting willingly into his arms, her face upturned, her lips parting under his, just as if she had indeed been waiting for it to happen, anticipating it, in the way he off-handedly remarked, 'Girls seem to expect it.'

Miranda had not expected it. It had been the last thing she had looked for. Nor had she expected the swooning, drowning sensation his embrace had invoked.

She could not help casting her mind back to Tony. She had loved him . . . or at least, she *thought* at the time that she did, but she did not recall his ever kissing her that way. His quick, impatient kisses had demanded an automatic response, efficient, mechanical, like the coffee machine in the dining-room—ten pence in, red light on, milk, coffee—presto!

But Alex's kiss had been an invitation to discover herself and him, to become what she could truly be, to understand her potential as a woman. Undreamed of vistas of pleasure had opened fleetingly before her.

Only—damn it!—he had not meant it! He had kissed

her merely because he thought that was what she wanted from him, and he might as well get it over with, once and for all, and that was insulting, because it needed no more than the basic requirements—that he was male and she female. He did not have to desire her acutely, or find her more than tolerably attractive, and he could either kiss her or let it alone.

He came upon her in the side ward, talking to the only patient who had refused to co-operate in the activities —thirteen-year-old Angela, who lay on her bed, wired up to her personal stereo, listening to endless pop music for most of the day, resisting anyone's attempts to involve her in more outgoing pursuits.

She had condescended to remove her headphones for long enough to convey shortly to Miranda that she was supremely uninterested in food.

'When I get out of here, I'm going to stop eating altogether!' she declared grumpily. 'Look at me—I'm getting so fat, I'm grotesque!'

Miranda was painfully aware that Angela, who was far from fat, was suffering from leukaemia in a state which was probably terminal, and it was difficult to resist the temptation to give way to her every whim. Difficult, but essential, if what remained of this young life were to have any kind of value or cohesion.

'I wouldn't recommend starvation as a diet,' she said cheerfully. 'Look at her—' she pointed down at the purple-haired, beanpole model in the teenage fashion magazine which lay open on the bed. 'She looks as though she could squeeze through a keyhole, but she probably lives on steak, yoghurt and fresh fruit.'

Glancing up as a shadow fell across the bed, she saw Alex approach, with Sister Robertson in attendance.

'Who does?' he asked, his casual smile making his appearance less like a consultant's call than a social visit.

'Oh—her. I expect you're right. Modelling is very exacting, or so I'm told, they need lots of stamina. What's on tape today, Angela? Tears for Fears or Frankie Goes to Hollywood?'

She favoured him with a grudging smile.

'Howard Jones, actually,' she said loftily.

'My sister's two girls are great fans of his,' said Alex. 'And what's the name of the two boys who went to China recently? They're mad about them.'

'You mean Wham!'

'That's right.' He grinned. 'I once got into a fearful row at school for playing truant to go to a Beatles concert. You're too young to remember them—even Sister would have to strain her memory, and as for Miss Lewis, their heyday was well before her time!'

Angela was fighting hard against the temptation to contribute more than monosyllables to the conversation, but curiosity finally overcame her, and as Miranda slipped quietly from the side ward, she heard her asking, 'Did you really and truly skive off school, Doctor?'

Wondering again at his ability to communicate with children of all ages at their own level, from tearful tots to rebellious adolescents, Miranda walked the length of the ward to the day room, stopping to look at several new badges en route, and out through the open french windows at the far end, which led to the garden.

The children's ward was fortunate in that it was on the ground floor, so that the young patients had access to fresh air and sunshine when possible, without causing too much hassle for the staff in transporting and supervising them. Several children were out in the garden now, since it was a beautiful sunny day, making full use of the swings and sandpit, under the watchful eye of one of the volunteer mothers who came regularly to help with tasks such as this, taking the pressure off the nursing staff.

Miranda watched too for a short while, hoping that Alex would have left by the time she went back in and she could avoid the necessity of coming face to face with him again. But it was not to be.

'The day room is ankle deep in half-finished badges,' he said in her ear, very close behind her. 'It's good to see the children so actively engaged.'

She turned around reluctantly and forced herself to think only of what concerned them both right now, blotting out that insidious memory which insisted on plaguing her.

'It's a pity we can't involve Angela,' she said. 'She spends too much time turned inwards on herself, and I feel such a failure because she's the only one whose imagination I haven't been able to grasp. Especially when one thinks . . .' she hesitated, unwilling to formalise the awful truth in words.

'Say it, Miranda,' he said quietly. 'It's better when it's out. Especially when one thinks she hasn't so very long to live.'

She winced.

'I just hate the thought.'

'Do you think that I don't? That Sister and the nurses don't? Because we're medical staff, we're trained to cope with death, we *have* to be hardened to it, or we'd crack. But we still resent it fiercely, particularly in the case of a young person, and feel impatient at the slow progress of research.'

Miranda sighed.

'I know. I just wonder if . . . well, if Angela knew, she'd try to get more out of the time left to her.'

'She knows,' he assured her gravely, and she looked up at him questioningly.

'You told her?'

'I didn't have to. She told *me*. The young are much more perceptive than we give them credit for. She's facing it in her own way, but don't give up on her. You'll find a means of getting through.'

He looked at his watch, causing Miranda to feel guilty for taking up his time, for all they were discussing a patient.

'I must see Dawn Littlewood's mother. The poor woman has been here day and night since the child was brought in, and I really think she might go home now Dawn is out of danger.'

'Yes. I was about to suggest that we might step up her food intake a little now. She could manage a small portion of steamed fish, I think, and there's milk pudding on the suppper menu tonight, which would be suitable.'

She accompanied him to the first of the rooms specially adapted to accommodate a parent who needed to stay with the child. Dawn, aged ten, had been rushed in with gangrenous appendicitis, needing an immediate emergency operation. Her mother had been distraught —Dawn was performing in a school play, and she had thought the pain and high temperature were merely a nervous reaction. Had she not had the operation when she did, Dawn might easily have died, but now she was on the way to recovery, given care and a little time.

'Do you really think I could go home?' the child's mother said anxiously.

'I don't see why not, Mrs Littlewood. How about moving into the main ward with the other children, now you are so much better, Dawn? You'd be able to watch the television. And Miss Lewis thinks you might have something a little more interesting to eat.'

Miranda nodded agreement, and over the child's pale

little face, framed in dark curls, met the relieved eyes of her mother.

'I ought to go home. My husband is coping, and the neighbours have been marvellous, but the other kids miss me, and I daresay there's a sky-high pile of ironing waiting!'

Her relief was almost palpable. Ironing. Children coming home from school. The normality of life, reaching out to take her back after the fraught days of worry and crisis.

'You can, of course, come in any time to be with Dawn,' Alex reassured her, 'although if you do, you'll probably be commandeered by the badge-making factory in the day room.'

'Can I make badges too?' Dawn piped up thinly.

'Dawn, you won't be able to escape it!' he smiled.

'Then I'll make one for you.'

'That's very kind of you. I was beginning to feel rather left out.'

Miranda slipped away. He had, she was sure, forgotten her presence anyway, his attention entirely focused on the child and her mother. The meeting she had anticipated with such dread had passed off quite smoothly. He had been calm, friendly and professional, no more. Not by so much as a look, let alone a word, had he indicated that those moments in each other's arms had ever taken place.

She supposed she should be relieved and grateful, but human nature is not so straightforward, and Miranda wished he had evinced just a little discomfiture. The reason he hadn't, she thought, with mingled shame and irritation, was because that brief kiss had not been important to him. The world had in no way moved for him when he took her in his arms. Perhaps he had actually forgotten about it, which was even worse—to have kissed her and so swiftly put it out of his mind, when she could not erase it from hers.

The best she could hope for was that she had appeared, this morning, as unconcerned as he. He could hardly have been in any doubt that it had given her pleasure, but pleasure is a transitory thing, and maybe, if he thought about it at all, he believed she had taken that temporary stirring of her senses in her stride.

Reaching her office, Miranda decided to waste no more time and emotion on something which was no big deal—a man, a girl, and a meaningless kiss. Instead, she set herself to thinking deeply about what she could do to help Angela.

If she could tempt the girl's appetite, it might be an initial step towards coaxing her out of her lethargy. What about a buffet-style meal for the children, on similar lines to the one in the staff dining-room? Or a barbecue in the garden? Lots of co-operation from staff and helpers would be needed, and first of all she had to talk to Jeff Thompson.

Anxious to waste no time before implementing her ideas, Miranda rang the Catering office, but it was Mick Mulligan who answered.

'Sorry, me lovely, but himself's not here today. Gone to an exhibition of catering equipment in Birmingham.'

'Oh, yes.' Vaguely, Miranda remembered Jeff's having mentioned it to her. 'It's today, is it? Never mind. I'll talk to him when he gets back.'

It was frustrating to be inspired with enthusiasm for an idea, and unable to get it off the ground, but that was the way it sometimes happened. There was no point in talking to Sister Robertson before she had sounded out Jeff and ensured that her proposals were feasible. Miranda hung up and turned her attention to more pedestrian tasks which, if less engrossing, nevertheless needed to be done.

When she arrived home, she found her father very smartly attired, ready to go out. He was accompanying Peggy Carson to a dog show somewhere near Brecon, and said they would probably stop for a meal on the way home.

'So be a brick, and do the hot drinks for the PGs tonight, will you?' he asked, straightening his already immaculate tie in front of the hall mirror.

'Yes, of course.' She wondered what he would have said if she had told him she would be out too? But no doubt he would phone up Lizzie from the village who 'did' for him, and arrange for her to come. 'You look very dapper.'

'Thank you.' He grinned. 'Have to make the effort, otherwise Peggy won't be able to differentiate between me and the hounds.'

'Yes she will. *They* have floppy ears.'

'Less cheek, my girl! Show a little respect for your aged parent!' he ordered humorously, and Miranda flashed him a wry smile.

'I will, if I ever see him around for more than five minutes at a time! My aged parent is conspicuous by his absence these days.'

He had indeed been seeing a lot of Peggy Carson lately, but this was the first time Miranda had referred to the fact, even obliquely, and his expression became serious as he asked, 'You don't mind? About Peggy, I mean.'

'Gracious, why should I? I like her very much.'

'I hoped you'd get on, but I didn't want you to think I was neglecting you.'

'Nonsense, Dad—you have your life to live, just as I have mine.'

'Well, that's the point I'm trying to make, Miranda. I know you have your work, which you love, and your friends at the hospital. But you don't, to put it bluntly, have much to do with the opposite sex.'

'You mean I don't have a boyfriend.' Her face clouded. 'Does it matter? I'm not interested in men right now, and I'm perfectly happy as I am.'

He shrugged, an apparently casual gesture which did not deceive her.

'If you say so. As long as you aren't still in a brown study because of that young man in London.'

'Tony?' Miranda said his name in surprise, realising that it was some time since she had even given him a thought. 'Oh no, it's not that.'

'Then what?' He looked closely at her, and it was her turn to affect the nonchalant lifting of the shoulders.

'Then nothing. There just isn't anyone.'

'Nor will there be, if you don't give them a chance.'

Miranda picked a flower from the arrangement on the hall table, stuck it behind her ear, and struck an exaggerated pose.

'You vant me to become ze scarlet woman of Ibsey?' she said flippantly.

'No, my dear. I don't see you as Marlene Dietrich, or Dorothy Lamour,' he told her drily. 'You aren't the stuff that scarlet women are made of.'

From outside, a car's horn interrupted them.

'That must be Peggy,' the Major said. 'We're going in her car, since it's better adapted for dogs.'

'Have a lovely time. Is Peggy showing Romeo and Juliet?'

'No, she doesn't show any more. She just likes to watch, and make acid comments, and chat to the other breeders.'

After he had gone, Miranda twirled the flower in her

fingers and gazed thoughtfully at herself in the mirror. Not the stuff that scarlet women are made of? On the whole, she would have said too true, but fleetingly she recalled that short interlude in Alex's arms, her eager, trembling response, and she wondered—was there, for every woman, one man who could unlock the doors of inhibition and let out the sensualist, the wanton she often did not know lurked behind them?

She fitted the flower neatly back into its place in the slab of oasis.

'Rubbish!' she said out loud to herself, and went to switch the cooker on, convinced that only imminent starvation could make her entertain such foolish notions.

After cooking herself an omelette, Miranda watched television for an hour or so, prepared the hot drinks, and went to bed with a book. A quiet, uneventful evening which held no warning of the maelstrom into which the next day would plunge her.

In the morning, she got up, washed and dressed for work. It was another warm day, already, at eight o'clock, promising to be much hotter, and Miranda ate muesli and toast, keeping out of the way of her father and Lizzie, who were cooking bacon and eggs for the guests. Yes, he replied to her query, while turning the bacon, they had enjoyed the dog show, only Romeo had suddenly decided to improve his image by taking off in hot pursuit of a lady Afghan hound, whose owner had not been amused.

Miranda was still chuckling over this as she drove off to Lenchester in her red Mini.

In retrospect, she wondered if perhaps there had been anything different about the hospital that morning, if she should have picked up indefinable atmospheric waves of trauma the minute she entered the main lobby. But in fact, she was absorbed in thought about the plan she intended outlining to Jeff Thompson, and she hurried up the stairs to her office in the administration wing without encountering anyone.

So it did not hit her until she entered the outer office and noted Miss Carmichael's widely gaping door, Maggie's stricken face, and the fact that the mail was all of a heap, instead of neatly sorted out in piles on the secretary's desk.

Every telephone in the block appeared to be ringing at once, the two on Maggie's desk and the private line in the Administrator's office shrilled out in unison. Maggie said, 'Yes . . . can you hold on . . . I'll phone you back,' left one on hold, slammed the other down, and ran into Miss Carmichael's room to take that call. Miranda heard her say, 'No . . . I'm sorry, she's not in the office. I'll get her to phone you as soon as she comes in.'

The other telephone trilled out again, and instinctively, Miranda picked it up.

'Administration—good morning, can I help you?' she said, wondering if all the world was going slightly mad around her.

'Maggie?' Jeff Thompson's voice demanded sharply.

'No, it's Miranda.'

'Get down here right away, please, Miranda,' he said tersely, and immediately rang off, just as Maggie returned, her expression more harassed than ever, resembling an apoplectic owl.

'Maggie, what *is* going on around here?' she demanded. 'I just had Jeff on the line, sounding most uncharacteristically curt, and this place resembles a battle station.'

Maggie passed a hand over her brow.

'That's what it is, Miranda,' she said dazedly. 'There

have been two deaths in Geriatrics overnight, and almost every ward has someone affected with sickness. I reckon it's some sort of food poisoning.'

Miranda said, 'Oh my God!' and was through the door almost before the words were out of her mouth. Her feet could scarcely carry her quickly enough along the corridors and down the stairs, and all the time her only thought, almost a prayer, was, please no—let it not be that. Let the deaths be isolated cases, the sickness coincidence. But she knew, even as she fervently wished otherwise, that it was almost certainly not so, that the stalking spectre all hospitals dreaded and feared had struck Lenchester.

There was a hushed and subdued atmosphere about the usually busy, noisy kitchen. Little groups of people were huddled together discussing the disaster in whispers, while others tried to look occupied and behave as though nothing had happened.

Miranda found Jeff and Miss Carmichael together in his office. His face was ashen, and she was tense and tight-lipped.

'You've heard, I take it?' he asked, looking up at her as she entered, and Miranda nodded helplessly.

'Do we know yet what the cause is?'

He gave a wan smile.

'No, but this department had already been tried, judged, and found guilty,' he said bitterly. 'As you know, we always keep food samples of everything cooked over a twenty-four hour period, and we shan't be able to pinpoint the organism responsible until these have been laboratory tested.'

'You've already been on to the Public Health people, I expect?'

'Yes. The Inspector will be with us shortly.'

Aline Carmichael's face was set in an expression of

extreme distaste at the mere idea of such an invasion.

'Nothing like this has ever happened in any hospital where I have been on the administrative staff,' she declared, her voice heavy with reproach.

The other two looked blankly at her. Two patients had died, and others were severely ill at this moment. Later, no doubt, they would all have to consider their professional reputations, but now, with a crisis still raging, it seemed hardly apposite.

'We'll worry about that when we have the time,' Jeff said. 'Right now, it's not my prime concern.'

'*You* won't have to be the one who speaks to the press,' she pointed out acidly. 'I suppose I had better go and prepare an interim statement, which, hopefully, will keep them quiet until we have the results of the tests.'

She swept disdainfully out of the office, and Jeff and Miranda raised their eyebrows at one another in mutual commiseration.

'Never mind *her*,' Miranda said briskly. 'She's never happy until she's said her fifty pence worth of criticism. Tell me what I can do to help.'

'Right.' He smiled gratefully at her and visibly pulled himself together. 'For the moment, until we have located the source of the outbreak and ensured that the kitchen area is sterile, the kitchen has been officially closed. We can't cook or prepare anything. All food for patients and staff will be brought in from the nearest suitable hospital, which is in Hereford.'

'So, first of all, you want me to sort out a list of all the patients who require special diets, and liaise with the dietitian in Hereford about those?'

'You've got it. Then we must get our heads together and see if we can simplify the menus, to make it easier on their catering staff. Things which can be delivered ready plated up, like salads, are one obvious solution.'

'Otherwise, one-container meals such as Irish stew,' Miranda supplied, grimacing. 'Can you imagine anyone wanting anything hot on a day like this? Jeff, speaking of Irish stew—where's Mick Mulligan?' she asked, as it suddenly occurred to her that she had neither seen nor heard the burly head cook, whose presence was usually difficult to miss.

'Now we come to the nub of the matter,' Jeff said. 'Mick is not here. Apparently, he went off duty shortly after lunch was served yesterday, because a neighbour phoned to tell him his eighty-year-old mother, with whom he lives, had fallen down stairs and broken her leg.'

'Oh dear! That must have been just after I spoke to him yesterday, and he told me you were away, too—in Birmingham.'

'That's right,' Jeff agreed grimly. 'Not that it makes one iota of difference. What happens in this department is my responsibility, whether I'm here or in Timbuktu!'

It seemed desperately unfair, Miranda thought, as they worked through the morning in liaison with the hospital in Hereford to ensure that meals could be provided for the staff and patients at Lenchester, but she knew he was right. Absence did not absolve one from responsibility. Jeff would carry the can for this, for all he had been eighty miles away, and was unaware that his head cook was also missing.

At eleven o'clock Miranda surfaced for long enough to make a quick dash to the drink vending machine for coffee, and there, to her horror, she found the usually cheerful and unflappable Sister Robertson biting back tears as she fought vainly to get her money into the slot.

'Here—let me,' Miranda said gently. She pressed the button and lifted out the steaming beverage in its plastic cup. Sister was leaning against the machine, taking deep, steadying breaths, and she closed her hands gratefully around the beaker.

'Are you sure you're all right?' Miranda asked concernedly.

Sister nodded.

'I will be. I had to get out of the ward for a minute—if my nurses saw me like this, they'd all crack, poor things!' She lifted a haggard face to Miranda. 'This dreadful food poisoning business—five children are down with it, and now we've lost that poor little girl who had appendicitis!'

'Oh, no—not Dawn?' Miranda could hardly breathe as the shock and horror clutched at her throat. She remembered the pale face and black curls against the pillow, only yesterday, and now she was dead. 'I hadn't heard that. I'm so sorry,' she said dully.

'It only happened just over an hour ago.' Sister Robertson gulped down her coffee. 'I must get back —Dr Emmerson is with the Littlewoods now, and Staff Nurse has her hands more than full on the ward.'

'Sister . . . before you go . . . can you remember what Dawn had for supper?' The question was tentative—she had no wish to upset the sister further, but the answer could be important. 'Was it the steamed fish?'

'No . . . now I come to recall it, she couldn't eat the fish. Said she didn't like it. All she had was the milk pudding. She had two helpings of that.'

'Thank you, Sister.'

Well before the Public Health laboratory confirmed their findings, she and Jeff had pieced together the alarming chain of coincidence which had led to the outbreak. The first link was the Catering Manager's absence, followed unexpectedly by that of Mick Mulligan, who was in charge in his absence. For all his blarney, Mick kept an eagle eye on the kitchen staff, and what had happened would have been virtually impossible had he been there.

The kitchen, short-staffed, was rushed off its collective feet, and in order to save time, the milk pudding had been prepared in advance, whereas normally it would have been freshly made.

'Which would have been all right had it been transferred to another container, cooled quickly, and put in the fridge,' Jeff groaned. 'I'm forever trying to impress on staff the vital nature of these hygiene rules. Train, train, train—I never stop training! Unfortunately, staff change, someone hasn't listened, or has forgotten, or is busy . . .'

'And the milk was left in the boiler it was cooked in, not cooled properly, and later heated up,' Miranda finished. 'On such a hot day as yesterday, the bacteria were off to a flying start.'

'Exactly. Salmonella poisoning.' Jeff rested his elbows on the desk, and lowered his head onto the palms of his hands for an anguished moment. 'Why? Why? Why? I wish I'd never gone to that wretched exhibition!'

Miranda knew that nothing she could say would alleviate the terrible sense of guilt which dogged him. It was an inescapable fact that the very people most at risk would be the ones likely to eat the milk pudding—old people in the geriatric ward, many of them in their eighties, like the two old ladies who had died, who could only manage soft food, patients on light, post-operative diets, and young children.

'I'll fetch us some more coffee,' she said quietly.

Throughout the day they were on tenterhooks, dreading the news that any more patients had died. But by that evening, all those affected were recovering, or at least stable, and the hospital began, tentatively, to breathe again. A number of nurses had been taken sick, but being healthy young adults, were not expected to suffer more than a few days' sickness and discomfort.

At six o'clock Jeff said, 'I think we might go home now, Miranda. There's nothing more we can do today.' He looked tired and drained, but relieved that the worst appeared to be over.

Miranda went back to her own office to get her handbag, and found Maggie just on her way out.

'What a dreadful day!' the secretary exclaimed wearily. 'The phone has been ringing and ringing, and the press were here . . .' lowering her voice to a whisper, she said, '*She's* still here. She said I could go home, so I'm off, but she's just sitting there, staring into space . . . it's weird!'

Miranda listened as Maggie's footsteps clacked away down the corridor, and an odd, unrestful quiet descended on the admin block. She paused, torn between conscience and inclination. She'd had a frightful day herself, and why should she trouble herself how Aline Carmichael felt? The Administrator had never exactly gone out of her way to make *her* life easier.

Miranda sighed. She couldn't just walk out. Crossing the room, she tapped lightly on the door and called out, 'Miss Carmichael?'

There was no reply, so she cautiously opened the door.

Miss Carmichael's chill grey eyes stared at her from a face stripped of every vestige of artifice. It was the face of a woman ten years older than the smart executive of this morning—bleak, emptied, contemplating an inner loneliness. Miranda was inexplicably shocked by this unexpected revelation.

'Miss Carmichael? Can I get you anything? Some coffee, perhaps?'

The Administrator looked blankly at her and waved a

dispirited hand in the direction of the wall cupboard.

'There's some Scotch in there. Have one yourself, if you want.'

Miranda didn't like whisky, but she found glasses in the cupboard, and poured two measures. She added water to hers from the jug on the desk, but Miss Carmichael drank hers neat.

Suddenly, without any preamble, she said, 'I suppose it's no secret that I opposed your appointment as Senior Dietitian? I told the interviewing panel that I believed the job should be held by someone considerably older —but I was over-ruled.'

Miranda took a sip of her drink and swallowed hard, hiding her distaste for it. She said, 'Miss Carmichael, I think maybe we got off on the wrong foot, and we'd manage a little better if you were to bear in mind that I am not Jean Davies.'

A wintry smile.

'Miss Lewis, I'm beginning to believe that. Jean was a pleasant, unexceptional, and in some ways rather silly girl. She could not have coped with today as you have.'

Miranda looked sharply at her, unsure whether to be suspicious of this remark, or to accept it at its complimentary face value.

'Don't ever doubt that I still have deep reservations about you,' she went on. 'Tomorrow will be business as usual, but try to imagine, will you, what it is like to endure a day such as this, and end it alone. Getting older. Getting harder.' She looked down at the contents of her glass, and tossed them off at a gulp. 'Getting maudlin,' she commented astringently, with a rare touch of self-criticism. 'Good night, Miss Lewis.'

Miranda set down her glass and stood up.

'Good night, Miss Carmichael,' she replied quietly. 'I'm sure we shall all feel better in the morning.'

Once out of the office, she ran down the stairs and out into the car-park as if some unnamed horror were close on her heels. As she got into the car and thankfully turned the key in the ignition, she recognised exactly what it was she was desperately trying to flee. In the face of the woman upstairs she had caught a glimpse of herself as she might be in ten years' time. Getting older. Getting harder. Getting lonelier.

Did it *have* to be that way?

CHAPTER SEVEN

MIRANDA's father met her as she walked in, with a cup of strong tea, freshly brewed.

'I heard the news on the local radio,' he said, 'so I can imagine what kind of a day you've had. We won't discuss it unless you want to.'

She smiled wanly.

'Thanks, Dad. Later, perhaps. Right now I'm up to here with it.' She indicated chin level with the flat of her hand. 'I do feel rather as though I've been run over by a steamroller, several times. Will something cold with salad do for dinner? I couldn't face food, but I'll get yours ready when I've come round a little.'

'Don't worry about it. I wouldn't dream of expecting you to cook tonight. Why don't we go down to the Green Dragon and persuade Mrs Evans to fix us something? You really should eat, you know. Physician, heal thyself, and all that.'

'I know,' Miranda agreed, 'but I just can't.' She finished her tea. 'First of all, there's something else I must do. Have you seen Alex Emmerson?'

'No.' Her father frowned. 'His car's outside, but I haven't seen him. Usually the first thing he does is change and get out into the garden. Ah . . . of course . . . he'll be feeling the strain of the day too, I expect.'

'There was a death on his ward,' Miranda said grimly. 'I must pop round and see how he is. I probably won't be either needed or welcomed, but still,' she shrugged. 'It's nagging at me that he might be there, alone, thinking about it.'

Her father did not appear to find anything abnormal about this.

'Quite. You cut across and see him,' he advised. 'If you want to join me in the pub later, please do.'

Miranda went down the garden and across the paddock. She had no idea of what kind of reception Alex would give her, but it made no difference. She had to go to him, and neither fear of his sarcasm nor memories of his embrace must be allowed to overcome this sure instinct that she was doing what must be done. She knew, in the deepest part of herself, how he would be feeling, and no one, she thought, remembering Aline Carmichael's bitter words, should be alone with such emotions.

She tapped on the door, and when no one answered it, knocked a little harder. All was silent, but she was convinced he was there. His car was outside, as her father had said, and besides, she could sense his presence.

'Alex,' she said. 'It's me—Miranda. Won't you at least answer the door?'

It occurred to her that she might be intruding quite unnecessarily. Maybe he had schooled himself to deal with such harrowing occurrences, and she was being presumptuous in believing there was anything at all she could do to help.

As she stood there, uncertain whether to go or stay, she heard his footsteps, then the door opened, and he leaned against the jamb, looking at her for a moment without recognition. He was still in his spruce, charcoal grey suit and pristine white shirt, but he had slackened his tie, and his hair was dishevelled, betraying the tracks of his hands through it. His face appalled her—it was lined with grief and guilt and despair, and all the barriers he habitually erected around himself were down, so that the anguish in his eyes went straight to her soul.

Wordlessly she stepped inside, closing the door behind her, and without thought or hesitation, put her arms around him, holding him close. His grip tightened, his hands pressing into her shoulder blades, drawing her into him, his pain draining into her, channelling itself through her until they were almost one, united in shared sorrow. She knew that it was comfort he sought when he bent his head to take possession of her mouth, and she did not deny it. At that moment, Miranda would have given him the world and herself with it, if it would have eased his unhappiness.

'Oh, Alex,' she sighed, as his lips began to explore her throat, and desire inevitably took over from the initial need to assuage grief. The touch of his hands became more immediate, more demanding, and she could find in herself no inclination to prevent him.

'Miranda!' Coming to his senses, he released her abruptly. 'I must have gone temporarily insane! It was unforgivable of me to try to use you in that manner.'

'It's all right,' she said shakily. 'I understand.' Taking his hands in hers, she said, 'Alex, you look all in. Come into the living room and sit down.'

Wearily, he subsided onto the sofa.

'I sent her home,' he said wretchedly. 'Dawn's mother. I told her to go home, because Dawn was on the mend, and then she had to come back and see her child die.'

'You couldn't have known,' Miranda tried to console him with reason. 'Don't blame yourself. You aren't clairvoyant.'

'Who do I blame, then?' he demanded with a flash of anger. 'A patient of mine died unnecessarily—a child who was recovering nicely, and should soon have been back with her family! Who do I blame? The hot weather, the Catering Manager, or some idiot in the kitchen? I'd like to go down there and have all their scalps, but it wouldn't make me forget that woman's face!'

'Alex, I *know* how you feel, believe me, and we would all like perfection, but it's a fact that carelessness and inexperience, and sheer ill-chance all played their part in this,' Miranda said. 'Each and every one of us is appalled and shaken by what happened—Sister Robertson and the nurses on Children's Ward and Geriatrics, Miss Carmichael, myself . . . as for Jeff Thompson, who wasn't even there at the time, the poor man knows this will follow his career like an albatross for the rest of his days.'

'Oh yes, we'll all suffer like hell!' he said balefully. 'However, none of us has to go home and arrange to bury our daughter. Mrs Littlewood has.'

He paused, studying the pattern on the carpet square as if he would commit it intimately to his memory.

'Did you know it was touch and go for Angela too for a while? We almost lost her, but she'll make it. God forgive me, I'm fond of Angela, but I had the most awful thoughts! I found myself asking why Dawn had to die, with all her life potentially ahead of her, while Angela's prognosis is for months, rather than years. Ironic, isn't it? One might almost say, unfair.'

'Life is mostly unfair, Alex,' Miranda agreed quietly, and was shaken by the violence with which he slammed down his hand on the sofa arm.

'That's why I'm in medicine—to correct that imbalance, to try to redress the unfairness. Today, I'm not succeeding too well.'

She could find no words which would be of help. There were no easy answers or platitudes in situations such as this, and she offered none. She longed to take him in her arms again and give him the only consolation she was capable of, but was afraid to. Earlier, she had acted blindly, instinctively, it had happened of its own volition. Now it would require a conscious overture on her part, and that she dared not make. Instead, she took refuge in the mundane.

'Have you eaten anything today?' she asked prosaically.

'You have to be joking!' He looked at her incredulously, and she gave a slight, nervous laugh.

'I know—that's how I feel too, but I think we should. It would do us good to eat, even if we didn't really enjoy it.'

She went into the minute kitchen and opened the fridge. There were two chops on a plate—a fair-sized portion, but a man with a good appetite could easily eat both. Oh well, neither of them was hungry, so perhaps it would do. There was salad in the crisper, and a bottle of decent Beaujolais on the wine rack. Miranda uncorked it and left it to breathe, then she washed the lettuce, sliced cucumber, tomatoes and green pepper.

In so confined a space it was impossible not to be aware that Alex had risen and was standing in the doorway, even though she had her back to him.

'What are you doing?'

'I'm cooking, isn't that obvious?' she said evenly, tipping new potatoes into the bowl, and reaching for the knife.

'Don't bother. I told you, I don't want anything.'

'And I told you, your objection has been overruled. Pass two wine glasses down, please. Being only five foot four, I can't reach your top shelf.'

'Five foot four inches of sheer obstinacy,' he grumbled, but he reached down two glasses and automatically filled them from the uncorked bottle. The wine was smooth and velvety, and they both drank deeply.

Miranda lit the grill and the hotplate, and very soon the potatoes were on the boil, and the chops sizzling.

'It does smell rather good,' he admitted as they carried the plates through to the dining-table. Across it, they met one another's eyes and soberly acknowledged a kind of complicity. Today had been as bad a day as either had known, but although it filled them with a vague sense of unease and guilt, they were young, healthy, and their lives had to go on.

'Leave the dishes,' he said, as she prepared to stack and wash them. 'That's an order from me, Miss Bossy-Boots. Let's take the rest of the wine into the garden, and drink it out there.'

They sat on the grass in the shade of the magnolia tree as the shadows lengthened across the paddock, the dusk deepened, and at last, the day's heat faded to a tolerable warmth. Miranda eased her feet from her shoes and leaned back against the tree. Like Alex, she was still in her office clothes, and was aware of how odd a picture they presented, dressed so formally, yet sprawling casually on the grass.

'Didn't that man you were going to marry realise what a culinary treasure he was letting slip through his fingers?' he asked idly.

'Any fool can grill a chop,' Miranda replied curtly, and then she realised that beneath the question he had apparently asked lay another, and it was one which she could answer now, without fearing those painful memories.

'I don't think Tony had any serious intentions of marrying me,' she said, looking straight in front of her into the concealing dusk, which made it easier for her to speak plainly. 'He works for the BBC. We met when I was at college in Leeds, and he was working for the local radio there. Then when he moved to London, and I graduated, he persuaded me to go down and get a job there, which I did. Perhaps I just fooled myself we'd be married, but what he'd intended was that we should live together. I . . . didn't feel I could do that. I know that must sound dreadfully prim.'

'For heaven's sake, Miranda, don't apologise for having old-fashioned values,' he urged her. 'So it broke up because you refused to live with him?'

'Eventually.' She sighed. 'But not as quickly and cleanly as that. It sort of dragged on for months, when we quarrelled a lot, and I suspected he was two-timing me. He disapproved of my job, too—he wanted me to get out of the hospital service and into some kind of commercial catering outfit. Finally I decided that enough was enough.'

Although they were not touching, Alex was close enough to pick up the vibrations of the shudder which ran through her, and she was not surprised when his hand covered hers.

'By the sound of it, you were well out of that,' he said. 'Marriage is no sure guarantee of eternal bliss or fidelity either, let me tell you!'

'No, I'm sure it isn't. My problems must sound fairly trivial compared to what yours must have been,' she said.

There was a short pause, which she expected to lengthen into his usual withdrawal behind the barricades of privacy. Then he said unexpectedly, 'Oh, what the hell! If this is confession time and we're being truthful, I have to take some of the blame for the failure of my marriage. I was mightily obsessed with myself and my work, and I took it for granted that Kay would accept that this was as greatly in her interest as it was in mine! She was young, selfish and immature, I was insensitive and intolerant. Someone else came along who she decided would be a better risk. It's as simple as that.'

Although he spoke lightly, as she had, about things which had hurt him in the past, Miranda was not deceived. It was never as simple as that, and she suspected that, unlike her, he was not fully recovered, which was not surprising. Several years of marriage, however unsatisfactory, could not easily be written off.

'What does her present husband do?' she asked. 'Is he another doctor?'

'Good grief, no! Kay made it clear she had had enough of doctors. He's a bank manager.'

For some reason she could not sensibly explain to herself, Miranda found this amusing. Or perhaps her levity was merely a way of defusing tension, but she could not repress the splutter of laughter which made her shoulders shake. Guiltily, she glanced at Alex to see if he was annoyed, to find that he was laughing a little too.

'Young woman!' he said with attempted severity. 'Has anyone ever told you that you have a highly anarchic sense of humour?'

'No,' she said. 'I've been told many things, but never that!'

His laughter faded, as did hers, and they gazed at each other through the gloom. Miranda held her breath, unable to look away, aware of a strange tightness in her throat.

'I never thought I should be able to laugh today,' he said soberly. 'You are an amazing girl, Miranda.' He drew her towards him, by the hand which still held hers, and kissed her very lightly on the lips, just once, before relinquishing his hold.

'I'd better let you go,' he said softly, 'because if you stay around here much longer, I'm going to find myself making love to you. And that wouldn't do. Would it?'

No, indeed, it wouldn't, Miranda thought seriously, making her way back across the paddock towards Meadowlands. She knew, now, why her whole being had flowed out to him with a need to share and alleviate his pain. That wasn't pity, that was love. She loved him, but she had already told him she had left one man rather than live with him without marriage, and maybe that was why Alex had let her go. She might, at that moment in the darkened garden, have seemed desirable to him, but he was still too involved with Kay to have anything lasting to offer another woman. He was still very much off limits!

'About last night, Miranda,' Alex said, catching her on the point of getting into her car the next morning. 'All I can say about my behaviour is that I must have been seeking some kind of emotional release from my problems.'

Miranda looked up at him, trying to ignore the unwelcome pounding of her heart. He was once again immaculate, dark suit perfectly pressed, hair brushed neatly, manner calm and only faintly apologetic.

'It's quite all right, Alex. I realised that,' she replied.

Sleep had been a long time coming to her, despite her exhaustion after the events of the preceding day. She could not deceive herself as to the need he had felt when he took her in his arms. It was primarily the warmth and comfort of another human being he had sought, which she had freely offered. Because she was after all a woman, comfort had veered dangerously close to passion, but she knew it was only that she was *there*, available.

If this were a book or a film, she thought ruefully, that would have been the mutually revelationary moment when he realised that he loved her as she loved him . . .

and when he had stopped her and said, 'About last night,' she had entertained a wild, desperate hope that this was how it would be.

But of course, it wasn't. This was real life, and in truth, he was not overcome by love for her, but by embarrassment because he had briefly lowered his guard and permitted her to get behind it.

'After the kind of day we had yesterday, I dare say we were both a little overwrought,' she said.

'That's very true. Thank you anyway for pulling me out of the depths.'

'Not at all.' She was as coolly friendly and polite as he, wondering all the while why she had never considered a career on the stage. 'It helped me to talk to someone, too.'

She put the car in gear and drove off down the High Street, hopelessly confused. Had she ever felt like this about Tony? Casting her mind back to the early days, when she was still in her final college year, she had to admit that there had never been quite this degree of painful intensity. They had simply been a young man and a girl dating—going out together, or with a group of friends. There had been no obstacles to their friendship. Neither of them was involved with anyone else, or recovering from heartbreak. It had been blessedly uncomplicated then, and Miranda had naively envisioned the smooth progression from courtship to engagement, and finally to marriage, step by step, a natural sequence of events. This was the way everyone seemed to go about it, as far as she could tell. No one she knew had ever fallen suddenly and ridiculously in love with a divorced man who was still emotionally shackled to his ex-wife.

When she moved to London, the difficulties began to arise. By this time, Tony had become part of the fabric of her life, and it was hard to imagine herself without him. He showed her a side of himself which she had not previously suspected, demanding of her a greater sophistication than she possessed. And when she had not fallen in with his plans, either to change her job or to move into his flat, he had retaliated by belittling her, undermining her confidence in herself as a woman, until at last she realised that the affection she'd had for him had turned sour, she neither trusted nor respected him, and the only sensible course was to cut her losses.

She'd had no intention of allowing herself to become involved with anyone else in the foreseeable future, but life, as she herself had said only last night, did not play fair, and here she was, only months later, loving Alex as she had never loved anyone before. How had it happened, against her will, in spite of her reluctance?

In the ensuing days, the shock waves that had rocked Lenchester General during the salmonella outbreak gradually receded, and things slowly returned to normal.

But Miranda could not recover from the *coup de foudre* which had smitten her that night at the cottage. She found herself watching eagerly for Alex's tall figure to appear along every corridor, or constantly glancing out of her office window, hoping for a glimpse of him crossing the car-park. But when they did meet, he gave her no peace, for his presence was more than she could comfortably bear. Always there was that heart-stopping surprise that anyone should affect her so strongly, simply by standing close to her, that breathless constriction of the throat, that churning sensation inside . . .

So I have done the very thing I vowed I would never do, she thought disgustedly. 'I've fallen in love with him, just as Jean Davies had. In the end, I was no more immune than she, no more sensible.

There, she pulled herself up sharply. Love, apparently, was a disease which could strike at will, against which there was no protection. But surely everyone had a choice as to how they reacted to it, how they behaved and allowed, or refused to allow it to influence them.

It was her misfortune that she loved Alex, who had neither the ability nor the inclination to return her love. But she could keep that misfortune locked inside herself, where no one need know. She would conduct herself with dignity and decorum, and she would not stoop to running along corridors after him or deliberately planting herself in his path.

They would meet in the hospital whenever it was necessary for him to consult her, or vice versa, and surely she was mature enough to discuss patients' requirements without gazing at him in lovelorn adoration. And when they met in Ibsey, as was inevitable when two people lived close to one another in a small village, it would be purely by chance, and they would talk about the weather, the cricket team's prospects, the garden . . . the inconsequential chat about unimportant matters which always composes the conversation of those who are no more than acquaintances.

As for the evening at the cottage, it would not be referred to again. They would both politely pretend it hadn't happened, and he would probably forget it. And that was the way it had to be.

A few days after she had given herself this formidable lecture, Peggy Carson rang to invite Miranda and her father to dinner at her house.

'Please do say you'll come,' she said eagerly. 'I've been looking forward to entertaining you, although naturally I'm nervous of cooking dinner for a fully-fledged dietitian!'

'Don't be,' Miranda laughed. 'I'd be delighted to come. I'm free any evening this week, so it's just a matter of fitting ourselves around Dad's various committees.'

'I've pinned him down to keeping Thursday clear, so shall we make it Thursday, at seven-thirty?'

'Lovely, I'll see you then.' Miranda was about to ring off when Peggy added suddenly,

'I've invited that nice Alex Emmerson, too. Four is a better number than three for dinner, don't you think?'

Miranda went cold, and almost dropped the phone.

'Oh . . . Alex is a very busy man. I shouldn't think . . .' she stammered.

'Nonsense. He said he'd be more than pleased to join us,' Peggy said brightly.

Miranda replaced the receiver slowly. Having already accepted gladly, how could she now wriggle out of what promised to be an ordeal? She had said she was free so could not plead a prior engagement, and if she rang up now to remember one, Peggy would simply alter the date, without changing the guests. She could not pretend to be ill, while still going to work every day, as her father would know that excuse was faked. The only way out would be to feign a sudden indisposition at seven o'clock on Thursday, when Peggy had gone to the trouble and expense of preparing a meal. She genuinely liked Peggy, and knowing that this friendship was important to her father, had no wish to offend either of them.

Could she face an evening seated at the same dinner-table as Alex, without betraying herself to him, to her father, or to Peggy, who was no fool?

'You'll have to, my girl,' she said grimly to herself. 'Don't be such an idiot. It will only be for a couple of hours. Surely you are capable of behaving normally for that amount of time. It would look far odder if you chickened out for some implausible reason.'

But her reluctance and her forebodings increased progressively as the week passed, and at Thursday lunch time she was gloomily stirring her coffee in the cafeteria, gazing into its depths, oblivious to Julie, who had spoken to her three times and not received an answer.

'Whatever's the matter with you? You look like a condemned murderer facing execution,' Julie remarked when she finally had Miranda's attention. 'Got a bad afternoon in prospect?'

Miranda pulled herself together and forced a smile.

'No more than usual,' she said.

'Sure? I think you're in danger of overdoing things, Miranda. You think of nothing but work lately and it isn't good for you. Fancy a workout on the tennis court tonight?'

An hour spent knocking a tennis ball to and fro across a net was a prospect Miranda would have relished far more than the one which actually faced her, but she shook her head regretfully.

'Sorry, but I can't. I'm having dinner with my father and his lady-friend, at her house.'

'That's bad enough to make you look as glum as you do now? Don't you like the lady!'

'Yes, I do. Very much. That isn't the reason at all.' Miranda got up, leaving her coffee untouched. 'I can't explain. Sorry Julie, but I must go now.'

She escaped hastily, aware of the puzzlement on her friend's face, and unable to remain for fear of further questions she couldn't answer.

So much for normal behaviour! That was a really good start, and it had taken only Julie, her friend, and the thought of tonight, to make her collapse into incoherent despair!

Arriving home at Meadowlands, Miranda went

straight to shower and wash her hair. The hot, sticky weather showed no sign of breaking, but apart from practical considerations she needed the morale booster of clean, fresh skin and shiny hair. Wrapped in a bathrobe, she surveyed her wardrobe's contents without enthusiasm. If only she'd had time to buy something new—her morale could do with all the help it could get tonight.

Then she remembered the red dress. It had been one of the last articles of clothing she had bought in London, from a little boutique off South Molton Street, and had cost far more than she was usually prepared to spend on clothes. The occasion had been her last outing with Tony, a cocktail party given by some television producer, and she had desperately wanted to look as smart and glamorous as anyone else there. She was trying hard not to see the writing on the wall for Tony and herself, but of course, she could not really ignore it, and she knew the party would be dreadful.

And it was. Everyone talked endless shop, which was not totally unexpected since they all worked for the same employer. But Tony didn't even try to draw Miranda into the conversational flow, or to explain any of the more esoteric technical chat which was way over her head. He was graceless and unkind, cutting her dead when she attempted to join in, talking down to her as though she were a complete idiot, and finally he abandoned her in favour of a mini-skirted production assistant, with whom she last saw him wrestling in a corner.

Miranda had walked out into the hall to phone a taxi, at the same time fending off the attentions of a heavily-bearded, half-drunken young man who followed her out and kept on trying to paw her.

The next day, glancing through the trade magazines,

she had spotted the advertisement for the dietitian's post at Lenchester.

She never wore the red dress again. It had too many unpleasant connotations. But now, pulling it out from the back of her wardrobe, she realised that it was a very attractive dress. It was vivid scarlet silk, with a fashionable dropped waistline, straight, slashed neck, and elbow-length sleeves. Miranda tried it on experimentally and decided it looked good. She didn't care any more about its past associations. They scarcely troubled her when the present was so fraught with difficulties.

'Very elegant,' her father said approvingly when she joined him in the sitting room. 'I haven't seen that before.'

'I bought it in London, but I don't wear it very often,' she said. 'Will Alex be coming with us?'

'No. He had an appointment in Hereford this afternoon, apparently, so he's going to make his own way there.'

Miranda exhaled a quiet breath of relief. At least she didn't have to sit with him in the car, and the moment of meeting was postponed for a little while. The condemned woman is given a short reprieve, she thought ruefully, and then realised how stupid she was being. However long it was delayed, that moment must come when she looked at him, loving him and knowing she must not reveal it. What was to be gained by putting it off?

Peggy Carson's house was twenty minutes' drive out of the village, and a short distance into another world. The lush, fertile, wooded valleys of Herefordshire dropped away behind them, and the bleak, bare uplands of the Welsh Borders stretched ahead, treeless blue-green wastes marching to a dark skyline of mountains.

'No wonder the Welsh came marauding down into Hereford so frequently in olden times,' the Major observed cheerfully. 'When one looks at the land the English have, from those barren mountains of theirs, it isn't surprising that they coveted it.'

Peggy's house was not a pretty black and white timbered showpiece, but a warm, squarely built red-brick building which had once been a farmhouse before the occupants gave up trying to wrest a living from their unyielding acres. But time had treated it kindly, a venerable ivy grew profusely up the front elevation, and from the comfortably spacious living room there was a breathtaking panorama of hills, misty in the heat-haze.

Major Lewis had brought flowers for Peggy, and she received them graciously, but with a humorous twinkle.

'Why, Charles—I didn't know you were so romantic! Roses!' she gurgled irrepressibly. 'Miranda, how charming you look! That dress has Bond Street stamped all over it!'

She set the flowers in a Staffordshire pottery vase, and poured glasses of sherry for the three of them.

'It's so warm, let's take our drinks out into the garden,' she suggested. 'I'm sure Alex will forgive us for being a round ahead of him.'

The garden was on a slightly lower level than the house, and approached by a short flight of steps. It was walled, and surprisingly productive, considering the nature of the land all around it. Shrubs and flowers rioted around the small terrace, and down at the far end Miranda saw runner beans, peas and raspberry canes, and there were apple and pear trees espaliered against the walls.

'Yes, my dear,' said Peggy, when she remarked on this. 'But you have no idea how many loads of topsoil I had to order to achieve such results! Come and have a look around, if you like. How about you, Charles?'

'Take Miranda. I'll sit here and enjoy my drink, and wait for Alex,' he said easily, and Miranda, trying not to react to the mention of Alex's name, followed her hostess on a grand tour.

'It's a beautiful garden, Peggy,' she said admiringly. 'The house is lovely, too.'

'Yes, but sometimes I think I made a mistake in buying it,' the older woman said soberly. 'We always had big properties, when we had the kennels, and I think when I bought this I must have temporarily forgotten that I was now a woman on her own, who didn't need so much space. The garden needs a lot of looking after. What's more, this place is very isolated in winter, and I'm not getting any younger. Nor do I really need four bedrooms.'

Miranda saw the point she was making, but thought that if *she* owned this house, she would be very reluctant indeed to move from it, and she said so.

'Ah well, perhaps I'll sell it to you when you get married,' Peggy laughed. 'It would make a splendid family home.'

'So it would, but you've got the wrong girl. Marriage isn't on my agenda!'

'It will be one day,' Peggy said, unperturbed. 'You've too much warmth, too much generosity of spirit to live all your life alone.'

'Thank you.' Miranda blushed. 'But don't wait for me to buy your house, much as I love it. I haven't even a likely candidate in mind for a husband.'

'You do surprise me,' Peggy said. Glancing back up towards the terrace she said, 'I see Alex has arrived. We had better go and join the men.'

Miranda didn't care for the juxtaposition of these two

ideas. Peggy was a delightful person, but she could be outspoken, and she had an unfortunate tendency to view Alex and Miranda as a twosome. It could easily become most embarrassing, Miranda thought, if she were not tactfully steered away from that subject.

'Alex!' Peggy made her way swiftly to the terrace, followed more slowly by Miranda. 'What a dreadful hostess I am! I should have been at the door to welcome you and fix your drink.'

'Don't worry. Charles did the honours in your stead.' Alex raised his glass.

'Oh, good. And you managed to find your way here without any trouble?'

'None at all. Actually I've driven past the house many times and admired it, before I realised that it was yours.'

Miranda emerged reluctantly from the concealment of the shrubbery, and Alex looked at her once, then did a double-take, his gaze concentrating itself on her in a manner she found most disturbing.

'You should wear that colour more often, Miranda. It's very becoming.'

She managed to stutter out her thanks, wishing now that she had worn something less noticeable. She had thought the dress would give her confidence, but all it had succeeded in doing was to make her feel conspicuous. He was still looking admiringly at her, and she wished he would stop. His casual approval was more than she could take.

Peggy was refilling their glasses, and at last Miranda managed to escape Alex's attention as the conversation became more general. But she could contribute little to it, to her intense discomfort. The other three were all content and at ease with each other, and only she was awkward, and unusually taciturn, and she didn't see how any of them could fail to observe this. 'I *must* make an effort,' she urged herself. 'Act naturally . . .'

'Excuse me while I disappear into the kitchen,' Peggy said cheerfully. 'No, no, Miranda, there's nothing you can do, my dear. Thanks for offering, but I think everything is under control.'

There was no escape. Even when they moved to the dining-room Miranda found that Peggy had placed her directly opposite Alex, and she toyed with her seafood cocktail without lifting her eyes above the level of his white shirt front more often than was unavoidable.

The meal was excellent. Peggy Carson was a first-rate cook. The crown roast of lamb was succulently tender and faintly pink at the centre, served with new potatoes and fresh peas which, she assured them triumphantly, were from her own garden. So were the raspberries, apples and pears in the fruit salad she gave them for dessert.

'Although I can't claim to have grown the oranges and kiwi fruit,' she laughed.

'I might be tempted to believe you if you did. Your garden is magnificent,' Alex assured her.

'Thank you, but as I was telling Miranda before you arrived, the place is really too large and too lonely for me. I ought to have somewhere more manageable, and closer to civilisation.'

'Well, if you do decide to sell, promise to give me the first option,' he said. Beneath the light, dinner-table manner, there was a seriousness his hostess grasped at once.

'Do you mean that?'

'Absolutely.' Alex turned the stem of his wine glass between strong, capable fingers. 'As I said, I've admired this house for some time. I've been house-hunting sporadically for the best part of a year, but I can't say I've seen anything else which appeals to me as strongly.'

'But Alex, old chap,' Major Lewis put in, 'is it practical for you? As Peggy says, it's too big for one person, especially a man with a demanding career. You'd need a housekeeper.'

'Don't be silly, Charles. Alex might be on his own at the moment, but he's planning for the future. Sooner or later, he'll have a wife.'

There was a short silence around the table, during which no one knew what to say. The Major coughed and made a great performance of draining his wine glass, and Peggy's smile faded as she realised she had committed a gaffe.

'Sorry!' she said, her innate directness going part of the way towards rescuing the situation. 'Have I put my foot in it?'

Miranda was compelled to look up and across the table at the man opposite her, although she didn't want to see that pained, shuttered expression which clouded his face whenever the subject of marriage arose. Under cover of the table, her hands were clenched, and once again his unhappiness was hers as that strange bond of empathy tied her to him. His pain at his own loss, and hers at his inaccessability mingled as they streamed through her, and only eased their grip as she saw the lines around his mouth relax into a smile.

'No, Peggy, not really,' he assured her. 'You couldn't be expected to know that I'm divorced, and it's no longer a matter for comment these days. However, once bitten, twice shy, as they say, and only a fool makes the same mistake twice.'

'My dear Alex, the only mistake you could make would be to pick the same kind of woman twice,' Peggy said equably.

He laughed. 'There's another kind?'

He spoke jestingly, and Peggy and the Major obligingly laughed. Miranda, who didn't miss the vein of bitterness beneath the levity, refused to play the game.

'As many kinds as there are women in the world, since we are all individuals,' she heard her own voice say, breaking a long period in which she had not said anything. 'It's ridiculous to suggest that we are all the same, like clones, and I, for one, find it offensive!'

They all looked at her, surprised by the fierce defensiveness, the ringing clarity and determination with which she voiced her statement. Confused and self-conscious, she looked down at the remains of her fruit salad.

It was Peggy who restored the balance between gravity and humour by saying lightly, 'Bravo! Spoken like a feminist!' and somehow, Miranda managed to join in the laughter.

Later, as Miranda was helping her hostess stack plates in the dishwasher, Peggy said, 'That was a frightful faux pas of mine back there, wasn't it? I had no idea Alex was even divorced, let alone that he was so touchy about it! Charles hadn't mentioned anything of the kind, but there—men never do tell you the interesting things about people, do they?'

Miranda concentrated on transferring glasses from the tray to the machine without breaking them.

'I doubt if Dad knows much about it. Alex rarely speaks of it himself. He's a very private person.'

'Hmm. I take it *she* left him—presumably for someone else?'

'Yes.' Miranda was extremely uncomfortable with this conversation, which made her feel that she was in some way betraying Alex's confidence, and she tried to change the subject. 'What a fantastic machine, Peggy. Dad really should get one—it would be no end of help.'

'What—and make all the washing-up ladies in Ibsey redundant at a stroke? It's a good thing Lizzie can't hear you.' She shot Miranda a particularly penetrating glance. 'I'll say one more thing about Alex, before you tell me not to be an interfering old biddy. I was under the distinct impression that you and he . . . what's the modern expression . . . had something going for you.'

Miranda shook her head.

'No, we don't. Not a thing,' she maintained firmly. 'I don't know where you got that idea, Peggy.'

The older woman looked slightly abashed, but unrepentant.

'He's an attractive man, you're a pretty girl, both of you are unattached . . . two and two frequently make four,' she said. 'And when I asked your father if I should invite your young man to dinner, he didn't contradict me.'

'Then I'm afraid I shall have to.' Miranda's voice was flat and definite. 'Dad is unnecessarily troubled by my solo state, so he's clutching at straws. But even if I were husband-hunting, I'd have to be crazy to set my sights on Alex. He's still in love with his ex-wife.'

'Is that a fact?' Peggy Carson said tranquilly. 'Since he's very wary, and still stinging from her desertion, it might be true to say he retains strong feelings about her. But he's the kind of man who would feel strongly about any woman to whom he committed himself.'

She programmed the dishwasher and started its cycle.

'*I* wouldn't be deterred by a woman who's no longer a part of his life. I'd say, well, I'm here, and she isn't, which gives me a very strong advantage!'

'And if, in the end, he rejected the reality of your love and chose the memory of *her*—wouldn't you be hurt?' Miranda asked carefully.

'Of course. But life is about being hurt and recovering, taking the knocks and getting up again, not just once, but as many times as it takes. Anything worthwhile, Miranda, is worth searching for, and fighting to keep.'

Peggy smiled. 'Goodness—how I do prattle on. Let's get the coffee made, or the men will think we've gone to Brazil to pick the beans!'

CHAPTER EIGHT

'BUT, Miss—can't I use any fat at all to cook Harry's meals?'

Miranda smiled at the worried little woman peering at her over the rim of her spectacles, her wrinkled hands anxiously clutching her handbag. She could only imagine how it felt to see your life's partner of more than forty years rushed into hospital with cardiac arrest, and to sit by his bedside watching the bleeping light flash across the screen, monitoring his heartbeat before your eyes.

'Yes, you can, Mrs Whittaker, but you must not use ordinary margarine or vegetable fats. Corn, olive or safflower seed oil are the best for your husband, and you can use polyunsaturated margarine for spreading on bread. Don't worry if that sounds technical—I'll give you a list of the brands which are suitable.'

'Oh dear! I thought Doctor said Harry was better now. A remarkable recovery—that's what he said.'

'Of course, or they wouldn't be planning to discharge him. But we have to keep him fit, and that's where this low cholesterol diet comes in.'

Patiently, she went through the details—red meat not more than three times a week, plenty of cod, haddock or plaice, but no oily fish, skimmed milk instead of whole, cottage cheese rather than Cheddar or Cheshire, clear soup and wholemeal bread. She knew it was often difficult for the elderly, brought up with different notions of food value, to relate to modern dietetic thinking, and so she didn't mind when the explanation overlapped into her lunch hour.

By the time she was free, she reckoned that there was bound to be a long queue in the cafeteria, and so she left the hospital and walked the short distance into the centre of Lenchester, taking a short cut down a narrow alley lined with boutiques and book shops. At the bottom, overlooking the square where the weekly market was held, was a small Italian trattoria.

Miranda went in and ordered a pizza and a cup of coffee, which she ate sitting at her favourite corner table by the window, where she could watch the shoppers crossing the square, and small children being pushed to and fro on the swings on the small, grassy central park.

Someone else was watching. Miranda's breath caught as her eyes followed Alex's progress across the square. She saw him pause to pick up a toddler who had fallen down, chatting for a moment with the child's mother, and although from this distance she could not discern it, she imagined the faintly wistful expression on his face. He should have been a family man.

If she kept still, and didn't attempt to attract his attention, she thought he wouldn't notice her, but he happened to glance in through the window of the café, and their eyes could not help but meet. He was still smiling from his conversation with the woman in the square, and Miranda was overcome by confusion because he had caught her watching him. Maybe her expression was wistful, too. She forced a casual smile to her lips, the kind of salutation one gives to an acquaintance passed in the street.

But he did not pass. He came in and made his way over to her table.

'Hello, Miranda. I assume you've no objection if I join you for coffee?'

'No . . . but I haven't much time,' she demurred uneasily.

'Nor I. But coffee won't take long, and we can walk back to the hospital together.' He ordered two coffees, leaving Miranda no option but to remain and drink hers.

'I didn't know you came into Lenchester during your lunch break.'

'I don't very often, but I was late today and the cafeteria gets so busy after one o'clock. I had to explain a low cholesterol diet to an elderly lady whose husband is due to be discharged soon, and I'm still not convinced she understands it completely. I must make sure of seeing her again before he goes home.'

She rattled on breathlessly, aware that she was talking too much, but needing the flow of words as a defence against her own nervousness.

'You've made your point, Miranda. I'm already aware of your dedication to your work,' he said.

She flushed at the implication that she was deliberately setting out to impress him.

'There's nothing wrong in that.'

'Not a thing,' he agreed. 'It's laudable in a world where so many are frankly bored by their jobs and exist only for their monthly pay cheques, and others are motivated only by personal ambition. Real commitment is rare.'

Miranda looked at the table, out of the window, at the colourful map of Italy hanging on the wall—anywhere but at Alex. There was a constraint between them which had begun the previous night at Peggy's dinner party, and avoiding his eyes did not dispel it. Nor did it help her escape the searchlight of his attention, under which she squirmed like a butterfly impaled on a pin board.

Quite how it had come about she wasn't sure, but the

evening had ended with his driving her back to Meadowlands, leaving Peggy and her father enjoying a final cognac. Alex had said something like, 'I have an early start tomorrow, so I hope you don't mind if I take my leave of you. Perhaps I could run Miranda home, too,' and before she knew it, she was in his car, purring through the scented darkness.

'Really, that wasn't necessary. I could have waited for my father,' she had murmured protestingly, and thought his smile was a touch grim.

'Oh, come on, Miranda—don't play gooseberry. Your father's of an age to be safely left alone with a woman, unchaperoned. Certainly neither of them objected to our leaving.'

Her smile was equally unamused.

'Somehow I don't see you as Cupid, Alex.'

'No? I wonder how you do see me. You certainly put me in my place back there. I haven't had my knuckles metaphorically rapped so hard since I was a junior registrar and had the temerity to disagree with the consultant.'

His voice was smooth enough, but there was an electric tension in his manner which put her instantly on her guard.

'I don't know what you mean.'

'I think you do. I'm referring to that pithy little speech about all women being individuals, which was neatly designed to deflate me. I hope you thoroughly enjoyed your small victory.'

'It wasn't intended to deflate you, and I saw it as a defence, rather than a victory,' she retorted. 'You blame all women because one gave you a rough deal, and I find that totally irrational.'

'Oh, you do?' Alex looked straight ahead of him at the white ribbon of the road, but his voice flung down a challenge Miranda could not ignore.

'Do you think you're the only one who has ever been badly treated, hurt or rejected?' she demanded. 'I have myself, and very well, for a while it made me cautious, but I'm not going to let it leave me an emotional cripple for the rest of my life!'

He drove the car into a lay-by and slewed it to a halt. The night was clear, with a bright full moon, and the angry gleam in his eyes caused Miranda to suffer a frisson of fear.

'Who are you calling an emotional cripple? When you've been put through hell, it seems to me eminently sensible not to risk repeating the experience.'

'All right, Alex!' Miranda exploded. 'Stay shut up in your fortress, with the drawbridge raised and the portcullis lowered. That's your privilege, but don't opt out on the pretext that all women are fickle adulteresses. It just isn't true!'

The silence of the hills and the night sky was serene and calm, but the silence inside the car hummed with strange vibrations. Alex was motionless, except for the fingers of one hand restlessly drumming the wheel.

'Damn it, Miranda!' he said softly. 'What is it about you that gets under my skin and makes me furious? Why do you turn all my reasonable arguments upside down and untidy my nice, peaceful, orderly existence? I don't *want* to be involved with you, so why is it that whenever we're alone together, I end up wanting to kiss you?'

It was beyond her to answer him seriously without also revealing her love for him, so she took refuge in levity.

'Damn it, Alex, how would I know?' she replied flippantly. 'I think you'd better take me home, or you might be overcome by the unfortunate urge to kiss me again!'

A moment later she regretted her own foolishness as,

crushed between the back of the seat and his body, she was all but deprived of breath. His mouth was hard on hers, forcing her lips apart, demanding capitulation in a declaration of power and strength. At first she struggled vainly for he was holding her too firmly, but deep inside her a different response was stirring, a white-hot, glowing warmth in which her resistance was all but consumed. And at the moment when he sensed her surrender he abruptly let her go.

She was still breathless, the world around her a spinning void as he turned the key in the ignition.

'Don't ever provoke me like that again!' he warned ominously, 'or I won't be responsible for the consequences!'

The remainder of the journey had been completed in total silence. Miranda was far too shaken to speak, and a covert glance at Alex's profile revealed his mouth sternly set in a firm line. He drove very fast, as though anxious to be free of her presence as quickly as possible, but all the same, when they reached Meadowlands he got out and walked with her to the door.

'Good night, Miranda,' he said shortly. 'I'll leave you now. This emotional cripple has some thinking to do.'

She groaned, wishing she had never allowed that epithet to be voiced.

'I wish you would forget I said that,' she begged. 'I didn't mean it.'

'I rather think you did,' he said quietly, 'and maybe you were right.'

The memory of those moments in the car hung heavy between them now, and Miranda tried to drink her coffee quickly, for all it was scalding hot. It was sweet torment to sit here with only the width of the small table separating them, but although part of her wanted to prolong it, she was terrified in case he made any mention of last night. She didn't want to be reminded of how she had succumbed so easily to the delight of being in his arms, even when his own desire had been fuelled by anger.

Casting around wildly for a safe topic of conversation to tide them over the next few minutes, Miranda said, 'The buffet-style lunch in the children's ward seemed to go quite well, according to Sister Robertson.'

'Indeed it did. All children like to pick and choose,' Alex agreed. 'It does create some extra work for the staff, of course, but the parents have been marvellous, helping to serve and generally fetching and carrying. It was worthwhile if only to see Angela taking an interest in food for a change.'

'Yes.' Miranda's face lit up. 'I had a long chat with her, and I think I managed to persuade her that high protein food doesn't make one fat. I must say she seems a little perkier of late.'

'We have to thank Dean Tempest for her renewed interest in life,' Alex said with a grin.

'Who on earth is Dean Tempest?'

His eyebrows rose, and he clucked at her in mock disbelief.

'You don't know? Which planet have you been living on recently? He's that long-haired lad who's currently taking the pop world by storm, and it so happens he hails from this part of the country, originally.'

'Obviously I'm not as *au fait* with the charts as you seem to be,' she riposted.

'You would be if you had teenage nieces, whose letters to Uncle Alex are full of such ephemera,' he laughed. 'Anyway, I suggested that Angela wrote to Dean Tempest, and the boy clearly has a heart beneath that dishevelled exterior. He wrote back. She's thrilled, and is trying to organise a branch of his fan club inside the hospital.'

'That's fantastic! What a good idea of yours in the first place. But how fortunate he responded—she'd have been so disappointed if he'd ignored her letter.'

'Credit me with a little sense, Miranda. I couldn't risk that. I wrote to him myself first, explaining Angela's situation, and he came up trumps. In fact I think there's even a possibility he might visit her.'

Miranda sat cursing herself as she watched him pay for the coffee. Of course he would not take the chance of Angela's being disappointed. He was far too caring and conscientious for that, and she should have realised that having planted the suggestion in Angela's mind, he would have done all he could to follow it through.

As they left the café together and walked back up the alley in the direction of the hospital, she said lightly, 'Can Lenchester General cope with a visit from a pop star, do you think?'

'We'll face that when we come to it,' he replied easily. 'Naturally, the press will have to be involved—they'd want a photograph—but too much prior publicity is out of the question. I won't have hordes of screaming teeny-boppers besieging the hospital. I've mentioned the possibility of such a visit to Aline Carmichael, who isn't too entranced. I think she's hoping it won't come off.'

'Oh, I hope it does—for Angela's sake,' Miranda said quickly, and caught him looking down at her with an odd expression on his face.

'So do I,' he said quietly. 'Having something to live for can make a vast difference in cases such as hers, where we can't effect a medical cure. The environment, the attitude, the quality of life, are vital. If Dean Tempest can help, who am I to argue?'

They reached the hospital gates, and as she was about to bid him goodbye, he caught her arm.

'Miranda.'

She recognised the alteration in his voice, the deepened timbre which told her that they were no longer discussing patients, or diets, or treatment. He was addressing her directly, man to woman, and panic assailed her.

'I have to go, Alex. It's almost two o'clock.'

They stood in the midst of a hubbub of activity. Cars pulled in and out, doors slamming. Two porters trundled past with a trolley of laundry. Nurses hurried on and off duty, telephones shrilled insistently from the open windows of several offices. And in the centre of this ebb and flow, Alex took her hand and held it in his, and she was powerless to detach herself from the spell which had descended on both of them.

'This is neither the time nor the place, I know, but I have to talk to you.'

She hesitated.

'If it's about anything I said last night, then I'm sorry. Can't we forget it and leave it at that?'

'*I* can't, and won't. You've successfully side-tracked me for the last half-hour, and tonight I have to go to London, to a conference. I must see you before I go.'

He's going to tell me to keep out of his life, to leave him alone, she thought desperately. Heaven knew, she had tried, but it hadn't worked, and now he thought she was pursuing him, and he was going to put her down, gently, perhaps, but very firmly.

'Alex, this is crazy,' she faltered. 'What if you hadn't seen me at the café? You'd have gone to London without seeing me, then.'

'No I wouldn't, because I would have phoned your office this afternoon. Stop hedging, Miranda. I intend to see you, and I'm not letting go of your arm until you agree. Don't struggle, or you'll only succeed in making this encounter far more interesting to whoever happens to be watching us from the hospital.'

Miranda remembered that the administrative offices overlooked the car-park, and Miss Carmichael's desk was handily placed next to the window.

'All right, Alex!' she gave in. 'I don't see why it can't wait until you get back from London, but if you insist, I'll meet you.'

He smiled triumphantly, but did not release her hand.

'My train leaves at six p.m. Can you be at the station by five-thirty?'

'Yes.' Her voice was no more than a whisper. 'Please let me go. We're causing a scene.'

She restrained herself from running, when he released her. Head high, trying not to think of all those curious eyes, Miranda walked at her normal brisk pace across the car-park without once turning to look back.

It was Friday, the day for her regular ante-natal clinic, and she wished it were possible to go straight there without calling at her office. Unfortunately, she had to pick up the white overall she wore for clinics, which she kept in the cloak cupboard in the outer office.

There was no sign of Maggie, but Miss Carmichael emerged from her sanctum just as Miranda was shrugging into her white coat.

'Oh, there you are,' she said disapprovingly. 'I do wish you'd get back punctually after lunch, Miss Lewis. Mr Meredith has been trying to reach you since half past one.'

Her expression was arctic, her voice withering, and any lingering hopes Miranda had cherished that she had not witnessed the episode in the car-park were instantly dashed.

'I didn't start my lunch hour until after one, Miss Carmichael,' she replied quietly. 'I left a message with Maggie to that effect.'

'Maggie has gone down to use the photocopying machine in general office and did not see fit to pass on the message,' the Administrator said nastily. 'You young women are all the same—no dedication whatsoever, your heads full of romantic trivia to which mere work is necessarily subservient.'

Since the salmonella outbreak, a cautious truce had been in existence between Miranda and her superior, and she thought she had, if not the older woman's acceptance, at least her reluctant respect. It had been hard won, and maintained with a determined politeness and a punctilious attention to detail. Now, at one stroke, she knew she was going to demolish all she had so painstakingly built up.

It could not be helped. She had personally written down the message and watched the secretary take it into Miss Carmichael's office, which was empty at the time. She was not about to stand by and listen to both herself and Maggie being so summarily and unfairly castigated.

'Excuse me,' Miranda said with frigid politeness, and stalking through into the inner office she quickly ran her eye over the papers lying on the Administrator's desk.

'Just what do you think you're doing?' Miss Carmichael demanded glacially. 'There are confidential documents on that desk which have nothing to do with you, so I would be obliged if you would kindly vacate my office!'

Miranda couldn't see the note! Miss Carmichael, hands on hips, was glaring at her, and the air was thick with impending confrontation, but she *knew* it had to be there.

'Miss Lewis, I'm warning you! I will not tolerate this insubordination!'

With blessed relief, Miranda caught sight of the piece of paper with her own handwriting on it. It was propped up by the ashtray, in which there were two cigarette stubs which had not been there before lunch. It was almost inconceivable that the ashtray could have been used without the note being seen.

Miranda picked it up. She did not say a word, but simply put it down again in front of Miss Carmichael's eyes. For a few seconds she was locked in antagonistic conflict with that icy glare, and then, amazingly, the Administrator shrugged and looked away.

'Yes, well, I cannot be expected to scrutinise every scrap of paper which appears on my desk. I'm far too busy,' she said testily.

You might if you were less busy watching other people from your window, was the retort which hovered on the edge of Miranda's tongue. She had sufficient sense and composure to swallow it. Instead, she went into her own office to phone Mr Meredith, spent ten minutes discussing the value of high fibre diets in bowel disorders, and then rushed out again to arrive at the ante-natal clinic with two minutes to spare.

The day had not been so entirely full of delights that she now looked forward eagerly to listening to Alex explaining why he wanted no further involvement between them. But she had promised to meet him, and there was no way she could avoid what was coming.

Wearily, Miranda dragged a comb through her hair, and after ringing home to let her father know she would be a little late, she got into her car and drove to the station.

Lenchester was only a small station on a branch line, and there were very few travellers waiting to catch the train which connected with the inter-city express from Newport. Alex was standing alone at the far end of the platform, and Miranda felt very nervous, very small and exposed, as she walked its length to join him.

'Here I am,' she said with an attempt at jauntiness, looking up at him and wishing she were braver, stronger, more prepared to take this.

'Yes, here you are,' he repeated, smiling gravely. 'Isn't it absurd, now you're here, I don't know what to say.'

'Oh, please . . . you don't have to say anything,' she assured him. 'I shouldn't have spoken as I did last night. It's none of my business after all, and I know how you must feel . . . about Kay.'

He appeared surprised.

'Then you know more than I do. It was more than three years ago, but my system took a long time to recover from the shock. When you have loved someone, and had faith in them, you can't quite believe they can deceive you so thoroughly. It makes a tissue of lies out of everything you once shared.'

Miranda was silent, and after a brief pause Alex went on, 'I suppose it was my own fault for not keeping an eye on what was happening in my own house, instead of taking too much on trust.'

'I think you are blaming yourself far too much,' she said. 'Surely marriage is about precisely that—taking one another on trust.'

'I must have thought so once. But then, the harder you fall when that faith is broken.'

'What you are trying to tell me,' she said, seized by a need to make this easier on both of them, 'is that you're through with women—full stop.'

'No! That isn't what I'm trying to say,' he contradicted forcefully. 'That's what I thought, until recently . . .

what I've been trying to make myself continue believing, since the day you rode into my life on that ramshackle bicycle of yours.'

He had taken both her hands and was holding them tightly.

'Miranda, I think I'm about ready to throw the crutches away,' he said. 'What I feel when I'm kissing you isn't merely the casual desire which is all I've known since Kay left me. I like you. I value your opinion. I miss you when I don't see you. Does any of this strike a chord in you, or am I presuming?'

It was all so different from what she had expected to hear, that at first Miranda could find no words. When her power of speech finally came back to her, her voice sounded to her own ears like a croak.

'No,' she whispered. 'You are not presuming.'

The sound of the announcer warning of the imminent arrival of the train to Newport drowned anything further they might have wanted to say, so they stood, still holding hands, as the train pulled into the station.

'I have to go,' he said. 'I'll be back on Tuesday. Have dinner with me then?'

'I'd love to, but . . . Alex . . .' Miranda was recalling the distasteful little scene in the Administrator's office. 'I don't want to tread on anyone's toes.'

Puzzled, he said, 'How would you be doing that?'

'Well . . . the word is that you and Miss Carmichael are . . . friendly.'

He almost snorted with amused disbelief.

'My, my! The things that get bandied around a hospital! I had lunch with her once, at her request. It transpired she wanted to discuss my plans for more parental accommodation on the children's ward, although why we had to discuss it in a restaurant she never made clear. She's a formidable female, but I'd be as eager to get friendly with a barracuda!'

The guard was bustling down the platform closing carriage doors, and Alex jumped quickly on board.

'Until Tuesday, Miranda.'

Before she realised it, the train had left the station, taking him on his way, the few dismounting passengers had hurried by, and she was alone on the now deserted platform, gazing incredulously into space.

'Miss.' It was the guard, nudging her elbow. 'That's the last train tonight. Unless you want to wait for the milk run to Hereford tomorrow morning.'

She favoured him with a smile of such radiance, he wondered what he had said that was so clever or amusing.

'No, I was just going,' she answered, and walked out into a world that looked the same, but was miraculously transformed.

Alex had not said he loved her. 'I like you,' he had said. 'I value your opinion. What I feel when I'm kissing you isn't just casual desire.' All these things were part and parcel of loving, but they were not the sum total —there was something more, an extra factor, and that he was not ready to admit to. Maybe, having been badly hurt, he was still holding back from that kind of total commitment. It was a leap into the unknown he was not prepared to take.

But Miranda was hopeful that given time, and patience, and her willing affection, he would come to love her, too. It was a chance she had to take, even at the risk of being once more and far more deeply hurt herself. This was the man she truly loved, respected, and wanted to spend her life with. As Peggy had said, anything worth having was worth searching for and fighting to keep —however great the risk to her own heart in the process.

* * *

The weekend loomed ahead unduly long for Miranda, who was keyed up and waiting in eager anticipation of Alex's return on Tuesday.

On Saturday she went along to score for the cricket team, but to her father's and Ken Digby's disgust, Ibsey could only manage a draw.

'That was a right old muddle-up of yours, Slogger, getting yourself run out for twenty,' the captain said as they held their usual post-mortem on the match in the bar of the Green Dragon. 'Anyone could see there wasn't a single to be had!'

'It was your Martin—he shouldn't have called,' protested the unfortunate Slogger. 'He was already half way down the wicket, so I had to go. Anyone can have an off-day, can't they? We could have done with Alex, though. Where is he today?'

'In London, so I believe.' Ken signalled to Mrs Evans behind the bar for a fresh round of drinks. 'That right, Miranda?'

'Yes. At a medical conference.' She accepted her glass of wine, unaware of the sparkle in her eyes as she spoke of Alex. 'He'll be back on Tuesday.'

'Good. Let's hope he'll be free to play next Saturday. We're going to need all the ammunition we can get for the return fixture against Angleton, won't we, Charles? Charles? Well, bless me, he's vanished! He was here a minute ago, and I've just bought him another drink.'

'I'll find him,' Miranda volunteered, setting her own glass down and picking up her father's scotch and soda. 'He's probably in the snug with Mrs Carson.'

Her father and Peggy were not in the snug, but glancing out of the door as she passed it, Miranda happened to catch sight of them in the garden, and she smiled to herself. No, she would not 'play gooseberry' as

Alex had said. The drink would keep until they came back inside.

Her father must have seen her as she turned to go back into the bar, for he called out, 'Miranda! Don't go. Can you spare us a minute?'

'Of course.' Joining them, she saw that both their faces were wreathed in smiles. Peggy looked as buoyant and eager as a girl, and her father was grinning bashfully from ear to ear.

'I say!' he exclaimed. 'You really must be the first to hear this, my dear! I can hardly believe it myself! Peggy has just—incredible as it seems—consented to be my wife.'

'What do you mean, "incredible"?' Peggy teased. 'I thought you'd never ask!'

Both of them burst into delighted laughter, and Miranda could not help joining in as she kissed first her father, then Peggy.

'It's wonderful news, but I can't say I'm surprised,' she told them.

'You don't mind having a stepmother?' Peggy probed a little nervously, and Miranda shook her head emphatically.

'Not in the least. I hope you'll be very happy, and I'm sure you will,' she said. 'When is the wedding to be?'

'We thought September, if the vicar can fit us in,' Major Lewis said.

'We're getting a little long in the tooth for extended engagements,' Peggy grinned. 'Besides, I'm not giving him a chance to change his mind!'

'*You* should be so fortunate, my dear lady!' he retorted. 'Come along—now we've told Miranda, let's go and break the news to the assembled company inside. I wonder if Mrs Evans has any champagne in her cellar?'

Later, after the excitement had subsided, Peggy said quietly to Miranda, 'We shall be living at Meadowlands, of course. Your father has his business to run, and I'd like to be as much help to him as I can. In fact, I think it was my hint the other night that I would be prepared to sell my house which persuaded him to pop the question. Men do need a little nudge in the right direction now and then!'

'I don't think he needed much nudging!' Miranda smiled. 'Seriously, though—Meadowlands will be *your* home. I can easily move out and get a flat.'

'I wouldn't hear of it!' Peggy protested. 'It's your home, too, for as long as you want it to be—although I don't expect it will be forever. But you must not think of moving out on my account, so let's hear no more about it. I shall offer my house to Alex Emmerson, as I promised. If he is really interested, as he seemed to be, then it's his.'

Miranda had a sudden breathless vision of living in that lovely place, with Alex. Sitting out on the terrace together, looking at the hills. Working together in the garden. Waking up every morning in his arms. It was almost too blissful to contemplate, and she dared not presume she would ever be that fortunate. Just because he said he liked her, and asked her to have dinner with him, she must not allow her mind to leap ahead to such delightful, but quite unfounded conclusions.

Arrangements for the wedding occupied much of Sunday. The vicar, when consulted, said he would be pleased to marry them on the last Saturday in September, which was fine, said Major Lewis, as the cricket season finished the previous week.

'I can see I'm going to be a cricket widow in no time at all,' Peggy said, unperturbed. 'Miranda, you must be my bridesmaid, naturally, and we can go into Hereford and choose our outfits together. I'd be glad of your help. Now, about the reception . . .'

'How was your weekend?' Maggie asked routinely, as Miranda arrived at the office on Monday morning.

'Amazingly eventful. My father has decided to get married.'

'No kidding!' Maggie listened avidly as Miranda regaled her with the details, until Miss Carmichael swept frostily into the office, demanding balefully,

'Doesn't anyone have any work to do around here?'

'Miranda was just telling me that her father is getting married soon,' the secretary said defensively.

Miss Carmichael looked Miranda up and down with icy scorn.

'Is that so? Romantic folly must run in your family, Miss Lewis,' she commented, and retreated into her office, closing the door firmly behind her.

'Gracious!' Maggie whispered in astonishment. 'Whatever is she on about? *You* aren't getting yourself spliced as well, are you, Miranda?'

'No, Maggie, I'm not. Take no notice.'

Miranda's smile was buoyant. It was too lovely a morning, and she was too full of optimism to let Miss Carmichael's sarcasm disturb her. She could only find it in her heart to be sorry for the woman today. The sun was shining, and she had driven to work through the lush, high summer of July, with birds singing, and hop-pickers busy in all the fields. Her father had found a woman to share his life, and there was wedding-talk constantly in the air. And tomorrow, in a mere twenty-four hours, Alex would be back.

She had told neither her father nor Peggy of the new closeness between herself and Alex. They were both deeply involved with their own plans, and their own happiness. Besides, she still thought of her relationship with Alex as a fragile thing, a bud rather than a flower, a promise rather than a fact. It would be foolish to read more into it than was actually there, and what was there to tell, after all, she warned herself soberly. Her father would instantly assume that his daughter had found a mate, and Peggy was already predisposed to scenting a romance. Better to let things develop at their own pace, to take it slowly, one step at a time.

It was hard advice to give oneself, and even harder to take when one was in love and wanted to inform the whole world. And this particular world, in which she spent her working days, was only too ready to snatch at and elaborate on the least scrap of titillating gossip which came its way. She was going to have to make a point of keeping extremely cool during her working encounters with Alex, so as not to add fuel to those already willing flames.

Tuesday was an odd sort of day. Miranda, knowing Alex would be back, was on edge with anticipation, although she did not expect to see him until she arrived home after work. Still, she could not prevent herself from counting the hours.

Coming back from a final chat with Mrs Whittaker, whose husband was to be discharged the following day, she realised with a start that she had been talking to her for far longer than she had thought, and it was already ten minutes to five. Her heart gave a wild lurch of anxiety and expectation, and she almost ran the last few yards along the corridor.

Maggie was folding up the day's mail and putting it neatly into envelopes, and she gave Miranda an odd, questioning look as she walked in.

'Miss Carmichael wants to see you immediately,' she informed her.

Miranda's spirits sank.

'Now? It's five minutes to five. Did she say it was urgent?'

A protracted session with the Administrator was the last thing she needed at this moment. Was Miss Carmichael a witch, she wondered? Did she know Miranda was anxious to be off on time, and had she perhaps divined the reason why?

'Absolutely. She said on no account to go home without seeing her.' Maggie lowered her voice theatrically. 'There's a lady in the office with her. I don't know who she is, but she came here asking for Alex Emmerson.'

Something cold and disagreeable clutched Miranda's heart, and for a few seconds she was actually convinced that she was unable to take a step forward. 'Riveted to the spot'. She had read the words many times in books, and discounted them, but now she knew it could happen. Some strong, psychological force prevented her from walking into Miss Carmichael's office, because she did not want to meet this woman, did not want to know who she was.

'Miranda?' Maggie said curiously. 'Are you all right?'

Miranda breathed deeply and deliberately.

'Yes. Fine,' she lied, forcing a smile. 'I'd better go and see what all this is about.'

'Into the valley of death' echoed a line from a verse of poetry learned in childhood, as she tapped lightly on the door and went in.

The woman seated in Miss Carmichael's visitor's chair was slim and blonde, ethereal-looking, with a wistful, elfin little face framed in short, natural curls. She wore a navy blue suit with a blue and white spot-print blouse, and her feet, shod in white high-heeled sandals, looked no bigger than a size two. Her equally delicate hands were twisting at a pair of fine white gloves.

'Ah, Miss Lewis,' Miss Carmichael said, with the voluptuous satisfaction of a cat who had unexpectedly found a forbidden plate of fish. 'This is Mrs Russell . . . our dietitian, Miss Miranda Lewis.'

Miranda nodded politely at the blonde woman, and Miss Carmichael went on smoothly,

'Mrs Russell is looking for Dr Emmerson, but unfortunately he's not in Lenchester today.'

'No. He'll be at his consulting rooms in Hereford,' Miranda said warily. 'His secretary . . .'

'Has already left, and so has he,' the Administrator interrupted her. 'I see from my files that Dr Emmerson lives in Ibsey, as do you. Mrs Russell has come by train, all the way from Edinburgh, and as you have your car and will be going that way, perhaps you would be kind enough to give her a lift.'

Miranda's thought processes froze for a short instant, as her feet had earlier done, then they swung into frenzied action. A strange woman could not walk into a hospital administrator's office and demand, and be given, the address of a senior member of medical staff, unless there was a very good reason. Unless, for example, she was closely related to him in some way. Miranda didn't need the look of almost gloating pleasure on Miss Carmichael's face to tell her who this woman was.

'Perhaps we should telephone Dr Emmerson at home first?' she suggested cautiously.

'Oh, please!' the blonde woman spoke for the first time, her voice tremulous and raw with nerves. 'I'd rather not. I really do need to see him, and it's not something I can discuss over the phone.' She looked up almost pleadingly at Miranda. 'I'm Alex's ex-wife,' she added softly, confirming what she had already, most unwillingly, guessed.

It was not in Miranda's power to force the ex-Mrs Emmerson to lessen the shock to her former husband by warning him of her impending arrival on his doorstep. And it was ironic that she had to be the one to deliver this bombshell. She wondered ruefully if that had any bearing on Miss Carmichael's enlisting her co-operation. She was not usually so sympathetic to personal dilemmas. Very well, she seemed to be declaring, *I* can't have him, but neither can *you*, for here is a woman with a stronger claim on his emotions than either of us could hope to have. Here is the woman he loved . . . and still loves?

'My car's outside,' Miranda said quietly. 'Would you like to go now, Mrs Russell?' And she walked helplessly towards her own destruction.

CHAPTER NINE

IT was difficult to have a reasonable, sensible conversation with Kay Russell during the drive from Lenchester to Ibsey. For a start, Kay was in a highly distraught condition. She kept on twisting the white gloves in her nervous hands, which she would occasionally clench tightly, she bit her lip, and blinked frequently, and Miranda half expected her to burst into tears at any moment.

Neither could she talk to this disturbed woman about whatever was troubling her, what had brought her on this unannounced journey to see a man from whom she had been legally separated for two years.

'It's none of my business' was the attitude Miranda tried desperately if unsuccessfully to adopt. But it *is* my business, because I love him, her heart objected violently. She wanted badly to know what was going on, but couldn't ask.

However, it was impossible to complete half an hour's journey without saying a word, so she tried politely to ignore her companion's agitated state, and asked safe, predictable questions about the journey from Edinburgh.

'Oh, it was perfectly ghastly!' Kay sighed dramatically. 'Either the trains were late and I just missed connections, or I had to hang around stations for ever. I don't know how I survived, but I just kept on telling myself I had to make it. I *had* to get to Alex, and then I should be all right.'

It seemed that this subject was not as safe as Miranda

had expected it to be, and she confined herself thereafter to observations about the countryside through which they were passing.

Kay was not particularly impressed.

'I can't visualise Alex living in such rural isolation,' she commented. 'I always think of him as essentially a "city" person.'

All topics immediately led to the one Miranda knew she should not attempt to discuss with Kay.

'I think he quite enjoys living here,' she responded carefully. 'Ibsey is not that isolated. It's a sizeable village, with a good range of community activities.'

'Yes. But what about the theatres, concerts, libraries? Alex would stagnate without civilised amenities.'

Miranda's personal opinion was that Kay was projecting her own needs on to a false image of her ex-husband, and she forbore to point out that the 'civilised amenities' were no more than fifteen miles away, giving anyone with a car the best of both worlds. Her carefully suppressed sigh as they drove up the lane to Cruck Cottage was both relieved and fearful. The last thing she wanted was to witness the meeting of these two people who had once loved each other deeply, at least one of whom was not completely cured. And maybe the other wasn't either, in spite of two years as someone else's wife, she thought darkly, casting a glance at Kay's taut, almost tearful face.

'This is where Alex lives,' she said. 'His car is there, so obviously he's in. Shall I leave you to find him yourself?'

Unexpectedly, Kay reached out and grasped Miranda's hand.

'No! Please don't leave me!' she begged distractedly, and looking dubiously at the cottage, added, 'What a poky little house. Are you sure this is the right place?'

'Positive.' Kay was still gripping her arm tightly and

Miranda found herself drawn into this reunion, however reluctantly. 'Look—I'll go to the door with you, and then I'll leave,' she suggested. 'I'm sure you'd rather talk to Alex alone.'

She virtually supported Kay to the front door of the cottage, but didn't have to knock. Alex must have heard the Mini's familiar engine, and came to the door wearing cords and an open-necked shirt, his dark hair tousled.

Like a mesmerised rabbit in the glare of a car's headlights, Miranda watched unwillingly as the welcoming smile froze on his lips, and the focus of his attention swung away from her, fixing itself exclusively on the woman at her side.

'Hello, Alex,' she said, her voice very faintly questioning, testing her welcome.

'Kay,' was all he said. He still had the appearance of a man who has been dealt a sudden, incapacitating blow on the head. The sound of his voice saying her name released something in her, and she rushed blindly into his arms like a homing bird.

'Oh, Alex, it's so awful, and there's no one else I can turn to, only you!' she sobbed, tears beginning to trace fresh rivulets down her cheeks. Automatically, protectively, his arms went round her, as they must have done many times. Miranda stood there, unheeded, superfluous, but still unable to tear herself away from this touching little scene she had no desire to be audience to.

Alex came to himself and looked at Miranda over the top of the fair head nestling against his chest. His eyes flashed her a message, almost pleading for her help, and she wondered if he had the remotest idea how hurtful all this was to her.

'Miranda . . . do you think you could rustle up some tea?'

It was not in her power to refuse. But her hands were trembling as she filled the kettle and put tea in the pot. So short a time ago she had been awaiting Alex's return with happy, if nervous, anticipation. A chapter had opened on the station platform as they'd said goodbye, and she had confidently expected it to continue.

But not with *you* as heroine, she told herself wryly as she got out cups and saucers. You have been relegated to assistant and helpmeet, and Kay is once again filling the role of romantic lead. She thought it took a special kind of effrontery to turn, in whatever trouble was affecting her, to the man who she had cheated and walked out on several years earlier. She must have more nerve, greater self-possession, than her delicate appearance suggested.

Miranda carried the tray into the sitting-room, where she found Alex and Kay sitting together on the sofa, his arm loosely round her shoulders. He had provided her with a large handkerchief, and she was ineffectually dabbing her eyes, somehow contriving to look wistful and lovely even in her distress.

Miranda set the tray on the coffee table before them.

'Oh, thank you,' said Alex's ex-wife sweetly. 'You've been very kind. I hope I haven't put you to too much trouble.'

'Not at all,' Miranda lied stoically. 'Will you pour, or shall I?'

'Would you, please? I'm all of a dither and not sure that I trust my hands.'

Likewise, Miranda thought, as she carefully poured the tea. Kay did not allow her presence to deflect her from the tirade with which she was regaling Alex. Perhaps she had gone beyond a point where she was able to stop, or perhaps she didn't think Miranda's being there was important enough to interrupt her. She had no reason to believe there had been any involvement between her ex-husband and the girl presiding over the teapot.

'It's all gone, Alex,' she said. 'There's nothing left, no feeling, no commitment, no . . . no urgency. We scarcely speak, apart from essential conversation. I'm about as noticeable to him as the paper on the wall, and sometimes I think I'm just another item on one of his wretched balance sheets. He loves that bank more than he ever loved me.'

Miranda hoped Kay took sugar in her tea. She looked the kind of woman who would, and certainly didn't need to watch her weight. Miranda was not about to interrupt her at this stage to inquire.

'You're probably blowing this up out of all proportion, Kay,' Alex said soothingly. 'Most men are preoccupied with work much of their time. It's in the nature of the beast . . . remember? I'm sure David still cares for you.'

Kay shook her blonde curls angrily.

'I'm not so sure—nor am I sure I care for *him* any more! Right now, I can't think what possessed me to leave you for him. I must have been a fool.'

Miranda only knew that she had to get out, and she did so, abruptly, without a word, not knowing whether either of them was aware that she had gone back to the kitchen. Staring dully out of the window, she asked herself with blind, unreasoning anger why this woman had chosen to turn up now, just when she was beginning to think that the tide had turned for Alex and herself.

She could piece it all together now, from what she had been obliged to overhear. Kay's second marriage, to the man for whom she had left Alex with his life in ruins, was going badly. Maybe she was the kind of woman who needed the constant, passionate attention of a man, and once the honeymoon period of marriage had passed and the relationship settled down to something quieter and less exalted, began to feel neglected and discontented.

Had she not been personally concerned in all this, Miranda might have had more sympathy for Kay, who struck her as being a trifle immature for a woman who must be in her thirties.

As it was, she was sickened by the growing suspicion, which she could not stamp out, that Kay wanted to walk back into her first husband's life as if she had never left. 'I can't think what possessed me to leave you for him.' She believed she still had rights in Alex, that he would take her back and rebuild her disintegrating world. Otherwise, why was she here?'

'Miranda.'

Alex's voice made her spin round, to find that he had followed her, and once again she had that odd sensation that he was appealing for her help.

'Do you know if your father has a room available at Meadowlands? Having just come all the way from Edinburgh Kay is tired and will need somewhere to stay the night.'

'I'm sure there is one free,' Miranda said, and overhearing the conversation Kay jumped up, looking suddenly far from exhausted.

'How many bedrooms does this cottage have, Alex?' she demanded.

'Two, both minute. But you can't stay here, Kay.'

'Why can't I? We shared a house for several years, or have you forgotten?'

'I haven't,' he said steadily. 'But we were man and wife then. Now you are married to someone else.'

'Who is many miles away and couldn't care less where I sleep!' she exclaimed pettishly.

'So you say. Nonetheless, it would be highly improper. Miranda's father has a guest house just across the way—in fact this cottage belongs to him too, and the gardens adjoin.'

Kay had sufficient shame to blush, remembering that she had referred to the cottage as a poky little house.

'And you'll be nearby? I have to talk to you. When I've settled in and changed, will you take me to dinner? Alex, I need you. You can't just abandon me here.'

He sighed.

'I won't abandon you,' he promised.

As they walked out to the car and Kay climbed back into the passenger seat, his gaze met Miranda's over the roof of the car, gravely regretful.

'It's all right,' she whispered quickly, and forced a lighthearted smile. 'I'll give you what the Americans call a raincheck on that dinner date.'

But she thought it would be raining for a long time.

Her father was out, but after ascertaining that the accommodation was still available, and that no reservations had been made during the day, Miranda showed Kay to her room. She looked round it only cursorily, and gazed out of the window at the cottage, still resenting her enforced, if temporary separation from Alex.

'I suppose the country is pretty in summer,' she conceded grudgingly. 'It must be ghastly in winter, though. Do you know Edinburgh? It's a marvellous city—we went to live there about a year ago, when David's bank promoted him to a main branch.'

Miranda confessed that she had never been to Edinburgh.

'I shall miss it,' said Kay, which seemed to make clear her intention of not going back. She sighed. 'Oh God, everything is such a mess!' she declared. 'I came down here like a bat out of hell. Some instinct told me I should be all right once I was with Alex. You can't be expected to know this, since you are single, but when two people have been married there is a tie that can't ever quite be broken. Even divorce and re-marriage can't sever it. What has once been is always there.'

Even when you've created a scandal that rocked the foundations of a man's life, and spent the last two years re-creating that unique, unbreakable tie with someone else, Miranda wanted to retort, wondering how anyone could be so incredibly self-centred.

But she couldn't bury a lingering suspicion that what Kay said carried at least a grain of truth. Marriage must wear grooves in a life, and in the partner the corresponding grooves remained. Two halves of a whole life which had once fitted together, and might again.

Her father arrived home a while later, accompanied by Peggy. They had been shopping together and were loaded with parcels.

'It's ridiculous, really,' Peggy said brightly. 'Both of us have had time to collect a life-time of possessions, and certainly don't need more, but all brides like to start married life with some new things, and I'm no exception. Miranda—you look as if you could do with a drink!'

'What Peggy means is that she'd like a gin and tonic, and wants someone to join her,' the Major twinkled.

'I certainly don't object,' Miranda said with feeling, as she fixed drinks for all of them. 'Oh, by the way,' she added with an attempt at a casual attitude, 'you have a new guest, a Mrs Russell. I put her in Room Four, and I think I should perhaps explain that she's Alex's ex-wife.'

'Gracious!' Peggy exclaimed. 'What's she doing here? Not trying to effect a reconciliation, surely?'

Miranda's silence confirmed that she had hit the nail squarely on the head.

'Oh, no!' Peggy said firmly. 'After what she did

—after all he went through, Alex wouldn't be such a fool.'

Miranda smiled weakly, and shrugged.

'Love is reputedly blind,' she said. 'You didn't see him when she arrived. He was stunned—knocked for six, as Dad might say.'

Her father looked intently at her, alerted by the sharp edge to his daughter's voice, but before he could say anything the doorbell rang. Miranda didn't need telling that this would be Alex, calling to take Kay to dinner.

'I'll go,' she said quietly. This was something she had to face, a private torture which no one could suffer for her, and she opened the door to him with a smile that was as friendly and equable as she could compose it to be.

He looked more darkly attractive than any man had a right to be, and she longed to transport them both back to the time, only a few days ago, when they had stood holding hands on the station.

'Please send her away,' she wanted to beg him. 'She had your love and discarded it. *I* love you—give me a chance to make you happy, as she failed to do.'

Instead, she heard her own voice saying calmly, 'Do come in, Alex. We're just having a drink. Won't you join us while you're waiting?'

Peggy smiled at Alex as he entered the sitting-room.

'Hello, Alex. I don't suppose Miranda has had the chance to tell you our news,' she said, and Miranda admitted that she had not.

'Peggy and I are going to be married in September,' Major Lewis said, and briefly Alex's harassed face brightened.

'That's splendid news! My congratulations to you both,' he said warmly. 'Although if ever I could have predicted a match, this is it!'

'Maybe this is not the time to ask if you are seriously interested in the house?' Peggy hinted cautiously.

Miranda saw him hesitate. Then he said, 'On the contrary. I think now is very much the time. But I'd be grateful if you would give me a few days' grace. I have one or two things to sort out.'

Now is very much the time . . . Kay had only just re-entered his life, and already, from the way he spoke, he must be thinking of taking her back again. A few days' grace . . . one or two things to sort out . . . they would have to talk, he would need to find out if she liked the house and would tolerate living in such a remote country location when her preference was for city life.

Miranda gulped her sherry more quickly than she had intended, and stood nursing her empty glass.

'May I come in . . . if I'm not intruding? I thought I heard you arrive, Alex.'

Kay had apparently packed very carefully for her headlong flight, and now presented herself in an exquisite little black jersey dress which contrasted dramatically with her pale colouring. She smiled very charmingly from beneath fluttering eyelashes as Miranda introduced her to her father—a woman who could not resist setting out to enchant men, and fully expected to receive their admiration.

'Will you be staying in Ibsey long, Mrs Russell?' Peggy asked sweetly.

Kay returned the smile with an equally calculated sweetness, which proclaimed that the two women had taken one another's measure, and she tightened her clinging grip on Alex's arm.

'I'm not sure yet, Mrs Carson. It would rather depend,' she said vaguely.

They talked desultorily for a while, comparing the

rival attractions of Edinburgh and London. Alex said very little, Miranda noted, and it was he who decided it was time for them to leave.

'But Alex—darling—I haven't finished my sherry,' Kay protested. 'Is it simply miles to the place where we're going to have dinner?'

'It's a fair drive,' he said uncomfortably.

'Where are you planning to eat, Alex?' Peggy asked casually.

'Bartesley Hall.' His reply was monosyllabic, and Miranda was uncannily certain that he would have preferred not to mention it. Peggy, of course, did not understand the reason for his reluctance.

'My dear Alex, the food is first class, but they get booked very quickly, and you'll never get in without a prior reservation,' she warned him.

'I have a reservation,' he said.

Miranda thought of the gracious converted country house with lawns sloping down to the River Wye. She knew he must have made that booking earlier, with her in mind, which was why the subject embarrassed him. *She* should have been the one to sit with him in the elegant, candlelit restaurant overlooking the terrace, from where the fragrance of the roses drifted in. It should be her walking with him later along the path which skirted the river bank. Now, most likely, she would never do those things, for Kay was back and everything was changed. The chance to win Alex's love had been almost within her grasp, but had been snatched away, for in such romantic surroundings who knew what might happen between two people who had once been lovers?

When Alex and Kay had gone, Miranda, unable to be still, took the dirty glasses into the kitchen and washed them. Peggy joined her and picked up a tea towel, and for a while they got on with their self-imposed task in sympathetic silence.

But Peggy was not of the nature to let things alone, and presently she declared, 'I'm going to burst if I don't say this. That scheming little hell-cat is going to have Alex right back where he started if you don't rescue him!'

'Alex is a man and in charge of his own life,' Miranda said bitterly. 'He has the option of telling her to go to blazes if he so wishes.'

'But my dear Miranda, the strongest, cleverest, most perceptive man in the world can be as putty in the hands of a determined woman. You have to *do* something.'

'I? I don't see what it is you think I should do. Or why it should concern me so intimately.'

Peggy cast an exasperated glance skywards, then back at Miranda.

'Don't be a goose! You don't have to hide it from me that you're crazy about the man. All I can say is, if he decides to go back to her, when he could have had *you*, then he's crazy too!'

Miranda laughed shakily.

'Thank you for those few kind words, ma'am! But Peggy——' her voice was serious now, '—please don't try to intervene in this situation. Don't say anything to Alex about me. Promise? He must work it out for himself and act as he thinks best.'

'Oh, very well!' Peggy agreed reluctantly. 'But you know my opinion about the judgement of men in these matters. I have small faith in it. They need a helping hand from the wiser sex! If you stand by and do nothing, you could lose him.'

'I think I already have,' Miranda said soberly. 'Let's not waste any more time talking about it.'

* * *

Kay was in the dining-room the following morning, having breakfast, and Miranda was astonished by the change in her as she calmly poured tea and spread marmalade thickly on her toast. The sobbing, half-coherent creature who had thrown herself into Alex's arms the previous afternoon had vanished, and here was a self-assured woman who, for all her porcelain looks, must possess an inner core of steel.

Miranda was obliged to listen for a while as Kay prattled on cheerfully about what a delightful evening she and Alex had enjoyed at Bartesley Hall, and what a charming place it was.

'I'll say this for Alex,' she added artlessly, 'he can be a positive beast at times, but he does know how to look after a woman—I mean, how to take over when she really needs him.'

Miranda waited to hear no more about how Alex had taken over. She wished Kay a polite good morning and hurried out to her car, virtually colliding with Alex in the doorway.

She could not prevent herself from looking up at him, and caught once more that fleeting regret in his eyes, perhaps because they had almost had something good, and now that possibility had ceased to exist.

'Miranda—give me a minute. There's something I have to explain to you,' he said urgently.

'Not now, Alex. I'm already late,' she protested quickly. She didn't want to hear his explanation. It was too obvious.

In contrast to Kay's insouciant mood, he looked tired and ravaged. Miranda thought that he was probably tormenting himself, because although his former wife had come back, she still belonged, nominally, to another man. No doubt that was why he had refused to let her stay at the cottage—he could not trust himself with her so near.

'You're not late. There's plenty of time, and you don't understand,' he began, but got no further before Kay hurried out into the hall, once more wearing her forlorn, bewildered expression.

'Alex—there you are at last! I didn't sleep a wink last night just going over and over everything in my mind,' she said, running a hand up the sleeve of his jacket and resting her head against his shoulder. Minutes ago Miranda had seen the brighter, sharper side of her, but in his presence she was all little-girl-lost, with the hint of a tear misting her eye.

Surely he was too intelligent to fall for that, Miranda thought disgustedly, as she excused herself and climbed into her car, slamming the door with greater force than she had intended. Then she remembered what Peggy had said last night about the gullibility of men, and the guilefulness of women, and the morning turned to ashes in her mouth.

'I take it you reunited the ex Mrs Emmerson with her former spouse?' was the first thing Aline Carmichael said to Miranda when she arrived at the hospital.

Now you are in the same boat as I, her smile said. You're nothing special. Just another woman who wants Alex Emmerson and can't have him.

'I wonder if there's any significance in the fact that he phoned in and arranged to take several days' leave?' she added.

And that, finally, despatched any faint, lingering hope Miranda might have had for Alex and herself.

'I'd fight if I thought, deep down, that he cared,' she confessed to herself. 'But it isn't so. It was all *me*, all one-sided, and deep down he still loves her, and always has. I can't untie the hidden strings holding him to her. So that's it.'

The day was a limitless torment, an endurance test which somehow had to be survived. Not only must Miranda carry around her own burden of misery, but it was added to by the fact that half of Lenchester General had also heard the latest item of spicy information.

Alex was going to loathe this, being the subject of scandal all over again, Miranda thought wretchedly, and after she had overheard Maggie re-telling the story to two girls from general office, she taxed her gently but reprovingly.

'Maggie, it isn't really in anyone's interests to have this spread all over the hospital. How do you think Dr Emmerson is going to feel when he knows that his private life is being treated like a television serial?'

The secretary's owl-eyes opened even wider behind her glasses.

'Gosh, do you think he'd even care what we lesser mortals said about him?' she asked naively. 'After all, he's a consultant.'

'Which doesn't prevent him from having sensibilities capable of being injured, like the rest of us,' Miranda pointed out.

Maggie's expression proclaimed clearly that the notion had not occurred to her.

'Someone should tell that to Madam Minotaur,' she said waspishly. 'I heard her holding forth on the same subject to Mrs Warner, the Domestics Manageress, only this morning, so I assumed it was common knowledge.'

No doubt it was, by now, Miranda thought glumly. There was nothing she could do to lessen the fervent interest in his personal problems. If he seriously intended getting back together with Kay—and that was the way it looked—then this was something he would have to bear, in the hope that it would soon blow over once another topic of curiosity took its place.

Miranda was only too glad to be out of the hospital once five o'clock came. But she was not anxious to remain in Ibsey, where there was always a chance of bumping into Alex and Kay, so she drove into Hereford and watched a film. Afterwards, she couldn't have given anyone a sensible resumé of the plot, but it filled the hours until she could safely return home and go straight to bed.

She had scarcely opened her mail the next morning before the phone on her desk started ringing insistently.

'Miranda.' It was Sister Robertson from Children's Ward. 'I hardly know how to tell you this. There's no easy way. Angela died during the night.'

Miranda leaned an elbow on the desk and cupped her forehead in her hand. Sister was right, she thought sorrowfully. There was no easy way. No amount of exposure to occurrences of this kind ever made the shock and the sadness less personal and immediate.

'Poor kid,' she said. 'I thought she had seemed so much livelier of late.'

'She was. These last weeks were the happiest she's spent since she was admitted. It was a sudden relapse, as can often happen in cases like hers. She'd had a good day, in fact, pasting up all her Dean Tempest pictures in her scrap book, and in the end she wasn't in pain. I thought I should tell you—you took a special interest in her and tried to help, and I know you were fond of her.'

Miranda sighed.

'One feels so helpless,' she said, and suddenly she remembered Alex and his fierce reaction when Dawn had died. She thought of the way he always insisted on talking to the parents, as only he seemed able to do so sympathetically. 'Have you got in touch with Dr

Emmerson?' she asked urgently. 'I know he's on leave, but he would want to be told, I'm sure.'

'I know he would, and that's just the problem,' Sister said worriedly. 'We can't get hold of him. His phone keeps on giving the engaged tone and I think it must be off the hook. Dr Daley, his registrar, is coping as best he can, but there's no one quite like Dr Emmerson in this kind of situation.'

Miranda frowned, but she hesitated only seconds.

'I think I can find him for you,' she said resolutely. 'Leave it with me.'

In the outer office, Maggie was busy filing.

'Crisis,' said Miranda. 'Can you hold the fort, take my calls and so on? I have to go out of the hospital for a while.'

'Done,' said Maggie, anxious to make amends for her earlier indiscretion. 'Don't tell me where you're going, and then I can tell *her*——' she nodded towards Miss Carmichael's door '—that I haven't a clue. I can be very vague when I have to!'

Miranda smiled gratefully, and almost ran out to the car-park. She took every set of traffic lights the instant the amber light went out, until she left Lenchester behind, and then sped along the country roads to Ibsey, almost running down a startled pheasant which shot across the road in front of her, and causing a farmer backing his tractor out of his gate to say a few well chosen words about women drivers.

She saw Alex's car parked outside as she pulled up by the cottage, and her heart began to thud painfully. This could be, at the very least, slightly embarrassing, at the worst, downright unpleasant. She had no idea how the couple inside the cottage were occupied. The phone was off the hook, so obviously they did not wish to be disturbed. They could be simply talking, or they could

. . . Miranda cringed. Over and above her reluctance to barge in on anything so private and intimate, she had no desire to have her worst fears confirmed.

But her own inclinations had to be set aside, because, compared to the fact of Angela's death, they were unimportant. So was Alex's reunion with his ex-wife, however joyful. Because she was part of the hospital, she believed this deeply herself, and what was more to the point, she knew that Alex would believe it too. Before everything else, he was a doctor, and would subjugate his personal needs, even his own happiness, to his duty to his patients.

Angela was gone, but her family, in Alex's code of practice, were an extension of her.

'The child is the family,' he had said once to Miranda. 'In paediatrics, more than in any other branch of medicine, the doctor must treat not only the individual, but the whole.'

Miranda lifted her hand and knocked resolutely on the door.

To her surprise, it was opened almost immediately. She had not expected that, and briefly robbed of speech she stared wordlessly at Alex. He was casually but immaculately dressed, and in no way dishevelled, and she was overcome by relief that she had not walked in on a compromising situation. Beyond him she saw Kay, curled up on the sofa with her feet tucked beneath her, and numerous empty cups littered around the room spoke of several brews of tea or coffee.

'I'm sorry to disturb you,' she said, recovering herself and remembering the urgency of her errand. 'Dr Daley and Sister Robertson have been trying to reach you, but they couldn't get through . . . so I had to come.'

'Why? What's happened?' he demanded promptly, realising, to her immense thankfulness, that only an emergency would have brought her to his door like this.

'Alex—it's Angela.' She watched his face closely and took a deep breath. 'She died last night. I'm so sorry . . . but we all thought you should know.'

He leaned against the door jamb and slammed one fist into the other, a gesture of impotent anger.

'Hell!' he said fiercely. Then more calmly, 'Yes, thank you, Miranda. You were quite right to come and tell me.'

Kay uncoiled herself from the sofa and sidled across the room to Alex's side. The look she directed at Miranda was oddly veiled. She seemed, for the first time, to look beyond herself and divine more than a working acquaintanceship between the other two, and Miranda sensed her resentment.

'Who is this Angela?' she demanded.

Alex had momentarily forgotten her presence, and she shook his arm. 'Alex? I asked you, who is this Angela who all the fuss is about?'

'Um? Oh, sorry, Kay,' he replied abstractedly. 'Angela is . . . was . . . one of my patients, a thirteen-year-old girl who has just died from leukaemia.'

'Oh, I see. What a shame,' she said with an attempt to feign concern which did not entirely come off. 'But there's nothing you can do about it now, is there?'

'No,' he admitted. 'There is nothing more I can do for Angela. But I can, and must, see her parents. You will have to excuse me, Kay.'

'But, Alex——' her voice throbbed with ill-concealed irritation '—you're on leave. Isn't there someone else who can do this? You have a registrar, I presume? Surely he can cope?'

'If he had to, he would. We all have to contend with this situation sooner or later. But I am here, and this is something I must do.'

'And what about me?' The wistful mask slipped to reveal a childlike petulance, and her voice rose shrilly. 'Wasn't that why we took the phone off the hook, so that we could talk without being interrupted?' She glared briefly at Miranda, and then switched her gaze, pleading again, to her former husband. 'You can't leave me alone now, Alex!'

'Kay, I'm a doctor,' he said, gently but insistently. 'You've known that all along, and it hasn't changed.'

'Patients always come first! They always did!' she accused him furiously.

He shrugged.

'This is wasting time,' he said. 'I must go now. I'll see you when I get back.'

He left both women standing in the doorway, and got into his car without a backward glance. They watched him drive down the lane and turn into the main road at the end—brisk, purposeful, a man with a mission.

'This is all *your* fault!' Kay said furiously, her fair face flushed with anger, the blue eyes no longer tearful but blazing with hatred. 'Why couldn't you leave us alone?'

She slammed the door in Miranda's face, and her footsteps could be heard echoing through the cottage as she ran upstairs.

Still shaking from the vehemence of so many strong emotions, both her own and those she had been obliged to confront, Miranda drove slowly back to Lenchester.

She could see very clearly that Kay would never make Alex happy. However much he might love her, all that lay ahead for him was an endless conflict of wills and desires with a woman who would always resent any time he spent away from her, any attention that was not lavished on her alone.

And she was amazed to realise that the ache of her

own loss, although ever present in the background, was eclipsed by the pain she felt on his behalf, knowing the kind of future he faced. It was no longer a simplistic choice between Kay and herself—she would give him up, if only she could somehow save him from falling once again into the old, disastrous pattern.

Maybe . . . just maybe, she could. Would he listen to her if she tried to spell it out to him? Would a man in love be accessible to such reasoning? The most probable result of any interference on her part would be that he would question her motives, would resent her for saying anything against Kay, and hate her for telling him what, in his heart, he must know, even if he had chosen to ignore the truth.

Anything worthwhile, Peggy had once said to her, was worth fighting for. Miranda didn't have the nerve, the effrontery, or the self-confidence to fight Kay for Alex simply because she loved and wanted him herself. But from somewhere within her she called up a courage she didn't know she had, to make a last ditch stand for *his* happiness, *his* future—even one that would not include her.

Picking up the telephone, she rang Peggy, and after she had finished speaking to her she swiftly scribbled a note on a slip of paper.

> 'Alex—I'm taking up my raincheck. Please meet me at Peggy Carson's house at six o'clock tonight. It won't take much of your time, but is important.
> Miranda.'

Quickly she folded it up, slipped it into an envelope and sealed it. Then, before she had a chance to change her mind, she hurried down to Children's Ward.

In spite of the nurses trying to go about their work in a normal, matter of fact manner, there was something stricken and awed about the generally bustling ward. The children were unnaturally quiet, and there was an unusual dearth of playful activity. Sister Robertson greeted Miranda with a smile, but even she was tight-lipped and restrained.

'Thank you, Miranda,' she said quietly. 'Not everyone would have taken the responsibility. Dr Emmerson can be . . . well, difficult, but in situations like this, he's irreplaceable.'

'That's all right. Actually, he reacted very reasonably. He's still with Angela's parents, I presume?'

'Yes, and has been for some time.'

'That's a task I would hate,' Miranda said feelingly. 'Are you expecting him to come back on the ward?'

'Oh yes. He intends having a word with the children,' Sister said. 'Dr Emmerson doesn't believe in trying to conceal from the others the fact that there has been a death. He says they are more frightened by the things we try to hide than by what we tell them. So he's going to talk to them.'

Miranda knew that Alex would have had a bad enough day, what with Kay's histrionics, Angela's parents, and explaining the death of a companion to a group of worried children. Would he be prepared, after all that, to listen to her trying to warn him against re-marrying the woman he loved, but who could only destroy his life yet again?

She decided wearily that there would never be a good time for what she wanted to say, and it was best behind them both. If she waited any longer her fragile courage might desert her yet again. Handing the note to Sister she said, 'Would you please give him this, when you see him?'

'Of course I will.' Sister, bless her, asked no questions, and Miranda escaped back to her office where she spent the rest of the day frenziedly trying to catch up with her paperwork.

Miss Carmichael, fortunately, was engaged in various meetings for most of the day, but passing through she took time to pause at the open door to Miranda's office.

'I trust you had a valid reason for absenting yourself from the hospital this morning, Miss Lewis?' she demanded acidly.

'Indeed I did, Miss Carmichael,' Miranda replied steadily. 'In fact, I was on hospital business. Sister Robertson on Children's Ward will be pleased to confirm that.'

The gimlet eyes regarded her unrevealingly for a moment.

'Yes? Well, I'm too busy to concern myself with it now,' the Administrator said loftily. 'I've a planning meeting to attend.'

Picking up her files and documents, she swept out of the office.

Maggie giggled.

'In other words, she would like to make something of it, but she's realised you have such a good excuse that she would lose any argument she started,' she commented irreverently.

'Nonetheless, I expect she'll have a few admonitory words to say tomorrow,' Miranda replied with a wry grin.

Tomorrow. She could face Miss Carmichael, face anyone or anything, tomorrow. Oh Lord, let her only get through tonight!

Peggy's house was still and quiet when Miranda arrived promptly at six.

'The key will be under a stone outside the front door,' Peggy had said, adding characteristically, 'Good luck.'

'All I require is somewhere I can speak to Alex alone

for a few minutes, without Kay including herself in the conversation,' she had replied.

'Well, she won't find you there,' Peggy had said, not without satisfaction. 'You should be undisturbed.'

Always presuming that Alex turned up, Miranda thought, as she let herself in and opened the doors to the terrace to relieve some of the heat. Would he come? He might be reluctant, but Miranda believed he possessed a fierce integrity which would not permit him to let her down. If he had not intended coming, he would have found a way to let her know.

Her heart fluttered uneasily, and taking deep breaths she gazed across the valley to the silent, empty peace of the hills. Something about this house and its setting exuded an incredible tranquillity. If she could talk to him anywhere, it would be here.

Going into the kitchen, she decided that a cup of tea was always helpful. She filled the kettle, and the noise of the running water must have prevented her hearing his car arrive. She had left the front door ajar for him, and the first she knew of his presence was his voice in the living room, calling out.

'Hello? Peggy—Miranda? Anyone there?'

Miranda set the kettle on the hob as he came into the kitchen. She turned to him with what she hoped was perfect composure, although weird flutterings were still going on inside her.

'There's only me here, Alex. Peggy is at Meadowlands with my father.'

'Oh?' A questioning smile touched his lips. 'Have you lured me here to be all alone with you, Miranda? How very intriguing!'

She had expected anger, or a tired, dispirited irritation, but not this tender, half-teasing manner which caught her off balance.

'I . . . I wanted to talk to you, and I couldn't with Kay there,' she started to explain, wondering how to go on from there, how she had ever thought she could succeed in this madness. It had seemed a sensible, if slightly hazardous proposition, in the safety of her office. Here, looking up into his dark, quizzical face, she was lost for a place to begin.

'You could have talked to me without Kay at the cottage, or at Meadowlands, or anywhere else for that matter,' he told her. 'She isn't in Ibsey. She's gone.'

'Gone?' Miranda's errant heart thumped more painfully than before. 'I don't understand. Where has she gone?'

'On her way back to Edinburgh, of course. Where else? I put her on the train this afternoon, after phoning David Russell to tell him his wife was on her way.' He pulled a face. 'Not that I especially enjoyed having to speak to him, but it was only fair. The man was frantic with worry.'

His tone was dry, but difficult to read. Miranda's brow puckered into a puzzled frown.

'Are you saying that Kay has gone back to her husband?' she asked faintly.

'Naturally. What did you expect?'

Miranda was adrift in the middle of a scenario the plot of which she had not read, with all the actors saying unexpected lines at the wrong moment.

'Well, I thought . . . that you and she were . . .' she stammered stupidly.

'Kay is pregnant, Miranda,' Alex said. 'She didn't tell you that? No, well, it took her a while to divulge it to me. At thirty-four, a first pregnancy can have a strange effect on a woman. But the fact that she's carrying David's child must indicate that her feelings for him are stronger than she knows, and certainly he's the one she should be with.'

Miranda reached out spontaneously and touched his hand. That must really hurt, she thought, to know that Kay was having another man's child, not his.

'Oh Alex, I'm sorry,' she said.

'Why should you be sorry? I'm not,' he stated firmly. 'I'm pleased and relieved for her. Perhaps this baby is just what she needs, and when it arrives she will finally grow up and start being a woman.'

'You're glad for her sake—even though that means you'll have lost her—again?' Miranda ventured, picking her way carefully.

'I lost her years ago,' he said. 'Or rather, I should say that the man I was then, lost her. I'm no longer that man. Seeing Kay again made me very sure that I'm light years away from him.'

'You don't . . . you don't want her back?' Miranda was nonplussed.

Alex shook his head.

'Emphatically not,' he declared without hesitation. 'There's nothing left of the love I once had for her. All I felt was a kind of irritated pity, but because she was once my wife, in a way she was my responsibility which I could not shirk. But never again. It's over now.'

They stared at one another, and in the silence the kettle began to whistle, filling the air with dense white steam.

'I think you'd better do something about the sauna,' he said lightly, and when she still didn't move he put both hands on her shoulders, shifting her bodily so he could finally turn off the switch. Neither of them troubled to pour the water into the waiting teapot.

'Did you inveigle me here so that you could warn me against making an utter ass of myself, the second time around?' he asked gently.

'Yes.' Miranda nodded, her eyes downcast, her voice very small. 'Silly of me, wasn't it? I fully expected you to flay me alive for my impertinence.'

His hand under her chin, he lifted her face, standing so close to her that she was overpowered by his nearness, by the subtly masculine scent of him, and the waves of warmth from his body.

'I will, too,' he said, 'if you disillusion me by saying you acted only out of kindness, because you felt sorry for me. I neither want nor need that kind of concern from you, Miranda. Tell me you did it because you love me, and I might just forgive you!'

The grey-green eyes flooded with emotion as she abandoned pretence.

'How can anyone supposedly so brilliant miss what's staring him in the face?' she demanded distractedly. '*Of course* I love you, Alex!'

'That's all I need to know,' he said. His arms went round her, holding her firmly, and Miranda's limbs suddenly acquired the consistency of blancmange. Only the fact that she was clinging to him kept her upright. Only the sweet, demanding exploration of his lips gave the world around her any semblance of reality. When at last he released her mouth, he refused to let her out of the circle of his arms, and they stood gazing at one another wonderingly.

'I thought about you all the time while I was in London,' he said. 'I couldn't wait to get back, to tell you what I didn't have the courage of my convictions to say to you before I left. That at last I had found a real woman, with warmth and character, beauty and understanding. That at last I was free of all the doubts I had lived with for so long. That I love you, and only you.'

Her expressive face grew serious.

'Oh, Alex—dearest, if only you had *told* me that at any time during the last few days! You can't imagine what I've been through!'

'You never gave me the chance for so much as a word in private,' he reminded her. 'And Kay was always around, intruding on us whenever I did try to speak to you. I suffered too, you know. I wasn't sure that you loved me—enough to share your life with someone with an ego a mile high and a poor track record!'

It was her turn to smile teasingly, as he quoted the words she had flung at him months ago.

'And are you sure now?' she asked.

'I sincerely hope so,' he replied. 'Otherwise, I shall have to tell Peggy to put her delightful house on the market and find another buyer. I'm not going to live here, unless it's with you, so you had better say you'll marry me, Miranda. This house, and you and I are all made for one another.'

She did not need to speak. The willingness with which she went back into his arms said it all for her, leaving no room for doubt.

After a while he surfaced, saying with mock annoyance, 'Miranda! All this passion is steaming up the kitchen again! Do you think Peggy would object if we helped ourselves to a cool drink from her fridge?'

'I'm sure she wouldn't.'

Miranda opened the fridge door, and both of them gasped, for inside, unable to be missed, stood a bottle of champagne, chilling nicely. A white satin ribbon around its neck was attached to a small note, which read, 'Congratulations. Don't hurry back.'

Laughing, Alex picked up the bottle, and with one arm around Miranda, swept her out on to the terrace.

'I don't think we are in any hurry, do you?' he

demanded. 'I prescribe a long, very leisurely celebration of our engagement.'

'Anything you prescribe is fine by me,' Miranda responded tranquilly. 'After all—you're the doctor!'

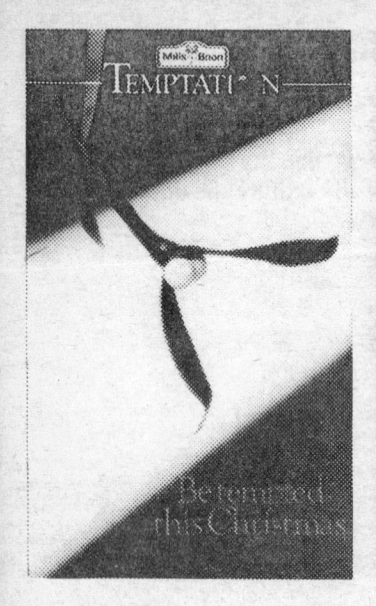

Merry Christmas one and all.

CHANCES ARE *Barbara Delinsky*	THE GIFT OF HAPPINESS *Amanda Carpenter*
ONE ON ONE *Jenna Lee Joyce*	HAWK'S PREY *Carole Mortimer*
AN IMPRACTICAL PASSION *Vicki Lewis Thompson*	TWO WEEKS TO REMEMBER *Betty Neels*
A WEEK FROM FRIDAY *Georgia Bockoven*	YESTERDAY'S MIRROR *Sophie Weston*

More choice for the Christmas stocking. Two special reading packs from Mills & Boon. Adding more than a touch of romance to the festive season.

AVAILABLE: OCTOBER, 1986 PACK PRICE: £4.80

Mills & Boon